Platinum B
www.pb-p

A Novel

Trice Hickman

Platinum Books, Inc.
www.pb-platinumbooks.com

Acknowledgments

God has blessed me to fulfill my dream for a second time with the publication of this book. He is so very good, and through him all things are possible. And again, I am humbled by his grace and love.

There are many people to thank.....

Thank you to my parents, Reverend and Mrs. Irvin and Henalmol Hickman, you are the two best people I know. Thank you to my husband James, for your partnership and steadfast support. Thank you to my sister Melody, your image on the cover makes the book shine! Thank you to my brother Marcus, for always caring. Thank you to all my relatives, I appreciate the tremendous love and support (a special shout out to the Trice Crew at the family homestead on Chestnut Avenue!). Thank you to Brian Little, our friendship has stood the test. Thank you to Barbara Marie Downey, I appreciate your friendship through the years.

Thank you to the following individuals for reading the manuscript in its infancy and giving me valuable feedback and suggestions. Your help and friendship means so much to me; Kimberly Riley, Cerece Rennie Murphy, Carmen Lathan, San Juan Johnson, and Dr. Regina Young.

I'm blessed to have an absolutely AMAZING group of sister-friends who have been by my side through thick and thin, coming through for me when I needed you!; Tammi Johnson, Tenya Grigsby, Monique Horton, Vickie Lindsay, Sherraine McLean, Terri Chandler, Bernadette Gatlin, Tiffany Dove, Melanie Trottman, Sondra Stephenson, Theresa Dillon, Gayle Walker, and Urania Brown. I love you all!

Thank you to the following talented artists who have taken this trip with me for a second time; Trina Cox, you've saved the day so many times I've lost count, thanks for making every page beautiful; Kea Taylor, your talent behind the lens helped me create another spectacular, eye-catching book cover; and Will Armstrong, you made my vision come to life with a fantastic web design.

Thank you to the many book clubs and literary professionals who have supported me; S.A.G.E. Book Club, Body & Soul Book Club, Sistah Confessions Book Club, The Sweet Soul Sisters Book Club, KC Girlfriends Book Club, Literary Divas Book Club, Rawsistaz Book Club, A Room Full of Sistahs Book Club, Senergy Book Club, Lubbock Public Library Book Club, APOO Book Club, B~More Readers with WISDOM Book Club, SistahFriend Book Club, Reading Divas Book Club, Reading Is What We Do Book Club, Savvy Book Club, Expressions Book Club, Sistahfriend Book Club, Get Your Read On Book Club, Lovely Ladies of Literature Book Club, Women of Wisdom Book Club, Phenomenal Women of Color Book Club, Shared Thoughts Book Club, Real Ladies Read Book Club (if I left out your club please forgive me...I'll get you in the next book!), EDC Creations, Urban-Reviews.com, AALBC.com, Book-Remarks.com, RAWSISTAZ.com, APOOObooks.com, Simply Said Reading Accessories, Linda Duggins, Carol Mackey, Janell Walden Agyeman, Troy Johnson, Ella Curry, Yasmin Coleman, Tee C. Royal, Radiah Hubbert, and two very special readers; Leyonta Sears and Rhonda Price.

Thank you most of all to the infinite possibilities...

If I've forgotten anyone, please blame it on my head and not my heart.

Peace and Blessings
Trice Hickman

KEEPING *Secrets* & TELLING *Lies*

Chapter 1

Still Going Strong…

"Listen," Victoria whispered. "Did you hear that?"

"V, it was nothing," Ted whispered back in a low moan, softly breathing into his wife's ear as he pressed his hard body against her soft curves.

"No…listen. I think she's up."

Knock, knock, knock.

There was no mistaking the faint sound of small knuckles rapping on the door. Victoria quickly adjusted the spaghetti strap of her silk teddy as she sat up in bed. She could still feel Ted's warm body next to hers as she gathered the sateen sheet around her waist.

"Mommy, Daddy…it's morning time," Alexandria called out in a high pitched squeal, peering into her parent's bedroom through the crack in the door. "Are you up?"

Ted sat up beside Victoria and sighed. As much as he loved his precious little daughter, he also cherished his alone time with his wife, especially since it was something they seemed to have very little of lately.

Over the last several months he'd been spending extra-long hours at the office in preparation for taking his company public next year. ViaTech had survived the telecom industry's down turn several years back, and was now poised to make a strong initial public offering next spring. And Victoria's days were just as long and hectic because her business kept her equally on the go. Divine Occasions, her event planning and catering company, was in its sixth year of full-time operation, and had established her as one of Atlanta's most sought after event coordinators.

But despite Ted and Victoria's jam packed work schedules, they always made sure to carve out time for their daughter. She was the single most important part of their lives. On evenings when Victoria didn't have an event to oversee she was diligent about spending quality time with Alexandria, making sure that she prepared dinner so they could eat together. And most nights when Ted wasn't out of town on business, he managed to return home from the office just in time to tuck her in and read her a bedtime story. After their professional and parental duties ended for the day, they'd steal a few treasured moments together before falling off to sleep.

"Yes, we're up, Sweetie," Victoria answered.

With that, Alexandria came barreling into the room, ponytails flying, and a grin on her face as big as the sky. She ran up to her parent's large four-poster bed, using the antique mahogany foot stool as a springboard to hop in between them. She giggled hard as she made an indention in the soft, jacquard-print comforter where she landed. "It's morning time, Mommy and Daddy!" she shouted again, full of all the excitement that a combination of Saturday morning cartoons and the promise of an afternoon playdate could bring for a five-year old.

Ted put his hand to his chest and fell back onto the bed, pretending to suffer an imaginary attack. "You yelled so loud, I think you gave me a heart attack," he teased.

Alexandria stopped grinning and stared at her father. "Daddy, are you all right?" she asked softly, putting her small hand on his broad chest. "Don't have a heart attack," she whispered, peering into his deep blue eyes.

Ted couldn't help but let out a laugh. Alexandria Elizabeth Thornton was the joy of her parent's hearts, and as they'd both come to agree, was one of the most serious five-year olds to ever own a pack of Crayolas. She was playful and exuberant, yet incredibly mature and cerebral for someone who could only claim graduating from preschool as her highest level of academic achievement to date.

She was what her Nana Elizabeth called an old soul. "That child has been here before. Any child who has that much common sense has walked this earth and seen things in another lifetime," Victoria's mother often said.

"No sweetie, your father's fine," Victoria reassured. "You just startled us. What have I told you about using your inside voice?" she lightly scolded.

Alexandria didn't answer right away. "Daddy, your heart's not right?" she said, tilting her head to the side, making it sound more like a pronouncement than a question.

Victoria didn't know why, but something in her daughter's tone put a chill on her arm.

"Daddy's fine, Princess," Ted smiled, grabbing Alexandria and tickling her until she dropped her frown and began smiling along with him.

Victoria tried to smile too, but she felt unsettled by Alexandria's comment and reaction to what should've been a playful moment. She looked into her daughter's eyes, wanting to reassure her again. "Sweetie, your father's fine, he was just playing around, okay?"

Alexandria nodded in compliance, but still didn't look completely convinced. "Can I watch *Big Bird*?" she asked in her small, high pitched voice.

"Sure, Princess. I'll set it up for you downstairs." Ted reached under the comforter, pulled his pajama bottoms up to his waist, then leaned over and whispered into Victoria's ear. "When I get back we'll pick up where we left off," he winked, then scooped Alexandria off the bed and headed downstairs.

Victoria watched her husband and daughter as their heads disappeared down the long hallway. She marveled at the way Alexandria had Ted wrapped around her finger. It reminded her of the relationship she'd shared with her own father when she was growing up. Alexandria was Ted's little princess, just as she'd been her father's little queen.

Victoria stretched her arms high above her head and thought about the busy day that lay before her. First on her list was dropping off Alexandria at her first Jack and Jill play date, then making a quick trip to her office to go over the remaining details for a large celebrity wedding she was coordinating next weekend. After that she planned to head back over to pick up Alexandria, drive across town to pick up Ted's dry cleaning, and then swing by the supermarket before she took Alexandria to their neighbor's house for a sleepover.

Sometimes, Victoria felt as though she didn't have time to think, let alone breathe. She always seemed to be going to this, hurrying to there, or coming from that. Running her business required her to put on a good face for the public, even when she felt crappy. Motherhood demanded that she appear eager and attentive, even when she felt exhausted. And being a wife meant she had to master the delicate art of compromise, even when she wanted to do her own thing.

But she knew there were worse things than having a busy life, and she knew that a lot of women would gladly trade places with her in a heartbeat. She was blessed to have a happy, healthy daughter who was smart as a whip, and whose loving spirit made her a joy to raise. And even though she wished her husband spent more time at home and less time away on business and at the office, she knew that he loved and adored her. She lived in a custom-built home in an exclusive, gated community. Her child-care service was reliable and trusted, and she was fortunate to have neighbors and friends who gladly pitched in to help. She'd quit her stressful corporate job several years ago to pursue the passion she'd loved since childhood, and to top it all off, she was in good physical health. Yes, she knew she was blessed, and she knew there were worse things than busy days.

After Ted secured Alexandria in front of the plasma TV with her juice box in one hand, the remote control in the other, and her favorite DVD playing, he hurried back upstairs, taking them two at a time. When he walked into the bedroom a smile slid across his face.

Victoria was waiting for him, perched on her knees in the middle of their king-size bed. Her silk teddy and lacy thong were tossed to the side, and the look on her face said she remembered his parting words. She was ready to pick up exactly where they'd left off.

Ted was struck by the fact that even though he'd seen his wife's naked body a million times, her sensuous allure and striking beauty never failed to stir him. He loved the velvety smoothness of her deep, chocolate-brown skin that always felt soft to the touch. He took pleasure in running his fingers through the silky thickness of her long black hair that draped the slender elegance of her neck. And he felt he could lose himself in the gentle curve of her lower back that gave way to the seductive pull of her soft, round behind. Motherhood had given her slim figure slightly more weight, and an added sexiness he loved.

"Damn, you're beautiful," he said, removing his pajama bottoms. He pulled the door in behind him and walked toward the bed.

Victoria smiled, enjoying the look that always came over Ted's face when they were about to make love. It let her know that he wanted her. He climbed into bed, covering her naked body with his. She embraced the feel of her husband's tall, muscular frame as she prepared herself for the pleasure to come.

He kissed her slow and deep, gently tweaking her hardening nipples with his fingers before moving down, alternating between his hands and mouth as he suckled her soft mounds of flesh. He eased his way further down her body, dotting small kisses along a man-made trail until his head rested between her legs.

"I love it when you're this wet," Ted breathed, gently rolling his tongue over her throbbing tenderness. Victoria threw her head back, digging her heels deep into the mattress as she clinched the bed sheet between her fists. He placed one hand under her hips and the other at the center of her warm middle. He worked with diligence, licking, sucking, and gently kissing her glistening folds. He took his time, devouring every inch of her sweet spot until she shuddered into a creamy orgasm that made her tremble. She released a deep, ecstasy filled moan that rumbled in the back of her throat.

After a brief moment, Victoria regained her senses, ready to give Ted the same intense pleasure she'd just received. She secured her hands around him, holding him in her firm but gentle grip as she stroked his hardness, massaging him with care. A long, slow, *"Uuuummmmm,"* escaped his lips as Victoria worked her magic. She opened her mouth wide and swallowed him, sucking and licking with controlled precision. When she squeezed the tip of his head deep into her tightening jaws, he could barely hold on any longer.

"Oooohhhhh, V," Ted moaned, perspiration dampening his skin. He shifted positions, gently laying Victoria on her back as she wrapped her long legs around his waist, arching her pelvis into the air to meet his. He slipped inside her with smooth, even strokes as they made love. Her body received him as he moved in and out, delighting and electrifying her all at once. Their rhythm was a slow and easy grind that flowed into a growing and heated frenzy as Ted went deeper, increas-

ing the speed of his thrusts. Victoria moaned, clinging to the sex drenched sweat pouring from his body while she worked her hips at an equally hungry pace. Finally, they both surrendered to a second wave of pleasure.

Victoria reveled in her husband's ability to fulfill her sexual desires. He knew exactly how to please her, anticipating her wants and knowing her most intimate needs. Over the course of their six year marriage, even though the frequency of their lovemaking had slowed, he'd never left her wanting. This was yet another one of her many blessings, and again, she knew there were many women who would kill to be in her shoes.

She'd heard more than a few of her friends and clients complain about their dead sex lives, citing disgruntled husbands, over-active children, and under-active libidos as major culprits. One of her best friends, Debbie Long, who was like the sister she never had, had recently confided that since the birth of her son seven years ago, her love life with her husband had dwindled to a state of near non-existence. "We're like roommates," Debbie had told Victoria a few months ago. "We love each other but the passion is gone. We're just going through the motions. As a matter of fact, I can't remember the last time Rob and I made love," she'd complained.

Victoria had been shocked to learn that Debbie and Rob's marriage had shriveled into the dull, sexless picture her friend had painted, especially since she and Rob had always been romantic and affectionate with each other. Aside from her parent's strong and lasting union, Victoria had held Debbie and Rob's relationship as the gold standard by which marriage could be measured.

But as Victoria would soon come to learn in the weeks ahead, time and circumstances were instruments that could change the tune of ones life in shocking and unexpected ways.

Looking at her own relationship made Victoria feel grateful that she and Ted were still going strong. She knew their marriage wasn't perfect, but they had love and trust as their anchors. The sex was hot, and he made sure that he pleased her. He was in excellent physical health, and his age-defying good looks made him appear a decade younger than his fifty-two years. His vanilla-hued skin was taut and supple with a hint of olive undertone that carried hardly a trace of any wrinkles, and the small hints of gray that now peppered his thick black hair added to his outrageous sex appeal. He kept his muscles strong and well toned with regular workouts, and jogged several times a week to round out his physical fitness regimen. Having a mate like Ted was what Victoria had always dreamed of, and again, she knew she was blessed.

After making love, Victoria lay next to her husband, running her fingers across the faint, dark hairs on his broad chest. "Alexandria's movie is probably half over by now," she said.

"Um-hm," Ted answered in a dreamy, after-sex voice.

"I'm gonna take a shower and go downstairs to make Alexandria's breakfast. We have a busy day ahead and I need to run a few errands before I drop her off at Susan's later this afternoon"

"Another sleepover?"

"Yep."

Ted pulled Victoria on top of him and grinned. "That means we'll have tonight all to ourselves."

"*Mmmm*, we sure will," she nodded.

They enjoyed another long kiss before Victoria rolled out of bed.

That Thing...

Fresh from the shower, Victoria headed downstairs. She walked into her large family room adjacent to the gourmet kitchen and found Alexandria enthralled in the classic, *Big Bird's Big Adventure*. The movie held her complete attention. It was a treat for Alexandria because Victoria and Ted didn't allow her to watch television during the week-day unless it was educational programming. Weekends were her time to *veg out*, as they liked to say.

Victoria poured Alexandria's Cheerios into her cereal bowl and sat it on the breakfast table along with a glass of orange juice. "Alexandria, come and eat your breakfast, Sweetie," she called out.

Alexandria walked slowly toward the breakfast table, pulling out the chair closest to the family room, angling it so she could see the large screen TV from where she sat.

"Wash your hands before you eat, young lady," Victoria said as she split a bagel and popped it into the toaster.

"Yes, ma'am." Alexandria made her way over to her step stool by the sink, singing along with the song that *Big Bird* was belting out.

A few minutes later Ted walked into the kitchen, still wearing his pajama bottoms and t-shirt. He came up behind Victoria at the large granite island and rubbed his pelvis against her curvy backside. He lifted her heavy mass of hair to the side and kissed the crook of her neck.

"Ted, your daughter's right over there," Victoria playfully cautioned, tilting her head to where Alexandria was sitting at the breakfast table.

"She's so into that DVD, she doesn't even know we're here."

"You're probably right," she laughed. "Didn't you get enough this morning?"

"Not hardly." Ted held Victoria close and kissed the side of her neck again. She was his second wife, but his first and only love.

After being trapped in a miserable marriage by a conniving, gold-digging wife for more than twenty years, Ted had given up on the possibility of emotional happiness, let alone the idea of love. Instead, he'd concentrated on his career, successfully achieving the professional goals he'd set for himself by following in his father's giant footsteps. But after moving from L.A. to Atlanta seven years ago to assume the position of CEO and part owner of ViaTech, one of the Southeast region's leading telecommunication companies, his plans all changed the day he met Victoria Small.

At the time, she worked in ViaTech's human resources department. When he first met her it was literally love at first sight. She was tall, elegant, and startlingly beautiful. Everything about her had captivated him. She had an MBA from Wharton, which told him she was smart, and in a few short years she'd risen to become one of the company's youngest senior directors, which meant she was ambitious and business savvy. They were qualities he admired, and she ignited a fire in him that wouldn't go away until he had her.

He'd spent months trying to get close to her under the guise of developing a professional working relationship, and his plan to woo her would have succeeded much sooner had it not been for Parker Brightwood. Parker had come into Victoria's life one weekend and swept her off her feet. Ted cursed himself for not acting sooner, or telling her exactly how he felt about her from the beginning. But he'd been caught in a delicate situation. He was her boss, and at the time he was still married.

He removed the largest barrier by filing for divorce, ending the paper thin façade he'd called a marriage. But there was still the sticky proposition of having an office romance, so he used discretion in his pursuit. Then there were the other issues; age and race. He was twelve years Victoria's senior. Although it wasn't a significant gap, and hadn't seemed to bother Victoria in the least, what Ted soon discovered was that the larger issue at hand was his race. He was white, she was black, and she'd made it clear that the two didn't mix in her romantic dealings.

Initially, Ted was disappointed to learn she felt that way. And to compound matters, his mother and Victoria's father had both expressed contrary views on the subject. He almost felt defeated because Parker had an automatic leg up by consequence of birth. His ethnic heritage guaranteed him a seat at the table. But after nearly a year of quiet, yet patient pursuit, Ted finally won Victoria's heart. He knew the love they shared was real, and it conquered a world of obstacles.

Victoria and Ted joined their daughter at the breakfast table, and soon each of them was immersed in their own worlds; Alexandria, chomping down on her cereal in between songs and giggles with *Big Bird*; Ted, reading *The Wall Street Journal* while trying to balance his bagel and coffee; and Victoria, checking her BlackBerry in between sips of her peppermint tea.

After a few minutes, Ted lowered his paper and turned his attention to Victoria. "What time does that thing start today?"

Victoria stopped in mid text and stared at him. She knew exactly what he was talking about, and she didn't like the way he'd just referred to Alexandria's first Jack and Jill playdate as "*that thing.*" She knew that Ted was still uncomfortable about their daughter's membership in the elite social organization for African-American children, but after several discussions on the matter she'd finally convinced him to let Alexandria join.

They'd gone round and round about the issue. "Ted, growing up I was a member of Jack and Jill and it was a wonderful experience," Victoria had told him several months ago when she filled out Alexandria's legacy membership application. "This will give Alexandria a chance to interact with kids who look like her, and it'll expose her to social and cultural experiences that I know you'll appreciate once you give it a chance."

For Victoria, their daughter's membership in the organization was not an issue that was up for debate. Alexandria was one of only a handful of black children in the exclusive neighborhood where they lived, as well as at the pre-school she'd been attending for the last two years. And while Ted was as white as any white man could be, thanks to Victoria, Alexandria's complexion clearly called into question the origin of her ethnic background. She was a lightly-toasted cream color, and she stood out in the sea of white faces that surrounded her every day.

"It's not a *thing*, it's a playdate," Victoria said with slight irritation, "and it starts at eleven. They'll have games and lunch for the kids and then I'll pick her up around two this afternoon."

When Alexandria heard the word playdate, she turned her attention from her movie to her parents. "Will there be lots of kids for me to play with?" she brightened.

"Yes, Sweetie," Victoria smiled. "There will be lots of kids there."

"*Yeeeaaa!*" Alexandria cheered. She was an only child, and she eagerly jumped at any opportunity to be around other children.

Ted shifted his weight in his chair. "Will there be other kids there like her?" he asked, this time with a little irritation in his voice too.

Again, Victoria knew exactly what he was hinting at, and decided to ignore his comment. "Certainly, all the children attending today will be in her age group, and from what I've been told, there's almost an even number of girls and boys. She'll have a ball," Victoria smiled, leaning over and tickling Alexandria on her side.

"That's not what I meant."

"I know exactly what you meant," Victoria responded in a sugary sweet voice, cutting Ted a look that contradicted her tone. She was happy that for once, her naturally intuitive daughter was so caught up in the excitement of her pending playdate that she hadn't picked up on the tension that had just blanketed the room. She pushed Alexandria's empty cereal bowl to the side. "Sweetie, why don't you go upstairs and start brushing your teeth. I'll be up in a minute to help you pick out a nice outfit for today, okay?"

"Okay, Mommy," Alexandria obeyed. She hopped down from her chair and headed upstairs.

Victoria and Ted sat in silence until they were sure their daughter was out of ear shot.

"What's wrong with you?" Victoria asked, peering into Ted's deep, ocean-blue eyes. "How could you ask a question like that in front of Alexandria?"

"V, you said that you wanted her to join this organization so she can be around kids like her. Well, she's not just African-American, you know." Ted folded his newspaper, placing it to the side. "Will there be any white kids or bi-racial kids there?"

Victoria let out a huff. "We've been through this before. You know full well that it's a black organization."

"My point exactly. I don't understand the necessity of her joining Jack and Jill. She's already in a play group at her school," Ted pointed out. "I thought we decided a long time ago that we weren't going to expose Alexandria to anything that was exclusionary."

Victoria threw up her hands, taking a deep breath as she looked out their large bay window. "Well, we better put the house up for sale. Take a good look around you."

"This neighborhood isn't exclusively white, but Jack and Jill *is* exclusively black," Ted responded.

"Other than the two black families in this neighborhood, whose children are in high school by the way, and a few others at her school, Alexandria's always in the minority in her everyday environment. I know what that's like, Ted…but you don't. And even though Alexandria just turned five, she sees the difference too."

"What do you mean she sees the difference?"

"You know that she's always been inquisitive and a bit more knowing than the average child her age…"

"Yes, I know, but what are you saying?"

Victoria put down her BlackBerry, locking eyes with her husband. "The other day Alexandria asked me, 'Mommy, if you're black and daddy's white…what am I?'"

They sat in silence again, staring at each other. Ted was at a temporary loss for words. He'd been warned by his mother that this day would come, and logically he knew this was a natural question for Alexandria to ask. But he hadn't anticipated it to come so soon. His little Princess was still so young.

"What did you tell her?" he asked.

"I told her the truth. That yes…mommy is black and daddy is white, and that she's the best of both of us," Victoria said, leaning back in her chair. "It seemed to satisfy her, but Ted, whether you want to face it or not, society has already labeled our child. There will be times when she *will* have to identify."

"Why do you always think she's going to have to choose one over the other?"

"Why do you think she'll never have to?" Victoria countered, shaking her head.

This was an issue that sometimes left them at odds; the struggle over their daughter's racial identity. Victoria knew that the discord would only grow as Alexandria matured in age, and the thought of having to constantly fight to infuse her African-American roots into her daughter's life was something that she knew would wear thin.

"Because we live in a global world," Ted continued. "Things have changed since we were Alexandria's age. You act like we're living in the Jim Crow era."

Victoria smirked. "Hah, Jim Crow was blatant. What I'm talking about is the subtlety of twenty-first century racism. It's cloaked so well that you don't even see it. Hell, it's got you drinking the Kool-aid. You haven't been ostracized in your social circle for being married to me, and it's only because of who you are and the economic status you hold. But trust me, they've talked about us under their breaths."

Ted shook his head, turning his eyes away from his wife, knowing she was right.

"As much as you love Alexandria and me, and as open minded as you are, you still have a blind spot when it comes to race. Are you just that oblivious, or do you purposely choose to ignore it?"

The air between them became thick with discomfort.

"I'm not oblivious about how things work," Ted answered. "I'm immersed in corporate America, remember? I understood the prejudice we were going to face long before we got married," he strained, squaring his shoulders. "We simply have different views on the subject. Alexandria's just five years old, V...five years old," he stressed. "I don't want her to feel like she has to choose anything right now."

"But, Ted, we've been teaching her how to make choices since she was old enough to speak her first words. Please, let's be clear about this," Victoria paused, "you don't want her to have to make choices when it involves race."

"V..."

Victoria interrupted him. "Before we got married I told you my concerns about us raising children and the struggles we would face, and *you* were the one who said you were ready to deal with anything that came our way, remember? Well, you better start dealing."

Ted let out a deep breath filled with frustration. He didn't want to argue so early in the morning, especially after they'd gotten the day off to such a good start. He decided that it wasn't the time to tackle such a delicate debate, so he reached over and put his hand on top of Victoria's. "I love my family, and I'll do whatever it takes to protect you and Alexandria. I'm not oblivious, and I won't make blind decisions that will hurt us. This is just something I feel strongly about."

"And so do I."

Ted leaned in close, prepared to give in, but only for the moment. "I hope Alexandria has a good time today," he smiled. "I really do."

Although Victoria knew that he meant every word coming from his mouth, they didn't arrest her worries because she knew what her husband didn't—that this was just the beginning. She wished she could wave a magic wand and change the last three hundred-fifty years of American history. This was a war she'd been suited up to fight all her life, but it was a new battle for Ted, and she knew that he would never fully understand the complexities of what it meant to be black in America.

"I'm heading upstairs because we've got to leave soon," Victoria said. She grabbed her BlackBerry and rose from the table. She leaned over and kissed Ted lightly on the lips. "We'll work through this, together."

Ted kissed her back and nodded his head. He watched his wife as she walked out of the room and thought about the question his daughter had asked...*What am I?*

He's Quite A Catch...

Victoria's stomach was a bundle of squiggly lines and nervous jitters. It had been that way since she'd arrived at Hilda Barrett's house a half hour ago. She looked down at her watch. *Damn! Thirty minutes to go.* That's how long it would be before she could get the hell out of there!

She couldn't wait to make a bee-line out the door and head straight to her car. Even though she'd have to return in a few hours to pick up

Alexandria from her first Jack and Jill playdate, she knew that she needed to leave now, before her temples throbbed any harder.

She was sitting on a large, paisley print sofa with her legs crossed, trying to concentrate on the information that Hilda, the current chapter president, was delivering to the parents of the newly minted crop of young Jack and Jill darlings. Even though Victoria knew the information like she'd written it herself, she tried to focus hard on the words coming out of Hilda's mouth. Focusing would help take her mind off the man sitting across the room. The one causing her nerves to fray at the edges.

She'd spotted him as soon as she and Alexandria had arrived. He was bent down on one knee, whispering something to an adorable little boy who looked like his "mini me." He rubbed his hands over his perfectly shaven bald head, then over the child's thick mass of black curls that mimicked the ones he'd briefly sported several years ago. When he stood, he looked as handsomely sexy as she remembered. His neatly creased trousers and white polo shirt hung well on his tall frame. She couldn't help but notice and admire the fact that his golden colored skin was still smooth, and his dimples were still alluring. His brown eyes were still piercing, and his muscular body was still in tip-top condition.

He looked at her, then down at Alexandria before returning his enticing baby browns back to focus on her again. He stared for a few uncomfortable moments before Victoria finally looked away. His gaze made her feel flush and nervous.

"Mommy, what' wrong?" Alexandria had asked, tugging at the light-weight material of Victoria's sundress, sensing the change in her mother's mood.

"Nothing's wrong. Everything's fine, Sweetie," Victoria softly reassured. When she looked in his direction again, she saw that one of the other parents had just come up and engaged him in what looked like a deep conversation, taking his attention off of her.

After one of the parent volunteers escorted Alexandria and the rest of the children back to the sunroom, Victoria tried to make casual small talk with two other mothers in attendance. They were standing in the large living room nibbling on fruit, waiting for Hilda to start the welcome meeting.

Victoria zoned in and out of the ladies' mindless Q&A; where do you live? What do you do? What sorority did you pledge? Are you a legacy? All the typical questions in that type of circle that usually bored her to tears. It wasn't until she caught the tail end of what one of the women was saying, did she realize that the new topic of conversation had shifted to *him*.

"He's the top gun in charge at the Carlyle Fraser Heart Center at Emory," the chatty woman said. Her name was Roberta Stevens. She was short and super-thin with a whiny voice, the kind that was primed for nagging. "He's one of my husband's top clients...with Merck you know," she smiled with a wave of her hand. "He's also president of the Association of Black Cardiologists, on the board of the Boys and Girls Club, and he's very involved with his son. He's quite a catch."

Tasha, the other woman who rounded out their group, looked across the room at him with hungry eyes. "So, he's single?"

Victoria quickly glanced down at Tasha's bare ring finger. There was something about her that was off-putting; a crooked line in her otherwise well put together countenance. She was attractive and her style of dress was hip and sophisticated, masking the ugliness that lay beneath. Victoria had known women like Tasha—ruthless! The cunning type who would stop at nothing to get what she wanted.

"Oh, yes," Roberta answered with a quick nod. "He's single and very much available."

"Really," Tasha pepped up, looking around the huge living room full of parents. "He's one of the few fathers who showed up here today, and probably the only single man in this entire room," she calculated. "But I bet he won't be single for long...if I can help it," she grinned, easing out the last part with a seductive purr. "So, what's the story on his son's mother?"

Victoria could see that Tasha was probing hard, probably already thinking of ways to make dinner plans with her intended prey.

Roberta shook her head. "They never married, but they share custody. She's general counsel for a huge lobbying firm downtown...a real workaholic if you ask me. That's why she's not here today, she's out of the country on business. The two of them used to fight like cats and dogs, but lately they've been getting along, which is a blessing for their son's sake. Poor little guy," Roberta sighed, shaking her head again. "What could be more important than spending time with your only child?"

Tasha nodded in agreement, but Victoria was motionless as Roberta went on. "She used to try to use the boy as leverage to get a ring...like that would ever happen."

"I thought you said they were getting along now?" Tasha asked with raised brow. "You don't think there's a chance of reconciliation?"

Victoria could see that Tasha was hoping there wasn't.

"Maybe when hell freezes over," Roberta smirked. "They're being civil for their son's sake. Besides, he's kind of, um...what's the word," she stumbled, scratching her head, "commitment phobic, that's it. I don't think he's the marrying type if you know what I mean. In the years I've known him I can't recall him ever dating anyone for longer than a few months at a time."

Victoria remained silent, listening as though the details of his life were of no concern to her.

"You seem to know a lot about him?" Tasha said, still keeping her eyes on the handsome man.

"Yes, Parker and my husband, Alvin, are quite close, and our sons used to attend the same pre-school. We do playdates and sleepovers all the time," Roberta responded. "That's his name by the way, Parker...Dr. Parker Brightwood."

Tasha grinned. "That's good information to know."

"Looks like someone's got their eye on the good doctor," Roberta giggled.

Tasha flashed a smile in Parker's direction that he seemed to return. "You could say that."

"Well, just be forewarned," Roberta advised. "He's a hard nut to crack, so good luck."

Back in the present, the other dozen or so parents looked on, actively engaged in Hilda's presentation. But Victoria felt as though she was sinking in her seat. She wanted so badly to get up and leave, to walk outside into the late morning sun to clear her mind. But she knew it would be rude to interrupt the session and she certainly didn't want to draw any attention to herself.

She focused on Hilda's speech so she wouldn't be tempted to look at Parker's sexy, soft-looking lips. She glanced up at the lovely silk taffeta drapes hanging above his head so her eyes wouldn't accidentally land on one of his deliciously inviting dimples. It had been six years since the last time she'd seen him and she still remembered his words from that day. "I'm gonna fight for you," he'd told her. "I'm not giving up on us."

He'd devastated her with a betrayal that had hurt worse than her first broken heart. She uncrossed her legs at the thought, then nervously re-crossed them, realizing that she was slowly melting away. She wondered if Parker was as uncomfortable as she was, if he was sitting across from her thinking the same thoughts that were running through her mind. She almost smiled to herself, remembering what a smooth operator he was. He could be sweating bullets like an infrared sauna and one would never know, that's how cool and controlled his outward appearance always seemed to be.

She wanted to steal a glance to see if she could discern his mood, but she was afraid he'd catch her in the act. Unlike him, nearly every move she made was obvious because she wore her feelings on her face. It made her think back to the night they first met. They'd been at one of her favorite restaurants, The Cheesecake Factory. She'd been alone, and he was on a blind date. He'd stolen glances of her the entire evening. Remembering that night made the smile she'd been trying to hide slip out before she could catch it. *Why am I thinking about this?* But the truth was that she knew exactly why those thoughts along with others were floating through her head, and it frightened her. It brought back to mind the recurring dream that invaded her sleep every so often. *I've got to get out of here right now!*

Just as she was about to rise from her seat, Hilda concluded her presentation. Victoria was relieved and tried to make a dash for the door, but just as she was headed out, Roberta stopped her.

"Victoria," Roberta smiled. "We should get together for lunch sometime. Do you have a card?" she asked, handing over one of her own.

"Oh, sure." Victoria tried to smile back as she fished through her overstuffed handbag for her silver-plated business card holder. She panicked when she looked up and saw that Parker was approaching. His eyes were fixed on her, as if he was taking inventory of her thoughts. Victoria quickly handed Roberta her card. "Call me and we'll get together," she said in a hurry.

Instead of thanking the hostess for her time and hospitality, or standing around and mingling with the other parents, Victoria headed straight for the front door.

Part Of The Package

Ted looked at his watch and rubbed his tired eyes. It was late afternoon and he'd been in his office since he left his house that morning. He was sitting at his desk, reviewing projection reports for an upcoming strategy meeting. He pulled off his reading glasses and leaned forward in his high-back leather chair, tapping his signature engraved Mont Blanc against a small stack of papers.

He was still thinking about the conversation he'd had with Victoria over breakfast. He didn't like arguing with his wife, but he knew the topic they'd discussed was one that would most certainly come up again, especially as their daughter grew in age. He hated the thought of Alexandria having to face the ugly prejudice of the world. She was his only child, and he wanted to protect her.

He let out a heavy sigh, pushing his papers to the side of his desk. This was what Victoria, and even his own mother had warned him about; part of the package that came along with being married to a black woman and raising a bi-racial child. When he and Victoria had first learned they were expecting a baby just a month after they married, he'd been elated. He couldn't wait to see a miniature version of the two of them running around the house.

But during Victoria's sixth month of pregnancy she began to verbalize her concerns more and more. "Ted, you're fooling yourself if you think that our child won't be treated differently," she'd told him.

Victoria had been speaking from a foreign place that he knew nothing about, and it had scared the shit out of him. He knew how racist the world could be, he'd worked in corporate America long enough to see it first hand. And he'd witnessed it up close and personal in his own family when he learned about some of his Knob Hill relative's reaction to him marrying Victoria. But he'd convinced himself that they were in the minority, and that things would be different for *his* child. His station in life had afforded him certain privileges that he intended to pass along to his son or daughter.

Ted had always prided himself on being a man of great will and prodigious determination. He was the son of Charles Thornton, legendary Boston businessman and real estate developer. He was a man's man, strong and immune to weakness, and like his father, he was always cool under pressure and calm in the face of adversity. But the thought of his child having to endure discrimination and cruelty, simply because of the color of her skin, was something he was ill-prepared for.

Ted leaned back in his chair and looked at the two pictures on the edge of his desk. One was a photo of Victoria, Alexandria and himself, taken last Christmas, all smiles and cheer. The other was his favorite picture of any they'd ever taken as a family. He and Victoria were smiling as they held their tiny daughter in their arms, joy and gratitude spread over both their faces. It had been a tender moment his mother-in-law had captured with her digital camera shortly after Victoria and Alexandria had arrived home from the hospital, two weeks after Alexandria had been born. They were all smiles and cheer in this photo too, but instead of celebrating the holidays and the miracle birth of Christ, they'd been celebrating the miracle that both mother and daughter were alive.

Ted rested his chin in his hand as he thought back to those days. They'd been the roughest weeks of his life, each day presenting the possibility that he might lose the two people who mattered most in his life. Victoria had suffered complications from an emergency cesarean and Alexandria had been born with health problems. Those had been bleak times, and it was only after his wife and child were safe at home, both out of danger, did Ted get a good nights sleep—his first in fourteen long days.

As Ted reminisced over those events, a thought sprang into his mind. It was something he'd heard one of the ladies say when he'd passed the nurse's station in the neonatal unit on his way to Victoria's room. "That Thornton baby is so beautiful, like a little black baby doll," the sixty-something, mocha-colored nurse had said to one of her co-workers. Then his mind took him back to small things he'd brushed off, times when he'd been out with Alexandria, taking her to the park or out for ice-cream when Victoria had weekend events to oversee for Divine Occasions. He thought about the quizzical stares that people had given him when they saw him with his daughter.

It was something that used to irritate him, and he'd attributed their behavior to plain ignorance, like the time a few months ago when a blonde woman who'd been sitting across from them in Baskin

Robbins leaned over, looked at Alexandria, and told him that she thought adoption was a great thing.

What dress to wear? What boy's offer to accept to the prom? What college to attend? Which academic major to pursue?—Those were the kinds of decisions he saw in Alexandria's future. Not what race she would claim? The thought pissed him off, and the fact that he knew there was little he could do frustrated him.

Right then and there, Ted made up his mind. Up to this point he'd been largely silent and ambivalent about the issue whenever Victoria brought it up. But now he was going to have to face the cold, hard truth that he realized he'd been avoiding. He knew that his daughter would need support and reassurance in ways that her everyday environment couldn't adequately afford her. He decided that when he returned home tonight, he would talk to Victoria and let her know that Alexandria's membership in Jack and Jill was just fine with him.

Chapter 2

A Roadmap For Chaos...

It was early evening and Victoria had just returned from dropping off Alexandria at Susan Whitehurst's house. Susan's little girl, Claudia, was Alexandria's best friend in the neighborhood. Since the beginning of summer their sleepovers had become a regular weekend ritual that both girls looked forward to. They'd play dress-up, eat their favorite snacks, and watch their favorite movies. Claudia, a freckled-face little sweetheart, was a year older than Alexandria, and in many ways their friendship, however elementary, reminded Victoria of the bond that she and her friend Debbie shared.

Ready to relax from her long and stressful day, Victoria went downstairs to the wine cellar in search of a vintage bottle of Rivesaltes. She needed it because ever since she'd seen Parker her nerves had been rattled like loose change. She couldn't get him out of her mind and she hoped that a good drink would help do the trick.

Her afternoon had been wrought with anxiety. After leaving Hilda Barrett's house, instead of going by her office to tackle the small stack of paperwork that she knew was sitting on her desk, and then picking up Ted's dry cleaning as she'd originally planned to do, Victoria found herself sitting in the park, camped out on a bench for nearly two hours. The fact that it had been an uncomfortably muggy, ninety-five degrees outside hadn't fazed her, neither had the stares she received from joggers and dog-walkers alike as they passed by, no doubt wondering why the woman in the stylish sundress and sophisticated three-inch designer sandals looked as though she'd just been given a fatal medical diagnosis. She didn't care because she had more important things to think about; like what she would do if she ran into Parker when she returned to Hilda's to pick up her daughter.

Why am I acting so silly? Victoria had asked herself. *He means nothing to me anymore. Why am I letting Parker Brightwood get to me!*

But again, Victoria knew exactly why Parker had stirred the emotions that were rumbling in the pit of her stomach. He was part of a recurring dream that still haunted her sleep, appearing on nights when she least expected. The first time had been six years ago, just a few months shy of her wedding day. In the dream, Parker had come to her doorstep in the middle of the night, begging for forgiveness and a second chance at their relationship. Despite her best efforts to resist him, they ended up in bed, making love until she awoke in a passion drenched sweat. And just as it had been when he'd entered her dreams that very first night, the thought of his touch still left a tingling sensation on her skin that felt as warm and real as her own flesh.

And yet another vision plagued her mind, one that was just as unsettling as her dream. She'd been lying in her hospital bed a few days after Alexandria had been born. She'd lost a tremendous amount of blood and was sedated from the drugs an IV was pumping into her system. She'd awoken in the middle of the night when a sharp pain gripped her. She opened her eyes and saw Parker as he was leaving her room. He wore a concerned but caring look on his face as he walked out into the hallway, disappearing from sight. She wasn't sure if she'd dreamed it, or if he'd really been there. But what she did know in the here and now was that she needed to stay the hell away from him!

Victoria knew she had to pull herself together. She had to go back to Hilda's and pick up Alexandria, and she knew that more than likely she'd run into Parker again, and this time there would be little chance of avoiding him.

But the closer she got to Hilda's house the more anxious she felt. Only hours earlier she'd managed to slip out the door like a thief in the night just as he'd been headed her way. But she feared this time she might not be lucky enough to dodge him.

When she arrived back at Hilda's she parked out front, rushed inside, and quickly looked around. She was thankful that Parker was nowhere in sight. She scooped up Alexandria and hightailed it back to her silver Mercedes SUV like she was driving a getaway car.

As Victoria stood at her kitchen counter uncorking the bottle of wine and thinking about her day, she tried to put the messy business of Parker Brightwood out of her thoughts. The fact that she'd handled the situation with the maturity of a tenth grader made her feel weak and silly, and it drove her crazy that Parker's face was still imprinted on her mind. And if that weren't enough to add to her growing discomfort, Alexandria had declared his son her new best friend.

"Mommy, PJ is my friend. He's nice!" Alexandria had announced with enthusiasm on their drive back home.

"Who's PJ?" Victoria asked, knowing who he was, but still needing confirmation.

"He's my new friend."

"*Oh*, and which little boy was he?" She had a thimble of hope that the PJ her daughter was referring to didn't answer to the name, Parker Jr.

"The nice one!" Alexandria exclaimed.

Victoria smiled. "No, sweetie, I mean...describe him. What color shirt was he wearing?"

"A blue one with a little thing on it right here," Alexandria said, pointing to the upper left side of her chest.

Victoria nodded with understanding. Her daughter was so observant, noticing the smallest of details, a characteristic she'd definitely taken after her father; Ted noticed everything!

"Mommy, can I go to PJ's house and play, *please*. He has a dog named Noah, and he said I can play with him!"

"We'll see," was all that Victoria could muster. The thought of having any involvement with Parker Brightwood gave her a shiver, the kind that ran from the top of her head down to the bottom of her feet.

*PJ is nice, and PJ is funny, and PJ knows the songs that I know, and PJ has a dog named Noah. PJ, PJ, PJ...*that was all Victoria heard from the moment Alexandria had climbed into her car seat until she'd dropped her off at the Whitehurst's house.

The sound of the garage door drew Victoria from her troublesome thoughts and back to the present. She reached into the cabinet for another glass and started to pour. She knew that after Ted's long day at the office he'd probably need a relaxing drink just as much as she did.

"Hey," she said, looking at her husband as he walked through the back door. She felt a twinge of guilt as he gave her an adoring smile. "Here," she nodded, handing him the glass of wine.

Ted gave her a peck on the cheek, then took a quick sip. "This is good, thanks." He put his glass on the counter and removed his jacket. "Let's go into the family room and relax."

After Victoria prepared a quick plate of cheese and crackers, and grabbed a handful of chocolates out of the Godiva box in the refrigerator, they settled into their familiar spots on the couch. Ted pressed the remote and threw back his head as Cassandra Wilson's smooth voice belted out a sultry tune from the stereo's surround sound system. The soft music and low lights were soothing, and just what they both needed. Victoria stretched her legs, resting her feet in Ted's lap.

"How was your day?" he asked, rubbing one of her ruby red painted toes. He wanted to start the conversation off slow.

"Um, busy. How about yours?"

"The same." He sensed that Victoria was uncomfortable, and that maybe somehow she knew he was going to bring up the conversation they'd had earlier that morning. "Listen, V, about Jack and Jill…"

"I know you don't want Alexandria to be a member," she said, looking away from him.

"No, I don't but…"

"Ted," she interrupted. "I think it'll be a good experience for her, but if you don't want Alexandria to be involved I will respect your decision because…" Victoria let her words trail off. She couldn't finish her sentence because she felt a mixture of relief and guilt about the choice she'd made, a decision she'd come to during her meditative hours on the park bench earlier that afternoon.

She didn't want to pass up an enriching opportunity for her daughter, but at the same time she knew there was danger ahead if she kept Alexandria in the organization. It was a danger that would impact their entire family more than a simple playdate ever could. Ted and Parker had been enemies. Their past encounters had been frosty at best, and Victoria knew she couldn't run the risk of Alexandria befriending Parker's son. That relationship would usher Parker back into their lives, and she had no doubt that it would be a roadmap for chaos.

Knowing that she had to nip the possible threat in the bud, Victoria continued. "We have to stand united in our decisions involving Alexandria, so if this is something that you don't want, I'll support you on it."

Ted was slightly taken aback, not expecting Victoria to acquiesce so easily, or at all for that matter. He knew that once she had something in her head, it usually took prayer on bended knee to change her mind. "You mean you don't mind if we pull her out of Jack and Jill? I thought this was something you wanted?" He didn't know why he was questioning her when she was basically giving him what he'd initially argued for, but what he did know was that this was very unlike his wife.

Victoria sat her wine glass on the coffee table and leaned forward for emphasis. "I want what's best for our family, and like I said, I want us to stand united in the decisions we make concerning Alexandria. We won't always agree on things, but I'm willing to bend on this one." She looked away and swallowed hard, letting her small lie slid off her tongue and down her throat.

Ted smiled, appreciating the fact that his wife was willing to compromise and stand by him in the decision he'd made, even if he'd changed his mind. He reached for her and pulled her into his chest. "V, do you know how much I love you?"

"Yes, I do. And I love you just as much."

Ted kissed Victoria on her forehead and stroked her hair. "Actually, I've been doing a lot of thinking, and even though I'm not one-hundred percent behind the idea, I think we should keep Alexandria in Jack and Jill."

Victoria pulled away, looking at him with surprise. This was something completely unexpected. "Why…what changed your mind?"

"Like you said, we need to stand united around the decisions we make in Alexandria's best interest, and I know this is something you feel strongly about. Besides," he paused, taking a deep breath, "what you said earlier…you were right. She needs to be in an environment where she sees kids who look like her."

Victoria didn't know what to say, and Ted could see the bewilderment on her face.

"V, I wanted to believe that things would be different for our daughter, but I know I have to face the reality that even though I see her as simply *my* child, the world will see her as a black woman, and I can't be the one who sends a message that there's anything wrong with that. Her mother is a smart, talented, beautiful black woman, and she will be too."

Victoria leaned into Ted's shoulder, resting her head there. She felt as though she was going to cry, but for all the wrong reasons.

Doin' The Nasty…

It wasn't how Victoria had planned to start her work week; frustrated and disjointed. Her calendar was jam packed with appointments and events in the days ahead. She was under pressure from duties and obligations, and she didn't have time to sit in the funk of her current mood.

Monday mornings seemed to always be her hardest day of the week. It usually took her a day or two to make the adjustment from her short-lived, hectic weekends spent with her family, to the frenzied and often chaotic world of event planning. And this particular Monday was even more challenging than most, given the fact that she'd been thrown for a loop that had sent her into overdrive. Her nerves were still on edge because she couldn't get Parker out of her mind.

She was on her way to work, moving slowly from her restless night. She'd been awake since three a.m., and her body had been shrouded in the same fleeting feeling she'd had since Saturday. It was a feeling that was frighteningly familiar, like life was about to take an unpredictable turn.

She remembered feeling that way at the start of her relationship with Ted, and again when she'd first met Parker. But even with the confusion and drama that those days had brought to her life, she was almost certain that this new turn would be much more complicated. Back in those days she'd only had to think of herself, but now she had a child and a husband, and it made the stakes much higher.

Victoria walked past the neatly trimmed shrubs and abundant

hostas that lined the walkway of the building leading up to her office suite. She opened the door, turned on the lights, and scanned the desk of the cubical to her left. It was empty. She let out a small sigh of relief when she remembered that Denise would be off until Wednesday. Although she loved her office manager and very dear friend, she wasn't up to facing her today. Denise was intuitive and could read people like a book. She would be able to see that something was wrong, and would ask questions that couldn't easily be answered.

Victoria walked down the small hallway that led to her spacious office in the back, turned on the light and dropped her large, leather handbag behind her desk. Unlike most people who dreaded going into the office, Victoria loved it. Ironically, her office had become her safe haven, providing a temporary reprieve from stress and worries.

When she was single, her home on Summerset Lane had been that retreat and she'd basked in its comforts. But now, when she returned home after a long day, it was motherhood and wifely duties that greeted her at the door, and sometimes she needed a break. Her office was the one place she could go to relax and shut out the world, even if it was for just a few hours. And its serene setting, tucked away in a quiet business park that was situated in the upscale Buckhead area, served as the perfect location. The added bonus was that it was only a ten minute drive from where she lived.

She'd taken the same meticulous care in decorating her office suite that she used with her own home. She'd painted the walls a golden bronze and dressed the windows with richly textured fabrics. The recessed lighting and accent lamps helped to cast a warm glow that set the mood to welcome visitors who came to do business. She'd even converted the tiny office adjacent to hers into a small kitchen, affording her the convenience of preparing a quick meal for herself or a delicious treat for prospective clients to sample. She'd thought of everything to make it feel like a home away from home. After all, she was in the business of making every occasion special.

Victoria sat behind her desk, uneasy about the emotions that her encounter with Parker had stirred, and at a loss for what to do about them. Then she thought about the one person who she knew could help her make sense of things. Her touchstone—Tyler Jacobs.

Tyler had been Victoria's best friend since their undergraduate days when she was a student at Spelman College and he was at neighboring

Morehouse College. Theirs was an unconventional friendship, challenging the myth that a man and woman couldn't be "just friends." They were both only children who'd found in one another a missing sibling. Over the years they'd been each others sounding board on everything from the people they'd dated to the business decisions they made, and right now she needed him.

She sat behind her desk and dialed Tyler's cell.

"What?" he answered in a huff on the second ring.

"My, aren't we cheerful this morning."

"Don't start, it's too damn early for jokes," Tyler whipped out in his Brooklyn born accent.

"You must not have had your coffee yet." Victoria knew that if Tyler didn't have his morning cup of Joe, he could be quite the bear to deal with.

"No I haven't, plus I'm tryin' to get around this idiot in front of me who doesn't know shit about merging," Tyler said as he navigated his Explorer through traffic. "What's up?

Victoria bit down on her lower lip, hearing the fatigue in her own voice. "Can you meet me for lunch?"

Tyler paused for a moment. "Not today, I have a meeting with a funder. But what's goin' on? You okay?"

"I had a rough weekend and I need to talk. I really need your advice about something."

"You at your office?"

"Yes."

"I'm in the area. I can stop by now if you have time?"

"I'll have coffee waiting for you when you get here."

Victoria hung up the phone and walked to the kitchen. She filled her Cuisinart brewer with Columbian Blend, reached in the cabinet and sat two mugs on the counter. *Maybe some coffee will get me going too.*

She strolled back to her office and plopped down on the maroon-colored chenille sofa that seemed to call her name. She closed her eyes, letting the coffee aroma tickle her nose, glad that she'd had the foresight to outfit the room with home furnishings instead of standard office fare—the comfort was priceless.

She knew she should be sitting behind her desk, responding to emails and returning phone calls, but she couldn't bring herself to move. Her body felt tired and heavy, the result of only a few hours of sleep over the last two days. Normally, she was a sound sleeper and nothing stood between her and eight solid hours of peaceful slumber each and every night. Ted often teased that once her head hit the pillow, not even an earthquake could wake her. But for the past two nights she'd laid in bed staring at the ceiling, thinking about Parker.

Victoria opened her eyes when she heard the musical chime of her front office door, signaling that a visitor was entering her suite. "Come on back, I'm in my office," she called out to Tyler.

Tyler walked into Victoria's plush office and over to the sofa where she was reclined. "You better be glad you're in this neighborhood," he said, shaking his head. "You're up in here stretched across your sofa with the door unlocked, lettin' any and everybody up in this camp. Do you know how dangerous that is? I could be a serial killer or some-thin'. You need to be more careful," he warned. "Plus, you need to pull down your skirt, I can see your pink *drawers*," he chuckled in a fake southern accent.

Victoria laughed as she crossed her legs and tugged at her short linen skirt, forcing it down her shapely thighs. "Tyler, I knew it was you. Besides, the only people who venture back into this area are clients who have business here. And by the way, I don't wear *drawers*. I wear thongs, boy shorts, bikinis, cheekies, and v-strings, and today's selection is a pair of boy shorts, which happen to be fuchsia, not pink."

"That's TMI. Your ass still needs to be more careful," he cautioned again.

Victoria rolled her eyes. "Let me get your grumpy behind some coffee before I have to curse you out first thing this morning."

Victoria prepared their cups, cut Tyler a slice of coffee cake that she'd baked yesterday afternoon, and then returned to the sofa where he was now sitting.

"Thanks, and I get coffee cake too," Tyler said, licking his lips. He took a sip of coffee and dug into his morning treat. His mood was brighter already.

Victoria watched him drink and munch as she quietly sipped her coffee.

"So what's up? What have you done that requires the expert advice of my steal trap mind?" Tyler said between bites of his cake.

"Who says that *I've* done anything?"

"Tyler, I really need your advice about something," he mimicked, imitating the urgency in her voice when she'd called. "I know you, so what's up?"

All Victoria could do was shake her head and slump her shoulders. She sat up and leaned forward, preparing to share her dilemma with the one person who she knew would give her the best and most unbiased advice she could find.

Tyler knew how to combine the right amount of clinical professionalism with a good dose of humor and compassion, helping a troubled mind walk through difficult situations. He'd perfected that skill over the last eighteen years, counseling at-risk youth through Youths First Initiative, or YFI as it was commonly called. He founded the nonprofit organization for inner city youths after graduating from Morehouse. Today, YFI was so successful that other non-profit and mentoring organizations often sought his counsel, using the curriculum model he'd developed as a diagram for their own programs.

Tyler had practiced his own form of therapy when he battled two crippling losses four years ago. The first tragedy came when his Aunt Beatrice, his mother's sister who'd raised him after his parent's untimely death, had a massive stroke and died. Then a year later he lost his beloved wife, Juliet. Had it not been for Victoria's calm, steadfast support, standing by his side through his grief and depression, Tyler had no doubt that he wouldn't have survived those devastating days.

Juliet had been the love of Tyler's life. She was his soul mate in the truest sense, but their journey hadn't been an easy one. They'd broken up after college, then several years later after more than a few failed relationships on her part, and an ill-suited marriage that lead to divorce on his, they'd reunited and tied the knot as they should have done from the beginning.

After loosing both his parents in a tragic car accident as a young boy, Tyler had finally buried the hurt he'd been carrying when Juliet became his wife. But two years into their marriage, Juliet's health began to decline. A doctor's visit revealed that she had developed an aggressive form of kidney disease. Over the next eight months she and Tyler prayed and waited for an organ donor that never came.

Victoria sat on the edge of her seat and looked Tyler in the eye. "I saw Parker over the weekend."

"Whoa." Tyler took a deep breath, sitting his mug and empty dessert plate on the small coffee table in front of him. "Okay, tell me how it all went down?"

Victoria told him about her weekend as he listened patiently. She began with her shock of seeing Parker at Hilda Barrett's house on Saturday morning, and then again in her dreams later that night. She admitted that he'd been the first person she thought about when she had woken up in bed the next morning, and that when she made a quick trip to the supermarket yesterday afternoon, she'd scanned the length of the produce aisle, wondering if she'd run into him again.

After she finished, she paused and let out a deep sigh, gripping the back of her neck which had stiffened from her stress. "Of all the people to run into…and after all these years."

"Damn," Tyler said. "So, is he married?"

"No, he's still single. Roberta, one of the parents whose husband is good friends with Parker, said that he and his son's mother share custody."

"Who's his baby mama?"

"Roberta said she's some high-powered attorney, so I'm assuming it's Pamela," Victoria said, rolling her eyes. "She's the heifer he used to date…the one who showed up for Christmas dinner when I went home with him to visit his family, remember?"

"Oh, I remember," Tyler paused. "I'm not detecting a little jealousy, am I?"

"Don't be silly."

Tyler cut Victoria a questioning look.

"I'm not jealous, but honestly…I can't get Parker out of my mind. I keep thinking about him, seeing his face, and remembering things…"

Tyler rubbed his fingers across his goatee, a feature that gave his boyish good looks a manly appeal. "What kind of things?"

Victoria dropped her eyes to the floor. She'd never told Tyler about her recurring dream. "Romantic things…um, sexual things."

"Doin' the nasty?"

Victoria let out a small laugh despite herself. "You can be so crude."

"But I'm always on point, and you know I'm gonna shoot it to you straight," Tyler said, laughing along with her. "But, on the real, that's some serious shit."

"Tell me about it."

"You haven't told Ted yet, have you?"

"No, and I'm trying to figure out a good way to break it to him."
Tyler folded his arms over his chest. "Just tell him like it happened."

"You make it sound so easy. You know the two of them never liked
each other. There's history there."

"And that's exactly why you've gotta tell him. You're bound to run
into Parker again, especially now that you've got my niece involved in
all that Jack and Jill bourgeoisie nonsense."

Victoria wagged her finger at Tyler. "Your Aunt Beatrice had you in
Jack and Jill just like I was, and both your parents, God rest their souls,
were legacies, so don't even try it."

"True, true, you got me," Tyler laughed. "You know I gotta mess
with you. But seriously, you don't want Ted to be caught off guard
about this."

"I know."

"And it'll look shady as hell if you two run into Parker at some
event and he finds out that you've had contact with the brothah all
along."

"I haven't had *contact* with Parker. I've only seen him once and we
didn't even speak."

"I know, but that's not how it's gonna look. Think about it. Wasn't
it your idea to put Alex in Jack and Jill?"

"Yeah."

"Basically against Ted's wishes, right?"

"Yeah."

"Now, all of a sudden Parker's son pops up there too. You
should've said something right away because now it'll look suspicious.
That's all I'm sayin'."

"I know, I know," Victoria sighed, running her fingers through her
thick mass of hair.

"I don't know what the big problem is. Hell, just tell him that
Parker's son happens to be in Jack and Jill too. It's not like you can control the organization's membership roster."

"You make a good point. But like you said, it's still gonna look suspicious because I didn't tell him right away," Victoria said before taking her last sip of coffee.

"But it'll be even worse the longer you wait." Tyler made the comment, hoping that some of what he'd said was sinking in. He recognized his best friend's familiar pattern of avoidance. Whenever Victoria didn't want to face an issue, she'd kick it to the side until it erupted into something she couldn't control. She'd been that way since childhood, when she learned how to tuck painful experiences away like a discarded toy.

"I feel so damn guilty because I keep thinking about Parker in ways that I shouldn't. What if Ted senses that when I tell him?" Victoria said, knowing how discerning her husband was.

"Then you better put on your game face."

"Oh, brother."

"Listen, if it's any consolation, it's not unusual to have these kind of feelings. You haven't seen Parker in years and he rekindled some old memories. Ol' boy had you strung out for a minute."

"Yeah, but why am I remembering the good times and the great sex? Parker was selfish and he cheated on me. Why can't my mind focus on that?"

Tyler cleared his throat and spoke with intensity because he wanted Victoria to face the reality of what he was about to say. "Maybe for the same reason you couldn't look him in the eye, or be in the same room with him, or tell your husband that you saw him."

The two friends stared at each other in silence. They both knew the answer to his questions, and it filled both their minds with worry.

Chapter 3

Why Are You Giving Me Attitude?...

It was hump day, and Victoria was glad that she'd made it half-way through the week. She had yet to breathe a word to Ted about her encounter with Parker, and despite her best efforts, the dashing doctor remained front and center in her thoughts. She was still sleep deprived from her worries, but had managed to doze off for a few hours the previous night. She was thankful for the rest that had come shortly after midnight because she knew she had a busy day ahead.

After dropping off Alexandria at summer camp, Victoria headed to Peachtree Country Day School, which was only a few miles away. She was there to register her daughter for kindergarten. She couldn't believe that her little girl was out of pre-k, and as Alexandria herself had declared, would be in big kid's school in the fall.

Victoria and Ted had looked at several schools before settling on Peachtree Country Day. It was one of the top private schools in the city and boasted a stellar reputation for high academic standards and a commitment to diversity, or as the headmaster of the lower school had stated on the school's web site, *inclusion.* That had been a major factor in both Victoria and Ted's decision.

Victoria arrived at the school and was once again impressed by the art covered walls and sparkling clean floors throughout the building.

She tried to center her focus on her task at hand as she walked down the long hallway toward the admissions office. Her sleepless nights were beginning to make her feel like a walking zombie. *Shake it off,* she told herself.

When she finally reached the main office and opened the door, she froze in her tracks. She wanted to believe that she was imagining things, or that she was witnessing a mirage, the result of sleep-deprivation. But as much as she wanted to dismiss it, she knew what she saw in front of her was real. Even though his back was turned to her, she knew it was *him.* The broad, muscular shoulders, and alluring scent of citrus and spice could only belong to one man. It was Parker Brightwood, and he was shaking hands with Katie Palmer, the Director of Admissions. *What the hell is he doing here?*

"We're so happy to have PJ with us this year," Katie said with a sincere smile. "I assure you he'll have a great experience here at Peachtree."

"I have every confidence that he will," Parker replied.

Victoria was about to duck into the empty conference room to her right when Katie called out her name. "Hello, Mrs. Thornton, you're right on time. I was just finishing up here," she said, nodding toward Parker.

At that, Parker turned around and looked Victoria dead in her eyes. She stood stock-still, unable to register a greeting in response to Katie's cheerful one. The room felt tight and stuffy. Parker's presence made her heart beat fast, just as it had at Hilda's last weekend. His sun-kissed skin looked soft to the touch, and his tan colored jacket, sky blue shirt and tailored trousers made him look casually sexy. It was a look he wore well, and judging from Katie's wide smile and eager eyes, she thought so too.

Parker extended his hand to Victoria. "Victoria, it's nice to see you again."

Slowly, Victoria slid her hand into his for a delicate, yet firm handshake. His palm was warm and electric to the touch. "Hello, Dr. Brightwood," she said, sounding much more formal in her greeting than he had. She felt her forehead turn hot as Parker held on to her hand.

Finally, after a few seconds, Victoria broke his intense grip when Katie interrupted them. "Oh, I see you two know each other?" she smiled, looking back and forth between them.

Parker spoke up, not taking his eyes off Victoria. "Yes, we do."

Victoria's only response was a simple nod as Katie quietly observed the subtle mixture of attraction-filled tension that bounced between them.

Parker could see that Victoria was having a hard time so he decided to give her a reprieve—at least for the moment. "I should be going," he said, turning his attention back to Katie. "Thank you for your time. I'll email you those contact numbers by the end of the day." Then he nodded to Victoria, "It was really good seeing you again…Victoria." And with that, he walked out the door.

Katie led Victoria back to her slightly cluttered office while they made small talk. The bubbly admissions officer was very cordial, making pleasant conversation that breezed by Victoria's ears. Over the course of the next twenty minutes, Victoria managed to complete Alexandria's paperwork by rote, filling out forms and answering questions until her daughter's registration was complete.

After a quick exchange of smiles and promises to become active in the PTA, Victoria shook Katie's hand, bid her good-bye, and hurried out of the admissions office and back down the hallway. She couldn't wait to get the hell out of dodge. But when she turned the corner to go out the door that led to the parking lot, she saw Parker leaning against the wall, arms folded, looking at her like she owed him something.

They both stared at each other, standing in silence.

"So…are you going to just stand there staring at me or do you have something to say?" Victoria asked, hoping she didn't appear as nervous as she felt.

Parker took his time appraising her, taking in her entire look from her stylish peep-toe heels that highlighted her manicured toes, to her fitted white skirt that clung seductively to her curvaceous hips, to her coral-colored silk blouse that made her chocolate skin shine with radiance. He thought her beautiful face was full of regal defiance, one of the many qualities that had initially attracted him to her. She was the woman he'd loved so deeply that he hadn't been able to eat for days after their break up. He shook his head with a slight smile. "Why are you giving me attitude, Victoria?"

"Why are standing here…obviously waiting for me? What do you want?"

"I want to know why you avoided me last weekend?"

Victoria shifted her weight to her right foot, feeling transparent under his gaze. Parker knew her almost as well as her own husband did, and even though it had been six years since they'd last spoken, he could still discern her mood. And right now, she knew that he knew she was nervous as hell. It was strange to her, but having that knowledge gave her a jolt of excitement. She wanted to smile, but she dared not give him the pleasure.

Parker uncrossed his arms. "I was just as shocked to see you at Hilda's as you were at seeing me. I wanted to say something to you, but I could see by the way you hurried away that you didn't want to talk…at least not to me" He said, motioning his head toward the long hallway that led to the school's main office. "You acted like I was a stranger back there. Are you still angry with me?"

Victoria looked at him, shifting her weight back to her left foot. He was still as straight to the point and free with his emotions as she remembered. His ability to express his feelings and thoughts, not afraid if it made him seem vulnerable, was a trait that contradicted his tough exterior. It was also a quality that had quickly won her heart when they'd dated.

Victoria bit down on her lower lip and tried to come up with a response. She wanted to tell him how she felt but she knew she couldn't, for fear of where it might lead. She knew those dangerous thoughts were better left stored in the safe place where she'd kept them buried over the years.

Parker reached into the breast pocket of his jacket and pulled out his card. "Call me. Maybe we can talk?"

Victoria surprised them both when she extended her hand and took the card without hesitation. She tucked it down into her handbag, stopping short of offering up one of her own in return.

"Are you going to call me?" Parker asked.

Victoria looked at him, shrugging her shoulders. "I don't know."

It was the only thing she'd been completely sure of since last Saturday.

Caught In Your Own Web…

Victoria practically made skid marks on the pavement trying to get out of the school's parking lot. Parker's black Navigator was close behind her. She knew he was watching her every move because when she glanced into her rear view mirror, his piercing brown eyes were staring right back at her. *Is he following me?* She made a sharp left, only to see him do the same. Her nerves were on red alert. Finally, when she turned at the next intersection his truck kept straight until he was eventually out of sight.

When she walked into her office, Denise was there, waiting to greet her. Victoria had almost forgotten that it was her friend's first day back from a much needed vacation. She prayed that Denise wouldn't notice how frazzled she was.

"Good morning," Denise smiled, lively as always. She popped up from behind her desk and gave Victoria a quick hug before jumping back into her work. "The phone's been ringing off the hook since I walked through the door. Denise Smith, at the Hilton Garden Inn Winston-Salem, called a few minutes ago about the WSSU Founders Day Luncheon this fall. I told her that we've already contacted the event chairs on the board and that you'll get back to her later today with a headcount and the exact date that you plan to arrive in town prior to the event," she said, handing Victoria a pink message slip. "That lady's a sharp cookie, and with a name like that, you know she's got to be good," she grinned at the mention of the woman who bore her same name.

Victoria tried to give her a small smile. "Yeah, Denise is great."

"And the director of Dress for Success wants to set up a meeting for next month to go over plans for their annual Gala. She also wants to know if you can do a Professional Women's Group workshop for them this fall. If you need me to drop off those business suits you're going to donate, just let me know?"

Victoria nodded her head again, not wanting to think about anything except how to ease the headache growing between her temples.

"Well, did you miss me while I was gone?" Denise smirked. "A *'Hi, Denise, welcome back,'* would be nice."

"Uh...yeah," Victoria smiled. "Welcome back."

Denise cocked her head to the side, staring at Victoria long and hard. "Girlfriend, what's wrong?"

Victoria tried to put on a good face. "Oh, nothing. I'm fine. Just really busy." She avoided Denise's eyes as she hurried down the narrow hall, heading straight to her office. After getting situated behind her desk she drank the last of her bottled water, swallowing hard as she washed down three extra-strength Tylenols. She kicked off her heels and leaned back in her chair, trying to block the image of Parker's face from her mind.

She turned on her computer and hoped for a few moments of uninterrupted silence. Unfortunately, her wish hadn't been granted and she cursed herself for not asking Denise to hold her calls until noon. Frustrated, she pushed the speaker phone button and tried to sound as cheery as she could. "Yes?"

"Bridezilla's on the line for you," Denise's voice echoed through the room.

Victoria put her hand to her head. It was her old college friend, Gigi Howard...*again!* Gigi had already called her cell phone three times and it wasn't even noon yet. She was getting married this Saturday and she'd hired Victoria to plan the event.

"This is going to be the wedding of the year!" Gigi had said six months ago after becoming engaged to Gary Hicks, star point guard for the Atlanta Hawks, who happened to be several years her junior. Before the announcement hit the papers she'd called Victoria in the middle of the night, begging her to coordinate the wedding. It was something that Victoria had agreed to against her better judgment— mixing personal friendships with business dealings. Aside from Tyler and his organization's annual Christmas fundraiser, it was her strict practice to never take on friends as business clients. Helping them plan a birthday or holiday party was one thing, but major events, particularly if money was involved, was where she drew the line.

But Gigi had been worrisome and persistent, insisting that had Juliet been alive she would have wanted Victoria to coordinate her special day. Victoria hated to admit that Gigi was right, but she knew deep down that Juliet would have been one-hundred percent on board with the idea. Gigi and Juliet had been best friends, and Victoria felt she owed it to Juliet's memory, if for no other reason, to make Gigi's day as elegant and special as possible....if one could imagine elegance and Gigi in the same breath.

"Denise, can you please take a message?" Victoria asked.

Denise rolled her eyes on the other end. "Girlfriend, you know I don't like dealing with this heifer. Besides, she's *your* friend."

"You don't have to carry on a conversation with her. Just take a message, I can't talk with Gigi right now," she said with biting irritation. She didn't mean to snap, and instantly felt worse than she had a moment ago.

Denise could hear the stress in Victoria's voice. "All right. I'll take a message," she said in a dry tone before disconnecting the line.

Victoria hung her head, disappointed in herself for the way she was behaving. Not only had she brushed off Denise when she came in, she'd just snapped at her for no good reason.

She and Denise had been friends for more than a decade. They'd met back in the day when they both worked at ViaTech. Denise had been her administrative assistant, and from the very beginning their professional relationship instantly blossomed into a sisterhood that each woman cherished. Two years after Victoria resigned from ViaTech and was running Divine Occasions full-time, she'd hired Denise as her office manager. She couldn't think of anyone more competent, qualified, or trusted to run the daily office operations of her growing business.

Denise was smart as a whip, loyal as a soldier, honest to a fault, and could see through bullshit; all attributes that Victoria valued, especially in a profession full of inflated egos and exhaustive personalities. They'd been there for each other through good times and bad. It was Denise who had kept clients on track and brought home-cooked meals to the house for Ted and Victoria's parents the week Alexandria had been born. And it was Victoria's shoulder that soaked up Denise's tears for a month after her mother passed away last year.

Victoria knew she shouldn't have taken her frustrations out on Denise. She was about to walk out and apologize when Denise came through her door holding two coffee mugs. She handed Victoria the one with the *Celestial Seasonings* tea bag string dangling from the side. "I figured you might need this."

"Thanks," Victoria said as she took the warm mug into her hands. "Denise, I'm sorry for snapping at you. I didn't mean to…"

Denise cut her off. "I want to know what's goin' on?" she asked, taking a seat in the upholstered chair in front of Victoria's desk. "I know *Ms. Thang* could make Job loose patience, but I don't think it's Gigi that's got your panties twisted in a knot this morning. You walked in here looking all distracted and stressed…and that's not like the confident business woman I know. Talk to me?"

Denise sipped her breakfast blend while Victoria strained with anguish as she unfolded the details of her two encounters with Parker.

"*Umph*, I can't believe Parker has a child. Is it a little witch or a little warlock?"

Victoria gasped. "Denise, you should be ashamed of yourself!"

"I know, I know, I'm sorry," she said, but didn't really appear to be.

"He has a son, and he looks just like Parker spit him out. He's so adorable." Victoria smiled even though she hadn't meant to. She couldn't deny that PJ was a handsome child with a face and smile that made you want to pinch his rosy little cheeks. "And before you ask, Parker is still single and I think that Pamela is his baby mama."

"The ice queen he used to date who showed up all big and bold at his parent's house for Christmas dinner?"

"The very one."

Denise threw up her hands. "Poor thing, that child doesn't stand a chance in hell, being spawned from the likes of those two."

"Denise, will you stop," Victoria said. "PJ's just a child. He can't help who his parents are."

"I guess you're right. Maybe being around those other kids in Jack and Jill will be a good influence on him. If you've got Alexandria in it, it can't be half bad," Denise said.

A line of worry sprang to Victoria's forehead. "We'll be seeing Parker and his son on a regular basis." She sat in momentary silence, taking in the thought. "Damn, what am I gonna do?"

"Girlfriend, you knew you were bound to run into him sooner or later, and frankly, I'm surprised it hadn't happened before now. It's a small world, especially in the circles you travel. It was just a matter of time."

Victoria looked at Denise with questioning eyes. She knew that her friend had never liked Parker, and once he showed his ass by getting caught cheating in the act, Denise had been through. "I know you have an opinion, so give it to me?" she asked.

Denise crossed her plump thighs and leaned back in her chair. "Well, you avoided him like the plague when you saw him last Saturday, and you could barely look him in the eye when you saw him again today. I think that says it all."

"Yeah, that I can't stand to be in the same room with him."

Denise rolled her eyes. "Please don't front. You know who you're talkin' to, don't you?"

Victoria looked away. Her hidden desires were finally bubbling to the surface. She let out a slow sigh. "Denise, this isn't good. I don't know what I'm going to do."

"Girlfriend, you act like you screwed the man."

Victoria flinched because in her mind she had.

"I agree with the advice that you said Tyler gave you," Denise continued. "You need to let Ted know about Parker. It already looks suspicious that you haven't told him before now."

"Yes, I know. I just have to find the right time."

"Girlfriend, the time ain't gonna get no righter than the present."

Victoria knew that just like Tyler, Denise was on the money. She knew that she couldn't continue to avoid the issue because the longer she waited, the more difficult it would be to explain to Ted why she hadn't mentioned running into Parker right away. Plus, she was drowning in the thoughts that had been dancing through her mind about the man she'd once loved. She hoped she would be able to keep those emotions in check while she delivered the news to Ted. "I feel so out of sorts," she said.

"About what? Nothing has happened…at least not yet," Denise responded, taking a small sip of her coffee as she eyed Victoria.

"What's that supposed to mean?"

"You know exactly what it means."

"*No, no, no.* I have a wonderful husband."

"Who's arguing that? Me, you, and everybody else knows that Ted's a rare gem. He's a genuinely good man. And that's hard to find, just like my Vernon," Denise said about her husband of over twenty years. "What I'm talking about is the reality of your situation. People slip all the time."

Victoria shook her head. "I would never cheat on Ted."

Denise was quiet for a second, carefully measuring her next words. "Just make sure you're being honest with yourself. Don't try to pretend that things are one way when you know they really aren't…'cause that's when you can get caught in your own web."

The two sat in silence for a moment. Victoria hated that Denise had made that statement, but more importantly, she hated that it was true.

Honey, What's Up?...

Later that afternoon, Victoria sat at her desk polishing off the last truffle in her box of Godiva chocolates. She looked at Parker's business card, *Parker E. Brightwood, M.D., The Emory Clinic, Chief of Cardiothoracic Surgery,* his title read. She smiled to herself, knowing this was what Parker had always wanted to achieve. He was ambitious, yet another quality she had admired about him. When they dated, Parker had been just as driven about his career as she'd been about her own. It was one of the many reasons why she thought they'd end up together.

She twiddled the card between her fingers and noticed that he'd written his home and cell phone numbers on the back. A quick rush went through her body. It was the same charge she'd felt when they were standing in the hallway at the school. She was temporarily drawn from her thoughts at the sound of Denise's voice.

"Okay, Girlfriend, I'm heading home."

Victoria slipped the business card back down into her handbag. "Enjoy your evening, and Denise, I'm sorry again about today. I really am glad you're back."

"I'm glad to be back too," Denise winked before waving goodbye.

As Victoria sat alone, surrounded by the quiet of her office, she thought about the immediate dilemma in front of her. She didn't know how to break the news to Ted that not only was Parker's son in Jack and Jill with Alexandria, but that he'd also be attending the same elementary school this fall. "With my luck, PJ will end up in Alexandria's class," she whispered aloud.

She knew that any kind of contact in close proximity to Parker would only lead to the worst kind of trouble. "Regardless of the consequences, I have to tell Ted," she whispered to herself. She realized that it would eventually come out anyway, so she may as well come clean with the truth. She decided she'd tell him right away, as soon as he walked through the door that evening.

After another half hour of emails and paperwork, Victoria prepared to leave the office, in route to pick up Alexandria from summer camp. She was about to log off her computer when her BlackBerry rang. She looked at the caller ID and saw that it was Ted. "Hey, Honey, what's up?"

He took a deep breath before delivering his bad news.

Ted had gotten a devastating call from his sister just an hour before. She'd told him that their mother was in the hospital, and that her condition was so grave the doctors advised that he leave for Boston within the next twenty-four hours.

Victoria knew that her mother-in-law's health had been on the decline for quite some time, but she'd kept the entire family in the dark about the particulars of her condition.

Carolyn Thornton's secrecy about things was something that had always bothered Victoria. The woman was about as open as a coffin, and it was a trait she'd passed along to her son. Ted kept information close to the vest, and at times, Victoria had to ask him what was going on with work and other projects because he rarely spoke of things that didn't involve their immediate family.

Initially, she thought it was great that Ted didn't bring up ViaTech or his other business ventures after he left work and entered their front door, but over the years she'd grown to want to know more about the various happenings in his life outside of their home. She wanted to feel connected to him in every way, but it was like pulling teeth. She'd tried over and over to get him to share other parts of himself, but he was hesitant to give her more than cursory information. And even when she was able to get small bits from him, she felt he was giving her just enough to keep her curiosity at bay.

"Oh, Honey…is there anything I can do?" Victoria asked.

"No, according to my sister it's pretty much a watch and wait situation. I need to fly out first thing tomorrow morning. I'll be home in an hour and I'll fill you in on the details when I get there."

To anyone else's ear they would have never been able to detect a thing in Ted's voice other than the power of his commanding tone. But Victoria knew her husband, and she could hear the shift. "Okay, I'll see you at home. I love you," she said before hanging up the phone. She walked out the door, her mind heavy with worry.

After dealing with Parker earlier that morning, and hearing Ted's terrible news about his mother later that afternoon, Victoria had begun to feel the weight of her long, stressful day. But her dismal mood was instantly erased when she walked into Alexandria's classroom and saw her daughter's smiling face.

"Hi, Mommy!" Alexandria yelled out. "Look what I made." She grinned and ran up to Victoria, handing her a brightly colored sheet of paper.

Victoria looked at the picture that her daughter had drawn. It wasn't a rendition of the stick figures that Alexandria normally drew. She'd crafted life-like images of a father, mother, and child. There was even a dog to complete the happy family.

"See Mommy," she smiled, "that's Daddy, and you, and me, and our dog!"

"Sweetie, we don't have a dog."

"I know, but can we get one? *Please?*"

Victoria didn't want a dog, and thankfully Ted had been in agreement about not having any pets. Not even goldfish. But apparently, Alexandria had her mind set on adding another member to their family.

"Please, Mommy? PJ has a dog and I want one too!"

Victoria blinked her eyes. *Damn!* "We'll talk about it later, okay," she said, helping Alexandria gather her things. She tried to remain calm, but right then and there she knew that Parker Brightwood was going to be a serious issue no matter how she couched it to Ted.

Alexandria was disappointed, but didn't drop her smile. "Okay. Can I get a Happy Meal?"

As Victoria pulled away from the McDonald's drive-thru window, she listened while Alexandria recapped her fun-filled day at camp, going on and on with the exuberance of someone who didn't have a worry in the world. Her daughter's bright spirit was the light she needed because she knew there was going to be rough patches ahead.

Face The Grim Situation...

Ted's afternoon had gone from bad to worse in the span of just a few short minutes. His meeting with the accounting department had been laborious, and his teleconference with the remote location supply chain directors and managers that followed hadn't been any better. But little did he know that those meetings would prove to be the highlight of his workday after hearing from his sister.

Even though all he wanted to do was grieve after learning the news about his mother's condition, he knew there was no time for that, at least not at the moment. He picked up the phone and instructed his assistant, Jen, to make arrangements for an early morning flight to Boston. After that task was handled, he dialed Victoria to let her know about his mother's fatal condition. It gave him comfort when he heard the care and concern in his wife's voice, and even though Victoria and his mother had never been close, he was thankful for the fact that they'd always been civil toward each other.

After he finished his laundry list of phone calls and sent out a few e-mails, Ted walked over to the mini-bar on the other side of the room in his large corner office. He was about to break one of his long-standing rules; drinking alcohol during business hours. He poured himself a gin and tonic, then walked back over to his desk and sank into his chair. He swished two ice cubes around in his mouth, letting the cold liquid drizzle down the back of his throat. The drink felt good and served as a temporary elixir from the news his sister, Lilly, had just delivered.

He learned that his mother was in the hospital, and from what Lilly had told him, she wasn't going to make it out. Ted knew she'd been feeling poorly for several months, but each time they'd spoken she had avoided giving him a straight answer about the full extent of her health. He'd suspected that it was worse than she had let on, but he also knew how private his mother was so he resisted the urge to push her.

Carolyn Thornton had always been secretive with information about herself and anyone else for that matter. She never gossiped; an astonishing feat for a woman of her age and social status. Carolyn was tight lipped about nearly every aspect of her life. It was an inherited trait that Ted had observed as a child and later perfected as an adult when his first marriage fell into tiny pieces.

It had been over a decade since his father had passed away, and in those first few years Ted had watched his mother's health slip little by little with each changing season. But when Alexandria had been born, she seemed to have undergone a rebirth. It was as though her youngest grandchild had given her a new reason for living. She'd *oohed and ahhed* over her son's first-born child. She'd said that she saw a lot of herself in Alexandria, although all Ted could see was Victoria through and through. When he looked at Alexandria's already prominently keen features and thick mass of curly black hair, it was plain to see that she looked every bit like her mother. The only biological footprint of the

Thornton clan that Ted had left on his child was evidenced by the light, cream-colored tint of her skin.

Ted loosened his tie as he finished the last of his drink. Finally, he rose from his desk, preparing to leave his office. Normally, he loved going home at the end of the day because he found comfort behind the stately brick walls. Victoria had made their house a home in every sense, providing love and nurturing care. Knowing that she and Alexandria were there waiting for him always made it easy for him to leave ViaTech and all his other business troubles at the front door. His home was the one place where he found peace of mind. But this evening was different and he wished he could linger at his desk.

As he looked out the window overlooking the city's skyline, he suddenly understood what Victoria meant about finding comfort in being at her office. In the early days of their marriage it had bothered him that she sought solace in going there rather than walking through the doors of their home as he did. "Ted, this has nothing to do with you or Alexandria. It's about me, and my time," she'd often said.

Now, Ted had the same feeling and understood perfectly. But he knew he had to leave and face the grim situation head on.

He thought about Alexandria and how his mother's death would affect her. He'd never known any of his mother's relatives, but he'd been fortunate enough to have his father's parents in his life until they passed away when he was in his early teens. And he'd been blessed to grow up surrounded by a cadre of the large Thornton clan, with tons of uncles, aunts and cousins. He knew that Alexandria was too young to understand that her Granny Thornton wouldn't be around much longer, and he dreaded having to explain it to her once he got home. He sighed heavily, thinking about the fact that his little girl had to deal with race and mortality, all in the same week.

The Last Ounce Of Comfort...

After Victoria cleared the table of her salad and Alexandria's chicken nuggets, she looked up to find Ted coming through the back door.

"Hi, Daddy! Look, look!" Alexandria said, jumping out of her chair. She ran up to the refrigerator where her picture hung affixed to the stainless steel door by a Dora the Explorer magnet.

Ted walked over to inspect his daughter's artwork as he removed his suit jacket. "Wow, Princess. That's a very nice picture."

"See our dog, Daddy," Alexandria smiled, pointing out the animal in the picture. She lowered her voice as she looked up at him. "We're gonna get a dog real soon."

Ted looked at Victoria as if to ask a question.

"Sweetie, I told you that's something we'll have to talk about later," Victoria corrected.

Alexandria looked from her mother to her father. "But I want a dog," she whined almost to herself as she tugged at one of her long ponytails.

Ted looked down at his daughter. "Listen to your mother," he said, winking in Victoria's direction. "This is something we'll have to discuss later."

Alexandria nodded her head.

"Sweetie, why don't you go upstairs, pick out a book for bedtime and get ready for your bath. I'll be up in a few minutes." After Victoria was sure that Alexandria was in her room, rummaging through her books and toys, she turned to Ted. She could see the stress clouding his face as she wrapped her arms around him for a gentle hug. "What exactly did your sister say?"

Ted let out a deep breath. "My mother has inoperable cancer, it's her pancreas. Lilly said she's been receiving chemo for months."

Victoria was shocked. "Oh, my Lord. I can't believe your mother never told anyone."

Ted shook his head. "Not a sole. She's been in the hospital for nearly a week, but Lilly just found out this afternoon when she got a call from mother's doctor. That's when she called Charlie and me. They're both at the hospital now. The doctor says she has forty-eight hours…maybe. She's been fading in and out of consciousness, but she asked for me specifically, so I'm leaving out first thing in the morning. This is my last chance to see my mother."

Victoria hugged her husband even tighter. "Oh, Ted, do you want me to go with you?"

"No, there's really nothing anyone can do at this point. Besides, you have Gigi's wedding this weekend, plus Debbie's coming to town tomorrow and I know you want to spend time with her." He paused, already feeling a sense of incredible loss. "By the end of the weekend, my mother will probably be...." Ted swallowed hard, not wanting to finish his sentence. "I'll get Jen to make arrangements for you and Alexandria to fly out once the burial plans are finalized."

The devastating news was happening much too fast for Victoria to process. Despite the fact that she and her mother-in-law had never enjoyed a particularly close relationship, she felt a sentimental longing that she couldn't explain. And seeing Ted in so much pain made her heart ache right alongside his.

"Are you sure you don't want me to go with you? I can call Susan, I know she won't mind letting Alexandria stay with them for a few days. Honestly, Gigi's wedding is nothing compared to what you're about to go through. Denise can run things for me, and Debbie will certainly understand," Victoria said, touching Ted's face with the palm of her hand.

"No, you should stay here and keep things as normal as possible for Alexandria. I need this time alone to say my goodbyes."

"We need to prepare her," Victoria said, darting her eyes up toward the ceiling above where they were standing.

Ted sighed. "I know." It was a task he didn't feel up to taking on, but he knew it needed to be done. Long ago he and Victoria had decided that they wouldn't sugar-coat life for their daughter, and that they'd raise her to be a strong young woman so she'd be prepared to deal with anything that life bounced her way.

Later that night after Ted and Victoria explained to Alexandria that her Granny Carolyn would soon be at eternal rest, Ted packed his suitcase in preparation for his early morning flight. He was filled with anxiety and dread. He wanted to get to his mother's side as quickly as he could, but he felt nearly crippled knowing it would be their last visit.

When he spoke to his sister to get an update before heading to bed, she'd told him that their mother was still hanging on, vowing not to breathe her last breath until he got there. An eerie numbness had overcome him. He couldn't put his finger on the feeling, but it was something that went beyond mortality, and it had unsettled him to his core.

Finally, he nestled into bed, lying close to Victoria. The feel of her warm body and the sweet scent of her skin helped him drift off to sleep. His mind told him that this would be the last ounce of comfort he'd have in the foreseeable future, and for the first time in his life, he hoped that his razor sharp senses were wrong.

Chapter 4

Vultures Always Circle Around...

The next afternoon, Victoria stood in front of Denise's desk as she told her about the situation with Ted's mother. She was glad that even though his heart was heavy, he'd managed to get a little sleep the night before. It was a sharp contrast to how she'd laid awake until the wee hours of the morning. She hadn't been able to shake the combination of sadness and grief that hung in the air from the moment Ted told her that his mother was dying. And now more than ever, she had a bad feeling that while this news was devastating, it was just the tip of the iceberg. Ever since her encounter with Parker last weekend, she could feel that things as she'd known them were about to change.

Victoria rubbed her tired eyes and yawned as she spoke. "I don't know how Ted's holding it together. If the situation was reversed, I'd be a basket case for sure."

"Wow," Denise said, shaking her head. "I can't believe his mother never told anyone how sick she was. No one had a clue?"

"Well, we knew she wasn't in the best of health, but we just figured it was the usual ailments that go along with being eighty-two years old. We had no idea she was battling stage four pancreatic cancer."

"She didn't even tell her daughter? I thought they were close."

"They are, about certain things. But Carolyn's always been very secretive. I guess everyone has their own little idiosyncrasies."

"*Hmph*, that's not an idiosyncrasy, that's just straight up strange," Denise said. "I hate to speak ill of the ill, but I've always thought something was up with your mother-in-law. Don't you think it's odd that in all the years that you and Ted have been married, you've never met a single relative from her side of the family, or heard about any childhood friends she may have had? If you ask me, that means she's got a checkered past with something to hide."

"Yeah, under any other circumstance it would seem a little strange. But she was orphaned at birth, so she never really had a family to speak of. When you think about it, it's kind of sad."

"I bet some long lost relatives are gonna suddenly appear out of the woodworks now. It never fails. When someone dies, vultures always circle around."

Victoria nodded her head, thinking about how Ted's older brother, Charlie, would be the first one lined up to pick the bones clean. "Good point," she agreed. "But like I said, she doesn't really have any family. The state of Louisiana bounced her from foster home to foster home until she was a teenager. That's when she left for Boston and never looked back," Victoria said, shaking her head. "Ted once told me that he was a grown man in college before he even learned that much. I think some pretty ugly things must've happened to her back then, and that's why she never talks about her past."

"Could be, but I still think she's a strange one. Remember how she acted at your wedding, smiling one minute, then running for cover the next?"

Victoria nodded her head as she remembered how strangely Carolyn had acted during their wedding reception. She and Ted were still giddy in the glow of their new union, and had been mingling with their guests, introducing their families to one another when she noticed a change in her new mother-in-law's behavior. One minute Carolyn was gracing everyone with her deep-rooted southern charm, laughing and talking up a storm, then the next she was cold as ice, withdrawing quickly from the crowd so she could return to her hotel room. She'd said she felt a migraine coming on and needed to rest, but that excuse hadn't rung true to Victoria because she sensed something inauthentic in Carolyn's words.

"Girlfriend, please. That headache excuse she gave was weak."

"I know," Victoria said, nodding in agreement.

"During your reception that old broad was throwin' back pomegranate martinis like spring water. I watched her, and it wasn't until your family started coming up to introduce themselves that she all of a sudden started feeling bad," Denise scoffed. "Like I said, I hate to speak ill of the ill, but the truth is, as much as her son loves your pretty black behind, she ain't too keen on our kinda people. I think she was overwhelmed by so many black faces crowded into one room. Think about it, she's a privileged white woman who lives in an estate on Knob Hill, how much contact does she have or has she had with black folks...other than in a service capacity?"

"I told Ted the same thing but he said I was making a big deal out of nothing. What is it about men that makes them blind to their mother's flaws?" Victoria's statement made her think about Parker. He'd been the same way when it came to his mother. Dorothy Brightwood was a shrew of a woman, but Parker thought she walked on water and floated on clouds.

The thought of Parker drew Victoria's mind back to him. No matter how hard she tried, she still couldn't get him out of her head. Even though she was concerned and saddened about her husband's dying mother, Parker was stuck in her thoughts. She wanted to come clean and tell Ted about her encounter with him, and brace him for the fact that they would likely run into her old lover at upcoming Jack and Jill functions and PTA meetings. But with all that Ted was dealing with at the moment, there was no good way she could find to ease Parker into their conversation. Even though Ted was a confident man, she knew he'd be uneasy about Parker's presence in their lives.

Denise continued talking but Victoria had zoned out of their conversation, consumed in her own thoughts. "Girlfriend, did you hear a word I just said?" Denise asked, snapping Victoria's attention back into focus.

"I'm sorry, what were you saying?"

"I said, given the fact that Ted's mother could pass away at any time, do you want me to stand in for you at Gigi's wedding so you can fly out early? The rehearsal dinner is tomorrow night."

Victoria knew that Denise didn't want any parts of the elaborate affair, but out of genuine friendship and professionalism she was ready to step up to the plate. "Thanks, Denise, but that's okay. We decided it would be best for Alexandria and me to stay for now. After talking with his mother's doctor, Ted seems to think she might hold on through the weekend. Then it'll just be a matter of making the final burial arrangements"

Denise let out a soft sigh. "Poor, Ted."

"I know."

"At least his mother led a full life and was able to see her children and some of her grandchildren grow up. That's a blessing some people don't get."

"Yes, it is," Victoria nodded. She was glad that Alexandria had the good fortune of being able to spend time with relatives on both sides of her family, a luxury that had escaped her growing up.

"Well, just let me know if you need me to do anything," Denise offered again.

Just then they were interrupted by the ringing phone. Denise picked it up and Victoria could tell by the scowl on her face who was on the other end of the line. It had to be Gigi!

Denise pressed the hold button. "You know who it is. I can tell her that you're in a meeting."

Victoria breathed out a heavy sigh. Gigi had just rung her cell phone a half hour ago, and now she was calling the office line for the fourth time that day. She couldn't imagine what Gigi wanted because they'd already spoken three of the four times she'd called.

"This woman is trying to drive me crazy," Victoria winced, loosing patience by the minute. She looked at her watch, not wanting to waste more of her time on Gigi's last minute hair-brained ideas. She'd made plans to meet Debbie for dinner, and she needed to leave soon. But she also wanted to get bridezilla out of the way so she could enjoy her evening. "Yeah, go ahead and transfer her," Victoria said as she headed down the hallway to her office.

After a painful and frustrating twenty minute conversation with the nervous and perpetually frantic bride-to-be, Victoria hung up the phone feeling like she'd just run a marathon. She gathered her things and prepared to leave the office.

"Gigi can drain the life out of a damn battery," she grumbled to Denise as she walked past her desk, trying to summon the last bit of energy in her reserves. She hadn't slept well since last Saturday, and now five days later she was moving like time was standing still.

"Don't let that crazy woman stress you out."

"I'm trying not too. That's why I got her out of the way so I can enjoy my dinner with Debbie."

"Hang in there, Girlfriend," Denise told her. "You know I got your back if you need anything, and tell Debbie I said hi and I can't wait to see her this Saturday."

Victoria hugged Denise on her way out the door, "I will, and thanks," she managed to smile, thankful to know that she could always count on her dear friend.

As she drove through the hustle and bustle of early afternoon traffic, Victoria wanted to do nothing more than go home and crawl into her bed. She wished she had asked Debbie to meet her at her house instead of agreeing to go out to a crowded restaurant. But she hadn't seen her friend in nearly a year, and from the way Debbie had sounded on the phone when they spoke yesterday, Victoria could sense that she was longing to have a night out.

She was about to hit speed dial and check in with Ted to see how things were going, when her cell phone rang. She looked at the caller ID and saw that it was him. "Hey, how is everything?"

"As well as can be expected," he said. Victoria could hear the tension in his voice. "I met with my mother's doctor a few hours ago. She's resting right now so I took a quick break to call you."

"Were you able to talk to her?"

"No, but when I walked into her room she looked at me and smiled, then faded off to sleep. I'm going to take Lilly to the cafeteria to get something to eat and then I'll come back and sit with mother until she wakes up again," he paused, "if she wakes up again…" Ted's voice was a whisper, trailing off like his thoughts. "How're you doing?"

"Hanging in there. I feel like I should be there with you, though."

Ted secretly wished she was there with him too because she made him feel invincible when she was by his side, and right now he was fighting to stay strong. But he knew that her time and energy were better served where she was. "V, the best thing you can do right now is keep everything together back home. Lilly's here for support, and soon, my mother will be in a better place. It's going to be all right."

"I'm glad Lilly's there, at least you two can lean on each other," she said, then a thought occurred to her. "Where's Charlie?"

Her question triggered a response that sparked a rise in Ted's voice. "Down at mother's attorney's office trying to see if he can get an advanced reading of her will."

"You're kidding!"

"Sadly, no. Lilly said she overheard him on the phone setting it up yesterday."

"I'm so sorry."

"It's no surprise. Charlie's always been a schemer." Ted thought about how he'd never trusted his brother when they were growing up, and still didn't to the present day. "Listen, I've gotta run. I'll call you if anything changes. Have fun with Debbie, and give my little Princess a kiss for me."

"I will."

After talking to Ted, Victoria gathered newfound strength. She knew that if he could marshal on in the face of such grief and sadness, she could certainly pull herself together. She needed to focus her attention and re-frame her thoughts on the things that really mattered. But all the while a nagging thought kept snipping at her conscious. It wasn't her dying mother-in-law, or her grieving husband, or the million and one things she needed to do before Gigi's rehearsal dinner tomorrow night. All she could think about was Parker's business card that was lying at the bottom of her handbag.

What's At Stake...

Victoria walked into Maggiano's Little Italy restaurant, and managed to find a seat in the tightly packed waiting area. She was tired and hungry, and she was looking forward to a good meal. Even though she felt stressed and sleep-deprived, the one thing that never faltered was her appetite. Nothing could stand between her and a good meal.

She arrived a few minutes early because she needed time to gather herself before Debbie got there. She was looking forward to spending time with her friend, and from the tone of their last few conversations, she knew that Debbie needed a listening ear. *Maybe helping her through her troubles will take my mind off my own,* Victoria thought.

Since Debbie had moved to Miami six years ago when her husband's job transferred them, the two had kept in touch, but they missed the kind of close friendship that being in the same city could offer. Debbie was only in town for the weekend to attend Gigi's wedding, but Victoria wished she could stay longer because she knew that once they started talking and catching up face to face, they wouldn't be able to stop.

The lobby had thinned out, and Victoria was busy responding to messages on her BlackBerry when she felt someone walk up to her. "Debbie?" she said with surprise.

"The one and only," Debbie smiled, standing before her with her hand on her slim hip, grinning from ear to ear. "Don't just sit there glued to that time-stealing *crackberry*, give me a hug," she grinned, opening her arms wide.

Victoria stood up and embraced her friend, trying to recover from the shock caused by Debbie's appearance. From head to toe, Debbie Long looked like a completely different woman from the one Victoria had known since they were roommates in graduate school at U Penn, or from the person in the Easter photo she'd sent just a few months ago.

Debbie had always been a free-spirited, granola kinda girl, preferring a look that unlike Victoria, screamed *Woodstock* instead of couture. The two women couldn't be more different in their taste from the clothes they wore to the men they'd dated, but they balanced each other out like salt and pepper, literally. Debbie was a decent looking woman, but she'd never really put a lot of time or care into her personal appearance. The new Debbie was a site that made Victoria do a double take.

"You like?" Debbie asked, striking a pose.

Victoria looked her up and down trying to make sure that it was really her friend standing before her. Debbie's long, unruly red hair was now a neatly tapered bob that rested just below her ears. Her customary t-shirt and torn, second-hand jeans gave way to a boat neck summer blouse and linen Capri pants. Her worn down Birkenstock's had been replaced with low-heeled sandals, and her pale, alabaster skin now boasted a serious tan.

"Girl, you look fantastic!" Victoria nearly screamed.

As the hostess lead them back to their table, Victoria still couldn't believe the drastic change in Debbie's appearance. She scanned her friend again as they perused their menus while their server poured them each a glass of Merlot. "I can't get over your new look," she told

Debbie.

"You really like it…I mean, I know I'll never be a fashionista like you," Debbie chuckled, "but do you really think I look good?"

Victoria reached for the hot, artisan bread that had just been placed on their table. "Yes! Girl, you look good. I know Rob's lovin' it," she grinned, dipping her bread in olive oil.

Debbie rolled her eyes.

"What?"

Another roll of the eyes.

"Okay, hold up. Stop rolling your eyes and open your mouth. What's going on?"

Debbie let out a long sigh. "I told you about the problems that Rob and I have been having in the bedroom, right?"

"Yeah, but I thought you two were just going through a little rough patch. I mean, you've always had such a hot and heavy love life…."

"*Had* is the operative word."

"Oh, I get it," Victoria nodded, giving Debbie an understanding wink. "You decided to get a makeover to spice things up. Is it working?"

"Um, not really."

Victoria looked closely at Debbie. She expected to see traces of worry, but her green eyes looked as bright as twinkling stars. "Debbie, what's going on with you?"

Just then their server came back to the table to take their orders. After making their selections, Victoria picked up where she'd left off. "Debbie, you're a woman who is completely comfortable in your own skin. That's one of the things I've always loved about you. You have your own style, however unconventional it may be," she said, making them both laugh. "So if you didn't make this drastic change in an effort to improve your marriage, what made you do it?"

"Another man."

There was a moment of complete silence.

At first, Victoria thought she'd misunderstood. But Debbie had said it so quickly and so matter of fact that she knew her friend was serious. She sat dumbfounded as Debbie told her about her new lover. His name was Stan, and they'd met at a local art exhibit where Debbie was one of the featured artists. He'd fallen in love with the five pieces she had on display and bought them all that very day. Over the next few weeks they exchanged their life stories over coffee and biscotti, they shared their goals and dreams through emails and secret phone calls, and they eventually gave in to their heated desire for one another in a hotel room at the Miami Marriott.

Victoria was still in shock as the server sat their piping hot plates in front of them. She watched Debbie dive into her gnocchi as her eyes danced each time she mentioned her lover's name. But with every detail she revealed, Victoria's heart filled with worry for her friend. "How long has this affair been going on?" she asked.

"A few months."

"Is Rob suspicious, I mean, has he questioned you about the sudden change in your appearance?"

Debbie shook her head. "He just thinks that since I turned forty I'm trying to reinvent myself. He doesn't really care for my new look, but he said if this is what makes me happy..."

Victoria put her fork down and gently wiped the corners of her mouth with her napkin. She'd been trying to reserve comment, but now she had to tell Debbie exactly what was on her mind. "I think you're making a huge mistake."

Debbie's smile dropped into a frown. "See, something told me to just keep this good news to myself."

"Good news?" Victoria said. "Is that what you think this is? Cheating on your husband and jeopardizing your marriage and family is good news?"

Debbie sat on the edge of her chair. "I thought you'd be the one person who would understand what it means to find real passion, but I see that I was wrong. Stop judging me, Victoria."

"Debbie, I'm not trying to judge you. I just want you to see what's at stake and realize what you're doing."

Debbie shook her head. "Forget it. You don't understand."

"Then help me to," Victoria countered, trying to keep her voice low. "I want to hear what's so great about this guy that has you sneaking off to hotels in the middle of the day while your son is at school and your husband is hard at work trying to provide a comfortable life for you."

Debbie put her hand to her head. "That's just it, it's all so *comfortable...*too comfortable. After Brandon was born, Rob and I eased into a routine that became predictable and boring. We used to take long walks in the park, hold hands at the movies, and spend hours making love. But then little by little it all stopped. Now, Rob spends most of his time at the office and when he's home it's like he's not really there, not fully engaged. Although I have to say, he does make time for Brandon, but as far as the two of us is concerned, the spark is gone."

Victoria listened as Debbie went on. "When I met Stan there was instant chemistry. He's handsome and exciting, and he looks at me like no other man ever has. A couple of weeks ago he told me that I had a hidden beauty that was bursting at the seams, waiting to be freed. The next week he took me shopping, made a hair appointment for me, and basically put together my makeover," she beamed.

Victoria held her tongue as their server approached the table, sitting Debbie's decadent Tiramisu in front of her. Victoria had forgone dessert, a first for her. This was a rare occasion that had stolen her appetite. She concentrated on her words, choosing them carefully because she wanted to say the right thing. "From what you've told me about this guy..."

"Stan," Debbie interjected.

"Excuse me, *Stan*...I still think you're making a big mistake, and it's not just because you're having an affair. Frankly, there are plenty of marriages that suffer infidelity and still survive. I think this is a mistake because this guy, excuse me, *Stan*, is trying to change you into someone you're not," Victoria said, taking a deep breath. "I listened to everything you said, and speaking as a sister who loves you, I don't like what I'm hearing. He's got you painting sunsets and baskets of fruit instead of the geometric abstracts you love. He has you wearing heels that you can barely walk in instead of your comfortable Birkenstocks. You even said that your new wardrobe has to grow on you," Victoria pointed out. "And now you're thinking about going back to the university to teach, when that was the very thing that burned you out and drove you to become a freelance artist in the first place." Victoria leaned in close, "Debbie, you were fine just the way you were."

Debbie looked up at the ceiling, totally exasperated. "But I wasn't fine the way I was. I felt like I was dying, Victoria. And, Stan...he makes me feel alive. Do you know what it's like to have someone literally wake you up from the dead?" she nearly pleaded, raising her voice.

"Debbie, calm down."

"You don't understand. You've got a handsome husband who bangs your brains out and shows you open affection. You're tall and beautiful and men drool all over you when you walk into a room. You don't know what it's like to feel undesirable, but I do. And right or wrong, Stan makes me feel desired, and wanted, and full."

Victoria sat back in her chair, taking in Debbie's words. She never knew her friend felt that way. She'd always seen Debbie as a confident, kiss-my-ass kind of woman who marched to the music playing in her own head, the rest of the world be damned. She had her own quirky style, and a genuine authenticity that made her one of the most sincere and honest people Victoria knew. Debbie's revelation about how she viewed herself was almost as startling as her admission to having an affair. "Have you talked to Rob about how you feel?" she asked.

"Yes, and it didn't do any good. He's oblivious."

Victoria looked her friend squarely in the eyes. "So, where are you going with this… where do you want this to lead?"

"Victoria, I honestly don't know."

"Well, you better start thinking about it because girl, you're playin' with fire."

"We're being careful."

Victoria shook her head. "All it takes is one small slip. Regardless of how oblivious you think Rob is, you know just like I do that even though he's a good-natured guy, he's got a little edge. If he finds out you're cheating on him, he'll put his Taekwondo lessons to use and kick some ass. The only question is, will it be yours or Stan's?"

"I told you, Stan and I are being very careful. We've stopped meeting in the city. We found a place that's a few miles outside of town, it's remote and secluded. Besides, Stan has just as much to lose as I do. He told me that if his wife finds out she'd surely take his children away from him."

Victoria's eyes bucked wide. "He's married with kids?"

"Uh-huh."

"Now you have two people to dodge. Women have great intuition about these kind of things. What if his wife is already suspicious? She could be tailing him for all you know. If you get caught you'll have another person ready to jump in your shit," Victoria said, trying to keep her voice low. "Girl, you've officially lost your mind."

"This is something I have to do for me. You're sitting there judging me, thinking why would I cheat on Rob? I know he's a good person and that he loves Brandon and me. But sometimes you need more than just love to keep you going. Do you know what it's like to find yourself drawn to another person who gives you that missing piece? Who electrifies you with just the sound of his voice? Who makes you want to be with him even when you know you damn well shouldn't?" Debbie sighed, returning Victoria's intense stare. "No," she shrugged. "You don't know anything about that."

Victoria shook her head, feeling her nose grow a full two inches as she thought about Parker's business card sitting at the bottom of her handbag. All she could do was say a silent prayer for her friend along with one for herself.

Later that night after Victoria tucked Alexandria into bed, she thought about her dinner conversation with Debbie. It had been disturbing on many levels, not only because she felt that her friend was making a potentially life-altering mistake, but also because of what it signaled.

In Victoria's mind, Debbie and Rob were the epitome of what a happy marriage was supposed to be. They were the perfect balance to each others personalities. His stable, conservative demeanor tempered her unpredictable, wild one. If their solid union was now teetering on the brink of disaster, she knew it was very possible that the waters ahead could prove to be choppy for her as well.

Ready to cap off her long day, Victoria drew herself a hot bath to soothe her tired body and mind. She lit two lavender scented soy candles, then sank down into the fluffy white bubbles as she relaxed in her Jacuzzi tub. She analyzed her actions, thinking about why she hadn't admitted the truth to Debbie; that she could understand how another man could capture her heart and make her think about throwing all caution to the wind just to be with him. She wondered why she couldn't bring herself to tell Debbie that Parker made her feel that way too?

Victoria rested her back against the tub, feeling still and numb. She knew she couldn't admit those things to Debbie because if she did, it would only be a matter of time before she found herself walking in her friend's troubled shoes.

Strange and Unsettling…

Ted watched the people hurrying to and from their cars in the crowded parking lot several stories below. He was standing at the window in his mother's dimly lit, private hospital room, wondering what medical tragedy had brought the visitors to the same place where he now stood. Had they come to grieve a loved one as he was doing, or had they received good news and were leaving with a piece of mind?

He dug his hands deep into the pockets of his khakis, trying to make sense of the last twenty-four hours. He'd been pouring over production reports when the call from his sister, Lilly, had come just yesterday.

The last few months had been particularly busy for him. Ever since he and Larmar Williams, his fifty percent partner in the company, had decided to take ViaTech public next spring, things had been moving at rapid speed. He'd been traveling the country, meeting with potential shareholders and company executives at their six remote locations, making sure their numbers were primed and ready for inspection.

It was a challenging task; running a multi-million dollar company, managing his various real estate investments, and finding time to spend with his wife and child. Some days were exhausting, others were exhilarating, but none had ever felt like the last few hours—strange and unsettling.

Ted walked from the window and sat in the stiff, vinyl covered chair beside his mother's bed. Waiting was the hardest part. He knew he had to stay busy, so he finished his copy of *The Wall Street Journal*, responded to several emails on his laptop, then made a few phone calls. An hour later the sun had faded into night. His sister had already gone home to her family, leaving him and his mother alone.

Carolyn had not awoken since seeing him earlier that morning, and now Ted was wondering if he'd ever see his mother's eyes staring into his again, or hear her voice one last time. Just as his thoughts were beginning to turn down a dark corner, he heard his name spill from her lips. At first he thought it might be wishful thinking, but when her eyes fluttered and her mouth fought to form a smile, he thanked God for one more chance. Springing from his chair, he moved to her side, taking her frail hand in his as he bent over to get closer.

"You made it," Carolyn whispered.

"Of course I did," Ted smiled back at his mother, looking at the skin and bones that lay before him. Carolyn had always been a beautifully put together woman, meticulous in her appearance. But as Ted scanned her pale, wrinkled face, looking at her sunken cheek bones and the gray strands sprinkled at the base of her temples, he realized that it was true, the human body was just a shell that wore out over time. The sight of his mother's listless body almost brought tears to his eyes, but he held them back.

"Theodore, there's so much I need to tell you," she said, struggling to pull her words together.

Ted shook his head. "Just rest. Don't strain yourself."

"No, you don't understand…there are things you must know."

The urgency in his mother's voice made Ted feel more uneasy than witnessing her visibly fragile state, because although her words were faint and barely audible, her intent was direct and serious. He leaned in closer, "What is it, Mother?"

"I need to tell you about my past."

Ted remembered her doctor mentioning that patients could become confused and disoriented, a result of the heavy doses of morphine used to ease their pain and keep them comfortable near the end. He thought that his mother might be experiencing that now. But as he studied her face he could see that her eyes were locked on his and her expression was as clear and coherent as it had ever been.

"Theodore," she breathed, pausing for a short moment, "I'm so proud of you. You've been a good son, a good brother, and a good husband and father. I always knew you were the strong one. Now, you must use that strength the deal with the truth, with the secret…"

"Secret?...what secret?"

Carolyn shook her head, casting her eyes toward the window. "I'll tell you tomorrow. I need to rest now…"

And like that, she was out.

Just as quickly as she'd opened her eyes, Carolyn Thornton had fallen back into a motionless sleep. A full minute went by before Ted realized that he was still hunched over his mother's bed, holding tightly onto her hand. After standing in a slightly startled haze for another few minutes, he reclaimed his seat in the uncomfortable chair next to her bed. He pondered what had just happened, stunned by his mother's words. He wanted to dismiss what she'd said as the ramblings of a sick old woman full of high-powered drugs, but he knew that wasn't the case. Carolyn had been precise in her delivery, and her tone told him that she was in command of her every word.

After the nurses persuaded him to leave for the night, Ted headed back to his presidential suite at the Ritz Carlton Hotel. He waited for room service as he unpacked his clothes. He'd brought three suits and several shirts and pairs of pants, knowing he might be there for a week or longer. When the food came he barely touched his plate. Usually, stressful situations didn't distract him from eating, sleeping, or carrying on business as usual. He was as steady as steel. But this wasn't business as usual, this was his mother, the woman he'd loved all his life. He was about to lose her, and he knew there was absolutely nothing he could do.

After he called room service to retrieve his mostly untouched food, Ted replayed the strange conversation he'd had with his mother. He didn't know what to make of it. What secret had she been keeping? Various scenarios ran through his mind from the possibility that he or one of his siblings might be adopted, to the far fetched notion that his mother had been leading some sort of mysterious double life.

Finally, he decided that he couldn't let his mind wonder off into far away places. Not at a time when he needed to be focused on more immediate things, like going over the arrangements with the funeral home director tomorrow morning, making sure that his sister didn't fall apart in the process, warding off his predatory brother from his mother's estate, and making sure that Victoria and Alexandria were safe and happy.

The mounting pressure, coupled with his hectic day was enough to make him fall asleep, but not before he spoke to Victoria one last time before the day ended. It was eleven o'clock, and knowing his wife the way he did, Ted knew that she was probably wide awake, waiting for his call.

He dialed the number and she picked up on the first ring.

"How are you?" she asked.

"I'm fine, back at the hotel getting ready to turn in. Did you and Debbie have a good time at dinner?"

"Uh, yeah," Victoria answered tentatively.

Ted heard her hesitation. "What's wrong, is she okay?"

Victoria knew that she couldn't reveal what she and Debbie had discussed during dinner. That admission would just open up a can of worms. "Oh, she's fine and crazy as ever. We had a great time, I'm just a little tired....how's your mother?" she asked, more than ready to change the subject.

Ted told Victoria about the strange conversation he'd had with his mother just hours before. "I'm sure she knew exactly what she was saying. It wasn't the rantings of a delusional, dying cancer patient. It was real, V."

Victoria sat up in bed, apparently just as confused and shocked as Ted. "Did she give you any indication about what kind of secret she's been keeping?"

"No, just that it has something to do with her past."

Victoria thought about the conversation she'd had with Denise earlier that day, and that ironically they'd talked about the fact that Carolyn had never mentioned anything about her past. It was as if her life had only begun when she moved to Boston all those years ago. "I wish you could find a relative or someone who knew your mother when she was a young girl growing up in Louisiana, that way you could talk to them about her past, especially since she may not be able to tell you yourself…I mean, do you really think she'll make it through the night?" It was a question Victoria hated to ask, but she knew she had to put it on the table.

Ted rubbed his tired eyes, shaking his head on the other end of the line. "My mother's a tough old bird. If there's something she wants to tell me she'll hang on until she gets it out."

"I pray that you're right."

Ted prayed that he was right too. "How's Alexandria?" he asked.

"She's fine. Just misses her daddy," Victoria said, knowing it would make Ted smile. "I called Susan and told her about what's going on and she offered to let Alexandria stay over with Claudia this weekend. She said she'd pick her up from camp tomorrow afternoon, and that's a blessing because it frees me up to deal with Gigi's rehearsal dinner and the wedding on Saturday."

Ted had been looking for a way to get out of making an appearance at Gigi Howard's wedding, but the death of his mother hadn't been the excuse he'd wanted. Nevertheless, he was glad that he didn't have to attend.

Gigi was Victoria's friend from their college days, and she'd briefly tried to pursue him before he and Victoria married. He'd never told Victoria about the succession of phone calls that Gigi had made to him after they'd met at Tyler's YFI Christmas Fundraiser, nor had he ever mentioned the email invitations to dinner she'd sent him for several months that followed. Although he thought she was a treat for the eye, Victoria had been his only focus, and every other woman paled in comparison.

"Good luck with the wedding," Ted sighed through the phone. "You'll need it with Gigi."

"Don't I know it. I just hope she behaves and that she and Gary don't cause a scene. The news crews will be lined up, primed and ready to capture their madness on film."

"Knowing Gigi, she won't disappoint," Ted paused. His voice was heavy with weariness and Victoria could hear it loud and clear. "I'm going to turn in now. It's been a long day and I need to head back to the hospital early tomorrow morning."

"Okay, Honey. Rest well and call me if anything changes."

"I will. I love you, V."

"Love you too."

As Ted lay in bed, he closed his eyes and tried to rest his mind. But his thoughts were steeped in his mother's words *"I need to tell you about my past."*

As far as he knew, his mother had led a fairly uncomplicated, straight and narrow life. She'd married his father a year after she graduated from Wellesly. Soon after, they had their first child, Charles Jr., then Lilly followed, with Ted rounding out their brood.

Carolyn and Charles Thornton had been the couple that other couples envied. Carolyn was tall, graceful, and classically beautiful. Her creamy, porcelain skin, deep-set eyes, and coal black hair were reminiscent of a young Elizabeth Taylor, and served to compliment her husband's blond haired, blue-eyed, all American boy next door good looks. They were a striking pair and had produced three equally handsome children. Add to that, they'd been madly in love, never leaving each other's side.

When Carolyn and Charles had first moved to Boston, the aristocratic Nob Hill establishment embraced the couple, which hadn't been hard to do since Charles had relatives in the area on his father's side, and hailed from a family base of old money and privilege by way of New York. The Thornton name was respected and highly regarded, giving Carolyn an automatic entrée into Boston's elite inner circle. And even though the old guard had initially wondered about her pedigree, her exquisite beauty and quiet charm eventually won them over and quieted their questions.

Carolyn had never been as outgoing or gregarious as her charismatic husband, nor had she ever put her education to use in order to carve out her own career path. But she wasn't simply a wealthy man's trophy wife who was good to look at either. She was the steady glue that kept the Thornton home and children in order. She was content with letting Charles take the spotlight, not wanting to draw any attention to herself. She quietly volunteered at her children's schools and sat on the board of a local charity. In addition, she tended to the details of overseeing the family's estate, and was a dutiful wife and mother to her successful husband and adoring children.

Thinking about his family made Ted realize just how intensely private and guarded his mother had always been about her life and her past. She was open with her love for them, but there was a side of her that was hidden and unknown, and before Ted knew it, long forgotten memories of his mother and his childhood began to race through his mind. As he drifted off to sleep in the distant comfort of a foreign bed, he wondered what secret he would discover in the morning.

Chapter 5

A Horrifyingly Hot Mess...

It was Friday night and Denise was ready to call it quits. "Can you believe this heifer! This is exactly why you should've never agreed to coordinate this wedding," she said to Victoria as she and Tyler looked in Gigi's direction. The bride-to-be had just finished a celebratory toast sprinkled with four letter expletives, then stumbled from the podium and down to where her fiancée was sitting at the head table.

"Damn, she's always bringin' the drama," Tyler added. "You'd think she would've grown up by now," he said in disgust, watching a clearly inebriated Gigi prance over to Gary.

As Victoria stood beside her two friends, looking around the opulently decorated ballroom of the Omni Hotel at CNN Center, she had to agree with Denise and Tyler. The elegant rehearsal dinner she'd planned had morphed into a scene straight from *Brides Behaving Badly*, and she was embarrassed to be a part of the debauchery that Gigi had managed to create. Not only were the happy couple both pissy drunk, nearly their entire wedding party was too. Victoria shook her head, knowing she should have expected no less given the combination of the bride's relatives and the grooms' friends. It was ghetto fabulous meets NBA bling, and the mixture was a horrifyingly hot mess!

Victoria knew she was taking a personal and professional risk when she signed Gigi as a client, but she felt an obligation to their friendship and more importantly, to Juliet's memory. She'd worked hard to build her reputation in an industry where very few people at the top looked like her. She'd carved a niche for herself by creating memorable affairs, not gaudy spectacles, and now she was regretting her decision. Gigi and Gary brought more drama than a daytime soap opera.

Victoria had taken care in cultivating Divine Occasions' client list that consisted of corporate giants and prominent non-profit organizations, civic and community groups, established business leaders, and some of Atlanta's most influential socialites. And although Gary was a well-known celebrity and something of a hometown superstar, he and Gigi were in a different circle. Their notoriety was for reasons that made Victoria shake her head. They were constantly stalked by the paparazzi for their drama-filled, off the wall antics in trendy clubs and at wild parties. They were a regular feature on *TMZ*, and at least once a quarter they were guaranteed to pop up in the *National Inquirer* or *Star*, making headlines for brawling at a night spot or causing some other kind of crazy scene.

The thought of a Divine Occasions event turning into a Jerry Springer like affair made Victoria cringe. The only thing that kept her from walking out the door that very moment was the thought that had been with her from the very beginning; that Juliet would have wanted her to be there.

Juliet, Gigi, and Victoria had all been friends when they met during their college days at Spelman, but it was Juliet and Gigi who had been inseparable. And despite the fact that they were as different as night and day, which was akin to her own relationship with Debbie, Victoria knew that their bond was strong.

Gigi had taken Juliet's death hard, barely able to function for the first few months after the funeral. Juliet's quiet strength had always been the perfect counter balance to Gigi's brazen boldness. Juliet came from an upper-middle class family of refinement and college-educated professionals, while Gigi's pedigree was tied to poverty stricken near-do-wells in one of the roughest neighborhoods in the Bronx.

She was the product of a drug addicted mother and a father she'd never known. But her brains, street smarts, and good looks carried her out of the tough housing projects where she'd grown up, and into a life that her late grandmother who raised her could have only dreamed of. She was the scholarship kid who'd done good, and today she was a successful sales director for an international cosmetics company, about to marry a multi-million dollar professional athlete.

But as Victoria looked at Gigi, who was now sitting atop the lap of her groom-to-be, straddling him as she simulated a sex act, all she could think about was the old saying, *you can take the girl out of the street!*

"This is ridiculous, she's one minute away from screwing him right here in front of God and everybody," Denise scoffed, throwing her hands in the air. "Do I have to come to the wedding tomorrow?"

"Frankly, I don't know if I'm going to show," Victoria hissed. "But I do know one thing, I'm getting ready to shut down this foolishness," she said, making her way through the crowd as she headed toward the podium up front. She adjusted the microphone before she spoke, trying to paint on a smile while the flash of several camera phones temporarily blurred her vision. "May I have your attention, please," she roared into the microphone, commanding the one hundred-twenty guests to look her way. "Thank you so much for coming out this evening to celebrate with Gigi and Gary on the eve of their big day. As you all can see...they're having a good time," she flinched, looking over at the happy couple who were now embraced in a heavy tongue lock. "So it's only fitting that we end now, on a good note."

Victoria wanted to strangle Gigi, but she remained calm. "For those of you who are members of the wedding party, please arrive at the church tomorrow, promptly at noon...sober," she threw in. "Thank you, and have a good evening."

Victoria pressed the button on her hotel issued Walkie-Talkie and instructed the concierge to alert the valets that a group of inebriated guests would need cabs waiting on standby out front. Next, she walked over to Gigi, grabbed her by the elbow and escorted her over to the other side of the room.

"Gigi, get a hold of yourself! It was bad enough that you showed up at the church for the rehearsal with liquor on your breath, cursing like a sailor. Now look at you, showing your behind on the eve of your wedding. What the hell's wrong with you?"

"Girl, I'm just havin' a good time. That's all," Gigi smiled, as if everything was fine.

Victoria looked at her friend's white lace blouse that was slightly askew and hanging off one shoulder. Her ultra tight, white leather mini skirt barely covered her round behind, and the four-inch rhinestone studded fuck-me-pumps on her feet screamed *Gigi Does Vegas!* She wasn't exactly a spokes model for what a blushing bride should look like.

"Don't you know that the media can't wait to see you act a fool so they can give people something to talk about?" Victoria said, shaking her head.

"Let'em talk, do you think I give a damn? They can kiss my ass. It's my wedding, and I'm gonna celebrate the hell out of it!" she slurred, Grey Goose reeking from her breath.

Victoria shook her head in total dismay. Over the past six years of Gigi and Gary's on-again-off-again, tumultuous relationship, the two had constantly made headlines with their Whitney/Bobby behavior. But in the wake of Juliet's death, they'd calmed their ways and seemed to have settled down...slightly. But in the months since Gary proposed, they'd been back in the saddle with their usual drama and had even kicked things up a notch.

Victoria was frustrated, knowing she had much too much on her mind to deal with Gigi. All she wanted to do was get home so she could call Ted. When she'd talked to him a few hours earlier, his mother was still hanging on, slipping in and out of consciousness. He had said that she briefly mentioned a few things about her will, but that it had been nothing significant, nothing revealing. Even though Ted seemed to be handling things well, Victoria wanted to talk with him again, just to hear his voice and give him comfort.

The thought of her husband's crisis in the face of Gigi's drama gnawed at Victoria's nerves. "Listen," she said. "The only reason I'm going to show up tomorrow is because we signed a contract. But so help me, if I smell one whiff of liquor on your breath, I'm walking out of the church. Do you hear me?"

Gigi looked at Victoria through her beautifully made-up, slightly glazed-over eyes. "I hear you...Victoria. I'm just having a little fun. Lighten up," she paused, her expression looking as if she was about to tear up. "If Juliet was here, she would be having fun too."

Victoria looked around, glad that Tyler wasn't standing nearby to hear the bullshit that Gigi was trying to feed her. "Quit playing the sympathy card. Yeah, Juliet would be having a good time, but she'd also be sober and she wouldn't have her ass hanging out for the world to see," Victoria hissed, reaching down to adjust Gigi's mini skirt. "And she'd tell you to act like you had some sense...and you know it."

Victoria looked at Gigi and was startled to find what looked like a combination of remorse and sadness on her face. Gigi had always done whatever the hell she wanted to do, regardless of place or circumstance, and it was actually one of the things that Victoria admired about her. But it was also her Achilles heel that crept up to bite her. Looking at her friend, Victoria felt compassion because at that moment she realized that Gigi was hurting. She was hurting because she was about to embark on something that neither she, nor anyone else in her family ever thought possible. She was getting married, and the one person besides her late grandmother who'd always loved her and had faith in her, wasn't there to share in her happiness.

In that instant, Victoria felt Gigi's hurt to. She took a deep breath and softened her tone. "I didn't mean to be so harsh. I just don't want this special moment to turn into a disaster. Hopefully this is something you're only gonna do once," she winked, "and you don't want to foul it up." She smiled, getting a small laugh out of Gigi.

"You're right, Victoria."

"The night manager and Gary's publicist both told me that there are several camera crews waiting outside, so make sure that you and Gary go straight to the limos I have waiting out front."

Gigi nodded. "Okay, we will."

"Now, I have to ask you to do me a favor?"

"Sure?" Gigi brightened.

"Please don't stop to pose for pictures, and for heavens sake don't say a word to the press."

Gigi nodded her head, knowing that Victoria was right. "Thanks, girl. You're the best," she slurred with a sincere smile.

"And tell Gary not to do anything stupid at the bachelor party. I want him and his boys at the church tomorrow, on time."

A mischievous grin formed on Gigi's lips. "Oh, don't worry, I have that under control. Me and my girls are gonna be at that party, okay?"

"What?"

"That's right, I'm not gonna let some random stripper get my fiancée off on the night before our wedding. If anyone's gonna get buck wild and give him a lap dance and some head, it's gonna be me!"

Victoria put her hand to her mouth, drawing in a deep breath.

"You're going to strip at his bachelor party…in front of all his friends?"

"Damn straight."

"Oh, my goodness."

"What?" Gigi asked, as if what she'd just said made perfectly logical sense.

"Gigi, please tell me you're joking?"

"It's not like I haven't done it before," Gigi boasted, hands on her hips.

Victoria could only imagine the hellacious scene that was going to take place later that night. She rubbed her temple in an attempt to stave off a growing headache. She couldn't find anything decent to say in response to Gigi's comment, so she bid her a good night and watched as she sashayed over to Gary. The happy couple walked out arm in arm with a thirty person entourage flanked behind them.

A few minutes later after settling the final tally and signing the remaining paperwork with the hotel banquet manager, Victoria found Tyler waiting for her as she walked out to the lobby. "I thought you were long gone. Where's Denise?" she asked.

"Probably walking through her front door. She left right after you went up to the microphone to restore some order."

"I don't blame her," Victoria sighed. "Thanks for sticking around."

"No problem. I wanted to make sure you're doing okay, besides, I need a ride. I took a cab over 'cause I knew I was gonna get my drink on tonight," Tyler laughed. "But damn, I apparently didn't get it on as much as the wedding party. You know you're dealing with some straight up ghetto drama, right?"

All Victoria could do was shake her head and pray that no one in the wedding party would wind up arrested or dead before the afternoon nuptials the next day.

Come Clean With Information…

Victoria and Tyler made small talk on the drive over to his townhouse. A month after Juliet's funeral he'd sold the house they had lived in, opting for a smaller place with empty memories.

Victoria pulled up to Tyler's unit and eased her car into the extra reserved parking space beside his SUV. The two friends sat with the engine humming as Victoria told him about Ted's mother.

"Damn," Tyler said. "Sounds like somethin' out of a movie."

"I know, isn't it strange?"

"When people start spillin' secrets on their death bed, watch out. You know whatever she's been hiding can't be good."

"Exactly, and what if she dies before telling Ted anything. He said that she's been slipping in and out of consciousness all day. I know my husband," Victoria paused, "and if he doesn't find out what she's been hiding, it'll eat away at him."

"I'd feel the same way. That's why you gotta come clean with information while you can. Speaking of which, you haven't told him about Parker have you?"

His question made Victoria's dull headache begin to throb. "No, and now how can I? I wanted to tell him the other day, but then this crisis with his mother happened...I can't possibly add to his worries."

"His worries or yours?"

"C'mon, Tyler. You know I don't want to put Ted through any additional stress. Loosing his mother is bad enough."

"I understand your point, and I feel for Ted because I know what he's going through," Tyler said in a solemn voice. "But you need to find a way to tell him because this situation with Parker ain't gonna go away, and I have a feeling it's only gonna escalate."

Victoria stared at her best friend, taking a deep breath before admitting what she'd been holding inside. "Remember when I told you that I've been thinking about Parker...fantasizing about him? Well, it hasn't stopped." She went on to tell him about the recurring dream that seemed to haunt her. "I went to register Alexandria for kindergarten the other day and he was there, registering his son.

Tyler leaned back in his seat. "You shittin' me?"

"Nope."

"You think he's stalking you?"

"No, it's just a coincidence. He's looking for the best organizations and schools for his child just like we are."

"Damn, this is gettin' a little too close for comfort."

"I know. He gave me his business card, and for a split second I actually considered calling him," Victoria sighed.

Tyler looked at her with worry. "But you didn't, right?"

"Of course not. But like I said, I thought about it."

Victoria knew that she should toss the card instead of letting it linger at the bottom of her handbag, reminding her of the past. "Tyler, what's wrong with me? I have a wonderful husband who loves me and needs me right now, and what am I doing…fantasizing about a man who cheated on me a million years ago."

Tyler put his hand on Victoria's shoulder. "You used to love him and it's only natural that seeing him for the first time after all these years would stir up some old feelings, especially since you never put them to rest."

"You think?"

"Of course. The bottom line is this, you know that you're gonna run into him at Jack and Jill and at Alex's school, so you're gonna have to deal with it. I'm sure that the more contact you two have, the more these fantasies will start to fade away," Tyler said, trying to reassure her—and himself for that matter. "Trust me, familiarity breeds contempt, especially with someone like that mutha…"

"I get the point," Victoria said, cutting him off.

"You're still gonna have to tell Ted about ol' boy, though. Let him bury his mother first, then break it down to him so he'll know the deal. Ted's a strong man. He'll be able to handle it because he knows that what you two have is solid….right?"

Victoria spoke quickly. "Absolutely."

"Then you should have no problem telling him."

"Right," she nodded, even though she knew it wouldn't be that simple.

Tyler unbuckled his seatbelt and opened the door. "And by the way, Debbie called me this afternoon to let me know that she made it to town. What's up with her?"

"What do you mean?" Victoria asked, raising her brow.

"What's that look about?"

"What look?"

"The look on your face that says somethin's up."

Victoria tried to sound casual. "Nothing's up."

"Okay, keep your little girl's secret. But I know that somethin's goin' on, I could tell by the vibe I felt in her voice when we talked."

Damn he's good! Victoria hoped that nothing had gone wrong, and that Rob hadn't found out about Debbie's affair. "You know how

Debbie is. She's fine, just crazy as all get out."

"All right," Tyler said, unconvinced. "Get some rest 'cause you'll need it to deal with Gigi and the wedding crew."

"Isn't that the truth."

"And one last thing, what you're feeling for Parker will pass."

Victoria drove from Tyler's subdivision and onto the highway, headed for home. Her heart sped up in her chest when she realized that for the first time since she'd known him, Tyler had been dead wrong."

Chapter 6

The Realm Of Possibilities . . . .

Time replayed itself in a strange déjà vu, reminiscent of the evening before as Ted found himself alone with his mother in her hospital room. She hadn't talked about the secret she'd spoken of, and he hadn't pushed her, fearing the stress of probing questions might be too much for her weakened state. But the unknown was maddening for him.

His sister had left to pick up her college-age daughter from the airport, and to prepare her home for the rush of grieving relatives and family friends she was sure to receive in the next few days. His brother hadn't come by the hospital all day, but had called for periodic updates, claiming that his appointments were keeping him too busy to stop by.

Ted thought about his brother's flimsy excuse. "Busy my ass," he whispered to himself as he looked over at his dying mother. She was on her deathbed and her first born didn't even have the decency to come and see her. Ted knew that his brother had done some pretty despicable things in his sordid life, but this took the cake.

He'd always been at odds with Charlie, who was usually involved in a half-baked lie to cover a crooked scheme. Ted knew that whatever his brother was up to now, it couldn't possibly involve anything legitimate. And he knew without a doubt that his brother couldn't be any busier than he was.

He thought about Charlie's situation compared to his own and shook his head. Charlie didn't have accountants breathing down his neck, or investors asking him probing questions, or production numbers that needed to be met, or tempers that needed to be clamed, or employees that needed to be reigned in. And those were just the demands of ViaTech. Added to his workload were the pressures of his involvement in several real estate development projects in two burgeoning Atlanta neighborhoods, a host of other business dealings, and family obligations that he juggled on a daily basis. But he didn't complain because unlike his brother, he thrived under pressure.

Charlie ran a small accounting firm that was always on the brink of either collapse, bankruptcy, or scandal, and sometimes all three. He was the oldest of the Thornton children, and his father's namesake. But it was Ted, the youngest, who their father had always favored, and for good reason. The elder Thornton could see early on that Charlie looked for the easy route and was prone to lie his way into and out of situations, many times dragging everyone else through the self-made chaos with him. There was something spoiled deep down inside Charlie, a natural inclination to go the way of wrong.

As Ted sat in the chair beside his mother's bed, watching her sleep, he prayed that Charlie would only cause minimal headache over the next few days. Charlie loved dominating people and exerting his gruff manner which made those around him shy away from confronting him directly, as was the case with Lilly. He felt comfortable bossing and manipulating Lilly and her mouse of a husband, Grant. And at times he'd even tried his shenanigans on Carolyn when she wasn't in her best of health. But Ted was another matter completely, and that was part of the reason he'd steered clear of the hospital since his younger brother had arrived in town.

"I can't let Charlie get to me," Ted mumbled to himself. His mind was tired from lack of sleep. Just as he was about to dose off, Carolyn opened her eyes.

Ted jumped to his feet and leaned against the side of her bed. "It's good to see you awake," he said, grateful to see his mother conscious again.

Carolyn mustered a small amount of strength to reach for Ted's hand. "Where are Lilly and Charlie?"

"Lilly's gone to pick up Sandra from the airport and Charlie had to take care of some business." He knew that his mother knew the latter part was a lie.

"But you're here…"

"Yes, I am."

Carolyn took a deep, labored breath. "Good, I'm glad we're alone. You're who I wanted to talk to anyway. There are things I need to share with you."

"All right." It was the only thing that Ted could think to say.

Carolyn swallowed hard, trying to hold onto her shallow breathing. "I shouldn't have held on to our secret for so long, or maybe not even at all. Your father told me that we should've let you children know the truth," she paused, focusing her eyes directly into her son's. "But I couldn't, I needed to protect you…once you hold on to something for so long, it's hard to let go. Especially when you know the damage it has the potential to do."

His mother's words made Ted nervous. He'd never known her to talk about her past, and now listening to her speak, it appeared as though his father's life was up for question too. Suddenly, his far fetched notion about secret, double lives didn't seem so far from the realm of possibilities. "Mother, I don't understand? What are you saying?"

Carolyn summoned her last bit of strength to grip her son's hand as tight as her frail fingers would allow. "There's a safe deposit box waiting for you at Boston Private Bank. Abe will give you the key tomorrow, after I'm gone. Soon, you'll find all the answers to the questions I see in your eyes."

It took a few seconds for her words to fully sink into Ted's ears because he couldn't make sense of it; *safe deposit box? Abe Brookstein?* He wondered what crime his parents had committed that required a bank's safe keeping under the watchful eye of their family's long-time attorney, Abe Brookstein. Disbelief covered Ted's face like a cold sweat. "Mother, who are you?" he asked, the question sounding foreign, even to his own ears.

"I'm the woman who raised you and loved you. Always remember that, Theodore…now, I need to rest so I can see you one last time when morning comes." And like a curtain coming down on stage, Carolyn closed her eyes and fell back to sleep.

Damn!

The wedding ceremony for Mr. and Mrs. Gary Leon Hicks had gone off without much commotion. The only hiccup during the lavish event came when Gary stumbled over his vows—several times! Still, there wasn't a dry eye in the church because despite the drama and madness that Gigi and Gary often created, it was clear that the two truly did love each other.

An hour after the ceremony, the reception at the Ritz Carlton Buckhead, was in full swing. People were laughing like old friends, drinking at the open bar like there was no tomorrow, and throwin' down on the dance floor like they were on the set of a music video.

Several floors above the ballroom as the celebratory guests danced the night away, Victoria was lying across the king-size bed in her club-level suite. She always reserved a room for herself at the venue of every wedding she coordinated, which served as her virtual office on location to store wedding gifts, extra flowers, toiletries for the wedding party, and any other important items for the day. Because of her working relationship with the luxury hotel, and the insane amount of money that the Howard/Hicks wedding event was shelling out for the big day, Victoria had managed to snag an upgraded suite for herself in the deal.

Victoria knew that she needed to be downstairs overseeing the festivities, but the thought of it made her head throb. All she could think about was the possible fiasco that awaited her several floors below. And this time, her worries about creating a scene had nothing to do with the bride and groom.

"Lord, why is this happening? And why now?" she said aloud to no one, holding her head in her hands. Three hours earlier she'd gotten the shock of her life when Debbie and her lover made an appearance at the church.

Victoria had been running between the sanctuary and the waiting room where Gigi and her bridesmaids where having their make-up applied by professional stylists, compliments of Gigi's company as a wedding gift. Although the paparazzi were parked outside the church, snapping pictures and trying to catch a glimpse of the rich and famous, things were actually flowing without incident. Victoria tossed her worries to the side, beginning to feel that the day was going to turn out better than she'd expected. She walked out into the vestibule to check on the progress the ushers were making with seating the guests when she ran smack into Debbie and Stan.

"Hey, Victoria," Debbie beamed. She was wearing a delicate, peach colored sundress that complimented her fiery red mane and sun tanned skin. Her makeup was light and fresh and her eyes sparkled like marbles. Victoria had to admit that she'd never seen Debbie look so good.

"I have someone I'd like you to meet," Debbie smiled, motioning to the man at her side. "Victoria, this is my friend, Stan…"

Victoria looked the man up and down. She thought he was cute in an average kind of way. But the most strikingly odd thing about him was that he could've passed for Debbie's husband; he looked just like Rob.

Victoria nodded politely in Stan's direction, then turned her attention to Debbie. "Can I speak to you in private?" She ushered Debbie off into one of the small meeting rooms adjacent to the main sanctuary. "What the hell are you thinking, bringing your lover out in public like this?" she nearly screamed after closing the door. "Have you lost your damn mind?" She knew she shouldn't curse in the church, but the situation had gotten the better of her.

"No one here knows who he is, and honestly, besides Gigi, Tyler, Denise and you, the majority of the people here don't know me either."

Victoria shot her a look. "Are you forgetting that you used to live in this city? Don't be fooled, people talk, and in less than twenty minutes this church will be spilling over with some of the most gossipy black folk from here to the North Pole. And some of them are going to be the very same people who attended my wedding, and you better believe they will remember the white girl with the fire-engine red hair who was my matron of honor," Victoria huffed, "not to mention the camera crews out front. For all you know they could've already captured you on film, and you and loverboy could end up on *YouTube* before the sun sets."

Debbie stood in silence, panic flashing in her eyes.

"You didn't think about that, did you? Those cameras aren't just flashing for the celebrities, they're catching everyone. How could you bring him out in public?" Victoria questioned again. "I hope you at least came in on separate flights?"

Debbie looked down at her brand new, ill-fitting pumps that Stan had purchased for her just days before, and shifted her weight back and forth. It was apparent that she'd done exactly what Victoria feared.

"Oh, my goodness. You *have* lost your mind."

"Victoria, you're making this seem way worse than it is. Stan and I saw this as a chance to get away. This is the first time we've been able to go out in public and actually spend the entire night together. We're having fun and we're being careful."

"Careful?" Victoria laughed. "Clearly you're not or you wouldn't be parading his ass up in here like it's no big deal. How are you gonna introduce him to Denise and Tyler?"

"As my friend."

Victoria sucked her teeth. "And he has the nerve to look just like Rob."

"No, he doesn't," Debbie snapped.

Victoria twisted her mouth but didn't say anything.

"Look, I know we're taking a small risk, but it's a calculated one. Believe me, we thought this through before we decided to make this trip together."

"Oh, just like you thought about the TV and newspaper reporters scattered out front, taking pictures and filming everyone who's coming in and out of the front doors?"

Debbie didn't have a comeback for that one. "Okay, so maybe we didn't anticipate on that, but…"

"This is a high-profile wedding with a guest list that includes some of the top names in sports and entertainment, how could you not think about that?"

"Damnit, Victoria, Stan and I aren't celebrities and no one is going to pay any attention to us with a guest list filled with hundreds of glamorous people."

"Okay, if you say so…it's not my ass that Rob's gonna kick if he finds out."

The two friends stood in silence with Debbie looking as though she was going to have a meltdown at any moment.

Victoria was afraid for her friend. She'd heard about people who had affairs and went completely nuts, loosing all sight of reason. But she never thought Debbie would be one of them...and over a man who looked exactly like her husband! Victoria thought her friend was risking everything for what she already had at home. "Debbie, I love you, and I'm only trying to help you the best way I can," she said, reaching out and giving Debbie a lingering hug.

Debbie sniffed back a small tear that had started to form. "I know you are, and even though it may not seem like it, I know what I'm doing."

Victoria wanted to talk some more sense into her friend but she didn't have time. She had a wedding to oversee, and as much as she loved Debbie, she had to be on her game because business was business. "They're filling up the church from front to back as people come in, but I'm going to walk you and Stan up to one of the ushers and get them to seat you in the back of the sanctuary, okay?"

Debbie breathed a sigh of relief. "Thanks, Victoria."

The two left the meeting room and found Stan still planted in the same spot where they'd left him. After Victoria made sure that Debbie and her lover were tucked away in one of the back pews, she made her way back out to the front of the church. Her mind was swimming with worry when she looked up and found herself face to face with Parker.

She was speechless, not wanting to believe her eyes for the third time in one week. He looked amazingly handsome in his custom tailored, navy pinstriped suit. She quickly scanned him, admiring his broad shoulders and gorgeous face. She thought he looked fine as hell, delicious in fact, and she could tell by the sly look in his eyes that he knew exactly what she was thinking. She wasn't sure why he was there and started to wonder if there was any truth to what Tyler had suggested. *Is he stalking me?* But her mind paused the thought when she saw the woman standing beside him and realized that he wasn't there alone.

"Three times in one week," Parker smiled.

Victoria didn't smile back. "What are you doing here?"

There was dead silence.

"Hello, Victoria. Do you remember me? I'm Samantha," the tall, thin-boned woman interjected, extending her slender hand.

Victoria immediately recognized Parker's favorite cousin. She had fond memories of Samantha from when they'd met several years ago during her disastrous Christmas visit with Parker's family. Samantha had been kind to her and had even snuck in a jab at Parker's mother when she'd tried to get under Victoria's skin. It had cemented her as an ally.

"Yes, of course I remember you," Victoria smiled, trading Samantha's handshake for a warm hug.

"Do I get a hug too?" Parker asked, sounding completely serious.

Victoria dismissed his comment but couldn't ignore his laser stare that penetrated her skin. She attempted to act casual as she tucked a stray strand of hair back into the delicate upsweep that highlighted the elegant angle of her neckline. She saw how his eyes zeroed in on her hour-glass silhouette, compliments of her small waist and curvy hips. She stood tall and erect in her knee length, apple-green chemise dress. Her long legs were accentuated by a pair of bejeweled stilettos, one of her many physical attributes that had always driven Parker wild when they dated.

"Are you a guest of the groom?" Victoria asked Samantha, remembering that the attractive woman was a bit on the wild side, and could easily be a friend of Gary's or maybe even a groupie.

"Actually, the bride," Samantha smiled. "Gigi and I work for the same company and we've known each other for years. She helped me get my job with Lancôme, and we've been tight ever since."

Victoria nodded, making the connection. Samantha was younger by several years, but she was a Spelman graduate as well. And even though Gigi led a crazy, drama-filled personal life, she was very active in business matters with their alma mater. She volunteered with the career services office on campus, and had helped several graduating seniors get jobs over the years.

Samantha spoke up again, feeling the tension that was building in the air. "I flew in last night," she continued. "My best friend who lives here was supposed to come with me, but she had to care for her mother who isn't doing well. I didn't want to come alone, so I asked my knucklehead cousin here to tag along." Samantha gave Parker a slight jab in the side. "Listen, Victoria, if I had known you were involved in this wedding I wouldn't have brought him with me and..."

"Don't worry about it," Victoria interrupted, not looking in Parker's direction. "You're here to help Gigi and Gary celebrate their special day, and I know they'll be happy that you came," she smiled, trying to put a good face on an uncomfortable situation. "And it's certainly good to see you again, Samantha. The ushers can show you to your seat."

Samantha nodded and smiled along as Victoria motioned in the direction of an usher who was standing nearby.

Parker's eyes never left Victoria's. "It's good seeing you, Victoria." Again, Victoria gave him no response, only a blank stare.

As she watched Parker and his cousin walk away, she felt a slight tingle in the pit of her stomach. *Damn!* she shouted in her head. She knew that the day was going to be filled with drama after all.

You Like Learning The Hard Way...

Back in the present, Victoria tried to take her mind off Parker because she knew that more pressing issues were at hand. She sat up in the middle of the king-size bed in her hotel suite as her thoughts turned to her husband and what he must be going through. She'd talked to Ted an hour earlier when she first came up to her room. He'd said that his mother was still holding on, but that the doctors had told them it was doubtful she'd make it through the night.

Victoria couldn't imagine the sadness he must be feeling. During their conversation he'd tried to be strong, but his tone told her that he was in pain. After they ended their conversation, she had to gulp down two Tylenols in her quest to bury her growing headache.

She knew she couldn't hide out in her room for the rest of the evening, so she finally rose from the bed and headed to the door. On her elevator ride down to the ballroom where the reception was still in full swing, she prayed that Debbie and Stan had exercised good judgment and left the scene. She also hoped that Parker and Samantha would be long gone as well.

I don't believe this shit! Victoria entered the room and spotted Debbie and Stan. They were joining in on a line dance that had just started. As she scanned the room her mood worsened. "Just my luck," she whispered aloud. Parker's gaze was fixed on her as they locked eyes. His stare made her forehead pop with tiny beads of sweat. She tried to play it cool as she walked over to where Denise was standing.

"You okay? You were up in your suite for a while," Denise said, with concern.

"I'm fine. I had to get away so I could talk to Ted," she responded, telling a half truth.

Denise nodded with understanding. She knew what it was like to lose a parent. "What's the latest?"

"His mother is still holding on, but it's just a matter of time. Alexandria and I will probably fly out tomorrow," Victoria said, trying not to look across the room in Parker's direction.

"If you need me to do anything just say the word and it's done."

"Thanks, but you've done enough already, holding things down here. How's it been going since I left?"

"Girlfriend, this wedding is really bringing out some strange happenings. What's the deal with Debbie and that man she's cheezin' with?" Denise asked as she and Victoria watched the two work up a sweat while they danced off-beat to the lyrics of Ludacris.

Victoria had been anticipating this question and hoped that she could throw Denise off Debbie's adulterous scent. "Well..." she began.

Before she could form her words, Denise cut her off. "How stupid is she? If you're gonna cheat at least be smart about it. Why in the hell did she bring her lover out in public? And I'll be damn if he doesn't look just like Rob."

Victoria knew there was no need to even attempt to try and clean it up. "I said the same thing," she sighed, shaking her head. "I don't know what's gotten into her."

"From what I can see, about six inches, maybe less...whattchu think?"

Victoria snickered. "That's hardly enough for the risk she's taking."

"Hmph, sometimes that's all it takes. You never know what makes folks do the things they do."

Victoria wrinkled her face. "I guess?"

"I'm gonna leave that one alone and put it in God's hands," Denise said, wiping her hands as if she was done with the matter. "And by the way, did you see who else is here?" she glared, rolling her eyes in Parker's direction.

"I know. I saw him earlier at the church."

"How'd he manage to get invited? I looked, and I didn't see his name on the guest list, but one of Gigi's hostesses obviously let him in. He probably smiled real hard and charmed his slick ass through the door."

Victoria shook her head. "He's here with his cousin. She's one of Gigi's guests."

"Umph, if she's a friend of Gigi's, she's probably no damn good too, which would explain why she's related to Parker."

Victoria wanted Denise to go easy on Samantha. "She's actually very nice. As a matter of fact, that's her over there." Victoria pointed toward the back of the room where Samantha was sitting at a table, talking with Tyler.

"I hope she's as nice as you say she is…for Tyler's sake," Denise said with skepticism. "They've been cuddled up in that corner ever since you went upstairs."

Victoria took a closer look, noticing the way Samantha and Tyler appeared to be flirting with each other. Samantha's long, thin body was nestled close to Tyler's, and his arm was draped over the back of her chair as if they were ready to embrace. Both of their faces were brimming over with smiles and something that looked close to lust.

Tyler hadn't dated much since Juliet's death. He'd thrown all his energy into YFI. And when he did meet someone of interest, it never went beyond one or two casual dates. Victoria had been wanting him to find someone for quite some time. The thought of her best friend going through life without someone special to share it with often made her heart fill with sadness. Tyler was a kind, good-hearted man who'd suffered many losses, yet had never surrendered to bitterness. He deserved happiness, and Victoria prayed that it would finally come his way.

But even though she liked Samantha, she wasn't sure that Parker's cousin was a good match for her best friend. Albeit, Samantha was smart, attractive, and had a good sense of humor, Victoria also remembered that for someone who was raised in DC's affluent Gold Coast community, by parents of a very distinct pedigree, in a family with deeply imbedded roots in the city's closely knit black elite, Samantha had a rough edge that she sported like a worn belt buckle; loose and ragged. She favored men who boasted prison rap sheets rather than sheepskin diplomas. She'd had a brief run-in with the law several years back, the result of a wild night of partying that had spiraled out of control. Had it not been for her father who happened to be one of the city's top attorneys, she would've no doubt done jail time.

As Victoria continued to study the two, she couldn't imagine what they had in common besides their libidos. Yet they were engrossed in what appeared to be a fluid and engaging conversation.

"Well, if you don't mind, I'm gonna head out," Denise said, looking in Gigi's direction. "I see that the blushing bride is starting up again and I want to leave before she turns this reception into a burlesque show."

Gigi was flicking her tongue, seductively licking the icing off of Gary's fingers one-by-one as they fed each other wedding cake, turning the time-honored tradition into a soft porn spectacle. A few of her cousins were cheering as their camera phones flashed, capturing the moment.

"Go ahead," Victoria said. "I'll call you if we fly out tomorrow."

"Okay, I'm outta here. And Girlfriend, watch yourself with him," Denise paused, rolling her eyes again in Parker's direction.

A few hours later the reception had finally started to wind down. Debbie and Stan had left shortly after their uncoordinated attempt to dance on beat. Their departure made Victoria glad that at least one headache was gone for the evening. Tyler had left an hour later, inviting Samantha to have a late dinner with him. And to know ones surprise, Gigi and Gary were pissy drunk, along with the rest of their ghetto fabulous wedding party. When Gary's best man announced there was a fleet of stretch Hummers out front, ready to take everyone to the after party at one of Atlanta's hottest night clubs, the remaining party-goers cleared the ballroom like someone had waved a gun.

All in all, Victoria was pleased that no one had gotten cursed out, injured, or arrested. She'd feared something bad might happen, given a few questionable characters in attendance.

After she signed the final paperwork with the banquet manager, Victoria headed back up to her room. She was looking forward to a peaceful nights rest, and since Alexandria was sleeping over at Susan Whitehurst's house, she planned to take advantage of an evening alone in the serenity of her hotel suite. She needed the peace and quiet because she knew the next few days were going to be somber ones.

She inserted her room key into the elevator which gave her access to the floors above. She pressed the button for the nineteenth floor, and just as the doors were about to close, Parker stepped in.

"What are you doing?" Victoria asked in a startled voice. "Why are you still here?" She thought he'd left some time ago because she hadn't seen him in the ballroom when the crowd began to disperse.

"I want to talk to you."

She stared at him with a silent, heavy glare.

"I sense that you're still carrying hostility toward me."

Victoria didn't open her mouth. Instead, she merely looked at him, unable to focus her thoughts. They rode in silence as people stepped into and out of the elevator on each floor. When they reached Victoria's floor, she made a bee-line for the hallway with Parker following close on her heels.

"Go away and leave me alone," she hissed as she hurried down the plush corridor.

"Why won't you talk to me? You can at least give me that courtesy."

"Parker, I don't have to give you shit," Victoria answered with irritation, not bothering to slow her gate or even look at him. "Now leave me alone before I call hotel security."

They reached her room and she was about to insert her keycard into the lock. "My husband is on the other side of this door, so you better leave now if you know what's good for you."

Parker shook his head. "No he's not. He hasn't been around all day, not at the church or at the reception. Are you two having troubles?"

Victoria knotted her brow and pushed against the door, intending to step inside and leave Parker out in the deserted hallway. But when she slipped into the room, Parker walked in behind her. "Are you crazy? Didn't I tell you to leave me alone?" she hissed again.

"Nice suite," Parker smiled, looking toward the window across the room. "You've got a great view."

Victoria couldn't believe his casual attitude, but she wasn't surprised by his bold audacity. "I guess you like learning the hard way," she said, walking over to the phone on the nightstand. "When I tell hotel security that a big, six-foot three inch black man just barged his way into my room, they'll have you out of here before you can blink. Now you have five seconds to get the hell out before I pick up this phone."

It was apparent that Parker didn't think much of her threat because he strode up to her in the same casual manner that he'd exuded when he entered her room. "Victoria, you're not seriously going to call security on me?"

She picked up the phone. "Try me."

"Put it down. We need to talk."

"Get out, I mean it!"

Parker reached for her hand that held the phone and gently coaxed it back to its cradle. When his fingers touched hers, Victoria stood stock still, unable to move a muscle. His touch was warm and exciting, making her think about things that created a small tingle below her waist. She could feel her weakness growing from the inside out and she knew that she couldn't trust her body's reaction to him. She had to do something to back him down, something to break his spell and prove to him, if not to herself, that she was unaffected by his presence. But as much as she tried, she was frozen in place.

They looked at each other, their breathing becoming more rapid, yet perfectly in sync. "Parker why are you doing this?" Victoria finally said. He was standing so close she could feel his body heat and smell the wonderfully intoxicating scent of his citrus-spice cologne. "This will accomplish nothing but some hurt feelings and a possible arrest."

Parker took one step back. It was a small step, but a step nonetheless, and it gave Victoria some breathing room. He gazed upon her with an intense stare that made her heart jump in her chest.

"Parker, I'm not playing with you. Please leave before this turns ugly."

"I didn't realize how much I missed you until I saw you last weekend, and I thought…."

Parker couldn't finish his sentence because he was caught off-guard by the way Victoria seemed to recoil from him. He'd been so sure about the chemistry he'd felt between them and he thought it was mutual. He couldn't believe he'd been so wrong. Feeling defeated, he turned to walk way, but then paused and spun around to face her. "I'm sorry for the way I've behaved. I apparently misjudged things. I thought there was still something left between us, something I thought I saw in your eyes when we were at Hilda's," he admitted, shaking his head. His voice was steady and his words were sincere. "I was obviously wrong. Please forgive me, Victoria."

This time when he turned to walk away, he didn't look back.

Live And In Living Color....

After Parker took a quick peek into his son's room and paid the babysitter, he settled in for the night. "Damn," he mumbled. He kicked PJ's Tonka truck to the side as he walked through his living room and headed to the extravagant gourmet kitchen that he never used. He loosened his silk tie and opened the refrigerator in search of relief. He popped the cap of his favorite ice-cold beer and turned the bottle up to his mouth. It didn't quench his real thirst, but it was a good, temporary distraction.

He polished off half the bottle in a few long swigs as he walked upstairs to his home office and settled into his worn leather chair, ready to check his email. He looked around the mahogany paneled room and thought about his encounter with Victoria.

It had been the third time he'd seen her in one week. He shook his head and smiled, thinking about how despite the fact that so many years had passed between them, she still managed to take his breath away.

When he first saw her a week ago at Hilda Barrett's house during his son's Jack and Jill playdate, he'd been shocked when she entered the room. She was the last person he'd expected to see. At first he thought his eyes were deceiving him, repeating the same cruel trick they'd played countless times over the last six years. There had been several occasions when he thought he'd seen Victoria walking down the street or sitting in a restaurant, only to find that it was a look-a-like, who upon closer inspection never measured up to the genuine article.

But when he saw the tall, beautiful woman standing in Hilda's living room, and then looked down to see the little girl standing beside her who was a cream-colored version of her spitting image, he knew it had to be Victoria. He wanted to go over to her and speak, but she was engaged with another group of women, one of whom was his friend's wife, Roberta. And knowing Roberta the way he did, he was sure that she was giving Victoria the lowdown on his life. He decided to approach her once the meeting ended, but she'd scurried away as though someone had been chasing her. He knew her pattern, and he knew that she was avoiding him.

Then a few days later he was standing in the admissions office of his son's new school when he heard the door open and smelled the undeniable scent of the only woman who'd ever made him want to settle down and repeat vows in front of an alter. When the admissions officer called out Victoria's name, he turned around to find her standing in front of him, looking as beautiful as he'd ever seen her. He could tell that she was shocked to see him again too, but he also saw a soft glimmer in her eyes when he shook her hand. He purposely hung around so he could talk to her after her meeting, and that's when he knew that the fire was still there. It wasn't what she did, but what she didn't do that gave him hope.

He knew from past experience that Victoria could be cold and distant if she was pushed to the edge, and considering the way their relationship had ended, he knew she was perfectly capable of treating him like yesterday's leftovers. But she hadn't done that. She wasn't welcoming, but she hadn't completely pushed him away either. And being a methodical thinker, he sensed an opening and took it. He handed her his business card and to his surprise and delight she took it.

It had only been recently that he'd finally given up on the hope of running into Victoria one day. He'd thought about her on many occasions since the last time he'd seen her—a time which even today he knew she was completely unaware of.

Sitting at his desk, mindlessly scrolling through his emails, Parker sighed as he thought about life's irony. When he'd come to Victoria in those dark nights five years ago it was the closest he'd ever felt to her, yet the most far away she'd ever been..............

On the day his son was born, Victoria had been heavy on Parker's mind. As he looked at his new "mini me" lying in the hospital nursery, he was overjoyed. But in that joy there was also sadness because although he instantly loved PJ on sight, he knew that having rebound sex with Pamela had been a bad idea.

He had regretted it almost from the start. They'd hooked up a few weeks after Victoria had gotten married. Seeing her wedding announcement in the newspaper had sent him into a mild state of depression, a very sobering experience for a man as admittedly confident and ego driven as himself. After moping around and shutting himself off for days, he decided that he had to get on with the business of living. He knew he was a damn good catch, and that he could have practically any woman he wanted. After all, who wouldn't want a tall, handsome, Harvard educated surgeon who was cultured in the ways of the world, sophisticated in his taste, and knew how to please a woman in the bedroom!

Parker decided that the best way to get back out there was to throw himself head first into the sea. When he ran into Pamela one night at a mutual friend's house warming party, she'd chatted him up and they agreed to have dinner the following evening. Over the course of the next week Pamela worked her charms, skillfully applying emotional salve on his wounds from his painful breakup with Victoria. She pulled out all the stops, luring him back into her bed. That night had been a blur for Parker after too many cognacs and sweet whispers in his ear, but Pamela had known exactly what she was doing. A month later she announced that she was pregnant.

Even though Parker clearly wasn't in love with her, he wanted to do the right thing by Pamela, so instead of giving her the engagement ring she'd been hoping for, he presented her with a carefully structured legal document that spelled out his financial commitment to their unborn child. Pamela was furious, but kept her true feelings tucked away while she patiently plotted to get the ring and marriage proposal she so desperately wanted.

During the months leading up to her delivery, Parker was ever diligent and caring, attending all her pre-natal appointments and joining her at lamasse classes. Pamela's enthusiasm about her impending bundle of joy began to wane as she grew bigger with each passing month, an emotional state that her OBGYN had attributed to stress. So Parker took it upon himself to order the crib, shop for baby supplies, and even decorate the baby's room in her house. "I don't want you to worry about a thing," he'd told her. "Our baby is going to be happy and healthy and I'll do everything I can to make sure you have a safe delivery."

When the big day finally arrived, Parker was overjoyed to cut the umbilical cord of his newborn son. His mother and Pamela's mother had come to town, and were equally as happy to welcome their grand-child. For them, it was a dream come true because the two women had been best friends for over forty years. They'd been making wedding plans for Parker and Pamela since they were children, building sand castles on the beach when their families vacationed together during summers on Martha's Vineyard. Now, they were ecstatic because they saw their new grandchild as the bridge that would finally unite their two children in matrimony. Everyone had high hopes except Parker, because he knew that his heart still belonged to someone else, even if she was married to another man.

The next day after PJ was born, Parker noticed a new baby in the nursery when he went to visit his son before starting his morning rounds. The baby was a tiny, beautiful little girl who trembled from head to toe inside an incubator. Normally, he would have paid no attention to any babies other than his own, but there was something about the helpless, angel-like infant that drew him in. He walked up to the side of the plastic encased bubble and stared at the little girl inside, then he looked at her name tag and realized why she'd captured his attention.

"Nurse," Parker called out to the ward nurse on duty. "Can you pull the chart on the Thornton baby?"

After reading Alexandria's chart, Parker immediately became concerned. She'd been delivered by cesarean section due to placenta abruption. She was full-term but underweight, and was suffering from severe jaundice, fluid build-up on her tiny lungs, and a weakened immune system. But his worry subsided a little when he saw that Keith Bloomberg, one of the best pediatric surgeons on the east coast, was already on the case.

"She was delivered early this morning," the nurse said as she stood near Parker, attending to another infant. "She's a tiny little thing, and she's got some breathing problems, but she's a real fighter," she smiled. "She gets it honest. I think she and her mother will both be all right, she's a fighter too."

Parker froze, but kept his outward expression calm and casual. He knew he had to find out the extent of Victoria's condition. Placenta abruptions could cause major bleeding and serious complications for the mother. After some quick snooping he learned that she'd hemorrhaged badly by the time she arrived at the hospital and even more during the emergency cesarean. Her blood pressure was dangerously low and she was still in intensive care.

Parker searched the floor for her room and finally found it. As he approached he glimpsed Victoria's mother and heard the unmistakable baritone of her father booming through the room. John Small had always been an intimidating figure, but hearing him speak now, Parker could feel the worry and fear in his voice. He wanted to rush in and let John and Elizabeth know that Victoria would be just fine, that he'd make sure of it. But he knew it would be a bad idea to insert himself into the situation, especially since he had no doubt that Ted was in the room with them. He tugged on his stethoscope and eased by the open door, looking inside as he passed. Ted was sitting at the edge of Victoria's bed, while her parents camped out in two chairs against the window.

Late that evening, long after visitor's hours had ended, Parker found his way back to Victoria's room. He remembered that she'd always been a sound sleeper, and now with the help of drugs, she was out for the count. He stood watch as she slept, checking the updates on her chart and monitoring her vital signs. He even ventured to hold her hand, then kiss her lightly on her forehead. This became his nightly ritual until she was released, safe and well....................

As Parker logged off his computer and went into his bedroom to undress, he felt a heavy weight sitting in the pit of his stomach. He reached in his pants pocket and fished out Victoria's business card that he'd picked up from the gift table at the reception. He looked at her business address, phone number, and email, committing them to memory before sitting the card on his nightstand. He let out a small sigh. Just when he thought he'd finally gotten her out of his system and off of his mind, she was back again, live and in living color.

Chapter 7

What's Inside That Box?...

It was early Sunday morning, and the waiting was finally over. Shortly after midnight, Carolyn Thornton breathed her last breath of life. It had been a tumultuous twenty-four hours. Ted and his sister had stood vigil over their mother's bed for most of the day, taking turns in between cafeteria breaks. Charlie had arrived late that evening, crying and grieving like the devoted son he never was.

Once all her children were gathered around her bed, Carolyn went quietly, but with a pained expression on her face. She'd awoken briefly, looked at Ted, Lilly and Charlie, and summoned the strength she needed to speak one last time. "I did the best I could. I loved you all." And with that, she was gone.

Carolyn's attorney had been posted at the hospital for most of the evening too. Abe Brookstein was more than just a legal advisor, he was a trusted and valued family friend. Abe had been the Thornton's attorney for over thirty years. His uncle and Charles Sr. had been classmates at Harvard, and had enjoyed a long-lasting personal and business relationship. After his uncle passed away, Abe took over where he'd left off. Watching Carolyn go was like loosing an aunt, and although at the moment all he wanted to do was grieve, he knew that he had serious work to do. He pulled Ted to the side, not hesitating so he could get to the bottom of the business at hand.

"Ted, can I speak to you for a minute?" Abe asked, inviting him to step into the hallway outside.

Ted could hear Abe's voice but he felt numb as he looked at his mother's lifeless body. He'd braced himself for this moment, knowing it would come, but it still felt unreal. He'd also braced himself for the conversation with Abe that he knew was coming. He stepped into the hall, leaving Lilly, Charlie and the nurse inside to wait for his mother's doctor. Charlie glared as the two men walked outside, wondering what they were up to, but not having the nerve to question them at such a delicately sensitive time.

"Ted, I know this isn't a good time," Abe began, getting straight to the point. "But I need to give you this." Abe handed Ted a small envelope with a number written one it. "Inside this envelope is the key to your mother's safe deposit box. She instructed me to give it to you the moment she passed."

Ted temporarily laid down his grief and picked up his focused mind. "Abe, what's this about? What's inside that box?" he asked, folding the small envelope before tucking it away in his pocket.

"I have no idea. Carolyn never told me...you know how private your mother is," Abe paused, still referring to her in the present tense. "All I know is that she was very adamant that I give you the key the moment she passed."

Ted shook his head, trying to deal with loss and newfound worries. He knew that whatever he found in the safe deposit box, it wouldn't be good, and the thought that he'd have to wait another day until the bank opened on Monday morning made the situation even more taxing. He didn't like the feeling of having no control over things, and as his fingers gripped the envelope in his pocket, his senses told him that this was the first of many situations that would leave him feeling helpless to the events around him.

After the doctor made the official death pronouncement, Ted began taking care of the solemn details that death required; signing hospital documents, and making funeral arrangements.

Charlie wanted to hold a family meeting right away to discuss their mother's will. Lilly was too despondent to be outraged that her brother wanted to talk about divvying up their mother's material possessions, instead of mourning her loss. But even though Ted was grief-stricken, he was still his commanding self. He told Charlie in a brutally firm tone that not a word would be discussed concerning their mother's estate until Monday morning, and for the moment, they'd have peace on the Sabbath and mourn her death.

After signing the necessary paperwork so the morgue could release his mother's body to the funeral home, Ted was exhausted from stress and fear of the unknown. For the first time since he'd arrived in town, he drove over to his mother's house. He didn't know if it was because of his mood or if it was a result of the years of quiet sickness that his mother had suffered, but the once grand Thornton home had taken on the look and feel of a mausoleum. It was the same house he'd grown up in and had visited frequently on holidays, but now, his mother's death had turned it into something else.

He climbed the spiral staircase, managing to drag his body up to his mother's bedroom. His thoughts were moving so fast they made his head swim. All he could think about were his mother's last words and the key in his pocket to the safe deposit box at Boston Private Bank. "What was Mother hiding?" he whispered to himself.

The smell of Carolyn's softly scented talcum powder filled Ted's nose. He looked around the large, neatly kept bedroom, as if answers would jump out at him. "What am I doing here?" he questioned. He knew that being there was a waste of time and that nothing would be accomplished by searching for a mysterious secret in a dark, empty house.

He'd considered contacting Bo Powers, the private investigator he hired years ago to uncover his first wife's sordid past. But upon further contemplation, he thought better of it because he knew that whatever his mother was hiding, it was something that was intended for him alone.

It was nearly three a.m. by the time he arrived back at his hotel room. He thought about calling Victoria, but decided against it. It was late, and he knew she'd probably had a long, hard day with Gigi's wedding. She hadn't been sleeping well lately, and he knew she needed to rest. Besides, the bad news he had to share could wait until the sun came up.

Riddles And Games…

Even though Victoria was surrounded by the serenity of her opulent hotel suite, a peaceful night's sleep had eluded her yet again. Now, she was up early because her mind was in a constant loop, thinking about Parker and their encounter. She could no longer skirt around what she hoped her head could trick her heart into believing—that she was over him.

More than a few times she'd wondered what their future would've held if Parker had never cheated on her. It was an act that had driven her straight into Ted's arms. Even though she and Parker had their problems, and it had frustrated her that he hadn't been supportive of her entrepreneurial dreams, she'd loved him, and he had loved her, and in the back of her mind the thought of *"what if"* challenged her to question what could have been.

She shivered when she thought about how close she'd come to embracing him, rather than calling hotel security as she'd threatened. And when he finally left her room, a quiet longing engulfed her because a part of her wanted to ask him to come back. Victoria knew that her thoughts were dangerous, and added to her worries was the fact that she could also see trouble ahead for Debbie and Tyler as well.

Debbie was clearly swimming in unfamiliar and dangerous waters. Victoria knew that her friend had always been wild and unpredictable, but never stupid and reckless. She prayed that Debbie would come to her senses before it was too late. All it took was one careless slip, one tiny mistake, and her life as she knew it would be over in a snap. She knew this because it was the very thought that kept repeating itself in her mind about her own tenuous situation.

And then there was Tyler. For months, she'd been trying to get him to start dating again. She could see that he was lonely, and hadn't been his usual upbeat self for some time. But his fear of getting close to anyone, only to lose them had kept him locked away in his own world. Victoria had tried to steer him in the direction of a few single women she knew through her Black Business Women's Association group, but he hadn't shown any interest. Now, to both her delight and chagrin, it appeared that he'd found someone who had captured his attention.

When she called Tyler late last night to see how his dinner with Samantha had gone, she was surprised that the two were still together. "She's there with you...it's almost midnight, what are you two doing?" Victoria had asked.

"Minding my own business like you should be doing," Tyler whispered into the phone. "Sam and I are still hangin' out. I'll hit you back later."

Victoria heard the unmistakable, beguiling laughter of a woman in the background and knew it could only mean one thing. When the dial tone rang loud in her ear, she hung up and hoped that Tyler knew what he was getting himself in to.

All Victoria could think about was how time had changed so many things. Six years ago she and her friends were all so happy. They were in love with their spouses, and didn't entertain the thought of being with anyone else. They were all living their dreams and everything seemed so perfect. But as she knew all too well, there was no such thing as perfection, and if one was able to briefly glimpse it, there was a hefty price to be paid for the experience.

Rather than sit in her restless state, Victoria decided to get on her laptop and tackle yesterday's back log of emails. When her cell phone rang, she looked at the alarm clock on the nightstand. *No one calls with good news before seven in the morning.*

Ted's voice came through on the other end. "She's gone," were his first words.

Victoria wanted to weep, but she knew he needed her to be strong, supportive and rock-solid. "Oh, Ted. Honey, I'm so sorry," she whispered.

"We were all there at her bedside when she passed shortly after midnight."

"She went quietly...no pain?"

"Yes, thank God."

"How are you holding up?"

Ted let out a deep breath. "Honestly, I don't know. On one hand I'm relieved that she's not suffering, but on the other..."

Although Victoria knew this was coming, it was still hard to believe that Carolyn Thornton was dead. So if it was hard for her, she knew it must be traumatic for Ted. "I know it's tough. There's nothing that ever prepares you for this," she tried to comfort.

"You're right, there isn't. But the truth is, and this is going to sound really terrible, but I'm pissed."

Victoria moved over to the couch by the window as she watched the sun struggle to make an appearance. She prepared herself to deal with the onslaught of her husband's emotions that were about to come rushing out. "It's natural to feel angry when you lose someone you love, especially a parent...your mother."

"It's not that. I've been thinking about the last two days of my mother's life, and the secret she talked about. All the riddles and games she laid out leading up to her death. I know she wanted to get things off her chest, but I wish she had just come out and told me whatever it was that she was hiding."

Victoria had been afraid of this. "She didn't get a chance to tell you her secret?"

"Well, yes and no. She told me that the answers would be in a safe deposit box that I'm supposed to open only after her death, but I can't get to it until the bank opens tomorrow morning."

Victoria's eyebrows shot straight up. "Ted, this sounds bizarre, like something out of a crazy movie. What do you think it could be? What could she have possibly been hiding all these years?"

"I don't have a clue. All I know is that I need you here with me. I'll call Jen and have her arrange a flight for you and Alexandria to leave out later this afternoon."

After they finished their brief conversation, Victoria sprang into action. She gathered her things, checked out of the hotel, then headed home to pack for the trip she knew she had to make, but didn't want to take.

Emotional Rollercoaster...

"How much longer 'til we see Daddy?" Alexandria asked.

"Not too much longer, Sweetie," Victoria answered, trying to make herself smile.

They were buckled into their first-class seats, ready for landing, both anxious to see Ted.

As their plane descended into Logan National Airport, Victoria handed Alexandria's apple juice to the flight attendant and braced herself for the emotional rollercoaster that she knew was coming.

Her mind was filled with so many thoughts, it was hard to keep up with them all. But at the moment her primary concern was for Alexandria and how she would react to her grandmother's death. She and Ted had tried to explain the sad details to her a few days ago, and she'd had another brief, but delicate conversation with Alexandria before they boarded the plane. Now, as Victoria thought about Carolyn's funeral, she wasn't sure how much her daughter truly understood about the finality of death.

Then her mind turned to Ted. Between his mother's mysterious secret and his brother's crooked greed, she wondered how he was coping. It was one thing to put on a strong front over the phone, but she knew the real story would be told once she was able to see him face to face.

And to top off all the worries floating around in her head, Victoria thought about what kind of secret Carolyn had been keeping. She remembered what Tyler had said about deathbed confessions, and she knew that he was right—nothing good could possibly come of it. Knowing her husband the way she did, Victoria was sure that Ted had readied himself with the same knowledge.

And even though she tried her best to fight the urge, her final thoughts landed on Parker. She knew that of all the complications pulling at her hem, Parker Brightwood was the thread that could unravel the entire spool.

Make Some Noise....

As soon as Victoria and Alexandria reached baggage claim, Ted was there waiting for them—strong and steady. It made Victoria feel guilty for the thoughts she kept having about Parker.

"Daddy, Daddy!" Alexandria squealed as she ran toward her father.

"How's my, Princess?" Ted smiled, grabbing his daughter up into his arms as he gave her a kiss on the cheek. He tugged at one of her neatly braided ponytails and made her scream out with giddy laughter.

Victoria walked up to her husband and daughter and they embraced for a family hug. Ted kissed her lightly on the lips and thanked God that the two most important people in his life were there by his side.

A few hours later after Victoria tucked Alexandria in for the night, she and Ted held each other close as they lay in the bed of their presidential suite. Looking at his wife, Ted realized how much he'd missed lying beside her at night. It had been over a week since they'd made love, and he was craving her, wanting her. He nuzzled his nose in the crook of her neck. "I'm so glad you're here," he breathed out as his lips found hers.

They kissed, letting their tongues dance and caress each others mouth in a slow, intoxicating rhythm. Victoria could feel Ted's erection growing. "We'll have to be quiet," she whispered, "I left the door open to Alexandria's room."

Unlike Victoria, who could sleep through a tornado, Alexandria had inherited her father's sleep habits and would awake from slumber at the sound of cotton hitting the floor. But tonight, her parents didn't have to worry because she was exhausted from the activities of her weekend sleep-over and an unexpected travel day.

"It's a good thing she's knocked out," Ted panted with a devilish grin. "I think we're gonna make some noise."

Victoria was surprised that with all the sadness and grief that had fallen onto his shoulders, that sex was even remotely on Ted's radar. She knew that if the situation was reversed and she'd just lost her mother, romping between the sheets would be the last thing on her mind. But judging from the large bulge in his pajama bottoms, it was at the front and center of his.

She looked into his eyes and saw a mixture of hunger and need, and then she understood. He was crying out for comfort, for a release from his frustrations, pain, and uncertainty, and she was more than willing and determined to give it to him.

Victoria kissed Ted deep and hard, letting her hands roam his body as she soothed him under her delicate touch. Slowly, she made her way down his chest and stomach, lightly kissing in certain places and sucking in others. When she reached the hardened thickness between his legs that always gave her pleasure, she licked and teased and kissed and swallowed until Ted nearly yelled out.

He was a man of unrelenting control, but tonight Victoria's mission was to render him helpless so he could release his burdens. The only emotion she wanted him to experience was pure and intense pleasure. She prided herself on being the only person who could make him lose complete authority.

Ted could feel himself about to explode. "V, come here...I want to be inside you," he moaned, trying to pull Victoria up from his lower body.

But she refused to retreat. She wanted him to fully enjoy the heat that she was about to bring him. She was glad that Ted was an unselfish lover, and that he didn't want to reach orgasm until he'd satisfied her first. But tonight she wanted him to think only of himself. She wanted him to reach nirvana, even if she didn't. He'd been through so much, and she was carrying such guilt, that she felt this act on her part would purge both their worries and troubles, at least for tonight. So she continued to suck, and lick, and envelope him into her warm, wet mouth, working the tip of his rounded head with her lips and tongue. His fingers dug into her scalp, pleading for mercy. His eyes were closed tight and his body pulsated with pleasure. Finally, he released himself as he moaned, delivering his promise to make some noise.

A few minutes later they were lying in the darkness with Ted spooning her from behind. Victoria listened to her husband's heavy breathing and prayed that the remainder of his night would be restful. They'd switched roles, and now it was she who was up during the wee hours, trying to drift off to sleep. As she said a silent prayer for Ted, asking God to give him the strength to bury his mother, she said one for herself, asking for the strength to bury her desire for another man.

Yet Another Twist To The Bizarre Puzzle...

The next morning Ted rose early, knowing that it may very well be one of the toughest days of his life. His mother's death was devastating, and her funeral in two days would without a doubt be the most heart-breaking thing he'd ever faced. But finding out the secret she'd been keeping, and dealing with whatever aftermath that came from it was something he was sure would be nearly as hard, and best left uncovered.

Ted dressed while Victoria thumbed through the room service menu, trying to decide what to order for breakfast because Alexandria would be up soon. "You sure there's nothing I can help you with?" she asked. She put the menu to the side and watched Ted as he slipped his navy blazer over his tan polo shirt.

"You helped me quite a bit last night," he winked, walking over and giving her a slow kiss on the lips.

Victoria stood in her silk robe and embraced him, inhaling his woodsy cologne. Even though Ted seemed to be in much better spirits than when he'd picked them up from the airport the previous night, Victoria could still see that he was emotionally fatigued. Death and secrets were a hazardous combination. He was about to go to the bank and open Pandora's box, and she knew that wouldn't be easy.

"Whatever's in that safe deposit box…we'll deal with it, together," Victoria reassured him.

"V, what would I do without you?"

"You'll never have to find out."

Her steadfast love and support made him smile. And he needed it because it would be the last time he smiled for several days to come.

Ted adjusted his collar and grabbed his attaché. "After I leave the bank, Lilly, Charlie and I are going to meet at the funeral home with the director, then we'll head over to Abe's office," he told Victoria. "My mother wanted her will read prior to her burial. It was a specific instruction."

"Really?" Victoria asked with surprise. She thought it was a rather odd edict to make. But then again, many things about Carolyn and the life she'd led were beginning to seem stranger and stranger by the minute. Reading the will before the burial was yet another twist in the bizarre puzzle she'd created. In Victoria's experience, wills were usually read after the last speck of dirt was thrown on the coffin, that way depending upon the document's contents, disgruntled family members wouldn't be able to show their asses until after the dead was six feet under.

She wanted to ask Ted why his mother would give those instructions, but at this point she knew that his guess was as good as hers. "After we eat and get dressed I'll take Alexandria to the park. Do you think you'll be able to join us for lunch?"

"Probably not, it's going to be a long day," Ted sighed. "I'll see you later this afternoon, but I'll call you after I leave the bank to let you know what I find out." He gave Victoria another quick kiss, then headed out the door.

Victoria went to Alexandria's room and found her coloring in her favorite Disney book. She watched as her daughter doodled and dabbled, trying to decide which crayons would make the plain black and white canvas spring to life with color. She thought about what kind of secret her mother-in-law could have possibly been keeping, and it suddenly became much more personal because whatever mystery Carolyn had been hiding over the years, it had the very real possibility of affecting Alexandria.

Now, Victoria became very concerned. Her mind raced and she wondered, *if Carolyn's secret was so bad that she had to keep it until her death, who was she and what kind of terrible thing did she do?*

Without Blinking An Eye…

An hour later, Ted sat alone in a small conference room at Boston Private Bank, trying to digest the information in front of him. He'd been sitting in stunned silence for nearly a half hour since opening his mother's safe deposit box and carefully examining its contents. He re-read the documents over and over again, as if what he'd seen in black and white would somehow change. He'd been prepared to find something shocking, and had braced himself for any number of far-out, crazy possibilities. But nothing in his wildest imagination could have compared to the reality that lay before him.

Ted wondered how his parents could have kept such an earth shattering secret hidden for so many years. *How could they have lived a lie for so long without blinking an eye?* he wondered in silence. Then he thought about his father, the man he'd always respected for his character and strength. He'd been Carolyn's partner in crime, an accomplice who helped to keep their shared secret from everyone, including their own children.

Ted pondered question after question as new ones kept rising to the surface. His fingers grazed the faded documents while his mind tried to grab hold of what the newfound information meant. He knew the implications would change his life forever and the very knowledge of what he was now privy to already had. Again, more questions flooded his thoughts. Finally, he realized that he had to stop before he drove himself completely mad.

Knock, knock, knock. "Mr. Thornton, is everything all right in here?" the branch manager asked, slowly opening the door. She stared at Ted as he let his mother's hand-written, death bed confession fall from his hands. "You've been in here for quite a while, so I wanted to make sure that you were okay. Does everything seem to be in order?"

"Yes, everything is fine," Ted nodded, pulling himself together.

"Great, then all you'll need to do is sign off on a few documents and I can release the contents of the safe deposit box to you," the pleasantly plump woman smiled.

"Sounds good, just show me what I need to sign."

After Ted took care of the necessary paperwork and secured possession of his mother's documents, he walked out into the late morning sun, trying to clear his mind. He was running behind schedule as he maneuvered his rental car out of the bank's parking lot and into the rush of traffic. He knew he should call Victoria as he'd promised he would, but the news was much too fresh and all too shocking to deliver. The only thing he could do at the moment was choke down his emotional confusion and concentrate on the many tasks that lay ahead.

And as he'd always done whenever he made a mistake or faced a challenge, Ted put the damage out of his mind and focused on how he would recover from it. For now, his immediate recovery meant meeting Lilly and Charlie at the funeral home and then heading over to Abe Brookstein's office for a reading of his mother's will, bracing himself for another shocker that was sure to come.

You Don't Know What I Know...

Victoria watched Alexandria as she played on the swings with another little girl who looked to be around her age. They were at Boston Common, enjoying the beautiful park in the heart of the city. Alexandria and her new little friend jumped from the swings and were now engaged in a spirited game of hopscotch. An older Latina woman who Victoria assumed was the little girl's nanny, hovered close by. It was almost lunch time and she wondered how Ted was holding up.

She was certain that he'd found bad news in his mother's safe deposit box, otherwise he would have called her by now. All morning long she'd wracked her brain trying to come up with possible scenarios. Had Carolyn killed someone? Did she have a criminal record? Had she been born a man and then had a sex change? These were all the questions that ran through Victoria's mind, but for the life of her she couldn't imagine what could be so terrible that Carolyn felt the need to hide it, literally under lock and key.

Victoria was deep in thought when her cell phone rang. She looked at the caller ID and felt a small relief. "Hi, Mom," she smiled into the phone.

"Sweetheart, you sound tired," Elizabeth said in her always cheery voice.

"Yeah, I am. I had a busy weekend, and Alexandria and I arrived here in Boston late yesterday," she said with a slight yawn. She hadn't slept all night and now she was craving a few hours of rest.

"How's Ted. Is he there with you?"

"No, Alexandria and I are out at the park and Ted left early this morning to take care of some business concerning the funeral and the reading of his mother's will. My guess is that I probably won't see him until later this afternoon."

Victoria's mother shook her head on the other end. "It's a shame, I tell you. Seems like it happened so fast. One minute all was fine, then the next, Carolyn's gone. You just never know when it's your time."

"Well, it wasn't as sudden as you might think," Victoria said, adjusting her over-sized, tortoise-shell designer sunglasses on her face. "Carolyn was diagnosed with pancreatic cancer several months ago, but she never told anyone. Ted's sister didn't even know she was in the hospital until a few days ago."

"Oh, no. That's just awful," Elizabeth groaned. "Ted must be devastated."

"Yes, he is. But you know him, he's holding up, trying to put on a strong face."

"My, my, my….besides loosing a child, I don't think there's any worse hurt than losing a parent."

Victoria heard the sadness in her mother's voice, knowing that she'd experienced the loss of her first child, a still-born baby girl, and the loss of both her parents, whom she'd been estranged from for years up until the day each of them died. Victoria felt a wave of emotion as she listened to the warmth of her mother's voice while she watched her own daughter laugh and play without a worry in the world. "Mom, even though he's trying not to show it, this is so hard for Ted, and I don't know what to say or do to ease his pain."

"Sweetheart, I'm sure that just being there is enough. In times like this there's nothing you can say that will take away the hurt he's feeling or the enormity of his loss, but your presence will make him feel loved. And trust me, that's all he needs right now."

Victoria held back the complicated emotions that were caught in her throat. "I hope that one day I'm half as wise as you, and that I'll make the right choices."

"You don't give yourself enough credit."

"You don't know what I know," was Victoria's response.

Elizabeth knew her daughter through and through, and she could sense when something was bothering her only child. The tone in Victoria's voice told her that something was weighing heavy on her mind, something that went beyond the hardships of dealing with the death of her mother-in-law. "Sweetheart, what's wrong? Talk to me." Elizabeth implored.

Victoria bit down on the inside of her cheek. "It's nothing, Mom…really. I'm just stressed out from Gigi's wedding, Carolyn's death, and lack of sleep."

"Gigi's wedding?" Elizabeth balked, sucking her teeth. "I'm sure it was an event for the ages. Did anyone get arrested?"

It was the first time in nearly a week that Victoria had laughed out loud. "No, Mom, but she practically gave Gary a lap dance at the rehearsal dinner, and then at the reception she…."

"Don't tell me anymore," Elizabeth interrupted, shutting her eyes at the thought. "That young woman should be ashamed of herself. I've read so many things about her and Gary in the newspapers, making spectacles of themselves everywhere they go, hanging out in night clubs and causing scenes. At first your father felt bad about us not attending the wedding, being that Gary is his oldest and dearest friend's nephew. But when he thought about the mayhem that might take place, we both agreed that a card and a gift from their registry was enough."

"Again, your wisdom prevailed," Victoria smiled. "Um, listen mom, I've gotta run. It's lunch time, and I need to take Alexandria to get something to eat."

Elizabeth knew that her daughter was withdrawing. It was what she often did when she didn't want to face a situation right away. She wanted to press Victoria about what was really bothering her, but decided that it wasn't the right time. "Okay, Sweetheart," she said, temporarily letting her daughter off the hook. "Tell Ted that your father and I send our prayers. Call me later and give me the name of the funeral home so we can send flowers."

"I'll do that."

"And, Sweetheart…"

"Yes?"

"Whenever you're ready to talk, I'm here to listen."

Victoria held her emotions close. "I love you, Mom."

"Love you too."

After she finished her conversation with her mother, Victoria and Alexandria ventured to a local deli for lunch, then shopped at a few specialty stores in the picturesque area. By late afternoon they'd both grown tired, so they headed back to the hotel.

It was after five o'clock, and Victoria still hadn't heard from Ted since he'd left their suite at eight-thirty that morning. She wanted to call him, to make sure he was all right, but she knew he needed time to sort through whatever terrible secret he'd discovered about his mother. "Just be there for him," she whispered to herself, repeating her mother's advice.

The Far Reaching Consequences…

Alexandria was playing with her dolls in her room, and Victoria was engrossed in work on her laptop when Ted walked through the door around dinner time. "How did things go?" she asked, putting her computer away so she could give her husband her full attention.

She could see a drastic change in Ted's demeanor. She studied his face and saw a type of frustration and worry that made alarm pulse through her veins. He walked over to where she was sitting on the couch and took a seat in the chair across from her. The fact that he chose a separate seat told her that he wanted space, but she was determined to be there for him, physically and emotionally. She wasn't going to let him shut her out, and she wasn't going to shut down on him either. She leaned forward, placing her elbows on her knees, focusing her eyes on his. "Do you want to talk about it?" she asked.

Ted responded with a vacant stare in the direction of the window across the room.

Victoria knew that she should exercise patience because of what Ted was going through, and she wanted to be the shoulder he leaned on, but not knowing about the secret that Carolyn had hidden in the safe deposit box was more than she could take. Her thoughts weren't just to satisfy her own curiosity, she wanted to make sure that her child would be safe from whatever crime his mother had committed.

Victoria decided to revise her approach. "Did you get all the funeral arrangements straightened out? My mother wants to know the information so she can send flowers."

Ted finally looked in her direction, letting out a long sigh as he reached into his attaché. "That's very thoughtful. Yes, here's the information." He placed a folder from the funeral home on the coffee table that sat between them.

They both stared at the burial documents, but neither of them said a word. Finally, Victoria spoke up. "Was your mother's secret that terrible?"

Ted looked at her with hollow eyes that sent a shiver through Victoria's body. She rose to her feet and went over to him, kneeling between his legs as she held his face in the palm of her hands. "Ted, I'm here for you. I know this is hard, but you're not in this alone. Just lean on me."

Ted wrapped his wife into his arms, rocking her back and forth in a slow and wordless trance. Victoria could feel his pain pouring out as he hugged her, but no tears came. So she held on tight, kissed the side of his cheek, and prayed for his peace of mind.

Ted tried to bring himself to tell Victoria the truth about the secret his mother had been keeping, but his mouth remained silent. All day he'd been thinking about how he was going to break the news to her. He'd already decided that it would take time before he revealed the truth to his siblings. His mother had been right. He was the youngest, but also the strongest of the three, and if he was having a hard time accepting what his parents had done, he knew Lilly and Charlie wouldn't be able to handle it. The secret affected them all.

The fact that he couldn't find the words to tell Victoria made Ted feel even worse. She was his soul mate, his closest friend, his lover and his most cherished confidant. She was the only person he trusted implicitly, and would willingly put his life in her hands without a second thought. But the information he'd learned today was so incredible that he didn't know what to do with it, and he was still coming to grips with how he felt about what it all meant. He didn't know how to tell her what he couldn't make sense of himself.

The far reaching consequences of what had been set into motion over six decades ago would have a profound effect on all their lives today. It was explosive, yet delicate, and until he found a way to deal with the truth in his own mind, and in his own way, he couldn't afford to expose it to anyone else.

Ted knew that Lilly and Charlie would surely ask a million questions that he didn't have answers to. But he also knew their curiosity would be nothing compared to the firing line of questions that Victoria would launch, and at the moment he didn't want to deal with it. He had to get through the next two days, attending his mother's wake tomorrow, and her funeral the following day. Then he would accompany his wife and child back home safely before he booked a flight to Jackson, Mississippi, where he could look for the answers to secrets that had been buried in lies.

Chapter 8

We Need Truth…

Victoria and Ted's uncomfortable evening rolled into a hectic day. Victoria still didn't know any more about Carolyn's secret than she did the day before, and even though she was desperate to find out what Ted had discovered, she was reluctant to push him while he was still so grief-stricken. For Ted's part, he was doing his best at holding up a strong exterior, while trying to tame Victoria's curiosity.

They made themselves busy by visiting Ted's relatives and family friends. Victoria knew most of them because they'd met when she and Ted got married, and had seen each other at family gatherings over the years since. She was glad that most were as warm and welcoming as Lilly and surprisingly, Charlie, had been when they first met. But there were quite a few new faces that she didn't recognize, and it was obvious that they weren't happy to see the prized Thornton son on the arm of one so dark.

Given their subtle, yet uncomfortable stares and near complete silence when she attempted to engage them in conversation, Victoria understood their reactions all too well, knowing exactly what they meant.

As she looked around Lilly's large living room filled with pale faces, her mind was focused on protecting her daughter from the ugliness that might rear its head. The sideways glances and hushed whispers made her want to tell a few of her bigoted in-laws to kiss her natural black ass! And if anyone had the bad judgment to exercise the least bit of prejudice toward her daughter, that's when the gloves would come off and the claws would come out. Victoria imagined that this must have been similar to what her parents had encountered in the beginning of their marriage. Elizabeth's light-bright-and-damned-near-white, color-conscious family was furious when she married a man whose skin was the color of night.

After an hour of forced smiles and tension-filled stares, Victoria assumed that the haters must have read her thoughts because even though they were distant and unsociable, they weren't outright hateful, and that was all that mattered to her.

She was given a small break when Lilly offered to take Alexandria with her to pick up a few things from the grocery store. It was therapy for Lilly because in her present state, she needed the innocent distraction of a child to make her forget about the loss and sadness that had been clinging to her for the last few days. Victoria had always liked Lilly because she possessed a genuinely good heart and kind spirit. And she was glad that Alexandria seemed to adore her aunt. She wanted her daughter to have a good relationship with relatives on both sides of her family, a luxury she didn't have growing up. Her mother's branch of her family tree was one she was largely unfamiliar with and had never really known.

Elizabeth's family had disowned her shortly after Victoria had been born. They'd cut off all contact following a heated confrontation. Elizabeth's mother had been greatly disappointed, and verbalized as much when she and a few other relatives came for a visit to see the new addition to their family. When she saw that little Victoria had inherited her father's dark skin instead of their family's prized alabaster hue, she was beside herself.

She'd held her nose and bit her tongue when Elizabeth married John, giving her a coal-colored son-in-law. But now, having a chocolate-brown grandchild was more than she could take. "At least you can tell she's going to have good hair, she's actually a cute little baby to be so dark," she'd said, her way of trying to turn a bad situation into something she could stomach.

John hit the roof. He threw his in-laws out of the house with

Elizabeth's approval and from that day forward there was no contact between them. Little Victoria often asked her parents why her mother's relatives never called on her birthday or came by to visit during the holidays like her father's family did. She'd seen pictures of them in her mother's scrapbook, but with the exception of Elizabeth's brother, Maxx, she'd never met any of them. John and Elizabeth skirted around her questions, telling their daughter that all her family loved her, whether they came to visit or not.

But the truth was that it didn't matter to Elizabeth's clan that John hailed from the wealthiest black family in their small, South Carolina town and owned considerable land and real estate, or that he was an Ivy League graduate who'd amassed a small fortune by founding Queens Bank, Raleigh, North Carolina's first black-owned, black-financed and black-operated bank, eventually expanding to four branches throughout the city. None of it had mattered because his skin nor that of his baby daughter's was light enough for their taste.

Victoria watched from Lilly's living room window as her sister-in-law backed her car out of the driveway en route to the store. Alexandria was strapped into the back seat, laughing with cheer because Lilly was obviously telling her a funny story.

Victoria prayed that Alexandria would never know the kind of hurt that she'd experienced when she was just a little girl. She was seven years-old when she awoke one night and overheard her parents talking about the fateful day when Elizabeth's family had come to visit. Discovering the ugly truth, that her mother's side of the family had distain for dark skin, had left a lasting mark. It made her feel inadequate and had nearly crushed her young spirit. She didn't tell her parents what she'd heard them discuss, and she kept the pain locked away for the better part of her adult life before finally opening up her old wounds so they could heal. But that night's discovery still lived with her today, because that's when she learned how to shut off the unpleasantries of the world until she was ready to deal with them.

Before Victoria could get too consumed in her thoughts, her cell phone rang. She tensed a bit when she saw who it was. "Hey, Debbie, how's it going?"

"That's the question I want to ask you…you okay?"

Victoria sighed. "I guess I'm as good as can be expected. Carolyn's wake is later this evening and the funeral is at noon tomorrow. Ted's holding up pretty well, but it's tough. We're just trying to make it through the next few days."

"Is there anything I can do?"

"Just keep us in your prayers."

"That's a done deal," Debbie said.

"How're things with you?" Victoria was praying that Debbie wasn't calling her with bad news, especially not right now.

"Umm, things are okay," she paused. "Ever since I got back home I've been thinking about everything you said, and you were right. I ended things with Stan."

"Praise, God." This was the best news Victoria had gotten in over a week.

"I knew that would make you happy. You can tell Tyler and Denise too because I'm sure they'll share your relief. And by the way, Tyler confronted me at the reception."

"For the record, I didn't initiate the subject with either of them. You know they don't sleep on anything. Besides, you practically gave yourself away."

Debbie nodded her head on the other end. "I know, I got carried away," she admitted, sounding deeply regretful. "Bringing Stan to Gigi's wedding was a dumb decision and one of the worst mistakes I could have ever made."

The tone in her voice gave Victoria alarm. "Oh, no...don't tell me that Rob found out?"

"No."

"Whew!"

"But I think I'm going to tell him."

"*What?*" Victoria nearly yelled, catching the questioning stares of a few curious eyes in the room. "Hold on a minute." She headed towards Lilly's back door. She knew she had to get out of earshot from Ted's nosy relatives.

Once she reached the back deck, she resumed their conversation. "I asked you last week if you'd lost your mind, but now there's no question that you have. Debbie, why in the world would you tell Rob if you haven't been caught?"

"Because we need a fresh start in order to repair our marriage. The only way to fix things is to come completely clean. We need truth."

Victoria closed her eyes, biting her bottom lip. "If you truly want to repair your marriage you better not say a word about Stan."

"But Victoria, I think the only way Rob and I can fix what's wrong is if we start with a clean slate. I had a long talk with him last night and I told him that I want us to start being completely honest with each other about how we feel and how we communicate our needs. If I'm going to hold up my end of the bargain there's no way I can get around not telling him what I've done."

Victoria was pacing back and forth on Lilly's patio deck. "In theory you're right, honesty is a great policy. But in reality you'll be making a big mistake if you tell your husband that you've been sleeping with another man. Most men can't recover from that kind of honesty."

"Well, I don't plan on telling him all the gory details, or even how long I've been seeing Stan."

Victoria couldn't believe she was having this conversation. "Then what's the point? What are you going to tell him?"

"Just that I made a mistake with someone at a weak moment, but now it's over, and that I want us to work on our marriage before it's too late to salvage. Funny thing is, when we talked last night, Rob told me that he knew that our relationship has been on the edge for a while, yet he's never said a word to me about how he's been feeling. If I hadn't pushed the subject I doubt he would've ever brought it up on his own. He thinks I'm just a little unhappy. He has no idea that I've been having an affair," she paused for emphasis. "So you see, I need to make him understand how serious this is. He needs to know exactly how I feel, and he can only know if I'm completely honest."

"Oh, Lord!" Victoria was starting to perspire, a combination of the ninety degree New England summer heat and what she thought was the pure lunacy of her conversation. "I know you want to purge your system, but if Rob doesn't suspect anything, why would you tell him? It'll only hurt him, Debbie. Just end things with Stan and keep your mouth shut, that way no one will get hurt."

Debbie let out a deep breath. "But that's dishonest."

"You snuck off to hotels in the middle of the day so you could fuck another man while your husband was at work, and now you're concerned about honesty?"

Victoria hadn't meant to be so blunt, but she didn't know what else to say. Her friend's naïveté about the decision she was about to make made Victoria all the more concerned.

"Don't lecture me, damnit," Debbie piped up. "I told you this because you're my closest friend and I thought you'd be glad that I'm going to do the right thing. Isn't this what you told me I should do?"

"Calm down," Victoria said, continuing to pace back and forth on the deck. "That's the problem, I don't think you're doing the right thing. I'm glad you ended things with Stan, but I didn't tell you to confess your sins to Rob."

"I want to make things right between us. Besides, what if by some chance Rob finds out on his own? He'd be devastated."

"What if he doesn't? What if he never finds out and never suspects a thing?"

Debbie was quiet for a moment. "I know myself, and I know my husband, and the only way we can fix this is if we have everything out in the open, no secrets, no lies."

"Okay, you know your relationship better than I do. But let me ask you a question?"

"Okay?"

"Do you want to confess to Rob because you want to make a clean start, or because you want to ease your own conscious?"

Debbie was silent again.

"Think long and hard about this. How is it possibly going to help Rob, or your marriage?" Victoria couldn't see Debbie, but she knew that her friend was biting her tiny nails on the other end of the phone. "I love you and I'm gonna be straight with you, just like you were with me back in the day when you called me out because I wouldn't admit I had feelings for Ted, just because he was white," Victoria said in earnest. "This isn't a movie or some kind of social experiment, this is real life and you're about to fuck up royally. Are you honestly ready to lose your family over an affair that Rob doesn't even suspect? Do you really think you can repair your marriage and make a fresh start by telling your husband that you slept with another man? Girl, that doesn't even sound right."

Debbie remained silent, taking in Victoria's words. And Victoria was silent, hoping that she'd broken through.

Debbie shook her head and lowered her voice. "Oh, Victoria...what am I thinking?"

The hell if I know, Victoria wanted to say but held her tongue.

"This is so hard for me, and I feel so guilty. I just want to get it off my chest," Debbie said, letting out a deep breath.

"Go to confession, do some volunteer work, or donate to a charity. Do whatever it takes to make you feel better, but don't tell Rob that you had an affair."

"Victoria, I'm so glad I talked to you about this. I don't know what I'd do without you. You're the only real friend I trust."

"I'm always gonna be here for you, no matter the situation."

Debbie nodded. "Well, thanks for sticking by me through all my craziness."

"I know you'd do the same for me. I just want you to be happy."

They settled into a moment of silence, each reflecting on their own personal dramas. "So, what about your situation?" Debbie asked.

"What situation?"

"Your situation with Parker?"

Victoria stopped pacing the deck and looked around as though everyone inside could suddenly hear her conversation. She swallowed hard, her throat instantly feeling parched and dry at the mention of Parker's name. "I don't have a *situation* with him."

Debbie gave a little smirk on the other end. "I was shocked when I saw him at the wedding. He tried to make casual conversation with me during the reception, and he purposely told me that he hadn't seen you in a long time, but now after all these years it was ironic that he'd run into you three times in one week. I know the only reason he said it was because he knew I'd come back and tell you."

"He told you that?"

"Yeah, now my question is why didn't you? You never mentioned a word about him when we had dinner."

Victoria ran her fingers through her hair which was beginning to frizz under the summer heat, giving her a slightly wild and sexy look. "Number one, you'd just dropped the news on me about you and Stan, so that was the major focus of our conversation. And number two, *Parker*," she whispered in a low voice, "obviously isn't important enough to bring up."

"I know I can be pretty green about some things, like confessing to Rob about what I've done. But Victoria, please don't tell me that seeing Parker again didn't warrant some kind of discussion?"

"It was no big deal. He's a part of my past."

"I saw the way he looked at you and believe me, it's a big deal."

"What are you talking about?"

Debbie's voice heightened. "I watched him, Victoria. His eyes lit up when he saw you. It's obvious that he's still in love with you."

Victoria couldn't say anything. She remembered Parker's stare, and it had made her feel warm, tingly, and dangerously afraid. She'd looked at him too, trying to convince herself that the thoughts she was having about him didn't amount to anything, that she was simply reaching back for a memory. But deep in her heart she'd known that wasn't true.

"Didn't you notice him looking at you?" Debbie asked.

"Yes."

"And you weren't the least bit affected by him?"

Victoria sat down on one of the patio chairs to collect her thoughts. "Okay, I'd be lying if I said that I didn't think he looked good, because he did."

"*FINE*, to be exact," Debbie grinned through the phone.

"Okay, yes, he looked fine as hell. But I know fire when I see it, and I don't have to smell smoke to know that any involvement with Parker could burn my ass."

"So you were tempted?"

"Why are we talking about this?"

"Because I don't want you to make the same mistake I made."

Victoria huffed. "You've got to be kidding."

There was a pregnant pause, then Debbie spoke in a serious tone. "I know that you and Ted have a wonderful marriage, and that you two love each other very much. But I saw the way Parker looked at you, and honestly, I saw the way you looked at him too. You have a history together, so I'm giving you advice just like you gave me. Be careful."

Victoria knew that she was as transparent as glass, so she decided she may as well come out with something close to the truth. "Alright, I admit it. I've been thinking about Parker ever since I saw him last week. I don't know why, I guess it's just lingering feelings from when we were together. But trust me, I'm not going to do anything to jeopardize my marriage."

"Victoria, I can't help worrying because I know what I saw between the two of you, and I know first hand how easy it is to land yourself in a compromising situation and end up doing things you never thought you'd do."

Damn, Debbie's right! Victoria knew there was a very real possibility that she could end up in a world of trouble behind Parker Brightwood.

That's why she was determined to stay as far away from him as she could.

They talked for a few minutes longer, with Debbie continuing to warn Victoria about what could happen if she wasn't careful, and Victoria trying to take in the fact that it was Debbie who had the level head in their conversation this time around.

As the two friends ended their call, both shared the same problematic thought—that the other was still in for a rocky ride ahead.

Instead of going back inside, Victoria sat on the deck, trying to push her conversation with Debbie out of her mind. With all she had going on at the moment, she didn't want to take on another emotional task. But try as she might, she kept hearing her friend's words in her ear, *be careful.*

She looked out at Lilly's beautifully landscaped backyard with its perfectly manicured shrubs, beautifully lined flower beds, and neatly cut grass. Her eyes focused on a creepy looking spider that had crawled atop a delicate yellow flower. A cold sensation ran down Victoria's spine—she knew that danger often lurked in beautiful places.

Her troubled thoughts were replaced by a smile when she looked up and saw Alexandria burst through the back door, bubbling with excitement. "Mommy, look what Aunt Lilly got me," she said, running up to Victoria with a brand new baby doll.

Victoria returned her daughter's smile, happy to see that Alexandria was having a good time. It gave her temporary peace of mind to know that in the midst of all the sadness and confusion around her, that her daughter was protected by her youthful innocence.

Just then, Ted came outside to join them. "There you two are," he said, walking up to the side of Victoria's chair.

"Daddy, look at what Aunt Lilly got me." Alexandria was all too happy to show her father her newest and now most prized, cocoa-colored doll.

"That's nice, Princess," Ted nodded, giving her a slightly uncomfortable smile. "I think we should head back to the hotel," he said, looking to Victoria.

She could see a significant change in his mood. "Is everything okay?" Victoria asked.

"Everything's fine. I just think we should go so we can rest and change before the wake."

Victoria sensed that something more was at play, judging from the urgency of Ted's tone and body language. But she knew he had a lot on his mind, so she resisted the urge to probe, which was something she was prone to do. She had to remind herself of the conversation she and her mother had the day before, *just be there for him.*

Ted held Victoria's hand as she and Alexandria followed him back inside. When they walked through the living room she noticed a decidedly strange tension in the air, different from the subtle disapproval his relatives had caste upon her earlier. *I wonder if their nosy asses overheard my conversation?* Victoria thought to herself, paranoid about her phone call with Debbie. As they moved through the room the same disapproving eyes that had met hers with hard stares when she'd first arrived, now shifted down to their feet, as if searching for change they'd dropped on the floor.

On their way out the door she noticed that Ted only said goodbye to a few of his relatives, while there were others who he walked by without parting his lips, as if they weren't even in the room. She made a mental note of those he'd avoided, and she suddenly understood the meaning of his actions and the reason for the tension.

―⸕∾⸕―

I Do A Lot Of Things, Be Specific?...

After they returned to the hotel, Victoria helped Alexandria settle in with her baby doll, and the thing that held her attention the most, the Dora the Explorer cartoon playing on TV. Victoria was glad that her daughter seemed to be handling the wave of activity swirling around her.

Once she made sure that Alexandria was sufficiently occupied, Victoria returned to their bedroom where she found Ted fresh from the shower, about to change into a stylish, black suit. He was getting dressed, preparing for his mother's wake that was to take place in a few hours. He, Lilly and Charlie had agreed to meet early at the funeral home so they could discuss the final details of their mother's burial. He paused when Victoria entered the room, "You look tired," he said, taking a long look at her.

"And you look very handsome," she smiled, walking over to take a seat on the edge of the bed. She watched Ted as he fashioned a

Windsor knot in his tie, and wondered what was really going on in his mind.

Ted blushed at her compliment, something only Victoria could make him do. "Thanks," he smiled.

She leaned back on her elbows, relaxing her body. "So…what did your relatives say about you being married to a black woman? I saw the looks a few of them shot my way, and they were the same individuals you intentionally ignored when we were leaving. What did they say to you?" Victoria asked.

Ted knew this conversation was coming and he was ready to discuss it. Unlike other times when he chose not to engage the ignorance of narrow-minded people, he was pissed by the reaction he'd received from several of his relatives, especially the ones who he'd once been close to. He hadn't seen many of them in years, and now given their hostile attitudes he didn't care if he ever laid eyes on them again.

He knew they'd speculated and gossiped behind his back about his marriage to Victoria, and that it had been the reason they'd refused to attend his wedding. His mother had told him as much when they were compiling names for the guest list.

When Ted first entered his sister's house and scoped out the slew of relatives gathered inside, he'd been tempted to walk up to each of them who'd been critical of his marriage and tell them to go straight to hell. But he knew that a family gathering during a time of mourning wasn't the proper time or place for that type of confrontation. Still, he was pissed and everyone who knew him knew it! His cool, smooth comportment was legendary, but so was his no-nonsense and sometimes ruthless side, a trait he'd inherited from his father.

So for the sake of appearance and civility, all the Thorntons in the room tried to get along. But when Ted's cousin Ronald, a notoriously well-known jerk, pulled him to the side, that's when the dominos fell. Ronald and Ted's fathers had been brothers. Ronald was only a year older than Ted, and had always been in competition with his father's favorite nephew, who the rest of the family also adored.

"Why'd you do it?" Ronald asked, looking at Ted as if he'd committed treason.

Ted stood nearly five inches over Ronald's head, looking over his bald spot and down into his bright blue eyes. "I do a lot of things, be specific?" Ted responded. He'd seen Victoria step outside to the back deck after she answered her phone, and he was glad that Alexandria had left with his sister only minutes before. He knew things could get ugly and he didn't want either of them to witness the scene.

Ronald could feel the anger building in Ted's veins, but he didn't back down. "After you got rid of that gold digger you were married to, you could've had your pick, but you chose…"

"Exactly who I wanted," Ted threw back, cutting him off. He uncrossed his arms, letting them hang at his side, and it made Ronald stand at attention. "Ron, you better stop while you're ahead because if you say one more word about my wife, I promise you'll end up lying beside my mother before the end of the day."

Ted delivered his words with an authority and loud base in his voice that made the hair stand up on the back of Ronald's neck. For a moment, everyone and everything stood still with tension. The room full of nosy cousins and family friends pretended to look the other way, busying themselves with imaginary tasks, all the while waiting to see what was going to happen next.

By this time, Ted's good friend, Barry, who'd flown in from L.A., stepped in to diffuse the growing escalation. Barry and Ted had been friends from their prep school days at an elite all boys' school, through their graduation from business school at Harvard. Barry knew Ted well, and he could see that the situation was headed downhill fast. "C'mon guys, let's calm it down," he urged.

Both Ronald and Ted ignored Barry's plea.

"Hey, buddy…hold on," Ronald foolishly continued. "She's a real looker, beautiful in fact. But Ted…."

Ted's French vanilla skin turned cherry red. "Say one more word about my wife, just one more," he threatened. "You must *want* me to kick your ass."

"Hey, hey," Barry intervened again. He gave Ted a friendly pat on the back, trying to calm him down. He knew that if his friend was mad enough to physically threaten someone, especially in a room full of witnesses, that he wasn't bluffing. Barry could see that cousin Ronald was getting ready to receive an ass-kicking that he and the rest of the Thornton family would never forget. "Ronald, this is wrong. Just shut your damn mouth," Barry advised.

Ronald was getting ready to open his mouth again but two things stopped him. The first was Ted's stance; a position similar to that of a man preparing to land a blow. And the second was Ted's precious little daughter who'd just walked through the front door hand-in-hand with her aunt.

Now, standing in the present and thinking back on the situation, Ted's blood boiled all over again. He looked at his beautiful wife reclined on the bed, staring back at him with loving eyes. He knew that half of Ronald's comments had been rooted in prejudice, but the other half were steeped in envy. He saw the hidden fantasy behind his cousin's eyes when Victoria had walked past him on her way out to Lilly's patio. It was a look he'd seen many times on the faces of many men, including his dear friend Barry. But he forgave it because he understood it.

Ted wondered if Barry knew his truth, would it create a shift in their friendship. He knew it would change many of his relationships, especially within his family, and perhaps even with his own wife. It had already changed something inside of him.

Ted took a deep breath and answered Victoria's question. "Ninety percent of my family loves you, V," he said, speaking the truth. "What you experienced today was the ten percent who no one gives a damn about, least of all not me."

"I guess it's no different from some of my cousins who talked about me marrying *that white boy*," Victoria said, shrugging her shoulders.

Ted chuckled. "Correction, as Tyler says, *that cool ass white boy*."

They both laughed, the first they'd shared together in almost a week. At that moment, Ted wanted nothing more than to crawl onto the bed and lay beside Victoria. He didn't want to think about burials, disputes over wills, or secret revelations. But he knew he had obligations that required his attention, so he prepared to face them.

After he finished dressing, Victoria walked him to the door. He reached for her hand and squeezed it. "I'll see you and Alexandria in a few hours."

"All right, be safe." Victoria watched as Ted walked down the hallway before disappearing around the corner. She had wanted to bring up the topic of his mother's safe deposit box again, but since they'd ended their conversation with laughter, she decided to table that discussion for later.

Ted walked to the elevator and stepped inside. He rode down to the lobby with what seemed like a gigantic boulder pressing on each of his shoulders. As he entered the lobby and waited for the valet to bring his rental car around, he prayed the evening ahead would go quiet and smooth. But like the shock he received yesterday, he had a feeling it was going to be turbulent.

Grown Folks Business...

Victoria and Alexandria were in the back seat of a Yellow Cab, on their way to Carolyn's wake. They were running behind schedule, but Victoria didn't mind arriving a little late because she wasn't exactly thrilled about having to bring Alexandria in the first place. Death and funerals were hard enough on adults, so she could only imagine the impact it might have on a five-year old. But she didn't have babysitting options, so she was left with no other choice than to bring Alexandria along.

As they sped through traffic she decided to give Tyler a call. She was preparing to leave a message when he picked up on the fourth ring. She was glad to hear her best friend's voice.

"I'm sure it's really tough on him, he'll be in a bad place for a while," Tyler said as he talked to Victoria about Ted's state of mind. "Give him time, he'll be okay,"

"I know, I just feel like there's something else that's wrong, like it's more than grief," Victoria said. She was glad that Alexandria was too engrossed with looking out the window at the new and unfamiliar landscape to pay attention to her conversation. It was another reason why she was thankful to have a curious child.

"This is new for you because it's the first time you've seen Ted deal with something this devastating," Tyler sighed. "Believe me, loosing someone you love can take its toll and everyone handles it differently."

Victoria could hear the hurt in his voice and it made her feel the weight of his pain. "You're right. But I know my husband very well, and this may sound strange, but something tells me that his detachment has just as much to do with the secret his mother was hiding as it does with her actual death." Victoria hadn't told Tyler about the safe deposit box because she felt there were some things that should remain private between a husband and wife.

"Did she tell him what it was?" Tyler asked.

"No, she died leaving him hanging."

"Damn, that's some shit. How you gonna get into heaven fuckin' with people's minds?"

"Tyler!" Victoria hissed, even though she felt the same way. "You can't speak ill of the dead like that."

"Why not?"

"Because, it's just not right."

"Says who?"

Just then Alexandria's ears perked up. "Mommy, is that Uncle Tyler? What's he doing that's not right? Can I talk to him?" she asked, ever the inquisitive child.

Victoria took a deep breath. "Yes, Sweetie, I'm talking to your Uncle Tyler, and right now we're discussing grown folks business, so you know what that means." That was Alexandria's signal to butt out and turn her attention back to sightseeing. She diligently obeyed, and was now glued back to the window.

"Tell my beautiful niece I said hello," Tyler smiled on the other end.

"I'll do that."

"How're you holding up?"

Victoria rubbed her temple for what felt like the millionth time. "Could be better, but could be worse, so I guess I'm okay."

"Listen, there's something I need to tell you," Tyler paused.

"Oh, Lord. By the sound of your tone I can tell it's not good."

"It's all good. Just a little, um, awkward."

"Well, spit it out. What is it?"

"You remember Samantha, right?"

Victoria's head began to throb even harder. The mention of Samantha's name brought Parker's face to mind. "Of course I do. Stop beating around the bush Mr. Straight Shooter. Tell me what's up?"

Tyler cleared his throat. "You know we hooked up and had diner and everything after the reception, right?"

"Yeah."

"Well, I'm diggin' her."

"*What!*"

"I said I'm diggin' Sam. Don't trip."

"Wow, you just met her."

"Yeah, well…that's usually how things start out. You meet some-one and then you spend time together, and then you get to know each other and…."

"Hold up, are you talking about starting a relationship with her?"

Tyler hesitated. "I didn't say all that. I just thought I'd let you know. She decided to extend her trip a few extra days, so we're gonna hang out this evening."

Victoria was silent.

"I know you don't approve, but Sam's cool people. You wouldn't even know she was related to that mothafucker you used to date."

Although Victoria knew that she shouldn't, she felt slightly defensive of Parker. But she held the emotion inside. "Let me set the record straight. I like Samantha...I have from the first time I met her. I just know that she's a little on the wild side."

"Who you tryin' to school? I already peeped that," Tyler chuckled. "But sometimes it's fun to walk on the wild side. And speaking of wild, what's up with your girl? Why the hell did Debbie bring dude to the wedding?" Tyler scoffed. "I pulled her to the side and told her she was messin' up."

Victoria shook her head and wondered if Rob would eventually find out too. "I know, she told me that you approached her when she called me earlier this afternoon. But don't worry, she ended it, thank God."

"Damn, just goes to show you that you never know what people are truly capable of. Fidelity is a funny thing."

Victoria kept quiet, mulling over her own hidden thoughts.

"And Ol' boy had the nerve to walk up in the joint looking just like Rob," Tyler continued. "That's crazy for real."

As the cab pulled up to the funeral home, Victoria adjusted her black skirt, looking out at the large, dreary looking building. "I'd love to continue this gossip session but we're here, so I've got to go."

"Give Ted my sympathies."

"I will, and just remember," she cautioned, "a walk on the wild side can be dangerous."

"Oh, really?"

"Yes, really...just because there's an attraction, it doesn't mean you have to act on it."

"You're right my friend. I hope you take your own advice."

Victoria wanted to say something smart but she knew there would be no good comeback. So instead of getting into a back and forth with her best friend, she quickly ended the conversation, paid the cab driver, and prepared herself for a meeting with death.

Chapter 9

Sweetie, What Are You Doing?...

Victoria and Alexandria arrived fifteen minutes before the wake was set to begin. When they walked up Ted was standing in the lobby, talking on his cell phone.

"Hey, Honey. You okay?" Victoria asked as Ted ended his call.

"I'm fine," he smiled, happy to see his wife and child. "Hey, Princess, don't you look pretty," he doted, admiring Alexandria's neatly braided hair and delicate sunflower dress. He loved the way Victoria always took meticulous care of their daughter's appearance, just as she did with her own.

"Thank you, Daddy," Alexandria grinned, walking over to his side. She was a true daddy's girl.

Victoria looked around. "Where's Lilly and Charlie?"

"Lilly's inside and Charlie...who knows?" Ted shrugged. "He never showed up to meet with us."

Victoria could tell by Ted's tone that he was completely fed up.

"Is that where Granny Carolyn is sleeping?" Alexandria asked, pointing toward a set of double doors down the long hallway.

Both Victoria and Ted looked at her, then at each other. "Yes, Princess," Ted answered.

"Can I go see her?"

Victoria sighed, wishing again that she hadn't had to bring Alexandria to the wake. The funeral itself would be bad enough, and she feared it might all be too much. She'd been up against a wall because she couldn't leave Alexandria in the hotel room by herself, and any relative of Ted's who she would've felt comfortable asking to babysit for a few hours would be at the wake themselves. She'd thought about not attending all together, but decided against it because she knew that Ted needed her emotional support.

"Sure, come with me," Ted nodded as he took Alexandria's hand in his. He gave Victoria a reassuring look. "It'll be all right," he mouthed as they walked down the hall leading to the funeral home chapel.

Once they entered the gloom filled room, they found Lilly sitting on the first pew. Her head was bent low in deep mourning. Her hair was fashioned in a neatly pulled chignon, but when she looked up her face appeared ashen and her eyes were red. She tried to form a smile at the site of her brother and his family.

"Hi," Lilly greeted with open arms.

Victoria welcomed her embrace as they hugged. She was about to tell Alexandria to give her Aunt Lilly a hug when she noticed that her daughter was no longer by her side. She looked up and saw Alexandria standing in front of Carolyn's ornately finished casket. Victoria drew in a sharp breath, as did Ted and Lilly. The site of Alexandria's small head barely reaching the top of the gold-trimmed box made them all pause. But their true concern set in when they heard her mumbling to the casket in barely audible tones.

Victoria and Ted walked over to her.

"Sweetie, what are you doing?" Victoria asked in the calmest voice she could muster.

Alexandria looked at her mother with a serious face, bringing her finger up to her lips, "Shhhh, I'm talking with Granny Carolyn. You have to be quiet so she can hear me," she said in a whisper.

Victoria and Ted exchanged horrified glances.

Victoria bent down and looked into Alexandria's eyes. "Sweetie, Granny Carolyn can't hear you. Remember what your father and I told you...she's at eternal rest. You know what that means, right?"

Alexandria nodded. "That she won't wake up anymore."

"That's right," Ted reinforced, trying not to show his growing concern.

"But I can still talk to Granny Carolyn, can't I?" Alexandria countered in a soft whisper.

By this time a small group of mourners had started to enter the chapel. "I hate to pull you away, but we need to greet the visitors," Lilly told Ted. She saw the concern in her brother's eyes as he stared at his daughter. "Is everything okay with Alexandria?"

"She's fine," Victoria said. "Come on Sweetie, let's go back outside." Victoria led Alexandria by the hand, breezing past the visitors as they headed back out to the main entrance.

Once they were outside the chapel, Victoria sat with Alexandria in the office area that the funeral home director was kind enough to let them use. She second guessed herself again for bringing Alexandria, wishing she had stayed at the hotel and forgone the service. As she watched her daughter thoughts of Carolyn's secret began to creep back into Victoria's mind. And again, she wondered what horrible thing Carolyn had done and if it would have any impact on her child.

Less than forty-five minutes later the service ended, making it the quickest wake that Victoria had ever attended. But it had been one of the most intense minutes of her life. She was worried about her child, worried about her husband, worried about her friends, and worried about herself.

As they left the funeral home and headed back to the hotel, Ted made small talk about the arrangements for the next day. Victoria could see that he was talking just to fill empty space, which was very unlike him. She knew he was grieving, but now more than ever she was convinced that his shifting mood had everything to do with whatever he'd found in his mother's safe deposit box, and when they got back to the hotel she planned to find out the details.

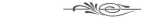

A Sanitized Version Of The Truth...

After a quick room service meal of grilled cheese and vegetables, Alexandria was out like a rock. Victoria was surprised but relieved that she'd gone to bed so easily, especially without her routine bedtime story from Ted.

Once she finished tucking Alexandria in, she went to join Ted in their bedroom on the other side of their suite. She didn't know where to begin, but she knew she had to confront him. She decided that she'd start by discussing the most important thing first, whether they should bring Alexandria to the funeral the next day, then she'd get to the bottom of the safe deposit box and the secret it held.

Ted had already changed into his pajama bottoms and t-shirt, and was sitting up in bed with his reading glasses perched on the bridge of his nose as he reviewed a small stack of business documents. He turned his attention to Victoria when she entered the room. "Is Alexandria okay?" he asked.

"She seems to be," Victoria nodded, unzipping her black skirt. She removed her top and finished undressing. "She was asleep before I finished tucking her in."

"She must be exhausted."

"Yeah, she was. I'm still a little worried about what she said at the funeral home tonight. I think for a minute she actually thought your mother was listening and talking to her," Victoria said. She slipped her silk teddy over her head and joined Ted under the soft cotton sheets.

"I know," Ted sighed. "Maybe it's just her way of dealing with death. Kids always have imaginary friends and conversations in their heads. She does it all the time when we're home."

"Yeah, but this is a little different. I'm not sure if we should let her attend the funeral tomorrow. It might be too much for her."

Ted pulled Victoria close to him. "I understand, V. We'll do whatever you think is best."

They held each other for a few minutes before Victoria slowly pulled away. "Ted, please tell me what you found in your mother's safe deposit box?"

Ted's face dropped as if he'd been punched in the stomach. Victoria saw his eyes shift. She put her hand on top of his, knowing that whatever the revelation, it was something very difficult for him to come to grips with. She looked deep into his eyes. "Honey, whatever it is, I'm here for you. You can tell me anything."

Ted knew it wasn't fair, or right for that matter, to keep the secret he'd discovered from Victoria. And besides, he knew that trying to keep anything from her was a task in itself because she was like a blood hound when she wanted answers. She could be relentless, probing until she found out what she wanted to know.

But he wasn't ready for her questions or to tell her what he'd discovered, so he gave her a sanitized version of the truth and hoped it would quail her curiosity. He removed his reading glasses, put his papers on the nightstand, and began a story filled with half-truths that would eventually lead to his undoing.

"My mother wasn't orphaned at birth, or born in Louisiana as she'd led us all to believe," Ted began. "She was born in Mississippi, to a teenage mother who had an affair with a much older, married man. Her mother died when she was five years old and that's when she was put into foster care. Eventually, she ran away from her last foster family before coming to Boston. Once she got here she changed her name and lived a new life."

Victoria looked at Ted with questioning eyes. "That's it? That's the big secret she was hiding."

He nodded, again hoping she'd accept what he told her and leave it alone.

Victoria tilted her head to the side and gave Ted a quizzical look, not sure what to make of what he'd just told her. "I don't get it? What you're telling me is that your under-age grandmother had an affair with an older, married man and had your mother out of wedlock?"

"That's pretty much it."

"Your mother made a deathbed confession like she was admitting to kidnapping the Lindberg baby. I can't believe she went through the trouble of putting that information in a safe deposit box?"

Victoria couldn't believe her ears. She'd been worried for days, thinking that Carolyn may have killed someone, or had a secret identity, or worse yet, had done something that would have direct consequences for Alexandria. And now to find out that she was simply hiding the fact that she was the illegitimate daughter of an underage mother was a far cry from what Victoria had imagined. The more she thought about it, the more it didn't make sense.

Ted could see the wheels turning behind Victoria's big brown eyes and he hoped that she'd cut him some slack and not ask too many questions. After all, it was late and they had a busy day ahead of them. Just when he thought she was going to let it rest, Victoria started again.

"I don't understand why she went through the trouble of keeping that information hidden for all these years…and in a safe deposit box? Why in the world would she go through all that trouble? It doesn't make any sense."

Ted realized how flimsy his explanation sounded, but he couldn't reveal the truth, a truth that he wasn't ready to deal with himself. "V, you have to understand. My mother held a certain position in her social circle, and this kind of thing was a huge taboo, especially back then. In a society where pedigree is your ticket, that would've been a hard pill for some people to swallow. That's why she was always so secretive about her past."

Victoria shook her head again. She knew that Ted's family was one of a certain social standing, and that outward appearance and reputation was of great importance to them. But the more she thought about what he'd told her, the more his explanation still rang hollow. "This is why you were so shaken up yesterday? You drug in here like you'd just lost your best friend," she paused, giving him a doubting look. "You're telling me that you were devastated because you found out that your mother came from less than pristine beginnings?"

Victoria knew there was more to the story than what Ted was telling her. Although he was well-heeled, sophisticated, and had a taste for the finer things in life, he was far from a snob and his mother's humble start in life wasn't something that would have ruffled his feathers. She knew that when he was a younger man he'd subscribed to his family's need for keeping up appearances during his first marriage. But since she'd known him, she could honestly say that he'd never been one to put much emphasis on pedigree, social standing, or even what someone did for a living.

Ted was privileged, without a doubt, but he was also the same man who she'd seen volunteer with inner city youth at Tyler's organization. He was the same man who ate fried chicken and collard greens at her family reunion and learned to play spades with her crazy cousin Willie. And he was the same man who put more importance on where people ended up than where they started out.

Knowing Ted the way she did, Victoria was sure there was something he wasn't telling her, and for the first time since she'd known him she could see a lie in his eyes. She nestled closer to him, searching for real answers. "Honey, you know that if there's more to the story, you can tell me, right?"

Ted tried to reassure her. "What more could there be?"

"You tell me."

"V, I've been a little shaken up by everything that's happened in the last few days. I didn't tell you this, but when we went to Abe's office for the reading of my mother's will yesterday, we all got a big surprise. She left everything to Lilly and me to divide equally…Charlie got nothing."

Victoria sat up straight. "You're kidding!"

"I'm serious. She named the two of us as her beneficiaries on her life insurance policy and left us the remainder of all her personal assets, and that includes all of my father's money, investments and real estate holdings that transferred to her when he passed away. It's tens of millions of dollars and she didn't leave Charlie a dime, didn't even mention his name anywhere in the will," Ted sighed. "I had to deal with him that entire afternoon, raising hell about how he'd been cheated and how he wasn't going to let it rest."

Ted's guilt was heavy but he felt a little better because at least that part of his story was true, although he'd left out a small yet significant detail—that there was one other person mentioned in the will; a person whose identity was a mystery even to him, but who he was sure was linked to his parents secret past. "Mother's will is iron-clad, but Charlie's talking to another attorney to see what can be done to divide her estate among the three of us."

"No reputable attorney is gonna touch that," Victoria said, shaking her head.

Ted raised his brow. "Since when has Charlie been involved in anything reputable?"

"Good point."

"I know he's going to try to get Lilly to sign over some of her inheritance to him, especially since her husband is basically a pushover for anything. But he won't get a dime from her if I can help it."

"So that's why he wasn't at the wake this evening," Victoria realized. "He's mad because he was left out of the will."

"Yeah, the selfish bastard. And that's exactly why Mother didn't leave him anything. She knew how he was, and she let him know it in the end."

"Wow."

Ted pulled Victoria into his arms again. "So, you see what I've been dealing with? Coming here to bury my mother, trying to calm Lilly in her fragile state, and trying to deal with Charlie…it all finally got the best of me," he sighed. "Not to mention everything that's going on at

ViaTech. Work didn't stop when my mother died."

Victoria felt bad for pushing him. "I'm so sorry, Honey. I wish there was something I could do." She gently kissed his lips, looking into his eyes. But when she peered close, despite his sympathetic plea, she still felt there was something missing.

Ted could see the doubt on her face so he tried to tie up the loose ends of his story. "As for my mother's secret, it's terrible that she felt the need to carry something so trivial to her grave. It's sad when you can't tell the people you love the truth." He felt his words slap him in the face, but he continued with his lie and forced himself to say, "V, I love you, and I'm sharing everything with you."

Victoria looked into Ted's eyes again, wanting to believe him, but unable to shake the feeling that there was something far more serious he was hiding. But with all she had on her own mind, she couldn't allow herself to obsess about it, so she decided to let Ted's explanation pass for now. She knew whatever the real story, she'd eventually get to the bottom of it because the truth always had a way of revealing itself.

When Jesus Comes...

"Get up sleepy head," Victoria smiled as she gave Alexandria's sheets a gentle tug. Normally, it was Alexandria who was the first one up at the crack of dawn. But this morning she was still lying in bed.

Alexandria rubbed her sleepy brown eyes and smiled back. "Morning, Mommy,"

"How're you feeling this morning?"

"Good. Can I have pancakes for breakfast with a smiley face on them like yesterday?" she asked.

Victoria smoothed the wild strands of hair from around her daughter's face. "Sure, Sweetie, but first I want to talk to you about last night," she said, trying to couch her words. "Remember when you said you were talking with your Granny Carolyn?"

"Uh-huh," Alexandria nodded.

"Did you have a pretend conversation with her like you do when you're playing with your dolls?"

"Kind of."

Victoria knotted her brow. "Sweetie, what do you mean, *kind of?*"

"Aunt Lilly told me that Granny Carolyn was sleeping until she can be with Jesus," Alexandria smiled, nodding her head.

"Okay?"

"So I talked to her to keep her company, so she won't be lonely 'til Jesus gets there," Alexandria answered as she sat up in bed.

Victoria marveled at the pure innocence and goodness that she saw in her child. She didn't have the heart to tell her daughter what was truly on her mind, that in her opinion Jesus wasn't going to be anywhere near Carolyn's final resting place.

"I want to see Granny Carolyn again so she won't be lonely."

"That's so thoughtful, Sweetie."

Alexandria grinned. "I want to talk to her when she wakes up again."

Victoria cleared her throat. "She's not going to wake up again. She's asleep forever, remember?"

"But Aunt Lilly said that Granny Carolyn's gonna wake up when Jesus comes to get her. So I can talk with her again when she wakes up a little later." Alexandria looked at her mother as if to say, *don't you get it?*

Victoria feared this would happen. She knew that Lilly hadn't meant any harm, but now Alexandria was completely confused. She was the kind of child who took things to heart, and she knew that if the wake had confused her, the funeral would throw her for a complete loop.

"After we get cleaned up and eat breakfast, I'm going to take you to the park again and then to the movies. Won't that be fun?"

Alexandria shook her head. "No, Mommy. We have to go see Granny Carolyn today."

"Listen, Sweetie. Your Granny Carolyn isn't going to wake up again. She's at eternal rest, that means she's going to sleep forever, and Jesus won't be coming to get her for a very, very long time...*if at all*." She let the last part pass through her mind but not her lips.

"But I want to see Granny Carolyn," Alexandria pouted, poking out her bottom lip.

Victoria looked into her daughter's bright eyes. "Alexandria, we're not going to the funeral today, okay?"

"Mommy, I have to go," Alexandria squealed. "I want to see Granny Carolyn when she wakes up."

"Sweetie, we're not going."

Suddenly, Alexandria burst into tears, leaping into Victoria's arms. "No, Mommy, no!" she cried. "I want to go, I want to go!"

By this time Ted had entered the room. "What's the matter, Princess?" he asked with worry as he approached the bed, looking at Victoria for answers. They both stared at each other with the same shocked expression they'd shared at the wake when Alexandria had walked up to Carolyn's casket. She wasn't a child prone to throwing fits or becoming emotional, so her behavior left them baffled, not sure of what to do.

"I want to go," Alexandria repeated through loud sobs.

"Go where?" Ted asked.

Victoria tried to calm Alexandria as she explained the conversation they'd just had. "I don't think she should go to the funeral," she whispered to Ted, rocking Alexandria in her arms. "She's all shaken up."

"Mommy, please let me go see Granny Carolyn," Alexandria pleaded, then she turned to Ted, "Daddy, please, *pretty please* let me go…"

At that moment the empathy Victoria felt for her daughter nearly flew out the window. She rolled her eyes and pursed her lips at Alexandria's sly manipulation. A *pretty please* could get Ted every time. Despite the fact that her daughter looked like her clone, Alexandria had inherited her father's character to a tee. She knew how to keep her wits about her even in the midst of a mini meltdown. Her *pretty please* was her ace in the hole and she often pulled it out to get what she wanted.

Victoria could see that Ted was on edge. In a few hours he'd have to bury his mother and he wasn't in the frame of mind to deal with a five-year old's temper tantrum, even if it was his own daughter. Victoria looked into his eyes and for the first time she saw indecision. He stared back at her as if asking what they should do. Finally he spoke up. "I think we should let her go."

Victoria wanted to disagree, especially since he'd said he would go along with whatever she thought was best last night. She had a bad feeling about what might take place at the funeral, and didn't think their daughter should go. Things had already started off with mysterious secrets and hidden lies, and she was very apprehensive about what might erupt before the days end. But under the heavy weight of Ted's grief and circumstances, she acquiesced and adjusted her position. "Okay, Sweetie, you can go," she said, calming Alexandria's hard sobs.

She and Ted sat there, looking at their daughter, hoping they'd made the right decision.

After Victoria got Alexandria dressed, she led her out to the living room area of their suite, armed with her dolls and two containers of *Play-Doh*. They had exactly two hours before the funeral was to begin. She and Ted quietly discussed Alexandria's behavior as they began getting themselves ready for what would no doubt be a stressful day.

"I hope Alexandria will be able to handle the funeral. She's acting so strangely, she never throws temper tantrums. This is all too much for her," Victoria said.

"I think she'll be okay as long as we keep an eye on her."

"But I've never seen her behave like this. It's almost as though she's a completely different child, and that concerns me," Victoria replied, helping Ted slip his sterling silver cuff links into the French cuffs of his crisp white shirt. "If she starts crying or having a hard time during the service I'm bringing her back here to the hotel."

Ted nodded in agreement. "Absolutely. Hell, you might have to bring me back too."

Victoria couldn't determine if he'd just made a bad joke or if he was really serious. Death had an uncanny way of making even the strongest people weak. Her husband and child were both acting like two people she didn't know, and she wondered what the long-term effects would be.

Why, Why, Why?...

Victoria knew that Carolyn Thornton's funeral would be one for the history books just by virtue of the way the day had begun. Her ordeal with Alexandria early that morning served to prepare her for the puzzling events that would unfold before her mother-in-law was laid to rest.

When they drove past the gate of the Thornton's large estate, the funeral home limousines were already lined up and waiting to transport the family to the church. After settling inside, Ted and Victoria stayed close together, keeping a watchful eye on Alexandria. Lilly, her husband, and their three children were there, along with uncles, aunts and cousins from their father's side of the family. But there was no sign of Charlie or his wife and kids.

"Damn, sonofabitch," one of Ted's uncles said. "Serves him right that Carolyn left him out of the will. Charlie's always been a rotten apple."

Charlie had quickly spread the news about his mother's last wishes, hoping to gain sympathy from other family members. "I deserve what's rightfully mine," he'd told several cousins. He thought that if he was able to get the support of his relatives it might help his case when he went before a judge to challenge the will. But his plan backfired. No one was willing to step forward to his side, and now he was more angry than ever.

As they piled into the limousines, Victoria prayed that the funeral service would end as quickly as the wake had the night before. The sooner they could leave the better. She planned to watch Alexandria closely during the service, and keep an eye on Ted as well.

When they arrived at the church, Charlie was already there—alone. He was standing off to the side of the sanctuary. Ted looked around for his brother's current wife, number three, and for any signs of his children, which included five in total. But none of them were there. Charlie was so angry that he'd instructed his wife and children to stay away from the service. None of them had ever been particularly close to Carolyn, so their presence wouldn't really be missed.

Ted had a feeling that Charlie was going to pull a ridiculous stunt. Before they'd left his mother's house, the funeral director approached him and Lilly, informing them that although Charlie planned to attend the service, he'd requested seating on a separate pew up front, and only after the rest of the family had taken their designated places.

"This is absurd," Lilly had said in a weary voice. "Why must he cause such headache and strife on today of all days?"

"Don't worry about him," Ted responded, in an even tone. "We'll get through this."

As the ceremony started, the organist played a beautiful selection composed of some of Carolyn's favorite songs. After the immediate family had been seated, Charlie slowly strode to the front of the large church and took his lone seat on a pew behind the last of his cousins. No sooner had the minister stood behind the pulpit to begin the service did Charlie break into tears. *"Why, why, why?"* he cried out.

Everyone in the subdued sanctuary looked Charlie's way. Those who really knew him wondered if he was questioning his mother's death or her decision to leave him out of her will. Either way, frustration was plastered on their faces, and on Ted's more than anyone else's.

Victoria held Ted's hand and could feel him squeezing hers so tightly she had to nudge him. "Stay calm," she whispered into his ear.

Ted was seething. He turned around and glared in the direction three pews behind him, giving Charlie a look that could have stopped a rattle snake in its tracks. He was pissed but not surprised by his brother's antics, so he tried his best to maintain his composure. The day before when they'd all gathered in Abe's office, Charlie had flown into a rage, yelling about how he'd always been misunderstood and mistreated by the rest of the family. Ted had warned him that he'd better calm down and if he didn't, there'd be trouble. He told his brother to respect their mother's last wishes. "For once in your life, act like a responsible adult," he'd said. Looking at his brother now, Ted could see that his words had fallen on deaf ears.

While Ted tried to ignore Charlie, Victoria kept a close watch on Alexandria. She was sitting beside her like a stoic little woman. Her serious demeanor was unsettling, and it made Victoria wish she'd followed her maternal instincts and stayed at the hotel, no matter how much Alexandria had pleaded. "Are you all right, Sweetie?" Victoria whispered.

Alexandria looked at her mother, smiled, and gave her a simple nod. It temporarily tamed Victoria's concerns, but she still kept an eye on her daughter just the same.

Victoria felt fatigued. Between her lack of sleep and dealing with her daughter and husband's emotional states, which seemed to be more fragile than she'd originally thought, all she wanted to do was take a week's sabbatical from life. And then there were her own troubling burdens still floating in her head. She tried to push her internal struggle to the back of her mind in order to be present her family, and she thought she was doing a pretty good job considering she'd only thought about Parker once all day.

After an hour of songs, words of praise for the life Carolyn had led, heartfelt condolences for the family she'd left behind, and occasional and inappropriate outbursts of grief from Charlie, the ceremony was over. All that was left to do was walk by Carolyn's open casket to view the body one last time before heading to the gravesite.

Victoria was extremely skeptical about this part of the service. Ted walked in front while she held Alexandria's hand as they approached the flower laden alter.

When they came to within a few feet of Carolyn, Victoria slowed her pace. She wanted to give Ted a moment with his mother because it would be the last time he laid eyes on her in this lifetime. She looked at the grief that seemed to grip his body and the sadness in his eyes as he gazed down upon the woman who'd raised him. Victoria held back her own tears, knowing how hard it must be for her husband. Then, thinking about her child, she picked up Alexandria and held her close, shielding her daughter's line of vision away from the casket as they walked by.

"I want to see Granny Carolyn, Mommy," Alexandria said in a bright, clear voice.

Victoria didn't know what to do as Alexandria wiggled her body and turned to face her grandmother's casket. Ted was still frozen in place in front of his mother's body, his head bent, his hand outstretched by his side, waiting for Victoria to walk up and take it. He was waiting for her to give him strength.

Victoria said a quick prayer, hoping the next few moments would pass without incident. She reached for Ted with her left hand, still holding Alexandria tightly in her right arm.

There they were. All three of them standing in front of Carolyn Thornton's lifeless body. Although Victoria wanted to move on and begin their recessional to leave the sanctuary, she didn't make a move because she couldn't believe her eyes. She'd been to many funerals, but she'd never seen anyone as beautifully preserved as Carolyn. The woman didn't look dead at all!

Carolyn's silk designer dress was a beautiful shade of pale blue, and her ears, neck and hands were adorned with stylish, understated jewelry. Her salt-n-pepper hair was perfectly coiffed, and her dainty lips bore her signature red lipstick that had always sealed the stamp on her trademark beauty. She looked as though she was simply taking a nap and was going to awaken any minute and ask what all the fuss was about. She was a far cry from the worn-down shell that Ted had described visiting on her deathbed.

Victoria was amazed by her mother-in-law's appearance, so full of life, yet as dead as any corpse in a morgue. She wanted to reach out and touch Carolyn to make sure she was really gone. But a mixture of common sense and fear stopped her hand from moving forward. She looked over at Ted and saw his sadness, then focused on Alexandria and saw that she was nodding her head, looking intently at her grandmother.

"Okay, bye Granny Carolyn," Alexandria said, barely above a whisper as she waved her small hand.

Victoria felt a shiver go through her bones. She looked from her daughter and over to her husband who was still standing in a motionless state. Even though Alexandria seemed to be in better shape than Ted, she knew that they were both experiencing a similar trauma.

"It's okay, Honey," Victoria whispered to Ted, rubbing his hand. They stood for a few more moments, suspended in time before he pulled himself away.

Slowly, the three of them moved on, allowing the rest of the family to come up behind them to mourn. As they walked back up the aisle to leave the church, Victoria looked out over the beautifully detailed architecture of the sanctuary and noticed two black women sitting in the back row on the very last pew. They stood out like lions among kittens. They caught Victoria's attention because other than Alexandria and herself, they were the only faces of color in the entire church.

The ladies were beautifully dressed in all white, a stark contrast from the rest of the mourners who all wore black. Their sophisticated, wide-brimmed hats and white gloves reminded her of an outfit that her mother would wear to a special Sunday service. Victoria tried to make eye contact with them as they walked by. She smiled and they nodded their heads, smiling back to acknowledge her. She made a mental note to find out who they were.

As they reached the vestibule, Victoria let out a sigh of relief. They were halfway through the sad day and she couldn't wait for the rest of it to pass. As they prepared to step outside into the waiting limousine, they heard a blood-curdling howl from Charlie. *"Why, mother, why?...Oh, God why?"* he cried out.

Up until that moment, Alexandria hadn't been phased by her uncle's outbursts when they were in church, but now she looked visibly shaken as she clung tight in Victoria's arms.

"Let's get out of here," Ted nearly shouted as he gathered Victoria and Alexandria by his side, leading them toward the open doors of the waiting limousine. He was glad that Lilly and her family were already situated in the first car in the procession, ready to make the last leg of their mother's eternal journey.

They sat in the back of the car, silent and somber as they arrived at the gravesite. Victoria and Ted's hands were locked tightly around each other while Alexandria rested in her mother's lap, drifting off to sleep.

"She's worn out," Victoria said, rubbing Alexandria's back in a soothing motion. "I'm going to stay in the car with her and let her sleep this one out. She doesn't need to witness the burial...it's just too much."

Ted nodded. "I'm worried about her...about both of you," he whispered. "She's been sleeping like a log and you've been up all night." He'd been clearly shaken at the church, but now he was putting his own grief aside in concern for his family.

Victoria leaned over and gave him a light kiss on his cheek, then wiped away the small imprint of plum berries that her lipstick left in the spot. She felt foolish about her lustful delusions over Parker. *I have a wonderful husband who loves me and our child, that's all I need*, she reminded herself.

Ted hugged Victoria one last time before the driver opened his passenger door. He stepped out of the car with a clearer head and purpose because he knew what he had to do. He walked toward the gravesite with his sister and her family as the gathering mourners cleared a path to let them through. He reigned in his grief and innermost thoughts, knowing he was about to put his mother and her secret in the ground, but not to rest.

Chapter 10

Bring It To A Stop...

Carolyn Thornton was dead and buried, and Ted and Victoria were snuggled in bed, talking in quiet tones about the events of the day.

After the gravesite burial, they decided it was best that Victoria take Alexandria back to the hotel instead of to the family gathering at Carolyn's house. "It's as if she's been drugged," Victoria had said with a worried expression.

Alexandria had slept through lunch and had only awakened for a few hours after Ted returned to the hotel later that afternoon.

Seeing that none of them was in the mood to go out for dinner, they ordered room service again. Alexandria was unusually quiet during their meal and afterward she turned down a chance to watch cartoons in favor of going to her room to play with her new doll before going to bed.

"What's wrong, Sweetie? Do you want to talk about what happened at church today?" Victoria had asked as she helped Alexandria into her nightgown.

Alexandria shook her head. "Mommy, I'm sleepy," was her answer before she curled up and fell into a hard sleep.

"I'm worried about Alexandria," Victoria said as she nestled close to Ted. "I hope she'll be all right once we're back home and she gets settled into her normal routine."

"Me too," Ted nodded. "I should've let you lead on this one. I know you didn't want her to attend the funeral."

"It's over and done with now, let's just move forward. Isn't that what you always say?"

"You're right," he smiled.

"I know you'll probably be here a few more days, but I think Alexandria and I should fly back tomorrow."

"Actually, I was thinking I'd fly back with you, get some things situated at home, then come back here next week to tie up a few loose ends. I'll call Jen first thing in the morning so she can make the reservations."

Victoria looked into Ted's eyes. "How're you feeling?" She was amazed that he was as calm as he appeared to be, given the circumstances. He'd told her that Charlie didn't show his face at the gravesite or back at the house, which had probably been a good thing for everyone involved.

"I'm okay," Ted replied. "It's been hard and I'm glad it's all over." He rubbed his tired eyes. "With the exception of my lunatic of a brother, Mother's service was exactly what she'd wanted."

"Speaking of the service," Victoria said, adjusting her head on his shoulder. "Did you see the two black ladies in the back of the church who were dressed in all white?"

Ted shifted his arm, pulling Victoria closer into his body so that her head rested on his chest. He didn't want to have to look her in the eye while he prepared to feed her more lies. "Yes, I saw them," was his brief response.

"Who were they?"

Ted knew he had to play it calm. "I'm not sure, probably some old friends of my mothers."

Victoria shifted back to her previous position, resting her head on Ted's shoulder so she could see his face. "I saw them walking up together when we arrived at the gravesite…you didn't get a chance to meet them?" she inquired.

Ted knew that she was preparing to interrogate him, and he needed to find a way to quickly bring it to a stop. "No, they didn't. But they shook hands with Lilly and me and told us that they knew mother and were sorry for our loss." He threw in a yawn, signaling that he was tired and didn't want to continue the conversation, then he leaned over and turned off the light on the nightstand for added measure.

But even in the dark, Victoria continued. "I didn't know your mother had any black friends, especially friends from the south."

Ted's jaw flinched, but he kept his tone even. "What makes you think they're from the south?"

"Wearing white to funerals is an old southern tradition."

Although Ted knew exactly who one of the two ladies was, he wasn't going to let on because he knew that one answer would lead to ten more questions. He decided to change the subject. "V, how are you feeling? You haven't slept in days."

"I'm good," Victoria lied. "You know how wound up I get. I'm just worried about you and Alexandria."

"I'm worried about Alexandria too, but I'll be fine, don't worry about me."

Victoria snuggled even closer to Ted, running her fingers over his chest, feeling the rise and fall under the weight of her hand. She wanted to erase his pain. Other than her father, he was the strongest man she knew, a quality that had always made her feel safe with him. But she also knew that even the strongest of men had their breaking point, and she wondered when his time would come. She wanted to tell him that it was okay to cry, something she hadn't seen him do yet. She made out the shadow of his face and raised her head up to his. "I love you, Ted."

"I love you too, V."

She enjoyed the softness of his lips, and his steady hand on her back as he gave her a slow, gentle goodnight kiss, quieting her worries.

I Knew He Was Gonna Be Trouble…

It was Wednesday morning, one full week since Victoria had attended her mother-in-law's funeral. And although it was the middle of the week, it was her first day back in the office. From the moment since their plane had landed, Victoria had made herself busy working from home, meeting with clients at on-site venues, running errands, and most importantly, keeping a watchful eye on Alexandria and Ted.

She was still sleep deprived because she hadn't gotten a moments rest, and now her body was beginning to betray her, making her feel sluggish and tired. But her one bright spot was that she was glad to be back in the comfort of her office, and now she was sharing the events of her trip with Denise.

"Girlfriend, shut up!" Denise gasped as Victoria recounted the events of Carolyn's funeral. "You mean to tell me that Ted's brother carried on like that?" she said, shaking her head.

Victoria nodded as she stood in front of Denise's desk. "You should've seen him. Charlie cried and whaled like he'd just lost a limb. You'd never know that other than visiting Carolyn at the hospital right before she died, he hadn't been to see his own mother in over six months. And that's a real shame because he only lived fifteen minutes away."

"Umph," Denise scowled. "That's low-down. The ones who cry the loudest are always the ones you have to watch."

"You got that right. And that's why she didn't leave him a dime."

"Well, I'll say one thing, your mother-in-law may have been a strange woman, but she knew a rat when she smelled one. Every mother knows their child," Denise said, shaking her head again. "He got what he deserved."

"I think that's the general impression the entire family shares."

"I know this must be hard on Ted. How's he doing?"

"You know him, always so strong and resilient. He'll be okay, but it's certainly taken a toll on him. Especially with the number his mother pulled about that crazy death bed confession."

Victoria knew it was wrong to be mad at a dead person because it was a wasted emotion, but she was upset about the unnecessary aggravation that Carolyn had caused. Not only had she kept her terminal diagnosis a secret from everyone, something she should've immediately shared with her family, she'd carried on about her secret like she'd been hiding the location to buried treasure. She'd caused Ted to worry over something so miniscule, and Victoria couldn't understand why. Carolyn certainly wasn't the first person to rise from less than dignified beginnings.

"I never pictured Carolyn as the overly dramatic type," Victoria continued, "but that little act about her big secret took the cake." She didn't want to reveal that Carolyn had gone through the trouble of keeping the information locked away in a safe deposit box, so she simply told Denise and Tyler that Ted had learned about his mother's past from their family attorney after her funeral. And what she also didn't say, despite her natural inclination to believe her husband, was that deep down she felt there was something still hidden about her mother-in-law's past.

"Girlfriend, I told you there was something wrong with that woman, and how much you wanna bet that there's more to that story than meets the eye."

Victoria wanted to say she agreed, but simply nodded her head in reply.

Denise sucked her teeth, "*Family,*" she huffed as she leaned across her desk to answer an incoming call. She frowned when she looked at the caller ID displayed across the shiny black phone. "Divine Occasions," she said in an unusually stern voice.

Victoria knew it couldn't have been Gigi because she and Gary were still on their honeymoon in the South of France, and it couldn't have been anyone Denise knew because she would've called them out by name. And she was fairly certain that it couldn't have been a client because Denise always treated everyone with courtesy. "Who is it?" Victoria whispered.

Denise waved her hand and flicked her wrist. "She's not in, but I can take a message?"

"Who is it?" Victoria whispered again.

"No, I can't transfer you to her voice mail because it's full," Denise lied. "But as I said, I can take a message."

Victoria knew that her voice mailbox wasn't full, and that whoever was on the other end of the line was someone who Denise clearly didn't like, given her harsh tone and bold lie.

A second later Denise hung up the phone, mumbling to herself. Victoria sat down on the loveseat across from her desk in the small reception area of their office suite. "Who was that?"

Denise rolled her eyes. "Dr. Parker Brightwood."

Victoria's throat went dry and the air became thick and muggy despite the cool BTUs pumping through the central air vents. "You've got to be kidding."

"He's been calling for the past two days but he refuses to leave his name or a message," Denise said. "But he knows that I know it's him. He tried to get the number for your direct line but I wouldn't give it to him, so now he wants to leave voice messages. You know I'm not about to let that happen. Girlfriend, I knew he was gonna be trouble."

Victoria raked her fingers through her hair and scooted to the edge of her seat. "Are you sure it was him?" she asked, knowing it was a silly question.

Denise looked at Victoria like she was crazy, choosing not to respond to what they both already knew. "I know you've got a lot on you with Ted grieving, plus worrying about Alexandria's emotional state too, but you've gotta handle this before it gets out of hand. You can't have that man calling up here for you, tryin' to chase you down," she warned.

Victoria knew that Denise was right. Parker was persistent, the type who wouldn't stop until he got what he wanted. She bit down on her bottom lip and closed her eyes. "Shit," she hissed.

"Yeah, that's exactly what's gonna hit the fan if you don't get this under control."

Victoria stood and paced back and forth. She didn't want to deal with Parker. He'd emailed her the day she left Boston, and she'd received another message from him two days after that. She'd deleted them both and had barely thought about him again, managing to push him to the back of her mind so she could give Ted and Alexandria her full attention.

Even though Alexandria seemed to be returning to her old self, Victoria was still worried about her. She wondered what lasting effects Carolyn's funeral might have on her daughter's young psyche.

After talking to her mother and telling her about Alexandria's behavior, Elizabeth offered to keep her granddaughter for a week. Although she and Ted had already planned to send Alexandria down to North Carolina for a visit at some point during the summer, Victoria wasn't sure that now was the right time. She wanted to keep her daughter close by her side so she could monitor her mood. But Elizabeth's plea finally convinced her that taking the trip was exactly what Alexandria needed.

"She needs to know that even though her Granny Carolyn went away, Nana Elizabeth and Grandpa John aren't going anywhere," Elizabeth had said. "Besides, it will give you and Ted a break during this difficult time. And with all the cousins and family friends we've got down here, she'll have a ball," Elizabeth reasoned, making her case as solid as stone.

Once she and Ted discussed the pros and cons, they both agreed that a visit with her grandparents would be good for Alexandria, and it would also give them time to decompress. Ted still needed to tie up a few loose ends in Boston, and Victoria needed to catch up on her rest and business activities that had gone neglected over the last two weeks. Elizabeth booked a flight to Atlanta, and would be there tomorrow to pick up her grandchild, then head back to Raleigh, where Alexandria would spend the next week and a half.

Victoria's anxiety level rose another notch as she continued to pace the small lobby area, thinking about her daughter, thinking about her husband, and now thinking about Parker. It seemed that he was determined to get under her skin and back into her life.

"Girlfriend, don't let that fool get on your nerves," Denise said. "You need to get him straight, real quick!"

Victoria stopped pacing, knowing exactly what she needed to do next. "Hold my calls," she said as she headed back to her office.

You Feel So Damn Good...

Ted sat behind his desk, ready to end his long day. He'd been up to his neck in meetings and phone calls since he returned home last week. When they landed at the airport, his car service had chauffeured Victoria and Alexandria in one direction, headed for their home, and took him in another, headed to his office. Normally, Victoria would've complained if they'd returned from a family trip and he headed straight for the office. But this wasn't a normal family trip. She knew that he needed space and she did too. So she kissed him goodbye and told him that she'd see him later that evening.

Since returning home they'd both been coming and going like passing vehicles on a crowded highway. Victoria had been busy with the everyday juggling act that came with being a wife, mother, and business woman. Ted had been preoccupied with the pressures of ViaTech and wrestling with the knowledge of the family secret he'd discovered. They hadn't been connecting with each other and he knew that the stress of everything was beginning to take over his life.

He leaned back in his chair, trying to focus his mind on the financial prospectus in front of him instead of the complicated thoughts running through his head.

"Ted, do you need anything before I leave?" Jen asked as she stood in the doorway of his office.

Ted looked at his watch. It was almost eight o'clock and he knew that his assistant was more than ready to get home to her family, but she was loyal, and would stay until midnight if he asked her to. Even though he was in no hurry to return to his own home, he knew that she needed to get to hers. "No, I've got things under control," he smiled. "Go home and have a good night."

The petite brunette peered at him through the thick lenses of her tiny, retro inspired glasses. "Ted, you really should get out of here too," Jen said. "Go spend some time with Victoria and Alexandria. You all need each other right now."

Ted knew that no truer words had been spoken. Jen was his trusted right hand, and other than Victoria and his good friend Barry, she was one of the few people he could share things with in complete confidence. He'd learned long ago how dangerous it could be to open up his world and his heart to the inspection of others. His first wife had taught him that lesson.

"You're right, I'll be leaving out behind you in a few minutes," he nodded.

Jen didn't know whether to believe him, but she hoped he wouldn't stay too late. In the nearly seven years she'd worked for him, she'd never seen Ted crack under pressure, not even in the face of turbulent times. The closest she'd ever seen him come to panic was during the days after Alexandria's birth, and even then he still carried on business as usual, not missing a single meeting or deadline.

But this was different. He was dealing with the loss of his mother. And Jen knew it had taken him to an emotional place he'd never been. "All right, have a good night," she said. "And I hope you're really going to leave soon."

Ted gave an affirmative nod as he watched his assistant leave the office. He wanted to linger at his desk for as long as he could, but he knew she was right, he needed to go home.

Going home at the end of a long, hard day had always been something he looked forward to. He loved his wife and he loved his child. They were the two most precious things on earth to him, and knowing that they were waiting to greet him when he walked through the door was the comfort that soothed him. But since unearthing the long-buried secret, each time he came home and looked them in the eye, he felt a well of guilt and uncertainty gripping at his heart.

Before they'd left Boston, when they were lying in bed the night of his mother's funeral, Ted had wanted to tell Victoria about the secret his mother had finally revealed. But he knew that he couldn't. When she asked him about the two black ladies dressed in white, he thought that somehow she'd read his mind, or worse, that she'd gone snooping through his attaché and found out the truth. But he knew that Victoria wasn't clairvoyant, and she'd never invade his privacy. He was suffering from a guilty conscious and it was beginning to cloud his rational thinking.

He couldn't tell Victoria that when he was sitting in front of his mother's coffin at the gravesite, receiving condolences from the line of mourners as they passed by, that the two ladies walked up, hugged Lilly's neck, then his, and quickly handed him an envelope. He tucked it away in the pocket of his suit coat and read it once the limo dropped her and Alexandria off at the hotel. The contents of that envelope was one of the reasons why he was about to make a trip to Jackson, Mississippi.

He planned to fly to Boston as he'd told Victoria he would do, so he could spend time with Lilly and meet with Abe Brookstein again. But instead of staying until Monday as he led her to believe he would, he planned to cut his trip short and head to Jackson, where he knew he would find the answers he was looking for.

Keeping secrets and telling lies was something he didn't want to do. He'd been lied to in his first marriage and deceived at the highest level. He knew how wrong and damaging keeping secrets could be. He'd seen how telling Victoria one lie had already led to a string of others. But right now he felt he had to continue down that road, so he could find resolution within his own mind before exposing the truth to those he loved.

Ted stood and stretched, trying to relieve the tension that had seized his chest and upper back. He looked at his watch again and knew he needed to get home soon so he could read Alexandria her bedtime story. Victoria's mother would be in town the next day to take her back to North Carolina, so he wanted to spend as much time tonight with his daughter as he could.

A half-hour later, Ted pulled into his four car garage, turned off the engine of his vintage, black jaguar and sat for a few moments of quiet reflection. He took a long, deep breath, then opened the door and entered his house. Everything was quiet on the first floor. The large, gourmet kitchen was dim, the spacious family room was dark, the stately dining room was pitch-black, and the elegant formal living room was motionless. His home felt as dead as his mother's hospital room had.

But as he approached the banister at the bottom of the sprawling mahogany staircase, everything suddenly came to life. He saw light and heard the soft voices of the two people he loved most, making his heart rejoice and ache at the same time.

He thought about the effect that knowing the truth might have on them. For Alexandria, it wouldn't cause her much consequence, especially since she was still so young and couldn't understand such complicated matters in the first place. But for Victoria, he knew that finding out the long-buried truth would have a huge impact. The truth would throw her for a loop and he wondered how life and the dynamics between them would change.

He climbed the stairs, taking them slowly as he listened to the hushed whispers and soft giggles of his wife and daughter. When they heard him approach Alexandria called out to him. "Daddy, you're home!" she said with excitement.

Ted marveled at the feeling of pure joy that ran through him every time he heard the word *Daddy*. He stood in the doorway of his daughter's room and smiled, realizing that his dread of coming home had all been for naught. Seeing his wife and child was the dose of medicine he needed, and even with the heavy troubles on his mind, they were still the best part of his day.

He loosened his tie as he leaned against the open door. "Yes, Princess. Daddy's home."

"Mommy," Alexandria said softly, "Daddy can finish reading me my story now."

Victoria wasn't the least bit phased that her daughter had basically dismissed her. She simply smiled and held the big story book up in the air for Ted. She knew that Alexandria always looked forward to this part of her evening when her father would read her a bedtime story.

Victoria rose from the bed and walked toward her husband. "You can take over from here." She gave him a quick smile and headed to their bedroom.

Less than ten minutes later, Alexandria was out before Ted finished the book. He kissed her on her forehead, turned off her light, and headed down to the end of the hall, longing for the peace of mind he hoped would be waiting for him. When he entered their bedroom and looked for Victoria he found it empty, then realized she was in the shower when he heard the sound of running water.

He stepped out of his shoes and dress socks, spreading his toes over the cool hardwood floor beneath his feet. He smiled as he listened to the quirky, off-key tone of Victoria's voice, making him laugh at her attempt to sing in the shower.

The steamy heat and sweet smell of her shampoo lured him in as he watched her through the frosted glass encased shower stall. He looked at the flickering, scented candles that lined the Jacuzzi tub on the other side of their master bathroom. Victoria had decided to jump in the shower at the last minute instead of taking her requisite long soak in the tub that she usually reserved for long, tiring days. Other than their chef-inspired kitchen, the bathroom was her second favorite room in their house. It was her in-home, private spa retreat.

Ted inspected her long, lean body as she stood under the showerhead. He studied her movements as she seemed to meditate in the relaxing stream of water kissing her smooth, chocolate skin. She threw her head back, rinsing the last of the shampoo from her hair.

At that moment, Ted wanted her so badly he hurt. He stripped down in a matter of seconds, leaving his clothes in the middle of the floor where he'd been standing. He walked over and opened the shower door. "Want some company?"

Victoria jumped, slightly startled at first, but then smiled and turned to face him. When she saw that he was dripping with desire, it ignited a flame in her that was ready to match whatever he had in mind.

He stepped in, wrapping his arms around her wet body, rubbing himself against her warm skin. He kissed her deep while his hands slid down her behind, cupping each of her soft, round cheeks. His tongue met hers, darting in and out, grazing her lips and teeth, making her moan. She reached for her bottle of shower gel. "Scrub me down," she purred, squirting a generous amount of the delicate smelling liquid onto her netted sponge before handing it to him.

Ted did as he was instructed. He loved the way the sudsy white lather coated Victoria's silky brown skin. Slowly, he rubbed the sponge across her shoulders, moving down her back, and on to her hips, concentrating his efforts there. He made circular scrubbing motions with one hand while he held her steady in place with the other.

His excitement was building and so was hers. He positioned himself behind her, letting the sponge fall to the tiled floor near the drain, ready to move on to a more immediate task. He gently guided his hands down the front of her thighs before landing in the soft spot that always made her quiver. She let out a small gasp as his skilled fingers danced inside the warmth that greeted him between her legs. *"Mmmmmmm,"* Victoria moaned.

"Oh, V," Ted panted into the back of her neck, rolling his tongue over her delicious tasting skin. He pressed his erection against her backside as he moved one hand up to her breast, gently tweaking her nipple while his other hand continued to pleasure her below. "You feel so damn good," Ted whispered into her ear.

Victoria leaned her slender back against Ted's broad chest, tilting her head until it rested on his shoulder. She spread her legs further apart as she grinded against his nimble fingers. The mixture of warm water and her hot wetness drove him wild. Gently, he turned her around to face him, positioning her against the shower wall. Victoria's back tensed when she felt the cold tile touch her skin, but the sensation was quickly replaced by Ted's heat. He lifted her left leg, holding it in place around his right hip as he plunged upward, going deep inside her, working her middle at a slow and deliberate pace.

"Oh, yeah," Victoria moaned as Ted filled her inch by inch. His thrusts were hard and powerful, pumping in and out as he leaned against her body for balance. She grinded against him, lifting her other leg around his waist. She locked her ankles together above his hips and let out a deep moan as he gripped her bottom in his hands, holding her steady while he pounded and stroked her at the same time.

This was one of Ted's favorite sex-in-the-shower positions. He closed his eyes, enjoying the pleasure he felt surging through his body as he made love to his wife against the shower wall. *"V, I love you,"* he moaned against her shoulder, continuing his pace as the warm water beat down on his back.

Victoria's rhythm started to slow, and she felt herself ready to explode.

Ted could see that she was reaching her breaking point and it turned him on even more. *"Are you almost there?"* he whistled into Victoria's ear, delighting in the fact that he knew she was. He used steady but gentle force to lower her body, sliding her down the wall for deeper penetration as he plunged into her, gliding in and out while he moved his hips. He buried his head in the crook of her neck, his favorite spot, not missing a beat of the rhythm he'd established. He stroked her up and down in an urgent frenzy as they both moaned, inhaling the warm steam that filled the room. When Ted heard the slow and familiar, high-pitched sound escape Victoria's lips, he pumped her with even more determination. *"Ohhhh, Teeedddd. I'm there,"* she called out.

Ted's pleasure quickly met hers, slowing his hips as he emptied himself inside his wife. They stood still, locked together in place, letting the water rain down to soothe their skin. They kissed each other in hungry little nibbles, enjoying the pure exhaustion of their love making. After they caught their breaths, they bathed one another, taking their time to caress each other's skin.

Victoria blow dried her hair, a feat that always took no less than twenty minutes, while Ted unwound in bed. He waited patiently until she finished and finally slipped under the sheets, snuggling close beside him. He spooned her from behind, feeling the first small bit of peace he'd had in over a week.

He needed what he and Victoria had just shared. He wanted to purge his family's secret from his lips to her ears, yet nothing, and everything held him back.

He hugged her body closer to his, listening to the steady sound of her breathing. She was resting, but she wasn't asleep and that worried him. He knew she'd been concerned about him and Alexandria. He ran his fingers over her still slightly damp hair, and thought about his upcoming trip.

Never in a million years would Jackson, Mississippi, have been a travel destination on his itinerary, but right now he couldn't wait to get down there because it was where he'd find all the answers that his parents had kept hidden from the world.

Are You My Husband?...

Victoria, Ted, and Alexandria stood together in the baggage claim area of Atlanta's Hartsfield-Jackson Airport. They'd come there to meet Elizabeth and deliver her granddaughter into her trusting hands. Victoria and Ted knew they could've let Alexandria travel under the escort of an airline provided guardian, but after the trauma she'd recently experienced, they felt better knowing that she had the familiar comfort of family by her side.

Initially, Victoria had been worried that her parents might not have the energy to keep up with an active and very inquisitive five-year old. Even though they were in great shape for their age, she knew that small children could be a test for anyone's stamina. But looking at Elizabeth's spry steps and glowing smile as she practically jogged up to greet them, Victoria realized that her mother was actually doing better than she and Ted were.

"Don't worry about little missy here," Elizabeth said, looking at her granddaughter. "She's going to be just fine."

"I get to stay with Nana and Grandpa!" Alexandria exclaimed with a big smile.

Victoria nodded her head. "Yes you do, and I want you to behave yourself, mind your manners, and do as your Nana and Grandpa tell you, okay?" She bent down and kissed her daughter, praying this trip would be healing for everyone.

"Yes, ma'am," Alexandria nodded back.

Ted picked her up and hugged her tightly. "We'll see you next week, Princess."

Once all the goodbyes were said and done, Alexandria and Elizabeth headed into the terminal to catch their flight. Victoria and Ted waved until the two disappeared out of sight, then walked at a quick pace back to their car in the parking garage. They were in a hurry, on their way to another terminal because not only was Alexandria flying out, so was Ted.

As they approached the garage, a small crowd of travelers rolled by, taking up over half the sidewalk with their luggage. Ted put his hand on the small of Victoria's back and gently guided her in front of him to give the group more room. As they side-stepped out of the way, Victoria caught the indignant stare of an older black man who looked at her and Ted like they'd just spat on his shoe. Victoria knew that she should've been used to it by now, but each time she encountered the subtle signs of prejudice it still stung, and it made her think about what might be in store for Alexandria down the road.

Victoria held her tongue until they were in the car, securely fastened in their seatbelts. "Did you see how that old man stared at us back there?" she asked Ted.

"Yes, and if he'd been just a decade or two younger, I would've asked him what the hell was his problem."

Victoria couldn't believe her ears. She hadn't expected the reaction or the comment that came out of Ted's mouth. Usually when they encountered a situation involving race, he nearly always brushed it off, choosing to either ignore or condemn it to plain ignorance.

Victoria looked at Ted closely, wondering what had caused the sudden change. Then she thought about all that he'd been through, dealing with the death of his mother and the chaos his brother was still trying to stir up behind Carolyn's will. She knew that loosing a loved one could have life-altering effects on one's outlook and emotions, and it certainly appeared to be the case with Ted. She'd noticed that ever since they left Boston he'd been a little different.

"Wait a minute, are you my husband?" Victoria joked, pretending to look around in search of someone else. "Where's the man who says, 'It's their problem, not ours,'" she mocked.

Ted nodded and leaned over, pulling her face toward his for a soft kiss. "It's me, I thought I proved who I was last night."

Victoria could only smile as she thought about the night before. They had both needed to reconnect in that way, giving one another the physical release that freed their hidden burdens. But even as she thought about the beautiful love they'd made, she couldn't let go of the feeling that something was missing. Something was wrong.

She couldn't put her finger on it, but something in Ted had changed, she was sure of it. And again, she felt it had something to do with whatever he'd found locked away in his mother's safe deposit box. Her gut told her that there was more to the story than what he'd shared. She wanted to question him about it right there on the spot, but she didn't have time because of two things; the fact that they were in a rush so Ted could make his flight, and the event she'd set into motion that required her immediate wits and focus for what she was about to do after he stepped on the plane.

They parked curb-side at the passenger drop off area outside the terminal. They both hopped out as Ted hurriedly removed his two bags from the back, sitting them to the side. They stood facing each other, holding hands. "I'll call you tonight," he said.

"Okay, be safe."

When they kissed goodbye, Ted held Victoria tightly, as if he didn't want to let her go. "V, I love you so much." The tone in his voice was urgent, like he'd never get the chance to say those words again.

Victoria looked at him, wanting to attach his behavior to grieving, but knowing there was much more lying beneath the surface. And just as her spider senses had tingled when they were in Boston, the same feeling overcame her now. Her better judgment told her to let it go because he had a flight to catch and she had a plan to carry out that she'd hatched the day before. But her natural and ever persistent curiosity grabbed hold and forced her hand. "Ted, what's the matter? Honey, talk to me?"

Ted shook his head. "Nothing's wrong, I'm just tired…that's all, really." He tried his best to smile as though all was fine, and he would have succeeded in the exercise if he'd been dealing with anyone other than Victoria. She was the one person who knew and understood him almost as well as he understood himself. Lying to her was becoming a habit, one that he wanted desperately to break. But for now he knew it was best to keep the truth from her, at least until he discovered the full details and came to terms with it himself. So he kissed her one last time. "Don't worry, I'm fine. I'll call you tonight."

They embraced again before Ted grabbed his bags. An airport security officer was about to tell Victoria to move her vehicle when she jumped back inside. She watched Ted walk into the terminal as she'd just done with her mother and daughter, hoping that his trip would bring healing too.

Victoria pulled off onto the ramp leading her from the airport back to the highway. She turned up the volume on her Ledisi CD as she sped past other fast moving drivers, preparing herself for what was about to come next. She knew she should call it off, but the plan had already been made. She took a deep breath and prayed again, this time for what she was about to do.

Chapter 11

Back And Forth Game...

Victoria pulled into the parking lot and spotted his vehicle almost immediately. They'd chosen a place located in a deceptively upscale, quaint little building tucked away in a quiet section of Dunwoody, a suburb right outside the Atlanta city limits.

Victoria's hands trembled as she eased her key out of the ignition and took a deep breath. She attempted to steady her nerves as she prepared to walk into what she knew could turn into a minefield. But she knew it was something she had to do.

She removed her large, tortoise-shell sunglasses from her face as she looked beyond the four-star restaurant's tastefully decorated entrance in search of him. He was standing over to the side, waiting for her, looking dapper in his black trousers and lemon-colored shirt. Her nerves were bubbling over as she walked toward Parker. *What the hell am I doing?* But she knew it was too late to turn back now.

His smile was warm and sincere as he greeted her. They didn't hug or shake hands, they simply nodded a cordial hello. Victoria was noticeably on edge, but as usual, Parker was as cool as a fan, acting as though it was a regular occurrence for them to meet for food and conversation during the middle of the week.

Parker took a moment to appraise the tan-colored, slim fitting linen skirt that hugged at Victoria's shapely hips, and the delicate design of her pink, cap-sleeve blouse. "Thanks for coming," he said.

They followed the hostess to a table up front. "Is there a more private area where we can be seated...like in the back?" Victoria asked, pointing her finger in the opposite direction.

Normally, neither of them would have wanted to sit in the very back of a restaurant, close to the kitchen, but in this case they both knew it was best. Victoria couldn't risk running into anyone she knew and she was glad that the place was practically bare of patrons. Meeting at an off hour, in between lunch and dinner had proven to be a wise choice, even if being there in the first place wasn't.

They sat in silence as the server filled their water glasses. Victoria knew that Parker was looking at her as she perused her menu, and could feel his eyes dissecting her every move. She tried to concentrate on the variety of food choices in front of her rather than on the undeniable attraction she felt slowly creeping through every part of her body.

The day before, when she'd gone back to her office to call him after Denise had practically hung up in his face, she had no intention of ending up where she was at the very moment. She'd fished his business card from the bottom of her handbag where it had been living for over two weeks, and dialed his work number, determined to put an end to whatever he was trying to start.

"This is Victoria," she said before he had a chance to say hello.

Parker's response was immediate. "I've been waiting for your call."

"Parker, why are you calling me?"

"Because you haven't responded to the emails I sent you."

Victoria had deleted the two emails he'd sent, each containing a brief but polite request for her to contact him when she could. She'd prayed that he would simply go away. But she knew that she was merely hoping against hope.

"There's nothing for us to talk about. We'll see each other from time to time at Jack and Jill activities and at our kid's school events, but other than that there's no need for us to have any communication," she said.

"There are a few things I want to talk to you about. I need to clear up some issues."

"We don't have any issues," Victoria countered.

"Oh, but we do…and I think you know it too." Parker paused for a moment as a group of interns walked by. He was at the hospital and didn't want his business overheard. He got up and shut his office door before he continued. "There's still tension and unresolved issues between us and I want to clear it up. As you said, we're going to see each other quite a bit and I think we should just get everything out in the open because it will make things a lot easier."

Victoria shook her head on the other end of the phone. "There's nothing that I need to get out in the open."

"Well, I do, and I'd appreciate it if you allowed me the opportunity to get it off my chest. I'm only asking for an hour of your time."

In spite of the small voice inside her head that whispered *no*, Victoria agreed to meet him. A coffee shop had been Parker's initial choice, but she thought it would be too exposed. There would be too much foot traffic and she didn't want to risk being seen with him in the light of day. She knew it would be a mistake to meet him anywhere at night, so when he suggested a quiet place outside the city limits and off the beaten path, she agreed, bringing her to the defining spot where she currently sat. In the back of her mind she wondered if this was how Debbie's situation had started.

After the server took their orders, they were left alone—no menus to distract them, just silence separating them.

"Your daughter is a beautiful little girl," Parker started.

Victoria's lips formed a smile. "Thanks, she's a handful, but she's the joy of my life. You've got a handsome little guy yourself."

"He's my mini-me," Parker laughed. "PJ's a handful too, but I wouldn't trade fatherhood for anything in the world."

Victoria was taken aback by the genuine light in Parker's eyes when he talked about his son. She could see his entire demeanor soften at just the mention of his child's name. Right then and there, the hard, icy spot she'd been trying to hold for him started melting away.

They spent the next hour covering a lot of ground, talking about their children and the ups and downs of parenting. She told him about the recent passing of Ted's mother, that she was worried about the long-lasting effect it might have on Alexandria, and how she hoped the visit with her parents would help bring her back to her old self. Parker listened with concern and told her that he could recommend an excellent child psychologist at the hospital if the need arose.

As they shared more tidbits of information about their personal lives, Victoria soon discovered that just as she'd thought from chatty Roberta's description during the Jack and Jill meeting, Pamela was indeed the mother of his child. They shared joint custody, but it was clear that Parker was the primary care giver.

From what Parker described, motherhood had never been something that Pamela really wanted, she simply saw it as a means to an end. In her mind, a baby equaled a ring, and a ring equaled marriage and happily ever after. But Parker's mind had thoughts of something completely different. When he refused to marry her, everything went up in smoke.

"Since the time PJ was about six months old, Pamela pretty much began to leave him at my place for longer and longer periods of time. Now, I keep him during the weekdays and she has him every other weekend. But even that's not always the case. Right now she's traveling for work and hasn't seen him in over three weeks. She gets back in town tonight and she's supposed to keep him this weekend…we'll see," he sighed.

Victoria could barely swallow the succulent chicken breast that was melting in her mouth. She couldn't imagine not seeing Alexandria for weeks at a time, business travel or not. As it stood, she couldn't wait to talk to her later that evening to make sure she was all right. "How does PJ handle not seeing his mother?" she asked.

"He's used to it. It's been this way almost from the beginning so it's all he knows."

Victoria shook her head. "So you're practically a single parent."

"You could say that. But I have a great nanny who works miracles. I couldn't make it without her. Plus, I've cut back on a few things at the hospital. I'm no longer teaching interns, which if you remember, I really loved." Parker stared at her for a moment, hoping to see a spark of nostalgia about the good times they'd shared. He saw a small flinch, but he couldn't get a good read, so he continued. "I'm strictly doing surgery and administrative work. It's a trade-off, but it's a small sacrifice to make for my son."

"Any dessert for you two love birds?" the cherub faced server asked.

Victoria's back stiffened at the comment, but Parker simply smiled. "If I remember, chocolate cheesecake is your favorite, right?"

After Victoria swept the server's misguided slip under the rug, they continued their conversation over chocolate cheesecake for her, and key lime pie for him.

"You seem happy, Parker...and I'm happy for you," Victoria said. She finally looked him dead in his eyes, wanting him to know that she truly meant it.

Parker dabbed his mouth, sitting his napkin beside his plate of half-eaten pie. "There hasn't been a day that's gone by over the last six years that I haven't thought about you or regretted how badly I hurt you."

Up until that moment, Victoria had felt surprisingly comfortable. But now Parker was stirring up things from their past, making her think about what she'd been trying to keep locked away in a dark, quiet place. She wanted to despise him the way she used to when he'd broken her heart, but she couldn't bring herself to do it. In the matter of an hour and a half he'd loosened the reigns and now the horse was out of the gate.

Why is he going there? Victoria screamed in her head. But then she reminded herself that this, after all, was the purpose of their meeting. He wanted to get things off his chest and now he was doing it.

"Is this what you wanted to clear up? The fact that you regret cheating on me over six years ago?" Victoria let out a tired sigh, pushing her dessert to the side. "Parker, you didn't have to meet with me to tell me that. I told you yesterday, what's done is done. We have a new understanding, so let's just put the past behind us and move forward."

They stared at each other, reverting back to the uncomfortable silence that had shrouded them at the beginning of their lunch. Victoria hoped she was doing a good job of hiding her secret desire. She was all too aware of the fact that Parker still knew her well, and she was praying that he couldn't see through her carefully manufactured facade.

Parker leaned forward in his chair, relaxing his elbows on the table. "I still care about you. Even though I made that horrible mistake, I never played games with you and I always let you know how I felt," he paused. "I still want you to know how I feel and I'd be lying if I pretended that I didn't want more from you than the casual parent-to-parent interaction we're going to have when we run into each other at meetings and at our kid's school."

Victoria could feel her heart beating fast inside her chest. Her palms began to sweat as she looked around the room, as if searching for something to rescue her from what rested inside her thoughts. She knew that Parker was reading her like one of his medical journals, so she had to put the tense moment to an end before it led to something she couldn't pull herself out of. She folded her napkin and placed it on the table next to his. "I'm glad that you've gotten *things* off your chest. But this doesn't change anything between us." Then she came right out with it, saying what was on both their minds. "I'm married, and I'm not interested in having an affair with you." The words she'd just spoken weren't convincing, not even to her, but it was all she had.

Parker looked at Victoria with intensity. If it hadn't been for the fact that they were in a public place and Victoria might freak out, he would've pulled her close and devoured her on the spot. He wanted to feel the heat of her flesh against his, run his hands over the softness of her velvety smooth skin, taste the flavor of her mouth, and fill her with the erection growing at the seat of his pants. These were all things he'd thought about since he saw her two weeks ago. And despite her valiant effort to uphold the fidelity of her marriage, he knew that she wanted him too…and that meant it was only a matter of time before she gave in to what they'd both been longing for.

He was a patient man. He'd waited this long, so he knew he could wait a little longer to finally have what he desired and needed. He decided to play along, but then his mind paused in mid-thought, causing him to quickly rethink the situation. He knew what he wanted, he knew what she wanted, and he wasn't going to sit around playing a silly back and forth game with her.

Parker leaned forward just a little more, close enough to reach over and plant the kiss on Victoria's lips that he'd been craving. He wanted her to know that he wasn't going to beat around any bushes or dance around the inevitable. "You and I both know there's an undeniable attraction and chemistry between us. It's natural and it's been there from the moment we first met. The only reason you're last name isn't Brightwood right now is because I fucked up."

Victoria's eyes grew large. "What makes you think that I'd cheat on my husband with a man who cheated on me?"

"Because you still love me."

There. He'd said it. The words she didn't want to hear. Victoria looked down at her dessert, pissed that she'd gotten herself into this situation.

Deep down she'd known what was coming from the moment she agreed to meet with him. And if she was being honest with herself, she'd have to admit that she'd been secretly looking forward to seeing him. But admitting those things would mean facing the reality that she was prepared to cheat on her husband, and she couldn't do that.

"I have to go," she said.

Before Parker could counter, Victoria pushed back her chair, stood up, and headed toward the door.

Parker quickly opened his wallet, tossed two fifty dollar bills on the table and followed on her heels. Once they reached her car that was parked in the back of the tiny lot adjacent to the restaurant, Victoria turned around and faced him. She could either continue to run and let the game drag on, or she could deal with it in the here and now. She took a deep breath and faced the music, knowing that she couldn't allow herself to give in to Parker's smooth talk and her own desires. "I'm ending this now," she willed herself to say.

Parker reached for Victoria's hand, and surprisingly, she didn't let go. He knew that was a good sign, so he moved slow, hoping to lead her back to a place they'd once shared. He stared at her fingers, interlocked in his grip. Her hand was shaking, but she didn't make a move. He looked into her eyes and when she returned his stare he was more sure than ever that she still loved him.

Parker knew that he didn't need to push her buttons any further because her true desires were written all over her face, and in the trembling palm of her delicate hand that felt so good resting inside his own.

No words were spoken as they shared the moment. Nothing else was required because their eyes confirmed what neither of them needed to say—that it was only a matter of time.

Slowly, Victoria withdrew her hand, stepped inside her car and started the engine.

Parker walked over to his truck as her car passed him. She didn't look back or wave goodbye, and that was okay with him because he knew he'd be seeing her again, very soon.

Tonight.....

It was Friday evening and Victoria was still at her office. She'd just finished talking to Alexandria and then to Ted. She was overjoyed to learn that both were doing better than when she'd last seen them yesterday. Alexandria had sounded playful and not at all ready to go to bed when Elizabeth put her on the phone. She'd been to the park, had ice-cream at the mall, made a new friend in Victoria's old neighborhood, and already had a playdate scheduled with her cousins for the next day.

Victoria's heart felt less burdened knowing that Alexandria was doing well, and the fact that her parents were enjoying their granddaughter's visit was icing on the cake.

Once her mind was put to ease after talking with her daughter, she hung up and dialed Ted's cell. She wasn't at all surprised that like herself, he was still fast at work. He was going over spreadsheets in his hotel room. His spirits seemed to be lifting, and she attributed it to the fact that he and Lilly were making progress with the final details of their mother's will. That, coupled with the fact that Charlie hadn't reared his ugly head since he'd shown his ass at the funeral, seemed to be just what Ted needed to start pulling himself into the light.

Now that she knew her family was safe and secure, Victoria sat behind her desk, at a loss for what to do next. This was the kind of quiet time she would've paid good money for just a few weeks ago…an opportunity to be by herself without worry or obligation to her child or her husband. She was essentially foot loose and fancy free, able to let her hair down and do whatever she wanted. But there she was, twiddling her thumbs, wondering how she was going to fill the next few days until Ted came back on Monday and Alexandria returned at the end of next week. She was about to start planning the details of a new corporate client's annual company retreat, when a message flashed across her computer screen alerting her that she had incoming mail. Her breath quickened when she saw that it was from Parker.

He knew she would be alone the entire weekend because she'd told him that Ted and Alexandria would be out of town when they'd had lunch. She looked at the screen and braced herself.

Date: Fri. August 4, 8:25 p.m.
To: victoria@divineoccasions.com
From: thebrightdoc@mailnet.com
Subject: Tonight

What are your plans for this evening?
Sent from wireless BlackBerry

Victoria read the email twice, clicking her neatly polished nails against the edge of her keyboard. She stared at the subject line, *Tonight*. That one word held a multitude of danger. She knew she shouldn't respond to his message, but she found herself typing anyway.

Date: Fri. August 4, 8:28 p.m.
To: thebrightdoc@mailnet.com
From: victoria@divineoccasions.com
Subject: RE: Tonight

Working late at the office. Have a good evening.

She took a deep breath, then exhaled slowly. She hoped the brief message had made it appear that she was knee-deep in paperwork and didn't have time for chatting, dinner, or anything else he might have had in mind. When she ended by telling him to have a good evening, it was her way of saying goodbye...period.

"Who am I fooling?" she whispered aloud. She knew that her staged attempt to brush him off was futile because Parker was a man not easily deterred.

Less than a minute later his next message came in.

Date: Fri. August 4, 8:28 p.m.
To: victoria@divineoccasions.com
From: thebrightdoc@mailnet.com
Subject: RE: Tonight

Ten minutes away from your office. Will be there shortly.
Sent from wireless BlackBerry

Victoria bit down on her bottom lip. Her hands trembled as she prepared to type a response that never made it past the keys under her fingers.

Someone's Gotta Drive This Train....

When the bell of her office door rang, Victoria closed her eyes and prayed. She'd been sitting on the couch in the reception area—waiting for him. She was nervous, but unlike the initial fear she'd had during their lunch meeting, second-guessing why she'd agreed to see him in the first place, she was clear about what she was doing now. Her trepidation wasn't from the unknown, it was from what she was very aware of.

She knew that her conscious denial and posturing would soon be tossed out the window with yesterday's trash. The inevitable wheels had been set into motion from the minute she'd tried to avoid him at Hilda Barrett's house a few weeks ago to the fact that she'd basically welcomed him to her office by not responding to his last message. Now it was time to play her hand.

She walked to the door, peeped through the hole and stepped aside to let Parker enter her office.

She watched him closely as he walked in. His tan trousers and black cotton tee clung to him from the stifling August heat outside, but he smelled of spring time freshness, as if he'd just stepped from the shower. She scrutinized everything about him, paying careful attention because of what his presence in that space and time meant.

She thought about the warning Debbie had given her, *"Be careful,"* she'd said. Victoria knew that if her friend could see her now she'd simply shake her head and ask, "Now who's lost their mind?"

Parker looked around, admiring the fine details of the sophisticated appointments that adorned the walls, and the chic, contemporary office furnishing that brought everything into perfect harmony. He took note of the colors, scent, and décor which all brought back familiar memories of when he and Victoria had been together; he knew her style. He was a man who appreciated the finer things, and he'd always loved Victoria's exquisite taste.

"Welcome to Divine Occasions," she said, a hint of jitters beginning to creep up in her voice.

"This is very impressive," Parker nodded.

They both looked around the small lobby; Parker as if in a foreign land, Victoria as if she'd never seen the inside of her own office. They each realized how awkward and slightly uncomfortable the moment felt, but neither of them was ready to let it go.

Finally, Parker broke their shared silence. "Can I have a tour?"

"Sure." Victoria started to feel a little more relaxed because she loved showing her small, but very chic digs. She waved her hand in the air. "As you can see, this is the lobby and reception area."

They both looked around the room again as Parker nodded his head, turning his attention to Denise's meticulously organized cubical. "I guess this is my friend's desk?" he winked with a chuckle, looking at Denise's family photos.

They both laughed at his joke. It was no secret that Denise couldn't stand him, and for his part, Parker could take her or leave her. Every exchange they'd ever had had been touchy and filled with angst. But he brushed his feelings about her aside because he appreciated the fact that she'd always looked out for Victoria and had her back.

"Yes, that's Denise's desk. She left ViaTech four years ago and has been here with me ever since. I don't know what I'd do without her, she's been invaluable."

"She's been a good friend to you."

"That she has." Victoria nodded her head, motioning toward the small hallway straight ahead. "The kitchenette, restroom, and my office are back here."

Parker peaked into the neatly decorated restroom with its vessel sink and bronze fixtures. The rich earth tone color on the wall reminded him of the bathroom in Victoria's old home. They moved on to the kitchenette, where he saw that she'd incorporated the creature comforts of home, making sure the small room was sufficiently supplied with scaled down, but high-end stainless steel appliances. "I know you do some serious cooking up in here," he teased.

She smiled. "You know it." They shared their first genuinely comfortable moment since he'd arrived.

They headed across the hall and into her office. Aside from the combined reception and lobby area, it was the largest space in the compact office suite. This was where Victoria held meetings, entertained clients, and finalized all the deals.

Parker walked over to her desk, running his hand across the top of the rich wood finish. He glanced at the pictures of Alexandria and Ted that populated one side of the space. A small jab caught him in his stomach when he saw how happy Victoria looked in the photos. He wished it was him holding her in the scenes captured from holidays and family vacations.

He quickly shifted his focus from the *what ifs*, forcing himself to look beyond what he couldn't change to what he needed to do in the here and now. He walked over to the conference table and upholstered couch near the back window. Her office looked like a mixture between a corporate boardroom and an elegant living space in a home and garden magazine. He nodded his head again. "You've done very well. I'm proud of you, Victoria."

His comment startled her. "Thank you. It's a lot of hard work, but I truly love what I do."

"You can never go wrong when you follow your passion." He let the double entendre linger as he took a seat on her couch.

"You never thought much of my passion when we were dating. You thought throwing parties and preparing food was beneath someone with an Ivy League MBA."

"I was wrong for that."

Victoria continued to stand by her desk, toying with a small string on the front of her floral print summer dress.

"You're uncomfortable, aren't you?" Parker asked.

"What makes you say that?"

"Because I know you."

The intensity in the room was as thick and heavy as a cinder block.

"Don't you have a hot date you should be on right now?" Victoria asked, hands on her hips.

"You know that I don't. I'm exactly where I want and need to be."

"Why are you doing this?"

"Because I want to be with you."

Victoria took a deep breath. "You know that's not possible... you shouldn't even be here right now."

"But I am." Parker stood and walked toward her. "And you want me here just as much as I wanted to come. I know it, and so do you."

Victoria couldn't deny the truth of his words. She *did* want him there.

And as he drew closer, her skin tingled with forbidden excitement.

"You could've told me to stay away, but you didn't," Parker continued. "That's why I'm here…because we both want this." He stood in front of her, allowing only a sliver of space to separate their bodies. "Let's stop playing games, Victoria. I'm ready to step out there if you are."

"Stepping out there is easy if you don't have anything to risk."

"Life's a risk. It's what you make of it that counts."

Victoria's mind was swimming with thoughts she couldn't control, thoughts that made her feel weak and exhilarated all at once. She desperately wanted to remain faithful to Ted, but she also wanted to feel Parker's soft lips against the side of her neck and his strong hands caressing her skin. She knew that she needed to back away and ask him to leave, because his being there was a mistake. But her legs and her desire held her in a steady yet dangerous place.

Parker looked into Victoria's eyes, sensed her wanting, and moved in for the kill. *Someone's gotta drive this train!* He took another small step forward until their bodies were touching. He enjoyed the feel of his hard pecs against her soft breasts that lay beneath the thin material of her sundress. He looked down at her, inhaling the sultry sweet scent of her Cartier perfume, a smell he'd missed. He felt the quick rise and fall of her chest and the nervousness that flooded her body. But he wasn't deterred because he knew her oh so well, even after all the years that had passed between them.

Without saying a word, he encircled his arms around her waist, not giving her a chance to move away before drawing her in to him. He roamed his hands along the small of her back and down to the base of her behind, gently resting there as he pressed his pelvis against hers.

Victoria knew that she needed to push him away, or do anything except what she was doing—standing there, enjoying the way her body felt in Parker's arms. So instead of resisting and fighting against what she knew she should do, she gave in to what she'd been wanting as she tilted her head, and welcomed his tongue into her mouth.

They kissed, swaying in the building heat of each other's embrace. Parker sucked her tongue into his mouth as he moved his body closer into hers, rubbing his hardness against her lower body. It made Victoria want to feel him deep inside her. She moaned as his hand reached for the hem of her dress, maneuvering the brightly colored fabric up her hips as he gripped her behind. She looked into his eyes, becoming lost in the desire staring back at her, making her feel warm, and wild, and free.

Victoria stood before him, wearing dead silence and wanton desire. Her mouth didn't open, but her eyes spoke the words that she couldn't seem to push out. After a moment, she finally forced herself to say it. "Yes, Parker…I want you too." But her common sense hadn't completely eroded because the next statement out of her mouth was, "But this is very dangerous."

Parker smiled to himself. It didn't matter that she'd equated being with him to eminent danger, what mattered was that she wanted him. He took Victoria by her hand and led her to where he'd been sitting on the couch across the room. He admired her beautiful, smooth chocolate skin, glowing against the brightly-colored straps of her sundress. He caressed her bare shoulders, thinking about how good it would feel to make love to her. Once again his hands traveled to lift her dress, pulling it up far enough for him to see the lacey edge of her orange-colored thong. He hooked his fingers around the silky fabric on each side of her hips as he attempted to guide them down her long legs. And just as she was beginning to loose all rational thought, she wiggled away.

"Baby, don't pull back," Parker whispered, planting a small kiss on her lips.

Victoria's mind was starting to tire of the wrestling match her emotions kept playing. She knew that she wanted him, but guilt mixed with a sense of honor were tugging at her to do the right thing. And therein was her problem. Despite all her doubts and fears, she had to be honest with herself and admit that being with Parker felt right.

"Not here," she said, shaking her head. "I want to be with you, but I can't do this…here. This is where I work."

Parker reached out, drawing Victoria back into him. "Okay, let's go to my place. Pamela has PJ for the weekend, so my house is free."

"What if someone sees me going up to your building?" Victoria asked with apprehension. She'd practically lived there when they used to date, and she didn't want to run into any of his neighbors.

Parker smiled as he slipped her a kiss on the neck. "I haven't lived downtown for nearly five years now."

Shortly after PJ had been born, Parker decided to trade in the trendy condo he owned in an ultra luxe building downtown for a large home with a big backyard in a subdivision in Buckhead. Not only did he want his son to have plenty of room to play, he wanted to give him the comfort and security of a traditional neighborhood. Having grown up in the elite Gold Coast section of DC, he knew the importance of being surrounded by the right kind of people in the right kind of environment.

"I live in Buckhead now. And actually, I'm not too far from your office. I bought a house in a subdivision called Eagle Point. I'm sure you've heard of it?" he said.

Victoria was stunned, so stunned that she had to move away and pull down her dress. "Eagle Point is only a mile or two from where I live."

Now Parker was startled. "You're kidding?"

"I wouldn't kid about that. You practically live in my neighborhood."

"Where are you?" Parker asked, obviously more excited about the prospect of being neighbors than Victoria was.

She cleared her throat, "Crest Meadows."

Parker nodded his head in silence. He was all too familiar with Victoria's grand subdivision. Eagle Point was exclusive, but Crest Meadows was practically restrictive. He'd initially considered buying one of the beautiful mini mansions that had been on the market at the time he'd been searching for a new home. But he changed his mind once his realtor informed him that he'd be paying nearly a quarter of a million dollars more for the same home in Crest Meadows that he could get where he currently lived. "That's by design," his realtor had told him. "It keeps the right people in and the not-so-right people out, if you know what I mean." Parker wanted to live in an exclusive area and could certainly afford it, but he didn't want PJ to grow up in a neighborhood where he'd be the only little black boy on the block.

Parker nodded his head, realizing that because of *who* Victoria was married to, the neighborhood in which she lived was probably of no consequence. "Whose decision was it to move there, yours or his?" he asked, assuming that more than likely it had been Ted's.

Victoria knew what he was implying and immediately became defensive. "It was a joint decision."

Parker was quiet, simply nodding his head again in reply to her guarded response.

"What does that mean?" she asked.

He shrugged his shoulders. "I didn't say a word."

"You didn't have to, I know that look…nodding your head like you know my business."

Parker chuckled, holding up his hands in surrender. "Don't get salty with me. Obviously there's some tension behind where you chose to live, and I suspect it's for the same reason I decided not to buy there a few years ago," he said. "You're living on the guess who's coming to dinner block, am I right?"

When Victoria and Ted had first talked about where they would live and raise their children, Ted automatically chose with good reason, to look in the very best neighborhoods. Victoria knew it was a perfectly normal thing to do, and given the amount of wealth they possessed it was logical. But the thing that Ted had never taken into consideration was the very issue she'd been concerned about and had dealt with all her life—race and class.

As a white man of wealth and privilege, Ted never gave a second thought about where he lived, worked, or socialized. It was a natural entitlement that had been a part of his constitution; it was a way of life. He never had to worry about how his race would impact or affect his experiences, and he'd taken for granted that his children wouldn't have to either. But Victoria knew differently. Even though she'd grown up in the vast comfort and privilege of an upper-class environment, she was black, so she understood what it was like to be the only one. And being someone who shared her same skin, no matter the difference in the gradient hue of their complexions, she knew that Parker understood what it was like too. "Black is black," her fair-skinned mother always said.

Issues like this made Victoria wonder from time to time how different her life might be if Ted was black. She knew that she wouldn't have to debate the issue of race, and that although being married to a black man wouldn't mean their relationship would be perfect, in a very real and powerful way it would almost guarantee they'd share a common place of understanding.

It was one of the things she admired about Parker. He was firm in his racial identity and how to operate in the world based upon it; he was a strong black man. She remembered how he'd always taken pride in his African heritage, even if his family wasn't as enamored by their darker roots. The Brightwoods were a color-conscious clan, just as her mother's family had been.

Parker wanted to make sure that his son was secure in who he was and as he'd told Victoria over lunch, he'd already taken PJ on a trip to the motherland last year. He was teaching his son about his rich ancestral culture through his extensive collection of African art, authentic masks and history books on the continent and its people. It was something Ted had never thought to introduce Alexandria to, but then again, neither had she, and for her part Victoria felt a particular burden of guilt.

She hadn't pushed the envelope on race and culture nearly as much as she thought she should have. Her first real introduction into the complicated waters had surfaced around Jack and Jill, and she saw how that had evolved into a game of push-pull.

Parker could see that Victoria was uncomfortable, and that her mind had wondered off to a distant place. He wanted to kick himself for breaking the seductive mood that seemed to vanish before he could save it, and he made a mental note not to bring up any subject again that involved her husband. "I made an assumption, and if I was wrong I apologize," he offered.

"No need to apologize."

They stared at each other in silence. Parker reached for Victoria's hand and caressed it, trying to recapture the heat before it was too late. He rubbed the inside of her forearm, sliding his finger across the small scar that stuck out against her smooth skin.

"It's from an IV gone terribly wrong," Victoria grimaced. "I had complications delivering Alexandria…one of the nurses in training had a little practice on my arm and…"

"I know…."

Victoria looked at him, studying his eyes. "How do you know?"

Parker held her hand as he reached back into the past and told her about the nightly visits he'd made to her hospital room after Alexandria's birth. He told her how he'd reviewed her chart every night, and that he'd asked the staff not to mention his presence. "I wanted to take care of you, but I also didn't want to cause you any troubles. I knew the situation, and all I wanted…all I prayed for, was for you to get well."

Victoria didn't know what to say. The memory she'd thought was a dream had actually been real, and now, a very live Parker was standing in front of her, making her desires and fears come to life. "I remember you leaving my room one night, but I thought I had dreamed it."

"Victoria, I didn't know how to love you the right way back then, and I apologize for that now."

Victoria stared at him, touched by the thought of Parker's care. He leaned over and kissed her gently as she parted her lips, welcoming his mouth to hers and his hands around her waist. He whispered into her ear. "Let's go to The Mansion on Peachtree."

Chapter 12

Let The Chips Fall Where They May...

Less than ten minutes after arriving at the ultra-luxury boutique hotel, Parker called Victoria on her cell to let her know that he'd gotten the room. She hung up the phone and closed her eyes, still feeling the warmth of his touch and the revelation he'd shared. She knew her connection to him was something that couldn't be denied.

Minutes later, Victoria found herself standing in the elevator, riding up to the tenth floor. Her nerves were surprisingly calm given the situation, and it made her feel awkward in an off kind of way.

When she reached the room, she stood frozen in front of the door. She thought about her life, her marriage, and the little voice inside her head that vacillated between exercising restraint and doing what she wanted. She thought about the weight of the moment and the impact it would have on everything once it ended. She thought about the very real and true desires she'd pushed to the back of her heart and mind; fear not allowing her to fully acknowledge her true emotions until now. And she thought about the man on the other side of the door who she'd loved in another lifetime.

Her logical mind told her that she was about to cross a line of demarcation that would eventually run jagged. But her heart and her body led her to knock on the door and let the chips fall where they may.

When Parker greeted her, the warm smile on his face made Victoria forget about the worries rumbling in her stomach. He ushered her inside the plush room, glad that she hadn't backed out. Victoria stood near the edge of the king-size bed, looking down at the elegance of the comforter's muted tapestry and the reach of Parker's hand as he took hold of hers.

"I'm glad you're here," he said.

Parker brought her into his embrace. Their hungry mouths began to kiss while their hands searched each others bodies, exploring what was both familiar and altogether new. Victoria enjoyed the softness of his lips, letting his tongue roll around the inside of her mouth. She allowed her body to sink into his as he held her tightly, roaming his hands across the bend of her back and the curve of her hips. He knew how to handle her, and it made her moan, anticipating the pleasure she was sure would come.

Slowly, they removed each other's clothes, reacquainting themselves, standing before one another, naked and exposed.

"I need to see you again," Parker whispered. "I mean *really* see you, Victoria."

He backed away at arms length, taking a slow and thorough inspection of the woman he'd been craving. It was a sight he'd reminisced and envisioned many times over the years and now felt honored to see. He took in the newfound beauty that his eyes were seeing for the very first time. He moved her hair behind her shoulders, gliding his hands across the smooth contours of her pronounced collarbone, and over the delicate rise of her full, soft breasts. He saw that their perky perfection had diminished slightly, no doubt a combined result of breastfeeding and age. He smiled, letting his fingertips trace the dark outline of her erect nipples as he tweaked them, making them stand on edge. He allowed his hands to travel down to her waist as he knelt on bended knee before her.

Victoria looked down at him. "Yet another memento from my delivery. It's my forever reminder of motherhood," she whispered, watching as Parker slid his index finger across the smiley-face shaped scar that rested under her lower abdomen. Her waist was still small and trim, but the cesarean cut had left her with an ever so tiny tummy bulge that one could only see if they were in the position where Parker presently sat.

He nodded and smiled, enjoying the full sensuality of what her body had always been, and had now become. He kissed her stomach, then circled his tongue inside her navel. Victoria let out a small gasp, her legs already starting to tremble. He revisited her scar, gently kissing his way from one side of it to the other, letting her know that he appreciated the special brand of beauty that only motherhood could bring to a woman. "You're breathtaking," he whispered, looking up at her, licking the wetness that had begun to drip down the inside of her thigh.

Victoria tilted her head back and closed her eyes, holding his head against her pubic bone. She trailed her fingers over the slickness of his freshly shaven scalp, allowing herself to give in to the moment they were about to share.

Parker stood to his feet and led Victoria to the bed, guiding her down to the center of the soft mattress. He lowered himself in front of her, looking into her eyes. She laid back, relaxed, and spread her legs, like an involuntary reaction. She took a deep breath, opening herself up to him. They never lost eye contact as Parker began his journey between the meeting of her thighs.

Her body tingled when his mouth covered her moist middle, lapping up her wetness in gentle, hungry gulps. He parted her lips with his fingers, granting him greater access to suck her quivering folds before sinking his tongue deep inside her. The moments of second guessing she'd initially fretted over faded away as he removed her doubts with each swipe of his tongue. She could only whimper as he kissed, and plied, and nibbled away at her sensitive flesh, creating tiny bursts of bright light that made her want to scream out loud as she bucked against his mouth.

Parker licked his lips, savoring the taste of her in his mouth and on his chin. His tongue followed her rhythm as she grinded against his gentle lapping, making sure that he ate her dry. He gave her one last lick before making his way back up to her hardened nipples, squeezing one while gently sucking the other, enjoying the feel of a different part of her flesh inside his mouth.

After a few minutes he pulled away. "Victoria?"

She couldn't hear him because she was lost, caught up in the euphoria of his passion.

"Victoria…Baby, look at me," Parker asked, almost begging.

Victoria had to concentrate so she could focus on the words coming out of his mouth instead of the lustful pleasure she was receiving from it. Finally, she realized that he was calling her name, demanding her attention. When she looked into his eyes she knew what he was both asking and saying without him having to utter a word. She knew because her eyes spoke the same language and the same feeling. It had been lying in wait, ready for this moment.

"I've never stopped loving you," he said.

Victoria trembled. Her words were caught in her throat and she couldn't push them out. So instead she gave him all she could at the moment. "Just love me right now."

Parker was already two steps ahead of her. Victoria looked on with surprise as he reached over to the nightstand and grabbed the small, plastic package lying next to the alarm clock. She didn't know when he'd found the time to take the condom out of his wallet and place it there, but she was glad he was so efficient. She watched as he leaned back, sliding the super magnum latex glove over his rigid hardness. She'd almost forgotten his impressive size, both in length and thickness, and now she was ready to take the trip down memory lane.

Parker repositioned himself on top of her, rubbing his pelvis against her wetness. Everything about her turned him on. She was the only woman he could truly say he'd ever loved. He knew that second chances rarely came around, so he was determined that this time he'd make the most of his good fortune. *No fuck ups. Show her that you've changed. Show her your true heart. Love her the way she deserves to be loved,* he told himself as he looked into her eyes.

The moment of first entry was always the most powerful, and as Parker slid into her, it was as hot and as sweet as he'd imagined it would be. He remembered what Victoria liked, so he took his time filling her with his entire length, rocking her back and forth as her body obeyed his rhythm.

She kissed the side of his neck, clinging to the satisfying fullness pulsating below her waist, in between her legs. She moaned as he increased the intensity of his penetration and the speed of his thrusts. Their voices saturated the room with lustful cries. Parker wanted to consume her and she obliged him. He arched his back and plunged deeper, hitting the magic spot that he remembered so well. Victoria gasped. *"Oh…Parker,"* she panted, nearly helpless to his rhythm.

"Is that what you like?"

"You know it is," she said in a breathless whisper.

He continued, giving it to her slow and steady, just the way he knew she wanted it.

She placed her hands at the base of his lower back, grazing her nails against his muscular behind. She hugged him tightly as she moved her hips to greet his fluid strokes. When she matched his rhythm beat for beat, it was Parker's turn to call out, *"Ooohhh, Baby."* He tried to hold on because he wanted to please her before his appetite was satisfied, but he wasn't sure how much longer he could resist the sweet sensation.

He got his wish when he felt her movements slow to a crawl and her body tense around his. Victoria felt the heavy pull between her legs, like an internal ball about to burst. She allowed the powerful orgasm to flow out like the wetness smeared against her leg. *"Ooooohhhhhhh, Yeeeesss,"* were the words she repeated over and over into his ear, and it was all that was needed. Parker was right behind her with a chant of his own.

They spent the next few hours exchanging gentle kisses and six years worth of information about their lives and details they'd tip-toed over when they had lunch. They lay entangled in each others arms, their bodies swirled together like the stripes on a candy cane.

Victoria couldn't believe the change in Parker, and she wondered if they'd stayed together would he still be the changed man he was today? Would he still be proud of her entrepreneurial spirit and dreams, or would he have crushed them because of his own ideas about success and his selfish wants?

The man caressing her skin and stroking her hair admired and respected her business accomplishments, citing again how wrong he'd been for not being more supportive when she needed him to be. The man holding her close and kissing her gently seemed to put her concerns before his own, instead of trying to control things in his favor. The old Parker she knew would have balked at the very idea of having to sneak around or share her with another man. But the one on whose shoulder her head now rested, told her that he'd take whatever opportunity he was given to be with her, and be thankful for it.

As Victoria lay in Parker's arms, a myriad of emotions ran through her mind. But the most unsettling of all her thoughts was that she was already beginning to regret what she'd done.

Impulse?...

Parker wanted Victoria to remain in bed with him for the rest of the night, but she told him that she couldn't. She had to get back home.

Even though Victoria had spoken to Ted earlier that evening, there was a chance he might call back to make sure she'd gotten home safely from working late at the office, and she knew she couldn't be in Parker's arms when her phone rang. "I have to leave," she said.

Parker sat up beside her, grazing her left shoulder with his lips. She trembled when she felt his mouth against her skin. "When can I see you again?" he asked.

This was one of the things that Victoria had thought about when she was standing outside the hotel room door—what it all meant and how they would operate once the moment ended. She knew it was only natural that Parker would want to see her again, and the reality was that she wanted to see him again too. But just as she knew deep down that a part of her would probably always love him, she also knew that she couldn't sleep with him again. The guilt was already eating at her. She'd made the same mistake that Debbie had made and had warned her against, and now she'd have to follow her own advice that she'd given her friend.

Victoria bit down on her bottom lip, casting her eyes away from his. "This can't happen again."

Parker shook his head, about to say something but Victoria stopped him. "We rekindled some old feelings that were never put to rest. But we're different people now, with different lives, and new responsibilities."

"Baby, we may have different lives, but we're the same two people who loved each other then and still love each other now. You can't deny that."

"I have a husband."

"Who you never should have married in the first damn place."

A moment of silence fell between them before Victoria spoke again. "Regardless of what you think about my marriage, the bottom line is that I have a husband who's going to be calling me soon, probably telling me how difficult it's been for him to return home knowing that he'll never be able to see his mother again."

Parker lowered his head and let out a sigh. "I'm sorry about that." Although Ted was far from one of his favorite people, Parker felt compassion for the man at the thought of loosing his mother, and for that reason he let it go.

He watched Victoria as she dressed, carefully putting on her clothes. He pulled on his boxers and t-shirt. "I reserved this room for the entire weekend. You're coming back tomorrow, aren't you?"

She ignored his statement and his question, slipping on her sling back sandals as she grabbed her handbag, preparing to leave.

Parker walked over to where she was now standing. "Can I call you tomorrow?"

"Did you hear a word I just said?" Victoria asked, looking at him with concern. She knew from past experience how persistent Parker could be, and she didn't want him causing trouble, although she'd already set the barometer high in that area by sleeping with him in the first place. "Parker, I'm already having serious regrets about what we've done…we can't do this again. I know we're going to run into each other from time to time at events for our kids, so we need to cool it and let this little impulse fade."

"Impulse?" Parker placed his arms around Victoria's waist, drawing her in close as he rubbed his pelvis against hers. When she didn't move away or resist, he knew he had her. "You don't mean that. I can look into your eyes and tell that you don't believe what you're saying."

This time Victoria took action. "Parker, stop." She released herself from his embrace. "I've got to go. And please, don't try to call me or get in touch with me…please. Let's just let this pass."

"All right," Parker smiled, stepping away. "I'll just wait for you to call me."

Victoria eyed him with a mixture of contempt and lust. She knew he wasn't trying to be cocky, this was just who he was. As he stood before her half-dressed, he looked gorgeous, confident, and wildly dangerous. All she could do was force her feet to move as she walked out the door.

Twenty minutes later Victoria pulled her car into her garage. She walked through her big, empty house, wanting her mind to free her of what she'd just done. She'd been fantasizing and secretly wanting Parker for the last six years, and now that she'd had him she felt a new world of worries flood her soul. "Damn, that old saying is true," she whispered aloud as she headed upstairs. "When you look for trouble, you find it."

You Want Answers....

It was bright and early on Saturday morning as Ted found himself sitting at Hattie McPherson's breakfast table. He was still a little sleepy because he'd arrived in town late last night on a half-empty flight into Jackson, Mississippi. He'd found her house without much problem. When he pulled his Enterprise rental car into the driveway of Ms. Hattie's neatly kept brick home, she was standing on the porch, waiting to greet him with Southern hospitality.

Just like Ted, Ms. Hattie was an early riser, so having him over for breakfast at the crack of dawn fit perfectly into her schedule. She had a busy day planned with a full slate of activities, from a meeting with her seniors group that afternoon, to her bridge game with her Order of the Eastern Star group later that evening. And in between she had errands to run and people to visit. Yes, Ms. Hattie was a busy bee!

For a woman of nearly eighty-two, the retired school teacher was as spry and in as good of shape as anyone half her age. And even though she was only five-foot two and barely weighed one hundred pounds, she possessed the type of presence that made one sit up and take notice. Mother Nature had been good to Ms. Hattie, blessing her with the kind of brown skin that stood the test of time, and if it were not for her full head of silver hair and the few minor wrinkles that kissed her eyes and mouth, one would never be able to guess her true age.

Looking at Ms. Hattie made Ted think about the saying he'd heard Victoria and her family repeat whenever they saw another black person whose looks defied their age, *black don't crack!*

Ted sat patiently at the neatly set table as Ms. Hattie poured him a cup of steaming coffee. "You're just like me," she smiled. "An early riser who likes your coffee as strong as it'll come."

"Yes, ma'am," Ted nodded. He watched as she walked back to the stove in the kitchen. "Are you sure you don't need any help?" he called out.

Ms. Hattie fanned her hand, placing it on her tiny hip. "No child, I raised six children, ten of my nineteen grandkids, and buried three husbands. Handlin' breakfast is like a walk in the park."

Ted was in awe of the little dynamo. When he'd first spotted her sitting in the back of the church at his mother's funeral, with a woman who he now knew was her oldest daughter, he had no doubt she was a direct link to the secret his parents had kept. Then after reading the letter she'd handed him at the cemetery, her presence there made perfect sense. She'd made the trip as soon as she received the call from Abe Brookstein, that Carolyn had passed.

The delicious smell of food and seasonings wafted through the house as Ms. Hattie scurried about in her tiny kitchen. Ten minutes later she sat a plate in front of Ted that was filled with down-home goodness. Thick, hickory smoked bacon, scrambled eggs, cheese grits, home fries, fried apples, and home-made biscuits with strawberry preserves. Ted stared at the heaping plate of food, sure that the meal contained enough calories, fat, and cholesterol to give him a mild heart attack. But since the kind old woman was gracious enough to welcome him into her home and prepare a huge meal that was made with tender loving care, he had no intention of refusing one morsel of Ms. Hattie's food.

Ted bowed his head as Ms. Hattie said grace, something that Victoria had gotten him into the habit of doing over the years since they'd been married. "This is delicious," he complimented, diving into his plate, filling his mouth with a forkful of eggs.

Ms. Hattie smiled, pleased that he was enjoying the meal. "Well, thank you much."

"No....thank you."

"It's my pleasure, son. Carol Lynn used to send me pictures of you, Lilly and Charlie when you children were growing up. It's good to finally sit down and break bread with you."

"I really appreciate you seeing me."

Ms. Hattie stared Ted in the eye, cutting straight to the chase. "How could I not....you want answers and I'm here to give them to you." She wasn't one to mince words or waste time. "I never thought that Carol Lynn and Charles should've kept the truth from everyone for all these years, especially not their own children. But it was their choice, and I respected their wishes."

Ted listened in near disbelief as Ms. Hattie told him about the life that his parents had kept a secret for over sixty years. At times he felt pity, anger, and complete astonishment as Ms. Hattie filled in the missing pieces of the puzzle that made up the lives of two people he now realized he'd never really known.

Ted had seen, heard, and experienced a great deal in his fifty-two years on earth, and he didn't think there was anything or anyone that could rattle him. But the last few weeks had proven how wrong he'd been. Death had brought about a new life, and it was one that he wasn't sure he wanted to start living.

"I know this is a lot for you to take in all at once," Ms. Hattie said, giving Ted a pat on the shoulder as she cleared the breakfast table of their dishes. She sighed, shaking her head. "Honestly, it's a blessing and a curse that Carol Lynn finally told you the truth."

"What do you mean?"

"The truth always cleanses the soul," she said. "But now that you know it, you've got to decide what you want to do with it. Seems to me that's a heavy burden to bear. On the one hand, you can go on living your happy life with that beautiful wife and little girl of yours, just the way it is now. Or you can kick over the apple cart and see how your lives will change."

Ted nodded, rubbing the stubble under his chin that had started to form.

Ms. Hattie continued. "Your parents lived their lives wrapped up in their lie for so long that Carol Lynn could've easily carried it to her grave and not a soul besides me would've been the wiser. But she didn't do that. For whatever reason, she decided to tell you, and leave you with the knowledge of something she wasn't strong enough to face herself," she said, taking a deep breath. She raised her head, looking up at the ceiling. "Sometimes living in the truth can feel just like dying."

Ted looked at Ms. Hattie as though she'd been reading his mind. He didn't want to resent his own parents, especially not his mother. But the more he learned about her past, what she'd done, and how his father had helped her hide it, the more he grew to distain the fraudulent life they'd both led and the burden it now placed upon his shoulders. He thought their actions and decisions had been selfish and reckless. "Why did my mother do it?" Ted asked in genuine frustration.

Ms. Hattie sat back down in her chair and thought for a few minutes before she attempted an answer. "I guess she thought it was a matter of survival. Son, I knew your mother and believe me, it ate her up inside, always having to lie and keep things bottled up. Imagine what it was like for her…living every day in fear that what she did might catch up with her."

Ted wanted to, but he felt no sympathy. "It was a life she willingly chose…and my father too," he said, looking into Ms. Hattie's wise old eyes.

She nodded her head, but didn't say a word because what he'd said was true, and it was the very thing she'd often thought herself.

After spending the entire morning with Ms. Hattie, Ted finally left. He agreed to stay in touch and promised to let her know when, or even if, he decided to share the secret with his family.

Before Ted closed Ms. Hattie's door, he handed her the envelope that Abe Brookstein had entrusted in his care before he left Boston. "You deserve much more. Friendship is invaluable," he said, giving Ms. Hattie a warm hug and a kiss on her cheek. He truly meant it and didn't think the one million dollar check he'd just placed in her hand was nearly enough to repay over seven decades of loyalty.

As Ted drove away from Ms. Hattie's house he thought about all the things she'd told him. He'd found out more about his parents in the span of a few hours than he'd known his entire life.

Later that afternoon he returned to his hotel. He was mentally weary from the thoughts and guilt that plagued his mind. Sitting at the small desk in his room, he stared at his computer screen as if the work at hand would take care of itself. Other than the uncertain weeks following Alexandria's birth, this was the first time in Ted's life that he couldn't bring himself to focus on the important tasks before him. There were urgent ViaTech matters that required his attention, but he knew they would have to wait until he could clear his thoughts of the clutter floating around inside his head.

His mind raced with memories that until now had never really meant anything to him. But with his newfound knowledge, he finally understood the meaning behind some of the things his mother and father had said and done when he was growing up. Now it made sense to him why she'd always been so secretive about her past, why she'd never socialized outside of a very few and select group of friends, and why his father was so protective of her. He remembered the warning she'd given him before he married his first wife. "Theodore, you really don't know a lot about this girl, or her family for that matter…You never know someone until you look closely into their background. Trust me on this. I know what I'm talking about," she'd said.

His mother's eerie foreboding had sent a chill down his spine even back then. And now he knew exactly what she meant. He shook his head, wondering how she and his father could have gone through life masquerading a fraud.

Ted moved his laptop to the side and opened the large envelope that Ms. Hattie had given him. It contained several old photos and hand written letters, all dated before he'd been born. It all seemed like an incredibly crazy dream, but when he looked at the black and white pictures and the faded papers, he knew it was real.

His mind rushed back to the past again, remembering how Carolyn used to tell him and his siblings that they were not to discuss family business with anyone outside their immediate circle.

Carolyn had instilled a sense of privacy in each of her children, but especially in Ted. With the exception of Victoria, and on occasion his friend Barry, Ted rarely, if ever, let people into his private thoughts or personal life. Marrying Victoria had opened up a new world for him, allowing him to trust another person without reservation. She was an open book, free with her emotions and giving with her love. He knew that at times his need for privacy frustrated his wife. She wanted him to share more, but he was operating from a learned behavior, still trying to navigate his new course.

His mother had taught him at an early age that information was power, and that as long as he held information to himself, no one could use anything against him. Confidentiality had been her brand, and reputation and honor had been his father's mantra. He wanted to laugh at his parent's teachings, knowing it had all been a farce to cover up the truth.

At that moment he needed clarity and peace, and he longed for the one person who could give him both. He reached for his cell and dialed Victoria.

"Hello," she said, practically yawning into the phone.

"V, you sound exhausted. Did you rest at all last night?"

"Um…a little."

"I bet you didn't leave your office until after midnight, did you?" Ted knew that Victoria could spend hours on end at Divine Occasions. He'd voiced his concerns more than once that even though her office was in a safe area, he didn't like the idea of her being out in the business park all alone at night.

She hesitated in her response, and it told him that he'd been right. "V, I don't think it's a good idea for you to be out there late at night."

"Sometimes that's when I can get the most work done, when it's late and it's quiet," she said as she bit her lower lip, feeling a mountain of guilt creep up.

"What are your plans for the day?"

"I'm going to the grocery store, the cleaners, and then a few shops…the usual routine. But right now I'm just lounging around, trying to catch up on some sleep. I'm actually still in bed."

Ted knew it was highly unusual for his super energetic wife to be in the house on a Saturday afternoon, let alone in bed. This had to mean that she'd reached her limit. He wished he could be there for her because he knew his mother's death had caused a deluge of stress for her as well. She'd been restless and worried, losing sleep because she was concerned about his mental state as well as that of their daughter's. And he knew she was still obsessing about the explanation he'd given her surrounding his mother's secret, not fully convinced that he was telling the truth.

Ted didn't want Victoria to doubt him. He knew she was a smart woman, and could see when something wasn't right, especially in matters affecting her family. And he knew she wasn't going to let it rest until she eventually got to the bottom of things.

"How're you doing?" she asked, sounding a little more awake.

"I'm fine. Just sitting here in the hotel going over some reports."

"Have you and Lilly gotten everything taken care of?"

Ted didn't miss a beat. "Um, yeah, pretty much."

"She must really be glad you're there. It helps when you don't have to go through difficult times alone."

Again, he played his role on cue. "Yes, we've gotten a lot of mother's financial matters straightened out. Lilly's much more comfortable with things now."

"Hey, speaking of Lilly, are you going to see her later this evening?"

His next answer was one that he could be completely honest about. "I hadn't planned to…why?"

"I never properly thanked her for getting Alexandria that beautiful baby doll when we were there, and I was hoping you could tell her. But on second thought, I should probably call her myself. That would be the more hospitable thing to do."

"Oh, don't worry about it," Ted replied in a smooth, even voice. "You need to get some rest, I'll relay the message to Lilly this evening."

"You sure?"

"Absolutely," he reiterated, not wanting to run the risk that Victoria might call his sister and find out that he'd left Boston yesterday.

"Thanks, that's one less thing I have to do."

For once, Ted was grateful that his wife was too exhausted to take charge of things. He quickly ushered her off the phone before she could ask more questions that would force him to tell more lies.

Ted hated deceiving Victoria, but for now it was what he felt he had to do. He walked over to his attaché and pulled out the thick manila envelope that held secrets to a hidden past. He opened it and placed the pictures and letters that Ms. Hattie had been kind enough to give him inside. He knew he had to find a safer hiding place for the information. He shook his head, thinking about how supremely ironic the situation had become, because despite his anger at what his parents had done, one of the first things he planned to do when he returned home was store the envelope in a safe deposit box.

Chapter 13

Getting Rid Of Her Evidence…

Victoria glanced at the clock as she rolled over in her big empty bed. She couldn't believe it was two in the afternoon. After she'd gotten home in the wee hours of the morning, she set the alarm clock so she could wake up a few hours later to call her mother and talk to Alexandria. She wanted to check in and see how things were going before they started their day of Saturday errands. Her parents still rose early, just like her child, so she knew if she wanted to speak to them she'd have to force herself from her sleep.

After waking briefly and hearing that all was well with her daughter, Victoria fell back into a deep sleep and hadn't stirred again until Ted's call pulled her from her slumber. She'd been knocked out for hours, and it had been the longest sleep she'd had in weeks. Her body had been aching for rest. But instead of feeling refreshed, she felt weighed down because the depth of her guilt was taking hold and sinking in.

She stretched her legs and sat up in bed, willing herself to rise as she headed to the shower. She stood under the stream of warm, flowing water, hoping it would soothe her mind. She grabbed her netted bath sponge and squirted it full of shower gel, lathering her body as she washed the remainder of Parker's scent from her skin.

She stepped out of the shower and wrapped a fluffy towel around her body. She walked over to the edge of the bed and thought about the night before. "What have I done?" she said to an empty room. She slipped into her robe and quickly stripped the sheets off her bed, holding them up to her nose, smelling the citrus-spice fragrance that was Parker's signature. She walked downstairs and stuffed them into the washing machine, getting rid of her evidence like a guilty person trying to cover up a crime.

She felt terrible about lying to Ted, and it was the first time in their relationship that she had been blatantly untruthful with him. This was more than a simple lie or a random omission, this was the ultimate betrayal. He was going through so much and a cheating wife was the last thing he needed to add to his loss. She felt low, hanging her head in shame as though peering eyes were watching her.

An hour later her cell phone rang. She looked at the caller ID and saw that it was Parker. She let it ring until *missed call* flashed across the screen. "Oh, Lord," she sighed. "I should've known better."

Victoria made herself a cup of chamomile tea to calm her nerves, and relaxed in the family room while she read the days paper. But the red light flashing on her BlackBerry called out to her to listen to Parker's message. When she clicked the keys she saw that he hadn't left a voice message, but he'd sent her a text.

Parker: How r u 2day

Victoria sat in pause for a moment, then decided to answer back.

Victoria: I'm good & u

Parker: Will b betr once I c u. I'm @ the hotel, waiting 4 u

Victoria: I told u we can't do this again. It has 2 stop. Goodbye

After a few minutes passed, Victoria glanced at her phone again. She was glad the red message light wasn't flashing. She finished her cup of tea, skimmed through the rest of the newspaper, and prayed that Parker would keep his distance.

No Matter The Cost...

Later that evening, Parker sat alone in his living room. The melodic sounds of his Earl Klugh CD floated through his Bose speakers as he reclined on one end of his leather sectional sofa. He propped his leg up on his mahogany coffee table, taking a sip of his favorite brandy as he stared down at a copy of the *Journal of the American Medical Association*, that sat in his lap. He was trying to concentrate on an article about new findings in the area of endothelial function, but all he could think about was Victoria.

It had been less than twenty-four hours since he'd seen her and he was already missing her touch. He thought about the night they'd shared and it brought a smile to his face. Not only had they made beautiful love, they'd connected emotionally, setting the stage for what was to come. He'd opened up his complete life for her inspection, sharing information about everything from his forgettable relationships of the recent past to his current dilemma of balancing a demanding work schedule and fatherhood.

Then it was his turn to listen to her as she told him about her new life. He paid close attention as she talked about the joys and pains of running her business and raising her daughter. He picked up right away on her reluctance to talk about the details of her marriage. He knew there had to be trouble in her relationship, otherwise she would-n't have been lying in his arms. But he decided to let it rest because he didn't want to be the one who introduced her husband into the conversation. So instead of asking the questions he was curious to know the answers to, he enjoyed the few hours they had left together.

The night had been exhilarating, and although they'd only been able to spend it in the confines of a hotel room, it was fine with him because he planned to change his course of action. He'd decided he was going to take her out for lunch the next day and maybe even catch a movie, then end the evening back at his place. He knew the last part of his plan would take some persuading, but he wanted Victoria to start getting acquainted with his home. Unfortunately, she'd thrown a glitch in his plans when she refused to see him.

As he put the magazine away and finished the last of the brandy in his glass, his mind returned to his curiosity about the state of Victoria's marriage. He knew it had to be bad, given the fact that she was willing to engage in an affair. But the particular cause of her unhappiness was still unclear, and he wanted to find out the details.

Although she'd refused to see him today, he didn't let it deter him. He knew this was fresh, and that Victoria had to come into it slowly. Ending a marriage, especially when a child and considerable financial assets were involved, could be a difficult proposition. But after being with her again and seeing how right they were for each other, Parker knew he had to take action and do what he should've done from the beginning—fight to win her heart, no matter the cost. He'd already waited long enough to have her and he had no intension of prolonging things any further.

Parker smiled as he thought about the new life they'd have together. After the Jack and Jill playdate, he wasn't surprised when PJ talked about his new friend, Alexandria. "She's nice, Dad," PJ had told him. Right away he knew she was Victoria's child. He remembered her name from when he'd seen her years ago in the neo-natal unit. The two children had hit it off immediately, and PJ had already asked if Alexandria could come over and play.

Parker didn't take his son's affinity for Alexandria lightly. Unlike him, PJ was quiet and introverted by nature. He was a loving, but sensitive child who didn't make new friends easily. But he'd warmed to Alexandria like they were the best of buddies. Parker knew that the two would have no problems adjusting to a blended family, and ironically, they were only one day apart in age and looked like they could be twins. From their light complexions, to their silky black hair, deep set eyes, and impressive height for children their age, PJ and Alexandria looked very much like brother and sister. Parker smiled again. Their instant family was picture perfect.

Somebody's Gonna Wind Up Dead...

It was almost nine o'clock later that night and Victoria was thinking about the conversation she'd had with Ted earlier that day. Their exchange had been brief and she could tell that something wasn't right by the sound of his voice. At first she thought it might have been her own guilt causing her mind to fixate on things that weren't there. But as she listened to him talk about his day, taking care of family business with Lilly and then returning to his hotel room to tackle ViaTech issues, her gut told her that something was simmering below the surface. She knew her husband well, and she was almost certain that whatever the problem, all roads led back to his mother's secret.

Each time she steered the conversation toward anything involving his activities in Boston, his tone shifted. She had a feeling that he was lying to her. She wanted to push deeper but she knew it was a waste of time. It was hard enough to get him to share information face to face, so she knew she wasn't going to get anywhere over the phone. Plus, in her guilt-ridden state she knew she was in no position to demand the truth from him, so she didn't mind when he quickly hurried her off the line.

She sat in her dimly lit family room, drinking a glass of wine and devouring a handful of Godiva chocolates as she thought about the mistake she'd made with Parker. She was regretful to the point of feeling tortured by what she'd done, and she couldn't keep her turmoil bottled up any longer. She needed her touchstone, so she called Tyler.

He picked up after a few rings. "What's up. You lonely over there all by yourself?"

"How'd you guess?"

Tyler laughed. "Why else would you be calling me on a Saturday night? I know you miss your man and your baby, so you're callin' your old stand-by. But that's all right. That's what I'm hear for."

Victoria sighed into the phone. "Can you talk?"

"Uh-oh, hold up. You sound funny. Did something happen?"

"That's an understatement."

Tyler took a seat on his sofa and readied himself for what he sensed was going to be bad news. "Are you at home?"

"Yeah."

Tyler shifted the phone to his other ear. "Okay, talk to me."

Victoria didn't know where to begin. She was silent for a second before she spoke. "I think I've gotten myself into something that I'm not sure I can get out of."

"This is about Parker, isn't it?"

Victoria stammered. "Um, yeah."

Damnit, Tyler said to himself, shaking his head. He knew what Victoria was about to tell him, and being the friend he was, he knew he had to deal with her straight. "Before you say anything, let me throw something out there, okay?"

"All right."

Tyler's voice was full of dead seriousness. "If you decide to sleep with him, or if you already have, don't tell a soul about it. Don't open your mouth to anyone, not Denise, not Debbie, not your mom...not even me. That's the kind of shit you carry to the grave...do you hear me?"

"But, Tyler..."

"I'm serious, Victoria."

Victoria's voice began to shake as a small tear escaped her eye. "But I need to let this out because it's eating me up inside"

Tyler let out a deep breath. "Please don't cry."

"I can't help it."

"You want me to come over?"

"Please."

A half hour later, Tyler was sitting on the other end of Victoria's couch, drinking a coke and listening to his friend pour out information that his ears didn't want to hear. He had never liked Parker, and the fact that not only had the man come back into Victoria's life, but that she'd slept with him, was a situation that he knew could only be described as a nightmare waiting to greet daylight.

Tyler had been afraid this would happen. From the moment Victoria had told him about running into Parker, he knew that trouble was on the horizon. He'd tried to calm her fears and push them aside by telling her that what she'd been feeling for Parker was fleeting, and would eventually pass. In retrospect, it was what he'd inwardly hoped. He remembered the love that Victoria had felt for Parker, but he also remembered how the bastard had hurt her.

"I feel so bad," Victoria said, looking Tyler in the eye.

He sat his coke can on the coaster atop the coffee table and rubbed his hand over his closely cropped hair. "I'mma be honest with you. This is a fucked up situation."

"Tell me something I don't already know."

"This *cannot* and *will not* end well. You know that don't you?"

Victoria was silent, her head bent with a complicated mixture of fear and shame.

Tyler scooted closer to her on the sofa. "I wish you hadn't told me, but now that you have it's my responsibility as your friend to give you the best advice I can. From this point forward you can't see him again, Victoria. I'm serious. Leave his slick ass the hell alone. Pull Alexandria out of Jack and Jill and register her at a new school if you have to."

Victoria's eyes grew big. "But, Tyler..."

He cut her off, holding up his hand, "But nothing. Listen to me," he implored. Tyler reached for her hand, holding it in his. "Do you think Parker's gonna be quiet about this? Do you think he's gonna just go away?"

"I told him it was over."

"I don't think you realize the gravity of what's going on here. If Ted finds out that you fucked around on him, and that it was with Parker of all people, somebody's gonna wind up dead."

Victoria's back stiffened.

"This is a very dangerous game you're playing," Tyler said, shaking his head.

"Ted would never kill anyone."

Tyler released Victoria's hand. "Never, ever, say what somebody won't do. Did you ever think you'd cheat on your husband?"

Victoria could only shake her head no.

"But you did, right?"

She couldn't speak. All she could do was look down at her feet in silence.

"I'm not here to make you feel bad, I'm here to help you. I love you, Victoria. You're my sister, and I only want the best for you. I'd be wrong if I didn't tell you with brutal honesty what I think. I'm not being objective about this, I'm being very biased because you've got some serious shit at stake."

"I know that, Tyler."

"Do you?" he asked in frustration, raising his brow. "I don't care how strong you think Ted is, he's just a man, and he just lost his mother…his first connection to this world. You don't know what that's like, but I do, and it's not something you can easily recover from. Ted's in a very fragile state right now."

Victoria nodded and was about to speak up but Tyler cut her off.

"Do you realize that if Ted finds out that you fucked ol' boy he could snap and kill you both?"

Victoria leaned forward and stared at him. "I told you, Ted's not a violent person. He'd be mad, hurt, and angry for sure, but he would never bring physical harm to me or even dream of doing anything as drastic as killing someone, no matter how mad he got."

"There you go again with that *never* shit," Tyler huffed, shaking his head. "See, that's the reason why you don't need to be creepin' in the first place. You have no freakin' idea what you're doing. There's no telling what a man won't do if you mess with his family, his money, or his pussy, and it doesn't have to be in that order. Victoria, I'm very, very concerned for you."

He was telling her the same thing she'd told Debbie. "Tyler, you're scaring me."

"Good, you need to be," he said, looking as serious as death. "When is Ted coming home?"

"Not until Monday afternoon."

"Okay, you have one day to regroup before he gets back."

"I don't know how I'm going to manage that. I'm a nervous wreck," Victoria said with guilt.

"You're gonna have to start by squashing lover boys plans, because trust, he's got plans for you. Parker's persistent and he's not gonna let up so you need to back him down. He's the kinda brothah you have to use force with in order to get your point across. What I'm about to advise you to do is gonna require you to be really strong and stand your ground."

"Okay, I'm listening," Victoria nodded.

Tyler knew his friend's history and pattern, and despite the fact that Victoria was curious and inquisitive, always seeking answers to questions, there was a side of her that had a tendency to avoid things instead of facing them head on. "Under any other circumstances I'd tell you to just ignore his ass until he goes away, but we both know that won't work in this situation because of his persistence and your avoidance. So you need to meet with him face to face, look him dead in his eyes, and tell him that it's over. He needs to know you're serious, and that you're not gonna let this linger. Nip it in the bud now, then first thing Monday morning you need to start looking for a new school for my niece."

Victoria sat back further into the couch, knowing that Tyler was right. She had to rectify the situation immediately. "Okay, I'll call him tomorrow and end this madness. She rested her back against the couch. "Thanks for the advice. I know what has to be done and I'm going to do it!" she said, sounding determined.

"Remember, you can't flinch, you've gotta look that muthafucker straight in his eyes and let him know that your not bullshittin'."

"I can do that."

Tyler looked at his friend, hoping she could get herself out of the catastrophe she'd created. They sat in silence for a moment, digesting their conversation before Victoria went into the kitchen and brought him back a fresh can of coke. They settled into a less tense line of conversation, changing the topic to how Alexandria was doing. It was a subject that Victoria welcomed, helping her to ease into a better frame of mind as she told him how happy she was that her daughter was enjoying her visit with her parents.

Victoria curled her legs under her hips, making herself comfortable on the couch. "Now that we've solved my problems, how're you doing?"

"Me?...I'm cool," Tyler smiled as he sat back and took another sip of his coke.

Victoria saw a glimmer in his eyes. "Um-hm...how's Samantha?"

"She's cool too?"

"So what exactly does *cool* mean?"

Tyler crossed his leg and chuckled. "Why don't you just come out and ask me if I'm hittin' it?"

"I don't want to know about your sex life," Victoria scoffed, raising her brow before asking, "Well...are you?"

They both laughed out loud. "I know what you're thinkin'," Tyler began, "and honestly, I'm as surprised about this whole thing as you probably are. I mean...I never thought I'd find a woman who would make me feel alive again, but that's what Sam does for me. I'm really feelin' her."

"It's only been two weeks," Victoria cautioned.

"Some things only take a minute."

"Damn, you're serious about her aren't you?"

Tyler nodded his head. "Maybe..."

"Wow," was all Victoria could say as she thought about Tyler's new-found relationship.

Her first concern was for his emotional safety. She knew that Samantha was wild, liked to party her ass off, and had a reputation for running through men like cheap pantyhose. And from what she remembered Parker telling her about his cousin, she seemed to gravitate toward men who either had a criminal record or were just one step ahead of the law. She preferred the thugged out, rough neck types, and Tyler definitely didn't fit into that group. Victoria didn't want her best friend to get hurt, especially after all he'd gone through. Then her second concern came to mind, the fact that Samantha was a direct link to a mistake that hit way too close to home.

"Tell me why you're so into her?" Victoria asked.

"I know what you're gettin' at. Sam's rough on the outside, but there's a real gentleness about her on the inside. She's not afraid of letting herself go to experience life to it's fullest, whether there's a chance she'll get hurt or not. She's a genuine person. She's smart, funny, and mad sexy."

"Interesting…I didn't think you were into skinny women."

"I didn't think you liked assholes, but you slept with one last night."

"That's not funny."

"Who's laughin'?"

Victoria could see that her comment hit a nerve, which let her know that Tyler's feelings for Samantha must be strong and growing. "It was just an observation. I didn't mean anything by it," she said, an attempt to smooth things over.

Tyler shrugged his shoulders. "No biggie."

"So where do you see things going between the two of you?"

"I'm flying to DC, to visit her next weekend. We're just gonna hang out, have a good time and see where it leads."

"You're prepared to have a long distance relationship?"

He smiled. "Like I said, we'll see where it leads."

"Tyler, you keep it real with me so I'm gonna keep it real with you." Victoria leaned in close to her friend. "Be careful with Samantha. Go slow and make sure this is for real."

"I'll take that under advisement. But believe me, I'm a big boy and I know what I'm doing. Besides, you have entirely too much shit on your plate to be worrying about me."

Victoria could only nod her head in agreement because he was right, and she knew she was the last person who was qualified to give anyone a shred of relationship advice. "I hear you."

A short time later, Victoria walked Tyler to the door. "Thank you for always being there for me. I'm so glad I can always count on you," she said, giving him a hug.

"I'm gonna always have your back, you know that," Tyler smiled. He gave her a hug and hoped that Victoria would be strong in the face of her current storm. But despite his hopes and best wishes, he had a

feeling that his best friend was already in over her head, and was speeding toward disaster.

No Wonder Tyler's So Scared...

After Tyler left, Victoria took a long soak in the tub. She slipped on her cream-colored, silk teddy and sprayed lavender scented body spritzer on her skin, preparing to relax her mind before heading to bed. But the harder she tried to clear her head, the more she kept thinking about the situation she'd gotten herself into and the conversation she'd had with Tyler.

It hadn't occurred to her that Ted might react violently in any situation. She'd thought about various scenarios of what might happen if he found out that she'd slept with Parker; loud arguments, possible separation, and threats of divorce being just a few of the things she knew could happen. But based on his nature, never in her wildest dreams had physical violence entered her mind. Ted was always cool and composed, especially in tough situations.

But the more she pondered the possibility, the more plausible it seemed. As it was, his behavior had started to change and she was pretty sure that he'd told her a few lies when they were in Boston, and then again when she'd spoken to him today. It was something he'd never done before, at least not to her knowledge.

Then a thought came to her, one that sent chills through her body as she crawled into bed. She remembered the hot summer night many years ago when he and Parker had nearly come to blows at her front door.

She'd just broken up with Parker after she caught him cheating, and at the time she was an emotional mess. Ted had come by to bring her dinner and comfort her, hoping to woo her in the process. After their meal when they were about to get cozy, Parker showed up unexpectantly, begging for forgiveness and a second chance. During the middle of his plea Ted had come to the door, and that's when things turned ugly. The two men cursed and threatened each other with physical violence. The only reason they hadn't rumbled like street thugs was because of her nosy neighbor who'd been taking her dog for an evening stroll. She'd seen the ensuing commotion and walked up, threatening them with pepper spray and a call to 911.

Like many things in her life, Victoria had pushed that memory to the side, but now as she lay in her empty bed full of uncertainty and fear, it was something that commanded her attention. "This isn't good," she said to herself. "No wonder Tyler's so scared." And now she knew that she should be too!

As Victoria nestled her pillow under her head, yet another thought sprang into her mind, something she'd completely overlooked. She was so focused on Ted's possible reaction that she hadn't thought about what Parker might do. He was a determined, strong-willed man, just like Ted, and he was persistent, the type who refused to take no for an answer. The very thought of how he might react once she hammered home her point tomorrow sent fear through her veins. "What have I gotten myself into?" she whispered in the dark.

Chapter 14

Whatever Road He Had To Take…

The next afternoon, Victoria found herself standing in the front entrance of the Spring Garden Chinese restaurant, waiting for Parker. It was a hole in the wall establishment, but its saving grace was a delectable menu and its virtual anonymity. It was situated in an area that was private and under the radar. Victoria hated creeping, but the fact that her short-lived affair was soon coming to an end gave her a little relief.

She looked at her watch, noting that Parker was running late. On her drive over she'd questioned whether she could trust herself to meet with him, thinking that she might be better off telling him what she had to say over the phone. But she knew she had to act just as boldly to get herself out of the situation as she had going in.

Victoria waited a few more minutes, but still no Parker. She was about to call him when he walked through the door. He looked sexy as hell in his faded jeans and Howard University t-shirt. He breezed in, confident and strong, giving her a smile that made her stomach do small flips. *Focus*, she told herself. *You know what you have to do.*

Parker gave her a warm hug that lingered a bit too long for Victoria's comfort before she finally pulled away. They walked to a table and were seated in a small booth near the back of the restaurant. After they placed their orders, Victoria looked at him as he unfolded his napkin, placing it on his lap. She wished she hadn't ordered, and now she was trying to decide whether she should tell him before or after their food came out. Now that she was sitting across from him, she was glad that she'd decided to meet him face to face. As Tyler had said, Parker was the type of man who required force and tangible proof, and even then that might not be enough.

She decided to jump straight in. "Parker, the only reason I'm meeting you here today is because I wanted to look you in your eyes and tell you that we have to end this. Please don't call, text, or email me. This has to stop."

Parker had known that Victoria was on edge from the moment he walked into the restaurant. From the stilted hug she'd given him when he greeted her, to the uncomfortable body language that had her shifting in her chair, he knew that she had something on her mind.

He didn't dilute himself. He knew that between the two of them it was she who was taking all the risks. Fidelity was important to her and it was plain to see that she was wrestling with the fact that she'd cheated on her husband. But he wanted her back, so he was prepared to walk down whatever road he had to take. He shook his head. "You don't really mean that."

"Yes, Parker, I do."

They were interrupted when the server brought out their food. Parker didn't even look at his pepper steak, and Victoria asked the server to take back her steamed vegetable platter altogether.

"Parker, I won't deny that what we shared was special. I don't jump into bed with men on a whim...it did mean something to me. But we can't continue to see each other. We've got to end this now before anyone gets hurt."

Parker sat back, looking at Victoria with intensity. "Are you happy?" It was a question and subject that neither of them had yet to broach.

"I have a good life."

"That's not what I asked."

They sat in silence staring at each other.

"Why did you sleep with me?"

Victoria took a moment. "I never got you out of my system. Maybe that's not a good enough reason, but it's an honest answer. And yes, Parker... a part of me still loves you. My actions might seem ambiguous and conflicting, but the one thing I know for sure is that we have to end this now. Too many people will get hurt if we don't."

"You mean your husband?"

And you too, she wanted to say, but remained silent.

"Does he make you happy? Does he fulfill your needs?"

Victoria nodded.

"All of them?"

"Yes, Parker. He does." Even though she knew her answer wasn't a hundred percent true, she could honestly say that it was damn close.

Parker shook his head. "No, he doesn't. I know you Victoria, and even though the love we share is powerful, it wouldn't cause you to cheat. If he was giving you everything you needed at home there's no way you'd be here with me right now, and you know it."

"Is that why you cheated on me? Because I wasn't fulfilling your needs?" She'd turned the tables, and she instantly regretted venturing down that road.

"We're not talking about me, but since you ask, no. I cheated because I was selfish and stupid. You were all I needed."

Victoria ran her fingers through her hair and let out a hard sigh. "Not everything is as cut and dry as you think. Sometimes people just make bad decisions, like you did."

"I know I made a big mistake back then, but is that what you think you did with me the other night, made a bad decision? I'm a mistake?"

"C'mon, Parker…"

"Let me tell you what I think," he interrupted. "I think you're cozy little life is just that…cozy, safe and predictable. You haven't had real passion since we were together. Even when we argued there was incredible energy in those moments. What we had was rare and there's no substitute for it. We know each others thoughts, wants, and needs. We're good together, and that's why you're sitting in this restaurant with me right now."

"No, I told you why I came here today."

Parker leaned forward, resting his elbows on the table. "Victoria, you don't know how many times I've wished I could go back and change what I did, but I can't. Like you said the other day, what's done is done. But what I can do is live in the present and look toward the future. Baby, when I see my future, I see you in it."

Victoria's back stiffened. "I'm married and I have a family. Ted and Alexandria are my future." She felt like a hypocrite, knowing that she hadn't been thinking about her husband or her child when he'd been caressing her breast and licking between her legs two nights ago. She felt a cold rush of shame and regret slap her face.

"As much as you love your family, you can't deny your true desires. Baby, I'm not the same man I used to be. Like I've said, I know that I was selfish and unsupportive when I should have been your biggest cheerleader, and I wish that I hadn't betrayed your trust. I was used to always having my way and not making concessions for others. But when I lost you it forced me to take a long, honest look at myself with a critical eye. Then when PJ was born everything became very clear."

A long silence settled over the table.

Finally, Victoria spoke up. "I'm happy that your life has changed for the better, I truly am. But I can't be a part of it."

Before their conversation could go any further, or Parker could stage a rebuttal to her words, Victoria pushed her chair back and stood. "Please accept what I've said. Goodbye, Parker." She put her large handbag on her shoulder and walked out the front door.

Parker sat at the table, starring at his untouched plate. He took a sip of his water and wondered how long it would take before Victoria stopped fighting the inevitable.

I Know What You've Been Up To...

Victoria pulled into her garage, deep in thought about the way her weekend had unfolded. Even though she'd known it was possible, if anyone had told her on Friday morning that she'd be ending an affair with her ex-lover on Sunday afternoon, she would have told them they were crazy. She still couldn't believe what she'd done.

Slowly, Victoria stepped out of her car and opened the back door that lead to her kitchen. She was drained after her encounter with Parker, and glad to be back in the comfort of her home. "I'm gonna take a nice long soak in the tub to clear my head," she said aloud, thinking about the relaxing serenity that the warm water would bring. But her heart nearly leaped out of her chest when she looked up and found Ted standing in front of the refrigerator.

"Hey you," he said as he twisted the cap off a bottle of Amstell

Light.

Victoria nearly jumped out of her skin. He wasn't supposed to be home until the following afternoon, yet there he stood in all his ruggedly handsome glory. His thick, five o'clock shadow told her that he hadn't shaved in a few days, and the tired look on his face let her know that he hadn't been getting much sleep since he'd been away. But the bright smile in his eyes spoke volumes to the fact that he missed her and was happy to be home.

"I didn't think you were coming back until tomorrow," Victoria said with nervous bewilderment.

Ted sat his beer on the counter and walked over to her. "I wasn't, but I decided to come back a day early." He gathered his arms around Victoria's waist and drew her in for a hug.

Victoria felt his body press against hers and prayed he couldn't detect the scent of infidelity lingering on her skin.

"It's good to be home," Ted whispered in her ear.

Victoria hugged him back even though she wanted to free herself from his embrace. She was afraid that he'd smell the faint trace of Parker's cologne on her cotton top from when she'd hugged him at the restaurant, or that he'd instinctively notice that her body and touch seemed different because she'd been with another man. She knew how intuitive and discerning Ted was, and very rarely did anything slip by him. But to her surprise he hadn't seemed to notice a thing. Victoria lowered her head in shame, resting it on his shoulder.

"V, what's wrong?" Ted asked, raising her chin with his index finger so he could see her face.

"Nothing, I guess I'm just tired."

He stood back for a moment and looked at her, taking in every detail from the top of her slightly tussled hair, to her fidgety posture, down to the strappy sandals on her manicured feet. He inhaled a deep breath and strained his face, looking her dead in her eyes as he shook his head. "I see…I know what you've been up to."

Victoria was too scared to even tremble, knowing that she couldn't hide anything from him. "You do?"

"Yes, I do. Despite the fact that you need to rest you've been at your office all day," he said. "I love that you're so driven, but sometimes you just need to relax."

She was so distraught, all she could do was nod her head.

"Tell you what, why don't we go upstairs and while I unpack, you take that bubble bath you were talking about when you walked through the door." Then a sensuous grin covered his face. "And who knows, I might join you."

As Victoria followed Ted up to their bedroom, she felt panic and guilt grip her stomach. Two days ago she was in the throws of passion with another man, but now there she stood, about to take a sensual bath with her husband. Her sins made her feel unnatural about something that should be familiar.

Only a few days ago the thought of taking a bubble bath with Ted while he stroked her skin and rubbed her back would've made her wet just thinking about it. But now, the visual made her feel almost claustrophobic.

She looked across the room as Ted began to shed his khakis and button down shirt. She studied his face and when she did, she noticed something that she hadn't seen when she first walked through the door. Beneath the sexy stubble lay a look of deep distress that bordered on nervous anxiety. She watched as his eyes darted toward his luggage sitting on the other side of the room—it was still unpacked.

"Ted, are you okay?" she asked, moving toward the edge of the bed where she took a seat in order to get a better look at him.

"I'm fine," he shrugged. "Just a little travel worn."

"Did you get a chance to spend time with Lilly last night before you left?"

Victoria wasn't sure, but she thought she saw Ted flinch, and when his eyes met hers she could see that his entire expression had changed. She knew his grief was still fresh and raw, but then again, she wondered if it was something else. "Honey, I'm sorry. I know it was an emotional visit for you."

Ted looked away, feeling the weight of his own guilt nipping at his heels. Rather than continuing to expand on the pack of lies he'd already fed her, he decided to change course.

"Why don't you take your bath, I think I'll just unpack and then check a few emails," he said, walking over to his luggage. He began unpacking his things, concentrating on the task as if it was a matter of life or death.

Victoria knew he was mourning, but she also sensed a strange uneasiness shrouding his presence. She noticed a complete shift from the man who'd held her in his arms not five minutes ago, to the one in front of her now, who seemed distant, frustrated, and bothered. But rather than question him again, she went into the bathroom and filled the Jacuzzi tub with bubbles. She decided to give him space, and herself some too.

She soaked in her bath so long, the water turned from steamy warmth to tepid coolness. Finally, she dried herself off and headed out to the bedroom where she found Ted, asleep on top of the comforter. He'd stripped down to his boxers and t-shirt, looking like a little boy as he lay curled in the fetal position.

Victoria walked to his side of the bed, noting that she'd never seen him sleep that way. He usually slept on his back or on his side, but never had she seen him nestle in as though he was searching for comfort. It made her pause with worry.

She forgot about her own heavy burdens and shifted to her husband's. Lately, he seemed edgy and distracted, and the fact that he hadn't even noticed the sheer panic on her face when she'd walked through the door was highly unusual. And now here he was, fast asleep and oblivious to the betrayal she'd committed. As she studied him closer, she knew without a shadow of a doubt that something was wrong with her husband.

If I Don't Seem Myself...

The next morning, Ted rose early as usual, but he felt as though he was recovering from a hangover. His head was pounding and his limbs were heavy, like they'd been weighed down in quicksand. He didn't remember falling asleep the night before, but he'd obviously been out cold because he awoke to find that Victoria had thrown a light blanket over him as he slept through the night. He looked over at her and sighed, wondering how long he could keep up his stories.

After a long shower and a quick shave he dressed and was about to head out the door when Victoria stirred. She looked at the alarm clock and yawned. Five-thirty was way too early for her to do anything except make an attempt to wipe the sleep from her eyes.

"Good morning," Ted whispered, walking over to give her a quick kiss on the forehead.

"How're you feeling?" she asked, still groggy and not fully awake.

"Good enough to start a new day."

"It's so early. You must have a busy one."

Ted bit his tongue, telling her another half-truth. "Yes, I have an urgent early morning meeting. That's part of the reason I came back a day early."

Victoria nodded her head as she let another small yawn escape her mouth. Even though the room was still dark, the light beaming in from the hallway shown bright enough for her to see Ted in the morning dawn. He looked dashing as usual, sporting a custom-made navy blue suit like an Esquire centerfold model. Physically, he looked like his old self; fresh, clean shaven face, neatly combed hair, and stylishly handsome good looks. But there was something off-kilter in his eyes. "Are you sure you're okay?" she asked.

Ted felt like he was going to scream if Victoria questioned him again. He knew she was simply concerned, and that her love for him was the reason for her constant worry. But it was starting to wear on him, despite her good intentions. The more she asked how he was feeling and if anything was wrong, the worse he felt.

He had to lie and pretend that all was well until he could figure out how he was going to live his life knowing the truth. But he also knew that he needed to make a compelling case to his wife, convincing her that he was fine because the last thing he wanted to do was cause her any further distress, or better yet, feed her growing curiosity.

"V, I know you're worried about me, but I'm okay. This has been a really trying time, and I'm facing challenges that I've never dealt with before. So if I don't seem myself it's because I'm not. But I'm dealing with it and I know that everything is going to be all right." Ted wanted his words to comfort and reassure her because he could see her doubts. "Knowing that you and Alexandria are by my side every step of the way is what's going to pull me through." He reached for her hand and kissed it gently.

Victoria looked into her husband's eyes. "I love you, Ted."

"I love you too, V."

They held on to each others words, hoping their love was enough to overcome their individual deceits.

A New Awareness...

After giving Victoria one last kiss, Ted left to start his day. He maneuvered his car down the deserted early morning streets and across town to his intended destination. He looked at his watch as he pulled up to the back entrance of a small, unassuming brick building. He parked beside the other lone vehicle that occupied one of the reserved spaces. "Thank God for small favors," he whispered to himself as he dialed his cell phone. "I'm here."

He got out of his car, taking large steps that led him up to a set of double-pane glass doors. A minute later a short, stout woman opened the back door and let him in. "Good morning, Ted. How are you?" Claire Langston, the bank president greeted with a cheerful smile.

Ted appreciated the fact that she was pleasant, even though he was sure she knew that whatever business he'd come to do must be unscrupulous, especially since it necessitated a pre-dawn meeting to ensure his privacy. Looking at Claire in her neatly tailored Brooks Brothers attire, Ted could see that she was the kind of no-nonsense person who normally followed strict protocol. But she'd made an exception for him because his old friend, Chip Langston, who happened to be her favorite and dearest brother, had called in the favor.

"Thank you for making this special accommodation, I greatly appreciate it," Ted thanked her.

Claire nodded, then gave him a quick handshake. "Any friend of my brother's is a friend of mine."

Ted followed her into the bank and down the hall as she led him to a small conference room. He looked at the medium-sized, black metal box and the small stack of papers that sat beside it.

"Just fill out the forms, put the necessary contents in the box and let me know when you're finished," Claire told him before leaving the room.

Ted took a deep breath and thought about what he was getting ready to do, ironically repeating his mother's pattern. Nearly twenty minutes later he found himself looking through the faded papers for a fifth time, straining his eyes behind the lenses of his smartly framed reading glasses. He scrutinized every line of each document as if he was seeing it for the first time.

He held his mother's birth certificate in front of him and rubbed his forehead. According to the age-worn document, Carolyn Thornton had been born, Carol Lynn Milleux. Her mother was listed as Sally May Turner, age nineteen, and her father, Jean Paul Milleux, age fifty. But what stuck out most in Ted's mind, and what still held him in a state of disbelief was not the fact that his mother had been born in Mississippi, and not Louisiana as he'd always believed and as the certificate plainly stated, or that there was a significant age difference between her birth parents. What made his heart race and his head pound was that Jean Paul Millieux was white and Sally May Turner was black…or Negro, as the birth certificate read, an so was little Carol Lynn.

Along with Carolyn's birth certificate were other documents which stood as evidence that she was born of a union between a young black woman and an older white man. Ted held a near pristine black and white photograph of a young black woman dressed in fine clothing, holding a white baby in her arms. The inscription on the back read; Sally May, 19 years old, and daughter, Carol Lynn, 6 months old. He looked at the woman who was his grandmother, and although she had a young, graceful face, her eyes were layered in what looked like years of hardship and sadness. But she cradled her baby as if she was her most prized possession, hugging her close to her body.

The more he read, the more Ted felt as though he was having an outer body experience, and none of it seemed any more real to him now than it had when he first made the discovery two weeks ago. He picked up a slightly tattered document from the Mississippi State Foster Care System, listing Carol Lynn Milluex as a mixed-race child who had been orphaned at age five, when her mother developed a fatal infection after battling a month-long bout of pneumonia.

Ted looked back at the picture of a grandmother he never knew, and the mother he now realized he'd barely known, and all he could do was wonder.

He ran his fingers over the edges of the two additional photographs that lay in front of him, showing little Carol Lynn with two different black families. In one photo she appeared to be a little older than Alexandria was now. No one in the picture was smiling, and little Carol Lynn looked especially subdued. In the photo with the second family, she was clearly a pubescent young girl, probably twelve years old. She was already showing her exquisite beauty, even if it was through sad looking eyes. Ted noticed that she carried the same burdened look on her face that her mother had. She was holding hands with a much shorter, but bright-eyed young girl, who he could clearly see was none other than Hattie McPherson. In both pictures, Carol Lynn stuck out as the lone white face in a sea of black ones.

Ted pushed the pictures to the side of the small conference table and picked up the long, hand-written letter his mother had penned, pouring out her confession. Even though he'd read every line nearly a hundred times over the last two weeks, it still seemed like a dream.

Dearest Theodore,

I am sorry that the truth had to come to you on paper, through my death, rather than from my own lips. But dear son, please know that I kept who I was from you because I wanted to protect you from the ugliness of this world. I did what I thought was best for my family.

My mother was a young domestic who worked for the family of a prominent businessman who had his sights set on a position in the Louisiana state legislature. She lived on the property with the family, but once she became pregnant by her employer, through a relationship that was not of her own choosing, the lady of the house put her out with only the clothes on her back. Her family shunned her for bringing shame on them by carrying an illegitimate child. She was sent to Jackson, Mississippi, to live with distant relatives and that's where I was born.

Although she died when I was a small girl, I have fond memories of my mother, and I can still see her smile when I close my eyes. You remind me so much of her. Please believe me when I say it was hard for my mother raising a mixed-race child, especially since I didn't look colored, or black as they say now. I was as white as snow, and it caused problems for her. She was a young, unmarried, uneducated black woman with an illegitimate baby by a white man, so opportunities were not plentiful. She scratched together a small living for us by cleaning houses and taking in laundry. But after she became ill and then died, I was all alone.

With no relatives willing to take me in, I was placed in the state foster care system. Although I looked white, black blood was in my veins and no white family would take me once they were made aware of my background. I was placed with several black families who took me in, but treated me harshly. I never quite fit in and my life was a living torment.

Thank God for Hattie McPherson, she was my salvation. I met Hattie when we were in second grade. While the other children in our segregated school teased me because I was different and accused me of thinking I was better than they were because of my white skin, Hattie embraced me like a sister. She was there for me through the cruelty and mistreatment I experienced. But even with Hattie's love and friendship, the weight of being mixed-race in the rural south was just too much. One is a lonely number.

I had heard about fair skinned blacks who were light enough to pass. I knew that if I left Jackson and went to a city where no one knew my background, I could live as a white woman and have a better life. So that's what I decided to do. When I turned sixteen I left Mississippi and never looked back. I moved to Boston, changed my name, lied about my age, got accepted to Wellesley on a scholarship and started a new life.

By the time I met your father I'd managed to graduate from college and had been living as a white woman for over six years. I loved him so much, too much to continue lying to him. I knew he deserved the truth, especially considering the reputation his last name carried. So I took a chance and told him. To my surprise he still wanted me to be his wife. The only thing I asked was that he agree to keep my secret, which he did. Your father even helped me get official looking documents and craft a better story than the one I'd made up. So we settled here in Boston, started our life together, and raised our family.

The only other person who knew our secret was Hattie. She and I never lost contact over the years. She's one of the best people I know and was a genuine and trusted friend, as I'm sure you will soon discover.

You are probably asking yourself why I'm telling you this now, if at all. Honestly, I planned to carry my secret to my grave, but from the moment Victoria became your wife I knew that I couldn't. You needed to know for reasons that Lilly nor Charlie will ever struggle with.

I know that over the years Victoria felt as though I didn't care for her, but I want you to know that was never the case, and in fact just the opposite. I always liked her very much. She is a good mother to Alexandria, a good wife to you, and is a smart and kind young woman. Most of all, I have seen with my own eyes how much she loves you. But I kept my distance from her. I couldn't allow myself to get close to her or her family. As I said, she is a smart and very inquisitive young woman who asks many questions.

Theodore, this information is for you and you alone. What you choose to do with it will be your decision. But if you want to learn more about my life, about who I was, contact my friend, Hattie McPherson, in Jackson, Mississippi, and she will lead you to the answers.

With All My Love,

Your Mother

Ted shook his head, remembering something his mother had said when he'd first told her that he was in love with Victoria. "It's hard for blacks and whites when they decide to intermingle…to marry. I've seen things in my day. The road you'll travel won't be an easy one, not even in today's time." Now he knew that she'd been speaking from direct experience.

He tucked the letter back in between the other pictures and documents he'd been keeping in his attaché. For the time being they would find a secure resting place within the safe deposit box in front of him.

After Ted completed the paperwork and left the bank, he headed to his office with thoughts of Victoria heavy on his mind. He could feel in his bones that something was slipping away between them. Normally, after returning home from a trip, especially if they were lucky enough to have the house to themselves, they would make love all night. But when he returned home yesterday they'd barely kissed. When she began to ask him questions about his visit to Boston, it took the wind out of his sails. His guilt and stress over lying to her had left him so deflated that instead of joining her for a pleasure filled bubble bath as he'd wanted to do, he fell into a deep sleep, not waking until early the next morning.

He felt awful about the recent decisions he'd made, all the lies he'd told, and the secret he was keeping. Even though there were certain things he didn't discuss with Victoria and never planned to, like the complex and often ruthless business dealings he crafted at ViaTech and through some of his entrepreneurial ventures outside the company, this was a situation that he knew he needed to share with her. Their relationship had been built on trust and now he was tearing down the very fabric of what held them together.

But telling Victoria the truth was more difficult than it seemed. He didn't know how or even where to begin because he'd have to explain why he hadn't told her from the beginning when she first asked, and why he found it necessary to continually lie even after she'd questioned him several times.

He wanted to tell her that he'd kept his mother's secret from her because of the unbelievable shock that still seemed to grip him. But deep down, he knew it was because he had yet to reconcile the jarring reality of who he really was. And deeper still, he'd have to admit a sobering truth—that he didn't want anyone to know about the black blood running through his veins. *What kind of awful hypocrite does that make me?* he asked himself. Victoria had often told him that he'd never know what it felt like to be black, and now that he had the opportunity, he wasn't sure that he wanted to experience how it would change him.

He thought about the sometimes heated moments and words that he and Victoria had exchanged over the years whenever they approached the subject of race. He shook his head, thinking about the irony of the situation. The tension they'd gone through over race and raising a bi-racial child had all been a waste of time, because in essence, he and Victoria were both black.

But after living life as a white man since the day he was born, Ted didn't know any other way to think of himself, and he'd never even pondered the issue of racial identity until he met Victoria. But for the last two weeks, race had been the one thing he couldn't get out of his mind.

When he looked in the mirror he saw himself with a new awareness. He'd begun to study his features more closely. He knew that his strong jaw-line, straight, angular nose, and piercing blue eyes were imprints that his father had passed on to him. But when he peered deeper he noticed something he'd never paid much attention to; his smooth, wrinkle-free skin carried a slightly olive-colored undertone that had always tanned to a beautiful, toasty color during the summer. He thought about how all his life he'd heard people say with envy, "I'd kill for a tan like yours." And he thought about the off-handed comment he'd overheard Victoria's cousin Patsy make last Christmas when she'd told her, "Girl, Ted's aging really well for a white man. There's hardly a wrinkle on his face. He's smooth and he's got rhythm. You sure he's not an undercover brothah?" she'd teased.

Now, when he looked at Alexandria, he knew that she was

black…on both sides.

As he approached the ViaTech building and parked his car in the executive garage, he thought about the fact that sooner or later he'd have to acknowledge the lineage that had been passed down to him from generations of people he'd never known existed.

When he arrived in his office, Ted was surprised to see that Jen was already there. It was barely seven o'clock and she was working like she'd been behind her desk for hours. Her quick fingers pecked at her computer keys, preparing his schedule for the week ahead.

"Didn't expect you in until later this afternoon," Jen said, equally surprised to see him. "You came back early."

"Yes, I decided to cut my trip short."

Jen handed him a folder full of papers. "The Dynamex account," she said. She knew that her boss was under a tremendous amount of stress since the death of his mother, and it amazed her how composed he still seemed to be. But even though he was strong, she knew that eventually something would have to give. "You want me to hold your calls this morning?" she asked.

Ted gave her a wink and a nod. "Thanks, Jen."

After he settled behind his desk, Ted jumped into the work in front of him, pouring over the complicated documents in the Dynamex folder. Conquering hard tasks was second nature to him, but today it was like working a math equation. He was stressed, but he couldn't let anyone see it. Even though his assistant knew him well, he was thankful she hadn't detected the anxiety that was making his chest pound like a drum.

His mind went back to Victoria because she was the one person he couldn't fool, the one person who had already noticed subtle, yet profound changes in his behavior. He knew she was wise to him, and that she sensed he hadn't been fully honest surrounding the details of what he'd found in his mother's safe deposit box. And he knew it was only a matter of time before she dug, questioned, and probed until she found out the truth.

He leaned back in his chair and looked out of his large corner office window, pausing in deep reflection. The early morning sun was making an attempt to shine over the Atlanta sky-line. He reached over and picked up the neatly framed photo of his family. "I've got to tell her," he whispered aloud. "I can't continue to live this lie."

Chapter 15

Things Still Weren't Right...

Victoria glanced at her watch and sighed. It was eight o'clock on Wednesday evening and she'd only completed half of the things on her long, *"To Do List."* The week had been busy, filled with meetings, site visits, and food tastings for upcoming events. Divine Occasions had become so lucrative that she would soon need to bring another full-time staff member on board. She loved growing her business and following her dreams, but it often caused an internal conflict between balancing her professional aspirations against her family's needs.

At times she resented the uneven load she was expected to carry. Ted could be out of town for days on end and work late nights at the office for weeks, all in the name of corporate business. But if she stayed away too frequently, or for too long, her absence was felt and noticed more than his, making her feel guilty whenever her work took her away from home.

She wanted to be home right now, having dinner with Alexandria, but her duties as a business woman had kept her chained to her office all day. It was times like the present that she was thankful she had a dependable childcare service. She picked up the phone and made a quick call to say good night to Alexandria, and to let the babysitter know that she needed her to stay for another hour. She'd already talked to Ted to let him know that she'd be working late, and not to her surprise, he'd told her that he'd be working late too—again.

Over the last couple of weeks they'd barely spent any time together or interacted much outside of their parenting duties. She shuddered when she thought about the current state of their marriage. They were becoming passing shadows in the night.

Two weeks had passed since Ted's return from his trip to Boston, and she was more worried about him than ever. Alexandria had come home a few days after, which had made her feel better because at least her daughter was back to her old self again. Victoria knew the trip to North Carolina had made all the difference. Since Alexandria had returned, she hadn't asked once if her mommy or daddy were going to go away for eternal sleep like her Granny Carolyn had. Her short-lived concern about mortality had been replaced by the excitement of her upcoming enrollment in what she called *big kid's school.*

Now, Victoria's biggest concern at the moment was for her husband. She'd hoped that Ted would return to his old self too, or at least open up to her about whatever the real secret was that his mother had been keeping. But to her disappointment, neither had happened.

Although she felt guilty for doing dirt of her own, she knew that Ted was up to something too. She tried to empathize because of the grief and loss he'd suffered, but her gut told her that he'd been lying, and that whatever Carolyn had been hiding must have bordered on criminal. It was the only explanation she could think of to justify his change in behavior and his constant preoccupation with hidden thoughts that seemed to be pushing him further and further away from her.

Victoria paused, rubbing her eyes as she looked at the wall clock across the room. It was approaching eight-thirty and she was still stuck on the same two lines of the catering contract she'd been looking at for the last half hour.

She rose from her desk to stretch her limbs, trying to shake off the bad feeling that had overtaken her—the knowledge that her marriage was in deep trouble. She and Ted were drifting toward shaky ground, not just because of his suddenly strange behavior, but also because of what she had done with Parker. The guilt was slowly eating at her like a sore that wouldn't heal, and she knew it was impacting her interaction with her husband.

The fact that Ted hadn't noticed that her behavior had changed, or seemed to care that their intimacy was eroding, had given her even more reason for concern. She thought about what had occurred between them a few nights ago while they were in bed. They were lying uncharacteristically apart, him on one side of their California king-size mattress and her on the other. He hadn't touched her in days, so she asked him outright about her suspicions.

"If your mother had done something bad, I mean really terrible, you know that you could confide in me, right?"

Ted had been silent for a moment before answering. "V, why are you still asking me about that? I told you everything there is to know."

Victoria reached out and draped her arm around his shoulder. "I'm asking because I know you," she replied. "And I know that there's something you haven't told me...I can feel it." She said this, peering deep into his eyes through the sliver of light that shined in from the hallway. She saw fear and vulnerability staring back at her. It frightened her, but at the same time it was the most honest and most connected she'd felt to him in weeks. Her heart sank because in that moment she felt like shit for sleeping with Parker. A single tear slid down her cheek at the thought. "I love you...I've made some mistakes," she paused, trying to hold back the flood that threatened, "but I promise you, I'll work hard to be a better wife. Just don't shut me out."

Ted's entire body exhaled, releasing the weight of his guilt into Victoria's arms. He pulled her close to him. He didn't know what to say to explain himself, so instead, he spoke a language that didn't require words. He stroked her back, kissed her lips, and removed her silk nightgown. Their love making veered between moments of sweet, gentle passion, and raw untamed heat. Their bodies swayed in sensual rhythm. Victoria dug her knees and the palm of her hands into the mattress, balancing herself on all fours as Ted knelt behind her. She gritted her teeth, receiving each powerful thrust as he gave her what they both wanted and needed—relief.

Afterward, they lay wrapped in each others arms. They wanted to stay in the safe place their heated passion had created, because despite what they'd just shared, things still weren't right between them. There were unanswered questions, secrets, and lies floating in the air, and neither of them had the courage to touch it.

Now, standing in her office with her mind on everything except work, Victoria knew it was pointless to stay any longer. Her thoughts weren't focused because the only thing she could think about was the fragile state of her marriage. She longed to skip over the next two days so she could get to the weekend. Even though she had a mountain of work to tackle, the weekend represented an opportunity for her to begin to repair the mess she'd made of things. She planned to start by taking Ted out on the town for a romantic dinner at his favorite restaurant, followed by a quick stop at his favorite jazz club, before capping off the evening with a moonlight stroll in the park.

Victoria was preparing to pack up her things and head home when a strange feeling hit her. It was a sense of impending danger that ran through her bones. She lowered her head. "Lord, please forgive me for what I've done and give me the strength to make things right again. So help me, from this day forward I'm going to act like I have some sense and hold my family together."

Just as she was about to turn off the antique art deco lamp on her desk, her cell phone began to ring. When she looked at the name that flashed across the screen, all she could do was close her eyes and pray harder.

Let It Go?...

Parker was glad that his long day had finally come to an end. It had been one full of frustrations, starting with a difficult emergency surgery that had stretched into the late afternoon, preventing him from picking up PJ from school. He was diligent about having his Wednesday and Friday surgeries scheduled for the early morning hours so he would have the afternoon fee to spend with his son, but when emergencies came he had to act. Then his new assistant abruptly quit, leaving him with a mound of paperwork and dozens of fires to put out. But even those complications didn't compare to the disappointment he felt when he thought about Victoria.

He steered his black Navigator out of the hospital parking lot, thinking about their last encounter. It had been two weeks since he'd seen or heard from her. Even though she'd tried to act tough by telling him that she wanted to end their affair, he knew it was simply a matter of time before she'd come back into his arms. So he decided to play along, resisting the urge to contact her. But now he was feeling agitated, and he realized that his plan to exercise patience wasn't going to work.

He was a man of means and unrelenting determination. The word *"no"* wasn't in his vocabulary. He'd been an overachiever all his life and was used to getting his way. If there was something he wanted he went after it, regardless of the roadblocks that threatened to sideline him. He'd always believed that life was too short to settle for anything less than what he wanted.

As he turned the corner, switching lanes, Parker shook his head when he thought about the fact that the woman he loved was married to another man. It killed him to know that Victoria was with someone else, but he withstood the injury to his heart and the insult to his ego because he knew he was responsible for his fate, and he knew that if he hadn't messed up they'd be a family today. So instead of continuing to dwell on past transgressions that he couldn't change, he decided to work on what he could. He turned down the volume on his truck's CD player, made a right turn onto Peachtree Road, and hit Victoria's number on speed dial. Just when he thought it was going into voice mail she picked up.

"Can you talk?" he asked, not giving her a chance to say hello.

Victoria let out a heavy sigh, "Parker, I thought we already discussed this. It's over. Why are you calling me?"

He felt like telling her that he was a grown ass man, that she was his woman, and that he would call her any time he damn well pleased. But only one of his points was valid so he held his tongue. "I need to talk to you."

"We have nothing to discuss. Please let this go."

"Let it go?" he said with incredulity.

Victoria sat silent on the other end of the line. "I'm hanging up now."

Parker tightened his grip on the steering wheel. He knew she must still be at her office working late, because if she'd been at home she wouldn't have answered her phone or called out his name.

He made a sharp left and headed in her direction. "I'm turning into the business park now. I'll be at your office door in less than two minutes." And with that Parker hung up and stepped on the gas.

Something Bad Was In The Air…

Ted sat at his desk, consumed by a sinking feeling that had settled over his body. He was thinking about the conversation he'd just had with Victoria only moments ago.

He'd managed to push his heavy personal burdens out of his mind in order to concentrate on the business at hand. His day had been surprisingly productive given his dower frame of mind when he first arrived at his office earlier that morning. He oversaw an executive board meeting with prospective shareholders, held a brain-storming session with key members of his executive management team, and then conducted a conference call with the VPs of ViaTech's six remote locations. Things had been going as well as could be expected until his cell phone vibrated and he saw Victoria's number light up the screen.

She'd called to let him know that she was still at her office, working late, and that she'd be there for at least another hour or more. When he told her that he planned to work late as well, he heard the gentle concern in her voice.

"Ted, you've been working day and night since we got back from Boston, you must be exhausted."

"I'm fine, but you on the other hand should probably head home," he told her.

He knew that Victoria always made a concerted effort not to work late during the week day unless an event pulled her away. The fact that she was still at her office let him know that one of two things must be going on with his wife, either she was snowed under with work that couldn't be put off for another day, or she was so stressed that she needed a few hours to herself in the empty solitude of her office. He suspected it was the latter, given that she was well organized and never let her workload get beyond a controllable manner.

"V, I really think you should call it a day," he reiterated. "You know I'm always uncomfortable when you're over there by yourself late at night."

"I'll be fine."

Ted tapped his expensive fountain pen against the edge of his desk.

He could hear an underlying tension in her voice. "Are you sure you're okay?" he asked.

"I'm just a little tired, but I'm good. Listen, I've gotta go so I can call the sitter."

She ended their call abruptly and it left him with the distinct feeling that something bad was in the air.

As Ted leaned back in his chair and replayed their brief conversation, his thoughts plunged deeper and deeper until they reached a place that was cold and unfamiliar. He was loosing Victoria and he could feel it. "I can't sit back and let my marriage fall apart," he said to himself. He knew he had to take action. He logged off his computer, grabbed his suit coat and attaché, and walked out the door, headed straight for Victoria's office.

You've Gotta Get The Hell Outta Here!...

Victoria refused to answer the door when she heard the bell chime. She thought about leaving through the back, but she knew she'd run into Parker if she did because she'd have to walk around to the front of the building where her car was parked. "I've been such a damn fool," she cursed herself. After the fifth ring she looked out the peep hole. "Go away, Parker," she said through the door.

"I'm going to ring this bell until you let me in."

Victoria knew she shouldn't be surprised, but it baffled her as to how a mature, confident man like Parker could act like a two-year old throwing a tantrum. She thought about calling the police, but then she'd have to fill out an official report, explaining his presence at her door. She was already paranoid and nervous about Ted finding out that she'd cheated, and at this point all she wanted him to do was go away.

After Parker rang the bell for a sixth time she knew she had to do something. She opened the door, stepped aside, and let him in. Even though the business park wasn't crowded that time of night, she looked around before shutting the door, making sure no one was in sight to witness him entering her office suite.

Victoria watched Parker as he stood before her. He was still in his scrubs, which meant he'd had a long day and didn't have the time or inclination to change. He hated going out in public in them, preferring his fashionable plain-clothes digs instead. His eyes looked tired and his face bore an agitated scowl.

Victoria put her hand on her hip, standing her ground. "You have a hell of a lotta nerve showing up here like this."

"You won't call me, you won't see me, so I have to take matters into my own hands."

Victoria shook her head. "There are a lot of things about you that have changed, but I see that your need for control is still the same. You're used to getting your way, and if things don't go according to your plan, you don't know how to handle it."

"We reconnected. We made love. Are you forgetting that?"

"Are you crazy?"

"Don't insult me, Victoria. You came back into my life, and now you want me to just act like it never happened? You want me to let this go?"

"I got caught up in the moment that night. It was a mistake that I completely regret."

Parker shook his head. "You don't mean that."

"Why do you keep saying that? I know exactly what I mean."

"Why are you trying to push me away?"

Victoria rolled her eyes. "Listen, the bottom line is this, we'll run into each other because our children will be attending the same school and participating in the same social organization. But outside of that we can't have any contact. I'm only going to say this one more time. DO NOT attempt to see me again," she nearly shouted. "*What* about that scenario do you not understand?"

Parker crossed his arms, organizing his thoughts. "You've been avoiding me, saying what you think you have to in order to make me go away. That's what you do, Victoria. When you don't want to deal with something you shut it off and push it to the side. But I'm not going anywhere. I'm going to fight for us to get back together. I know it's going to be hard, but I'm ready to put in the work."

"Damnit, don't try that arm-chair psychology with me," she said with irritation. "I was trying to be civil about this, but now you've really pissed me off. You need to go."

Parker smirked. He'd always loved her feistiness. "You're something else, you know that? Why are you fighting this?"

Oh, Lord. I've gotta get his ass out of here! Victoria could see that playing hardball with Parker wasn't working, and that her strategy had actually backfired. She needed to get him out of her office, so she tried to be calm as she attempted to reason with him. "We can't change anything that has happened between us, not the past or the present, but we can control what happens in the future." She folded her arms, resting them at her chest as she looked him in his eyes so he could see that she meant business. "I love my husband. What I did was selfish and irresponsible. I'm under no illusions about my reckless behavior, and that's why I'm trying to make things right." She paused briefly for a breath, saying her last words with conviction. "You need to accept what I've said and respect my wishes. This is it...this is the end."

"Are you finished?" Parker asked.

Victoria nodded her head and braced herself for another heated exchange. But the barrage of words she'd expected never came. Instead, he took two steps forward, put his arms around her waist, drew her into his embrace, and kissed her so deeply she couldn't breathe. "That's my response," he whispered.

He'd taken her by surprise. "You need to stop this!" she hissed, pushing him away as she released herself. They stared at each other; her with contempt, him with steadfast nerves.

Victoria turned and was about to open the door to show him out when the bell chimed, startling them both. The uneasy feeling of impending danger that she'd experienced before Parker had arrived, suddenly returned.

Victoria put her finger to her lips in a shushing motion, her eyes pleading with Parker to remain silent. When she tiptoed to the door and looked through the peep hole she nearly lost her balance. Ted was standing on the other side.

Panic shot through Victoria's body like a flash of hot lightening. She rushed over to Parker, pulling him by the arm as she ushered him to the back of her office. She led him to the exit door, trying to stay calm. "Ted's outside," she whispered in a hasty breath. "You've gotta get the hell outta here!"

Parker opened his mouth to object, but Victoria quickly covered his lips with the palm of her hand as she turned the deadbolt and opened the door. "Damnit, Parker. Don't do this. Please, I'm begging you. Just leave!"

They stood in the middle of the open door as the smoldering night heat seeped in between them. Victoria's BlackBerry started ringing in the holster on her hip. She knew it was Ted and she knew she had to pick up. Her car was parked out front, so he knew that she was still there. Again, she put her finger to her lips, motioning for Parker to keep quiet.

"Hey," she spoke in a nervous rush.

"Why haven't you answered the door, I'm standing outside," Ted said with worry in his voice. "Is everything all right?"

"Um, yeah. I'm in the bathroom," she lied as tiny beads of sweat began to form on her forehead. "I'll be out in a sec."

Victoria hit the end button and prayed he hadn't detected the panic in her voice. When she looked at Parker he was staring at her with a combination of emotions that she couldn't place and didn't have the energy to try. "Parker, you have to go. This can't happen again. Everything has to end right here, right now."

Parker brought his hand to the side of Victoria's cheek and stroked it gently. He shook his head and stepped away, granting her wish. Victoria exhaled a deep sigh of relief, but then held her breath because he turned around, walked back up to her and looked her in the eye. "Every goodbye's not gone," he whispered softly.

Victoria stood at her back door, speechless as Parker turned again and walked away into the darkness of night.

Serious, Deadly Serious...

Victoria quickly pulled herself together, smoothed her hair back with the palm of her hand and opened the front door. When Ted entered he looked at her with questioning eyes. "Are you sure you're okay? You sounded different on the phone…and you look flushed."

Victoria took a deep breath, trying to appear casual. "I'm fine, like I said earlier, I'm just a little tired, that's all." Then a thought occurred to her. In all the years since she'd opened her office, Ted had never shown up unannounced, not even when she'd been working late at night. "What made you come by?" she asked.

Ted removed his suit coat and unbuttoned the top of his shirt, loosening his tie for comfort. "Let's have a seat," he said, extending his arm toward the small loveseat near Denise's desk.

A fresh wave of panic reached out and grabbed Victoria's heart. She knew that something was very wrong. She sat down beside him, not wanting to look him in the eye, praying she could hold herself together.

Ted took her hand and held it gently in his. "You're trembling," he said in an unsteady voice that was unlike him.

Now he was scaring her. "Ted, what's wrong?" This time Victoria looked into his ocean-blue eyes and held his stare.

Ted squeezed her hand tight. "V, I love you with all my heart. You and Alexandria are my world, and I'll do whatever it takes to protect you. Sometimes things aren't as they appear, but eventually all things will be revealed in time."

Victoria withdrew, studying the serious look on his face. "What's going on? You're talking in circles." She started sweating like someone had poured water over her face. *Oh, Lord! Did he see Parker as he was leaving?* Then she realized that he couldn't have. There was no way that Parker could have possibly made it from the back of her office building to the front before she'd opened the door to let Ted in. She knew that because if the two men had seen each other, she wouldn't be sitting down talking with her husband at that very moment because the paramedics would've been there by now!

Ted reached for her hand again. He spoke softly, but with great intent. "The last few weeks have been difficult and I know you've noticed that I haven't been myself." He lumbered slightly, taking a deep breath to prepare himself for what he was about to say next. "You know me better than anyone else, and I don't want there to be any secrets between us. I love you and I'm sorry that I've had to lie to you."

Victoria's eyes widened. Normally, she would have been asking a million questions, because her curiosity was just that great. But she knew this was serious, deadly serious, and it left her in complete silence.

Ted continued. "I haven't been honest with you about my mother's secret. What I discovered about her was far more complex than I told you."

Now, Victoria was sitting on the edge of her seat, her thoughts swimming with confusion as Ted held on to her hand. His words tumbled out like a mystery movie plot starting to unfold.

"You know that old saying, 'You never really know someone,'...

well, it was invented for people like my mother. Her life wasn't what it seemed and she wasn't who any of us thought she was. This isn't the right moment for me to tell you what I found in her safe deposit box, but I want you to know that neither you, nor Alexandria are in any danger from it."

Victoria finally spoke. "I don't understand why you can't tell me? This is crazy."

"V, Sweetheart, please bear with me and trust me on this."

The irony of the situation nearly crippled Victoria's mind—he was asking his lying, cheating wife to trust him. But despite her duplicitous position, she wanted answers from him.

She withdrew her hands from his and stood to her feet as she began to pace the room. "You just told me that you've been lying to me and now you want me to trust you? How am I supposed to do that?" A small voice inside her head called her a hypocritical bitch. She immediately regretted her words, knowing that she had absolutely no right to stand in judgment or demand truthfulness when she'd just welcomed her husband through the front door after rushing her lover out the back.

Ted stood and walked over to her. "You have every right to feel the way you do. I've lied to you and I know it's built a wall between us. V, I'm still dealing with the shock that my mother revealed to me...it's been hard. But yes, I'm asking you to trust in me, and I'm asking you to give me just a little more time so I can make sense of it. I'll tell you all there is to know...soon."

She wanted to believe him, and he wanted to make the questions and pain on her face disappear.

Victoria could see that the weight that had been haunting Ted's eyes was no longer there. He looked tired, but he also looked relieved. She knew it must have taken a lot for him to come forward with the truth, even if he'd only given it in dribbles, and that whatever embarrassing indiscretion Carolyn had been hiding, it almost certainly paled in comparison to the secret she was keeping.

Now she knew how Debbie had felt because she wanted to tell Ted her truth too. She wanted to confess her sins and make things right, but she knew she couldn't. It was one thing for him to lie to her about a secret that his mother had been keeping, but it was another thing entirely for her to admit to him that she had slept with Parker.

Victoria sank into his arms and held on tight. She sniffed back a tear that threatened to fall. "Before we got married, I remember you said that we'd encounter a few hurdles along the way, but as long as we were together it would make life a hell of a lot easier," Victoria said, biting her bottom lip as she swallowed hard and continued. "I haven't been perfect either, but you've loved me anyway. I adore you, and I'm here for you whenever you're ready to open up to me."

That night Victoria and Ted made love like old times. All that had been said and done was washed away with tender kisses and gentle caresses. Everything that had been broken became whole again. As she lay in her husband's arms, Victoria drifted off to sleep. She knew they hadn't cleared all the hurdles in the road, but they were headed for recovery. Now her only worry was how she was going to keep Parker at bay.

Chapter 16

You Need Some Tough Love...

Victoria sat at her desk thinking about the roller coaster ride she'd had the night before. After barely escaping what could have been a catastrophic scene between Ted and Parker, she shuddered when she thought about the bullet she'd managed to dodge. She knew it was proof that God had been watching over her in spite of her poor decisions and careless behavior. She was grateful she'd been spared, and she knew it was time to get her act together.

She'd put all that she loved on the line, and when she thought about what she'd nearly lost she almost cried. She remembered how happy Alexandria had been when she dropped her off at summer camp an hour ago.

"You're the best Mommy in the whole wide world," Alexandria had said out of the blue.

"My, my, young lady. What did I do to deserve that honor?"

"Just 'cause I love you, Mommy" Alexandria smiled back.

Victoria gave her a big hug and a kiss on her forehead before watching her skip away toward her group of friends who'd already gathered in their classroom. She looked at her daughter, and thanked God for second chances.

She thought about the love she and Ted had made after they

returned home from her office last night, and about the passionate declarations they'd whispered to each other in the dark. She knew she'd been given a blessing that eluded most, and now she had to step up her game before she squandered it.

Morning slipped into lunchtime, keeping Victoria busy as she worked on new projects. Then out of the blue, an unsettling thought came to her, breaking her concentration and gripping her mind like it was caught in a vise. She heard the words that Parker had spoken, echoing in her ears. *"Every goodbye's not gone."* It had been his way of telling her that he wasn't giving up and he wasn't going away.

Suddenly, Victoria's optimistic mood took a one-hundred eighty degree nose dive. The more she thought about what Parker might do, the more nervous she felt. If she wasn't fearful before, she was terrified now. As she pondered her fate, she heard Denise walk through the door.

"You ready to go to lunch?"

Victoria looked up at her friend, startled and anxious, doing her best to mask her emotions. She'd forgotten they had planned to have lunch outside the office. "Sure," she said, grabbing her handbag. *Maybe a good meal will calm my nerves.*

Fifteen minutes later, Victoria and Denise settled into a booth at Houston's restaurant. They each ordered a salad and the soup of the day. Denise took a sip of her coke before she started in. "All right Girlfriend, what the hell's goin' on?"

"What do you mean?"

Denise pursed her lips. "Tell me what's got you looking like you just stepped into a room full of fog. I know it's been rough since Ted's mother died, but there's something else going on."

Victoria shifted in her seat, not sure if she was ready or that she even wanted to involve Denise in her complicated drama. She thought about the advice that Tyler had given her—the less people who knew about her indiscretions, the better.

Denise leaned forward. "A few weeks ago Parker was calling like a bill collector, then all of a sudden he stopped and that's when you started acting strange. Now, I'm not stupid…whatever's going on with you, it has something to do with Dr. Brightwood," she said, twisting her mouth.

Victoria could only nod her head, confirming Denise's suspicions.

"Girlfriend, tell me what kind of mess you've gotten yourself into behind that fool?"

Victoria couldn't keep it from Denise any longer. She spilled out everything as she told her friend from beginning to end about her affair with Parker, right up to what had happened in their very office last night.

Denise shook her head. "Well, I'm not even gonna lie. I knew this was gonna happen. You're sittin' in the middle of a serious shit storm."

"*Really?* I didn't know that. Thanks for your astute observation."

Denise craned her neck. "Don't get snippy with me. I'm here to help you."

"You could've fooled me. I don't need to hear, *I told you so right now.*"

"What else do you want me to say?" Denise said, doing her best to keep her voice low. "Listen, you messed up. You risked everything you have for some dick, and now you want sympathy? Uh-uh." She pointed her finger in Victoria's direction. "I thought Debbie had lost her mind, but you managed to top her."

"You didn't have to go there."

"But I did. You know I love you, but I'm not gonna coddle you. And you know I'm not one for all that pretending and bullshit. I'm gonna be honest with you because you're my girl. You need some tough love and real talk, not some hand-holdin', sugar coated mess that'll have you in worse shape than you're already in."

The two friends quieted their conversation when the server came back with their food.

"For the record, it wasn't just about the sex," Victoria said once the server left their table. "As much as I wish it wasn't true, and as much as I hate to admit it, I've always had feelings for Parker."

Denise paused for a moment, letting out a long and heavy sigh. She nodded her head, acknowledging what she also knew was the truth. "I know…and I'm sorry. I guess I just wish that you didn't."

"Me too."

Victoria picked over her salad while Denise dug into her soup.

"Parker basically told me that he's not giving up. He's not going away easily," Victoria said.

"Do you think he's bold enough to start popping up on the regular?"

"After the stunt he pulled showing up at the office last night, I really don't know."

Denise moved her empty bowl to the side and wiped her mouth with her napkin, carefully accessing the situation. "Parker's an arrogant bastard, but he's not crazy. If he wanted to show his ass and make a scene he could've done it last night, but he didn't."

"So you think he'll just fade away?"

"I didn't say that."

"Yeah, the chances of that look slim," Victoria said.

"When does school start?"

"Next Monday." Victoria desperately wanted to switch Alexandria to another school. The only reason she hadn't was because she knew she'd have to explain the move to Ted. They'd spent months searching for schools before deciding on Peachtree Country Day. They both loved the school, and she knew if she told him that she wanted to move Alexandria, she better have a damn good reason why.

Denise rubbed her chin. "My guess is that he'll try to start some mess at the first school event where he gets an opportunity."

Victoria shook her head. "I don't think Parker would cause a scene in front of his son. He loves PJ too much to do something ridiculous like that."

Denise raised her brow. "You love Alexandria more than life, but you risked Ted leaving you and a possible custody battle, so don't tell me what people won't do."

Victoria couldn't say a word.

"Girlfriend, I'm not tryin' to be a bitch about this, I just want you to see the light."

"You're right. If I'd been thinking with a level head, I wouldn't be sitting here unable to eat and worried as hell right now."

"If my aunt had balls she'd be my uncle. You can't worry about what you can't change. The important thing is that you're thinking on the right track now, and you need to make sure you stay there."

Victoria rubbed her temples. "Ted's going to eventually find out that Parker's son goes to Alexandria's school, and he's bound to find out about Jack and Jill too. I have to figure out a way to explain why I haven't said something before now," she groaned. "This is such a mess."

"But it's one that you can dig yourself out of. The next time you take Alexandria to a Jack and Jill function, tell him that Parker's son recently joined…it's not exactly a lie. In the meantime, you need to find a way to tell him about the school situation because that's more immediate."

"You're right. I'll just tell him that I needed to stop by the school to drop off some last minute paper work and that while I was there I ran into Parker, who was registering his son too."

Denise smiled. "Now you're thinking. You need to work this before it works you."

Just then, Victoria's cell phone rang. "It's him," she said, looking at Parker's reversed initials, *BP*, appear in bright letters across the screen.

"Don't answer it," Denise said, staring at the blinking light on Victoria's phone. "From this point forward don't answer any of his phone calls and don't respond to his emails or text messages. You need to cut off all forms of communication with him. If he conveniently shows up any place where you're at, leave immediately and tell him that you'll call his chief of staff at the hospital if he does it again. You've gotta back his ass down."

Victoria nodded her head, regretting the situation she was in, but knowing she was the only person to blame.

This World Is Too Damn Small!…

Two weeks had gone by, school had started, and Victoria and Ted were attending their first PTA event at Alexandria's school. They were pleased that she was adjusting so well to her new environment. She loved her teacher and had already made a group of new friends.

While Ted held court beside Victoria, listening to the PTA president outline their goals for the coming year, she tried to steady her nerves. She was on pins and needles at the thought that Parker might walk through the door at any minute. She still hadn't told Ted about seeing her ex-lover at the school because he'd been in and out of town so much on business trips that they'd barely seen each other at all. And she knew that she couldn't break the news to him as she'd planned on doing because now that he seemed to be back to his old self again, she was sure he'd be able to see through any attempt to cover up the truth. She would have to come clean and admit that she'd known for nearly two months that Parker's son was a student at Alexandria's school. But the fact that PJ was a student at Peachtree Country Day wasn't going to be the problem—Parker was.

She knew for certain that Ted wouldn't be pleased that Parker was back on the scene, but more importantly, he'd be pissed that it had taken her so long to mention it. That alone would raise his suspicions about their involvement. Her only saving grace was that he'd yet to tell her the full details about his mother's secret, and she knew she could use that as ammunition to back him off if she needed too.

And to make matters worse, just as she'd feared, PJ was in Alexandria's class. She hadn't been caught off guard when she ran into Parker and his son on the first day of school. She'd been prepared for it. But her blood pressure rose a notch when she found out that PJ was in Alexandria's class. As soon as the two kindergarteners saw each other they bonded again like Siamese twins. Parker was delighted but Victoria was more than a little nervous about their children's instant connection. She could see where it was going, and all roads lead straight to trouble.

Since that first day of school, all Alexandria could talk about was PJ, and the dog she wanted because he had one. And to throw Victoria's nerves into overdrive, Alexandria had practically begged for the two of them to have a playdate. "Mommy, can PJ come over and play, please, please," she'd asked just two days ago.

Luckily for Victoria, Ted had been gone so much lately that when he made it home, coming in late after business trips out of town and long days at the office, Alexandria had only briefly mentioned her new friend to him because she was too engrossed in the bedtime stories he read when he tucked her in.

Outside of seeing Parker at school a few times when she dropped Alexandria off in the morning, Victoria had managed to avoid contact with him since his surprise visit to her office. He'd called her several times, and sent texts and emails, but she hadn't responded to any of them. She was thankful that he hadn't done anything crazy so far, but she knew it was only a matter of time before Ted would find out that he'd re-entered their lives.

Victoria tried to relax and enjoy the PTA meeting, but her mind wouldn't allow it.

Ted eyed her with concern. "You keep looking around, like you're expecting someone. Are you okay?" he asked.

"I'm fine. Just checking out the room." Victoria gave him a quick smile, trying her best to ignore the intense stare of his piercing eyes. She could see that Ted was studying her, noticing every little detail, every little nuance, and every move she made. Even though he'd been traveling on business for most of the week and this was his first night home in several days, she knew that he'd begun to notice signs that something was wrong with her. She was jumpy, nervous and distracted.

The next hour went by without incident, and to Victoria's great relief, Parker hadn't made an appearance. After the school principal made the final remarks, the PTA president adjourned the meeting.

Minutes later, Victoria and Ted mingled with a few other parents. She was feeling a little more at ease until she felt a small tap on her shoulder. She turned around so quickly she almost gave herself a case of whiplash.

"Hi, Victoria. It's good to see you again," Roberta Stevens smiled.

This world is too damn small! Victoria hadn't seen Roberta since the Jack and Jill meeting nearly two months ago. "Hi, Roberta, it's good to see you too," she smiled back. "I didn't know your son was a student here."

"Yes, this is Al Jr.'s second year, and he loves it." Roberta beamed as the short, heavy set man beside her nodded with enthusiasm. "This is my husband, Alvin," Roberta said, introducing him as she exchanged glances between Victoria and Ted.

Victoria and Ted greeted him with warm smiles and strong hand-shakes. The two couples made pleasant small talk which mostly centered around their children.

"Victoria, I don't know what your schedule is like but we sure could use your help planning the Jack and Jill holiday social this year. We're having a meeting at Hilda's house next weekend. Think you can make it?" Roberta asked.

Victoria purposely hadn't mentioned Alexandria's membership in Jack and Jill since the disagreement she and Ted had ironed out, and she was glad that he'd forgotten about it in the wake of all that had recently happened. But now, Roberta was re-opening the can of worms. "No, I'll be tied up with an event next weekend. And actually, my schedule...our schedules," she said looking at Ted, "are so busy that I'm not sure how involved we'll be." She wanted Roberta to know that Jack and Jill wasn't a household topic, and she hoped the chatty woman would drop the line of conversation.

"Oh, I completely understand," Roberta squeaked in her high-pitched voice. "Well, since you're so busy I'd be more than happy to pick up your daughter and take her to the library for their field trip this weekend."

Victoria wished she could slap a piece of duct tape over Roberta's big mouth. "Thanks for the offer, but that won't be necessary," she smiled.

Roberta opened her mouth, ready to make another suggestion but Victoria interrupted her. "Look at the time," she said, glancing at her watch. "I've got an early morning meeting so I think we're going to call it a night." She looked at Ted, giving him a stare that said, *back me up.* He nodded in agreement.

"Okay," Roberta grinned. "We'll have to get together soon. I'll give you a call next week."

After they said their goodbyes, Victoria and Ted turned to walk away. "V, I know we had our disagreements about it, but like I told you, I'm fine with Alexandria being in Jack and Jill."

"I know, but I think she'll have enough things to occupy her time between the ballet lessons she started this week and the piano lessons she'll start next week. Not to mention homework and all the new play-dates she'll have coming up. I just don't want to overload her."

"You're right. I've been so busy and pre-occupied, I don't even know my own child's schedule."

"That's what you've got me for," Victoria winked.

Ted took her hand in his as they prepared to leave. They were nearly out the door when Alexandria's teacher, walked up to them.

"Hello, Mrs. Thornton," Emily Snow greeted with a perky smile.

Victoria smiled back, giving her a quick hug. "Let me introduce you to my husband." She made the introductions, glad that the two were finally getting a chance to meet. She liked Alexandria's teacher, who was a twenty-something, young black woman with a progressive and interactive teaching style. They'd had a nice chat on the first day of school when Victoria discovered they were both Spelman graduates. She appreciated the women's eclectic quirkiness and fresh innocence. She was a combination of bohemian meets elegance, with a hint of southern charm sprinkled in. Emily Snow had not yet been jaded by years of institutional bureaucracy or the politics that often came along with being a tenured teacher at a top-tier private school. She was a genuinely sweet person, and Victoria also appreciated the young woman's dedication to her family. She was the primary caregiver for her terminally ill mother.

"Alexandria loves you," Ted praised, giving Ms. Snow a warm smile. "She talks about how much fun she has in your class. When kids think learning is fun, it's a sign that somebody's doing their job."

Ms. Snow beamed, flattered by the compliment. "It's a joy to have a bright and inquisitive student like Alexandria. She makes teaching easy."

"Thank you," Victoria said.

"You two have done a great job with her. She's so smart and outgoing, she gets along well with her classmates, and the other teachers adore her," Ms. Snow nodded from Victoria to Ted. "She's a regular little Ms. Congeniality."

Ted slipped his arm around Victoria's waist. "She inherited her charm from her mother."

"I can see that," Ms. Snow smiled at Victoria. "That's a great quality to have."

"Thank you, both," Victoria said.

"Yes, Alexandria is a leader among her classmates, and she's made lots of friends already, especially PJ. The two of them are inseparable," Ms. Snow giggled.

Victoria felt a cold rush slide through her veins.

"I believe she's mentioned his name a few times," Ted grinned, not surprised that Alexandria had already learned how to steal men's hearts—she was, afterall, her mother's daughter.

"PJ is a joy too. His father couldn't be here tonight because he had surgery."

Victoria felt another jolt rush through her body.

"Oh, I hope he's going to be all right," Ted responded with concern.

Ms. Snow waved her hand in the air. "Forgive me, that came out all wrong. Dr. Brightwood isn't having surgery, he's performing surgery. One of his patients took a turn for the worse and..."

"Did you say Dr. Brightwood?" Ted interrupted.

Ms. Snow nodded her head with enthusiasm. "Yes."

"Dr. Parker Brightwood?"

Victoria's knees locked in place.

"Why, yes. You don't know PJ's father?" Ms. Snow asked, looking at

Ted and then back to Victoria. She'd seen Parker and Victoria interact during the first day of school, and Parker himself had told her that the two of them were old friends. Now, seeing the uncomfortable look on Victoria's face and the uneasy look on Ted's, Ms. Snow knew that he was old friends with only one of them and that the history wasn't good.

Then another thought came to Ms. Snow's mind. She quickly connected the dots and the picture became crystal clear. Her best friend, Samantha, had told her about a new guy she'd met when she came to town last month to attend a co-worker's wedding. She was head over heels for him, and he happened to be best friends with the woman who her cousin Parker used to date, and still loved. Emily had known Parker for years. They'd met when she went home with Samantha for school break during their freshman year of college, and just like Samantha, Parker had become like family. She was the reason he'd enrolled his son in Peachtree Country Day.

Samantha hadn't gone into specific details during their brief phone conversation because she wasn't one to gossip, but she was worried about her cousin. She mentioned that Parker was going through a rough emotional time. The woman he loved was married to someone else, but he still had hopes that they'd get back together because there were unresolved feelings between the two of them.

Looking at the pained expression on Victoria's face, and the tension that gripped her husband's jaw, Ms. Snow knew that she was the mystery woman who Samantha had spoken of.

The three stood in awkward silence before Ms. Snow politely excused herself and made a quick departure, sighting that she had to greet other parents.

Within minutes Victoria and Ted left the school auditorium and headed to their car. No words spoken between them. As soon as he closed the door, Ted turned on the engine and faced his wife. "So, that's who you were looking for?"

Victoria buckled her seatbelt and prepared for the bumpy ride that was about to come.

Your Big Girl Panties...

Tyler leaned back in the chair in front of Victoria's desk. After the tumultuous night she'd had, she called Tyler as soon as she dropped Alexandria off at school. He had just finished his morning workout at the gym and decided to drop by her office to give her moral support.

Tyler sighed. "I knew some shit like this was gonna jump off. This isn't good."

"I know," Victoria said, putting her hand to her head.

"So how bad did Ted go off?"

"He was pretty mad. He's not the type to rant and rave or raise his voice, but he was pissed for sure."

"You're lucky you're married to a white boy, 'cause a brothah would've gone the hell off."

Victoria rolled her eyes. "You know you're not right, right?"

"But you know it's true," Tyler said. "It's not like we're talking about a casual friend who you haven't seen in years. This is a man you used to be in a relationship with, a man you used to sleep with, who your husband can't stand."

"Loathe is a better word."

"See, that's even worse."

Victoria knew that Tyler was right. By the time she and Ted had reached their house, he was heated and she was remorseful. Fortunately, Alexandria had been fast asleep and the babysitter eased her way out so they could finish their war of words.

"I told you," Victoria attempted to explain for a third time. "Your mother had just passed away and I didn't want to upset you any further. Then one thing led to another and you were so distraught...I just didn't say anything."

Ted looked at her, trying to keep his voice calm. "We've always had a very honest relationship and you know you can tell me anything, no matter the situation, so why would you keep something like this from me?"

"You hypocrite," Victoria threw back at him. "Not only have you lied to me, you've asked me to be patient about it. And you still haven't told me the whole truth about the secret your mother was keeping. If we can tell each other any and everything, why haven't you told me that?"

"V, the situation with my mother is completely different."

"How so?"

"It's about family business, something that my mother intended for only me to know. It has nothing to do with a third party outside our marriage. Parker is your ex-lover, and you felt a need to keep this from me even though you've had contact with him on several occasions."

Victoria crossed her arms. "Well, no matter how you want to couch it, keeping a secret is keeping a secret...simple as that."

"Your entire argument about secrets is a misnomer. My mother was the one with the secret, not me." Ted paused staring at his wife with suspicion. "Do you have a secret that you're not telling me about? Is there more that I need to know?"

Victoria bristled. "Don't turn this on me when you're still withholding information."

Their conversation wavered through a laborious back and forth for another hour before they agreed to call a truce. Ted assured Victoria that he would tell her about his mother's sordid past in due time, leading her to believe that Carolyn had committed some small indiscretion that was unethical but not harmful. And Victoria told him that he had absolutely nothing to worry about with Parker, giving him the impression that their interaction had been brief and strictly platonic, centering around their children. After all was said and done they finally laid their heavy burdens on their pillows, falling into a restless sleep.

Just as quickly as they'd gotten back on track, the wheels had started coming off again.

Victoria shook her head as she thought about the way they practically avoided each other as they got dressed this morning, and the small, passionless kiss that Ted had placed on her forehead before heading out the door.

Back in the present, Victoria rubbed her temples as she spoke to Tyler. "I can't believe that your new girlfriend is best friends with Alexandria's teacher. Why didn't you tell me?"

"'Cause I had no idea. You know I don't talk about your business, not to Sam or anyone else. All she knows about you is that you're my best friend, my ace. Any other info she's gotten has been on her own or through Parker. But honestly, Sam's not the gossipy type. That's one of the things I like about her, she doesn't get into that he-said-she-said nonsense. And trust, if she did, your shit would've been blown up long before now."

"I can't believe that in the course of two months my marriage has gone from sugar to shit."

"It's called trials and tribulations. Right now you're in a *Splenda* stage."

"You think this is funny?" Victoria huffed.

"No, I think it's fucked up, but shit happens. As I recall, someone very smart once told me, and I quote, 'Tyler, everyone makes mistakes.'"

Victoria smiled, remembering the advice she'd given him years ago when he'd been lamenting over the mistake he made when he'd broken up with Juliet. The two friends sat in a moment of silence around his dead wife's memory.

"How's it going with Samantha?" Victoria asked, drawing both their minds back to the present moment.

Tyler smiled, but didn't show any teeth. "It's um, okay." He avoided Victoria's eyes.

She looked at her friend as she leaned forward, searching his face to confirm what her intuition already told her. "You're falling in love, aren't you?"

Tyler knew he couldn't skip around the truth with the one person who'd always been his closest confidant. With the exception of Victoria, he'd been afraid to open up his heart because it seemed that everyone he truly loved either ended up dead or walking out of his life.

But the connection he felt with Samantha was organic and he couldn't ignore it, even though he had tried. From their initial encounter he wanted her. They'd made love that first night and he was hooked. He liked the fact that Samantha was tough, yet gentle, and her genuine, authentically flawed nature made him fall for her quicker than a New York minute. He'd started looking forward to her phone calls and texts and thinking about her when they were apart. But the things he loved about her were the very things that scared him most, making him reluctant to get any closer. He didn't want a bad fate to befall them.

"I'm not gonna lie, I'm feelin' her. She's a good woman. But I'm not sure that she's the woman for me," Tyler answered.

"Why not?"

He shrugged. "It's complicated."

"Falling in love usually is." Just as Victoria was about to continue, she looked up and saw Denise walking through the door.

"I knew I heard the voice of one of the most handsome, intelligent, sexy men on the planet," Denise smiled wide, walking toward Tyler with her arms out-stretched for a hug.

"See, you know how to make a brothah feel ten feet tall. No wonder Vernon's been hangin' in there all these years," Tyler grinned, standing up to give Denise a big hug.

"You know that's right. How've you been?"

"I'm good."

Denise leaned against Tyler's chair as she turned her attention to Victoria. She instantly read the melancholy in her friend's eyes and knew that something was wrong, especially given that Tyler had made an early morning appearance. "What happened?" she asked with caution.

"Tyler, Denise knows about my salacious affair," Victoria said. "So now everything's out in the open among friends." If it hadn't been for the fact that Debbie was trying to rebound from her own messy affair, she would have patched her in by conference call so she could join in on the Pow Wow too.

Denise and Tyler looked at each other and shook their heads, both full of worry. Then panic spread across Denise's face. "Oh, sweet Jesus," she gasped, putting her hand over her mouth. "Did Ted find out?"

"No," Victoria sighed. "But he may as well have." She gave Denise a brief rundown of the incident that happened at last night's PTA meeting.

"See, I told you to leave Parker's slick ass alone. You should've stayed away from him from the very beginning. Remember, I told you he'd be trouble," Denise said, sucking her teeth.

Victoria looked from her to Tyler, then back to her again. "I sure am lucky to have friends who like to continually say, *I told you so*. Aren't you the one who said I should stop focusing on what I can't change and move forward to try and fix things?"

Denise nodded. "Yes, I did. And I'll say this too…Yeah, I'm the kind of friend who'll tell you, *I told you so*, but I'm also the kind of friend who loves you enough to give a damn and will tell you what you need to hear, when you need to hear it."

"Amen," Tyler followed up. "So dry up that sad face, put on your big girl panties, and start handling your business."

Victoria could only nod her head because she knew her friends were right. She didn't have time to sulk or contemplate. She'd made a litany of poor decisions, but now it was time to forget about the mistakes she'd made and work hard to repair the dents that had pierced her marriage. She knew she had to act quickly if she wanted to keep her man!

Chapter 17

The Shit Had Hit The Fan...

An hour after talking with Tyler and Denise, Victoria found herself riding up the elevator to the twenty-fifth floor of the ViaTech building. She decided that she needed to start making up for lost ground. Her marriage was in need of repair and she knew just the particular set of tools that would do the job.

She planned to strut into Ted's office and surprise him with a little mid-day pick-me-up—a quick afternoon romp on the top of his desk. And even if he was in a meeting, she'd wait because at the moment there was nothing more important than doing whatever it took to jump start their passion again.

She felt a sense of deja'vu when she stepped off the wood paneled elevator and headed toward the opulence of Ted's office on the executive floor. She remembered the days when she used to work at ViaTech and she'd walked those very halls. It all seemed like a life-time ago. She hadn't visited his office since she went to meet him there before the company's Christmas party last year, and now she had a party of her own in mind for him.

She greeted Ted's assistant with a huge smile. "Hi, Jen. How are you?"

Jen lit up like Ted had just given her the day off. She'd always liked

Victoria. They regularly kept in touch around Ted's schedule. Jen was his woman from nine to five, before handing him over to Victoria to claim at the end of the day. The two had come to develop a great relationship.

"Victoria, it's so good to see you!" Jen said, nearly leaping from behind her desk to give Victoria a warm hug. "Ted didn't tell me you were coming by."

"He's not expecting me. I thought I'd pop in and surprise him," she said, looking at Ted's closed office door.

"Well, he'll certainly be thrilled," Jen said, shifting her chipper smile to one of mild concern. "He needs a good surprise…he's been a little on edge since he came in this morning."

The one thing Victoria knew about her husband was that he was cool under any kind of pressure, and if he'd allowed his mood to show, he was probably more upset from their argument last night than she'd thought. "Is he in?" she asked.

"No, he had to step out at the last minute for an off-site meeting. But I'm expecting him back any minute. Would you like to wait in his office?"

Victoria nodded, and headed toward his door. "Oh, and Jen…don't tell him that I'm here. Remember, it's a surprise."

Jen clasped her hands together. "Excellent! I'm sure his spirits will lift when he walks through the door and sees you."

"Let's hope so," Victoria said under her breath. She stepped into Ted's office and closed the door behind her.

She looked around her husband's spacious office, noticing the meticulous way he kept everything in neat order. "Why can't he keep his closet at home this tidy?" Victoria whispered aloud, examining a heavy lead-crystal paperweight that rested atop a stack of perfectly centered, straight-edged papers on his credenza. Her eyes roamed over to the two pictures that sat on his desk. *I love this one*, she smiled to herself, picking up one of the framed photographs. It was her favorite; the picture they'd taken the day they brought Alexandria home from the hospital. She looked at her family, holding the picture to her heart, and prayed it wasn't too late to undo the damage she'd created.

She put the photo back where she found it and came up with an idea. She grinned as she slid into Ted's leather chair behind his desk, ready for a little fun. Knowing that he would walk through the door at any minute, she leaned back carefully, propping her seductively long legs on top of his desk, and raised her short black skirt up her thighs. She undid the top three buttons of her silk blouse to expose her lacy push-up bra, and waited to give her husband a thrilling surprise.

When a few minutes went by with no grand entrance from Ted, Victoria began to relax her pose. She let her arm dangle off the edge of the chair and hoped that her husband would soon walk through the door.

After an hour of waiting, Jen's periodic checks to see if she needed anything, and eating a snack of fruit and juice from Ted's compact refrigerator, Victoria gave up hope that he was coming anytime soon. "His meeting must've run over," Jen had offered twenty minutes ago. "Those last minute meetings usually require more time…putting out fires."

Victoria knew that she needed to leave soon. She had an afternoon appointment with the director of Dress for Success, to help the organization plan their annual gala. She looked at her watch, knowing she was cutting it close.

Disappointment was an understatement to describe her mood. She wanted to do something passionate and spontaneous that would excite Ted and reignite the flame in their marriage that was slowly fading away. As she looked around, something caught her attention, leading her eyes to fall beneath his desk. She had another idea that just might do the trick. She scooted the chair out and leaned forward, reaching for his attaché that was lying on the floor, tucked away behind the small cabinet that held his files.

She knew from experience that Ted always kept his attaché with him when he was out on business. She thought it was strange that he'd neglected to take it with him, but it was also her good fortune because it was perfect for what she had in mind.

She bent down underneath his desk and retrieved the leather bag. "This should get him going," she smiled, reaching over for his pen and stationary. She wrote Ted a quick, erotic love note that detailed what she had in store for him when he came home that evening. She pressed her berry-colored lips against the parchment paper, giving it her sexy seal, then stood up and slid her silk thong down the length of her legs. She opened his attaché to place the note and seductive undergarment inside and smiled again, thinking about the surprise that would greet him when he opened it. But her smile slowly faded when she examined the bag's contents. She put her panties back on and took a seat in the chair.

Victoria sat at Ted's desk in complete shock, confusion, and utter disbelief as she poured over the Xeroxed documents in front of her. She re-read each one, making sure that her eyes weren't playing tricks on her. She held a copy of Carolyn's birth certificate in one hand and her hand-written letter to Ted in the other. Her stomach formed into a ball of knots. "This is the secret his mother was hiding? This is what was so awful that he couldn't bring himself to tell me?" Victoria's heart sank as her temperature began to rise.

She sat back, letting the documents fall to Ted's desk, stupefied by her discovery. "He's been lying all this time because he doesn't want anyone to know that he's black," she whispered into the air. A sick sensation filled her, and just as she took a deep breath to hold back her emotions, Ted walked through the door.

He stopped in his tracks, surprised to see Victoria sitting behind his desk. He smiled at the sight of her open blouse and abundant cleavage, but he quickly lost the thrill of excitement when he saw the look on her face, and the all too familiar documents that sat on his desk. He'd been so busy rushing off to his meeting that he hadn't realized he'd left his attaché in his office until he was already half-way across town.

He could've kicked himself for not locking the copies away in a safe place as he'd planned to do ever since he'd stored the originals in the safe deposit box. He cursed himself for walking around with the copies he intended to hand-deliver to Abe Brookstein when he came to visit at the end of the week. He'd appointed Abe as his sole attorney, and in the interest of client confidentiality, he was bound by law to keep what had now become his secret too.

But now the shit had hit the fan, and Ted knew he had to deal with it. He closed the door behind him and walked toward his wife.

Victoria stood up from behind his desk, letting her anger fly out with her words. "This is what you were gonna tell me in due time?" she mocked, holding the copy of his mother's birth certificate in the air."

"V, calm down. I can explain."

"You should've explained when I first asked you about what you discovered in that safe deposit box."

"It's more complicated than you think."

"Yeah, being black can complicate the hell out of things, huh?" Right now I don't want to hear shit from you. Don't say another word to me."

"Lower your voice," Ted commanded in a tone that was as steady as if he'd asked her if she wanted a drink. Although the walls and doors were thick and well insulated, he knew they were no match for the pitch his wife could carry.

Victoria couldn't believe how calm he was acting, almost cavalier. "Lower my voice?" she yelled, ignoring him. "I'll turn this place the hell out if I want to."

Ted had witnessed this side of Victoria before, particularly during heated arguments with family members and on the rare occasions that a rude, demanding client tried to take advantage of her services. But up until now he'd never been on the receiving end of the wrath he knew she was capable of wielding, and it occurred to him that he didn't know if he could contain her. "V, you've got to calm down," he urged. "This isn't the time or place." He calmly raised his hands in surrender, but now his cool exterior was beginning to melt.

Victoria put her hand on her hip. She was getting ready to open fire but something inside stopped her. She parted her lips but nothing came out except a feeling of deep hurt. She knew she needed to get out of his office. Without a word, she grabbed her handbag and began to walk past him, headed for the door.

"Where're you going?" Ted asked.

"Don't say shit to me."

"Where're you going?" he repeated.

Victoria didn't answer, instead she opened the door and charged out like someone was chasing her.

Jen looked up as Victoria rushed past her desk with her blouse hanging open. She'd heard the muffled sounds of what she thought was an argument, and when she saw Ted take off behind her, hot on his wife's heels, she knew there was no longer a need to wonder.

Ted reached the elevator and stepped inside where Victoria had just entered. He held the button to keep the door closed as they rode down to the executive parking garage.

"V, I know you're upset, and I know what you're thinking…"

Victoria broke her silence. "You're ashamed to admit that you're black, even though you're married to a black woman and you have a black child," she yelled in his face.

"Please calm down."

"I'm gonna slap the shit out of you if you tell me to calm down one more time."

Ted looked at Victoria in disbelief, but he knew his wife and what she was capable of, and at this stage he didn't want to tempt fate so he changed his approach. "I just want you to relax so we can discuss this is a rational manner."

Victoria rolled her eyes. "There's no need to discuss anything. I already told you, I don't want you to say shit to me."

Just then the elevator door opened and Victoria nearly pushed Ted aside trying to get out. Again, he followed on her heels as she walked to her car. "Stop following me. Just go away," she yelled. She pulled out her key chain, pointing it toward the car as she pressed the remote. "Didn't I tell you to go away," she barked.

Now, Ted was beginning to loose what little calm he'd managed to maintain. "V, please. Just listen to me." He grabbed her arm, preventing her from opening her driver's side door. He didn't care about the security cameras that monitored the area, at the moment his only worry was centered around the situation in front of him. "I know you're upset, and I know I should've told you the truth before now…"

Victoria cut him off, jerked her arm away and turned around to face him. "Yeah, you should have, but you would've had to admit that you're black…now I know why you have rhythm and a big dick."

"Was that supposed to be a joke?"

"Nothing about this shit is funny." Her voice became low and venomous. "It's fine to fuck a black woman, but it's another thing to admit that you're a black man isn't it?" A small tear rolled down her cheek.

Ted reached for her, but she slapped his hand away. "Don't fucking touch me," she screamed. He reached for her again, this time taking hold of her shoulders and bringing her into his embrace. Victoria squirmed and hit him repeatedly, but he wouldn't let go. Her tears began to flow harder as her blows dissipated. Finally she stopped fighting, looking at Ted in dead silence. They stood facing each other, letting the stuffy air fill the small space between them.

"If you're so ashamed of who your mother was, of who you really are, what does that say about us?" Victoria said, pointing her finger into his chest. "What does that say about what you think of me...of our daughter?"

Ted fought hard to hold back the emotions that were lodged in the back of his throat. He looked Victoria in the eye. "Let's go home so we can talk...I'll answer all your questions."

The Shoe Was On The Other Foot...

Thirty minutes later, Victoria and Ted sat on opposite ends of the sofa in their spacious family room. The richly colored walls and elegantly cozy furnishings were a stark contrast to the gloomy mood and uncomfortable stillness that now owned the space.

Even though Ted knew that Victoria didn't want him anywhere near her, he moved over and sat close beside her anyway. "I want to start by saying I'm sorry," he began. "Some of what I'm going to say might make sense, and some might not. But please, just hear me out, okay?"

Victoria nodded her head.

"When I first read my mother's letter and discovered that she'd been living a lie her entire life, I was so shocked and stunned I couldn't even think straight. I felt like I'd lost her twice. I had to deal with burying her, trying to hold Lilly together and keep Charlie under control, and then making sure that you and Alexandria were okay. I'm not trying to excuse how I've handled things, but for the first time in my life I didn't feel like I was in control of what was going on around me."

Ted proceeded to tell Victoria about the trip he'd taken to Mississippi to find out more about his mother's life. He told her about his visit with Ms. Hattie and about the up and down emotions he'd been experiencing since his discovery. "I hated lying to you, V...but I didn't know what else to do. Imagine finding out that you aren't who you think you are. All my life I've lived as a white man, and then in the flash of a second I found out that I'm not, that I'm black, or at least a part of me is," he said with a chuckle that bordered between light and melancholy. "When I look at myself I don't see a black man and to be honest, it's hard for me to even think of myself as anyone other than who I am, which is simply Ted, husband and father, period. I had never even thought about the fact that I'm white. I just am who I am. And I never thought about race in any real context until I fell in love with you."

Ted reached for Victoria's hand and held it. He could see that she was apprehensive and doubting, but he pushed forward anyway. "Marrying you was the best thing I've ever done. It didn't matter to me that you were black. I loved you. I'm not ashamed of you, or of the fact that I'm married to you. I know that many, many men of any persuasion would love to be in my shoes. I'm a lucky man," he smiled. "You've given me a beautiful daughter who I adore, and you've enriched my life in so many ways. You and Alexandria mean everything to me."

Ted positioned himself so that he could look directly into Victoria's face, lifting her chin with his thumb and index finger so they were eye level. "When the world sees us, they aren't going to see a black couple, they're going to see a white man with a black woman; an interracial couple. I struggled with that part of it...who I really am. Am I black or am I white? I look white, but my mother was a black woman, and in this society I'm my mother's child. But I realized that regardless of race, I'm the same person I've always been."

Victoria couldn't hold her tongue any longer. "Like your mother, you have the option of choosing. It's very convenient to say, 'I am who I am,' when society accepts *who* you are. You made your mother's secret sound so shameful...hell, I thought she'd killed someone or robbed a bank or something. The only crime she committed was being black."

"Being black isn't a crime."

"You're acting like it is."

"I've just had a hard time accepting and dealing with everything that's been going on. Can't you understand that?"

Victoria looked at him in silence. "It's been nearly two months since you found out the truth, and in that time I'm sure you've done a lot of thinking. As a matter of fact I know you have because I've seen the distant, pre-occupied look in your eyes. Now I'm sitting here wondering, if I hadn't found out by accident, would you have ever told me?"

Ted looked at her, unable to answer.

"You locked away the evidence like your mother did, and you're meeting with Abe when he comes to town this Friday. Did you ever plan on telling me, or is this something you were going to take to your grave like your mother did?"

Ted shook his head. "Honestly, I don't know."

Victoria let out a heavy sigh as she shifted in her seat on the couch.

"V, I lost my mother and I found out that she and my father lived a lie. For weeks our daughter walked around worrying if you or I were going to drop dead at any minute, and then I watched our marriage start to crumble before my eyes. Damnit, V, this has been the hardest two months of my life." Ted shook his head, pausing for breath. "I don't have all the answers and I don't know how to explain things so that it makes sense to your ears because it's barely real to mine. And yes, the hard truth is that I didn't want to admit that I'm black because I thought it would take away from who I am."

Victoria looked at him, realizing how much the naked truth hurt. His last words stung.

Ted could see the pain in her eyes. He paused, trying to calm himself as his heart raced, beginning to literally pound inside his chest. "Does it freak me out to know that I'm black...hell yes. Am I ashamed of it...no. It's a vacillating feeling, but I can't say that it's shame. I just don't know how to deal with it. The way I handled things was wrong. " He looked into Victoria's eyes, hoping she'd see the truth and sincerity in his words. "Being ashamed of who I am would mean that I'm ashamed of who you are, and of the beautiful child we created."

"Then why did you make your mother's secret seem so...bad?"

Ted took a deep breath. "Because what she did was a terrible thing, it was wrong. She denied who she was, and that denial kept Lilly, Charlie and me from knowing who we truly are. She taught me how to live in secrecy, how to keep things locked away in private places. From the time I was Alexandria's age she drilled into my head that reputation and image was everything and that you should go to any lengths to guard it, even if it meant living an unhappy life and holding up a façade to the world that was total bullshit. That's how I operated until I met you. I'm not saying that my mother is responsible for the mistakes I made, those are mine and mine alone. When I spoke of my mother's secret, what you heard in my words and in my voice was frustration and sadness."

"Sadness...why?"

"Because my mother lived her entire life with pain and conflict always resting in her heart. Maybe that's why it was so difficult for her to get close to people." Ted cleared his throat, choking back a small tear that eventually traveled down his cheek. "I don't want to be like my mother, I can't live my life that way. Please forgive me, V."

Ted reached out for Victoria, and without hesitation she embraced him, hugging him close as they leaned back onto the sofa.

"Shhh," she whispered. "You can choose a different path." She stroked his hair, soothing him as she spoke. "I'm still not sure what to make of all this, but one thing I know is that we'll get through this together."

Victoria held him in her arms while he rested his head on her chest, unloading the last of his burdens from his heart. She ignored her chirping BlackBerry, switching it to vibrate in order to silence the annoying sound. She knew it was Denise, trying to get in touch with her to see why she hadn't come back for her afternoon appointment. But at the moment, she knew she was exactly where she needed to be.

She ran her fingers through Ted's thick, black hair, kissing the top of his head. She knew they'd both done things they wished they could change. Lies and secrets were a troubling combination, and she wondered when hers would come to light. But for now, she held on to the moment she had in her hands.

"I love you, V," Ted whispered, holding Victoria close.

"I love you too."

They laid together, side by side, still and remarkably peaceful for another full hour. Even though it wasn't the way Ted had wanted Victoria to learn about his mother's secret, he was relieved that everything was finally out in the open. He felt comfort and assurance in her arms. And although he knew that she still had mixed feelings about all that had just happened, and the many things he'd said, he knew they were headed in the right direction.

Victoria also felt relieved that the truth was finally out too. She still had questions though; not about Ted's mother's past, but about their future. She wondered if he would tell the rest of his family, or even acknowledge it to hers. *Will he just continue to live as a white man, because basically that's who he is?* A thousand thoughts ran through her mind but she didn't have the luxury to worry about them because other duties called. She looked at her watch. "I need to head over to the school to pick up Alexandria"

"I'll go with you," Ted offered.

Victoria hesitated. "You don't have to."

"But I want to. I've never picked her up from school before, not even when she was in daycare. This will be a little surprise for her."

We've had enough surprises for one day, Victoria thought but didn't say. And though she dared not mention his name, she feared it would be just her luck that they'd run into Parker.

They gathered their things and headed to the garage. Ted opened the passenger side door to let Victoria in. He took her hand in his. "V, I promise that from this moment forward I'll never keep anything from you, ever again. I know you've lost some trust in me, and I don't blame you, but I'm going to work hard to regain it."

Victoria felt herself shrinking. There he was, talking about trust and second chances, and all the while she was keeping a secret of her own. For a split second, in the spirit of open and honest disclosure, the thought crossed her mind to confess about sleeping with Parker. But then her common sense kicked in, persuading her to keep her mouth shut. So instead of standing in front of her husband with the taste of betrayal on the tip of her tongue, she swallowed her sins, jumped in the front seat, and wondered if he'd give her a second chance if the shoe was on the other foot.

Walking A Death March...

The minute Victoria and Ted pulled into the pick up line in the school parking lot, Victoria knew there would be trouble when she spotted Parker's vehicle. Even though he was parked several cars ahead of them and huge SUVs and mini vans were blocking her view, she could spot his black Navigator anywhere. She could see from where she sat that his truck was empty, which meant he'd already gone inside to get PJ. Most days PJ's nanny picked him up from school, but today of all days Parker had decided to do the honors. Victoria bent her head down, rubbing her temples. *I can't believe this!*

"What's wrong?" Ted asked.

"Slight headache." She unbuckled her seatbelt in a hurry. "You can wait here, I'll go in and get Alexandria."

Ted opened his door at the same time. "That spoils the entire surprise. I'm coming with you."

As they walked up the steps and entered the building, Victoria silently prayed the quickest, most desperate prayer she'd ever uttered.

Even though he was still worked up over their confrontation, Ted had the presence of mind to know that something was wrong with his wife, and it had nothing to do with uncovering his mother's secret or their terrible argument that had followed. Her body language and facial expression spoke volumes that her mouth didn't. He'd noticed her mood from the moment they left the house, and he knew the reason why she was so uneasy—her fear that they'd run into Parker Brightwood.

From the moment he learned that Parker's son was in Alexandria's class, Ted knew it was only a matter of time before they'd come face to face again...and he was ready. He knew there was a chance that Parker would be there to pick up his son, but that was of no concern to him because his priorities rested with Victoria and Alexandria. He was thankful that the burden he'd been carrying was lifted and that his family now had a chance of getting back to normal. And at the moment, all he could think about was seeing his daughter's face light up with surprise when he walked into her classroom. In his mind, he relegated Parker to a consequence he'd deal with when the time came.

"It's the last classroom on the right," Victoria said, looking straight ahead as though she was walking a death march.

Ted slowed his pace and came to a stop just outside of Alexandria's classroom. He gently rested his hand on Victoria's elbow. "Don't worry, it doesn't matter who's on the other side of that door," he said, looking into Victoria's eyes. "Like I've always said, the only thing that matters is you and me."

They looked at each other for a long moment. Victoria wanted to believe him, but she knew what he didn't. She exhaled, desperate to relieve the fifty pound weight that had lodged itself on top of her head. She had no doubt that whatever the situation, Ted wouldn't show his ass in public, and certainly not in front of their daughter. But suddenly she wasn't so sure about Parker. The last time the two men had faced each other it had turned into an ugly scene.

Victoria nodded her head and followed Ted as they walked through the door.

Chapter 18

The Volcano That Was About To Erupt...

Victoria's entire body stiffened when she saw Parker standing off to the side. He was talking with Ms. Snow while Alexandria and PJ were busy playing with building blocks on a mat in the playroom corner. She knew the only reason he was hanging around, chatting up his cousin's friend was so he could run into her. She was pissed that he'd never told her about the connection and wondered why he'd kept that information under raps. She took a deep breath and readied herself.

"Daddy!" Alexandria squealed when she looked up and saw Ted. She dropped the colorful, plastic toys and sprinted toward her father.

Ted bent down and scooped Alexandria up into his arms while Victoria tried to pace her breathing. "How's my, Princess?" he smiled, giving her a kiss on the cheek.

Alexandria hugged his neck tight, grinning from ear to ear. "I want you to see what I made," she said, pointing toward a wall full of finger painted pictures. She wriggled out of Ted's arms and led her parents over to look at the masterpiece she'd created during art period.

Victoria stayed close as they walked over to the wall to see Alexandria's artwork. She looked down when she saw PJ come up and stand beside them. He flexed his adorably dimpled cheeks and offered a smile. *"Hi, Mizz Thornton,"* he grinned. "Me and Ali made pictures today." He pointed to his own picture on the wall.

The way he sang Alexandria's pet name in his cuddly soft voice made Victoria want to give him a big hug. "That's a very nice picture, PJ," she smiled. His gentle-hearted demeanor, doe shaped eyes, and innocent charm made her nearly forget the trouble that was attached to him.

"So you're, PJ," Ted smiled, bending down to greet the little boy who looked so much like his father that he was taken aback.

PJ grinned and nodded like a bobblehead doll. "You're Ali's dad?"

"I sure am."

"There's my dad," he said with excitement, pointing toward Parker.

No sooner had the words come out of PJ's mouth, did Parker walk over and stand by his son. He'd been watching them like a hawk since they'd entered the room. "Hello," he said, looking directly at Ted. No smile, no hand shake.

"Hi, Mr. Brightwood!" Alexandria shouted.

Parker temporarily averted his eyes, looking down at his son's new best friend. "Hi sweetie, did you and PJ have a good time today?"

PJ interrupted. "Dad, can Ali come over and play? I want her to see Noah," he said. Alexandria had already declared she was getting a dog too.

Alexandria looked at Ted. "Can I Daddy, *pretty pleeeeaaaassse?*"

Victoria narrowed her eyes. "Not now, Alexandria."

Ted stared back at Parker as he spoke to his daughter. "We'll see, Princess."

Parker didn't look away and it made Victoria nervous as hell.

Parker wanted to say something to Ted, but he stopped himself because he could see the sheer panic and anxiety on Victoria's face. He hated the way Ted stood in front of him, holding Victoria's hand with the satisfied look of a man who'd just won a first place trophy. He wanted to tell him that he'd made love to his wife, and that he couldn't wait until their next rendezvous so he could feel the warmth that resided between her legs. Although he didn't speak it, he let his eyes do his talking. He wanted her, and he didn't give a damn if Ted knew it.

There they were, Victoria, Ted, and Parker, standing in complete silence as their children played and chatted away, oblivious to the volcano that was about to erupt.

Parker knew he should let the moment fade, that he shouldn't start what could become an ugly scene, but he couldn't resist. He saw an opening, so he eased into it. He looked at Victoria. "Roberta told me that she really wishes you'd change your mind about volunteering on the planning committee for the holiday social. I told her I'd ask you the next time I saw you."

Victoria nearly swallowed her tongue. She could see the small vein in Ted's right temple pop out, which meant he was pissed to high heaven. She'd never told him that she had seen Parker at the Jack and Jill meeting too. He was still under the impression that their first encounter had been during school registration. Ted dropped her hand and all she could do was look down at her feet.

"I think it's time to go," Ted motioned to Victoria, not taking his eyes off Parker. He knew he had to get out of there because despite his best efforts to remain calm, he was about to blow his cool. Now he understood why Victoria had suddenly lost interest in keeping Alexandria in Jack and Jill. The fact that she'd kept it from him made him wonder what else had gone on between the two of them. He caught every glimpse that Parker had thrown Victoria's way, and he wasn't about to stand by and watch another man lust after his wife. At least not without punching his lights out.

"Alexandria, go to your cubby hole and get your things. It's time to go home," Victoria said.

PJ followed Alexandria like he was her shadow. The two walked over to get their small backpacks, laughing and playing without a care in the world. Ted waited until the children were out of earshot before he spoke, letting out exactly what was on his mind. "Our kids are in the same class, so we'll run into each other from time to time. But I want to make myself very clear." He stared hard at Parker, giving a brief pause to set the tone for what came next. "Stay the hell away from my wife."

"Oh, Lord," Victoria said, barely above a whisper. She looked out of the corner of her eye and saw that Ms. Snow was staring with concern. Then she looked into Parker's eyes, silently pleading with him to back away from the trouble that was brewing. She motioned to Ted. "Let's go," she said, reaching for his hand, attempting to usher him away.

"You better listen to her," Parker said, never raising his voice. "You still don't know who you're fucking with, do you?" Although his tone was calm, his words were harsh and his jaw flinched as he spoke.

Just as things were heating up, Alexandria and PJ came walking up. "Let's go," Victoria urged again.

Both Ted and Parker calmed down because they didn't want to cause a scene that would frighten their children.

After saying goodbye to a watchful and worried looking Ms. Snow, they all headed out into the hallway. Alexandria and PJ raced ahead to see who could make it outside first. Parker strode in front as Victoria and Ted walked behind him in silence. Victoria didn't even attempt to say a word to Ted because she knew that his anger was beyond the pale. His nostrils were flared, his breathing was rapid, and the vein in his forehead was waving a flag.

Victoria took a deep breath when they finally made it out to the parking lot where Alexandria and PJ were already standing. Parker walked up to his truck, "Time to go big guy," he said, opening the back door. He buckled PJ in and closed the door.

Ted froze in his tracks, looking as if all the blood had been drained from his body. He stood for a moment, shaking his head from side to side in disbelief. He looked at the truck and remembered that it was the same lone vehicle that had been parked in the lot next to Victoria's office when he'd shown up there a few weeks ago. Since she had been working late, he'd made a mental note to scope out the area in case anyone was lurking around. He remembered the nervous pause he'd heard in her voice that night, and that she'd made him wait outside while she claimed she was in the restroom. "He was there," he said, turning to look at Victoria. "Sonofabitch!"

Parker looked up and saw what was happening.

"That was his truck I saw parked outside your office the night I went by to see you," Ted yelled at Victoria.

"I can explain," she pleaded. "Nothing happened. He just stopped by unexpectantly, and…"

"Stop!" Ted yelled again.

Alexandria looked on with confusion. She'd never heard her parents argue or even raise their voices for that matter. "Mommy, Daddy, what's wrong!?"

By now a few parents who were gathering their children were staring in Ted and Victoria's direction. Victoria reached in her bag for her keys and pointed the remote toward her car. She pressed the button and called out to Alexandria. "Get in, Sweetie."

Alexandria fumbled with the back door until she opened it, letting herself in. She was visibly disturbed, but she climbed into the back seat and did as her mother asked.

Victoria looked at Ted and pleaded again, this time with her eyes and her heart. "Let's go home," she said.

Parker watched with a careful and steady eye, preparing himself in case Ted decided to approach.

Disappointment and rage zigzagged across Ted's face. He looked at Victoria, and the hurt she saw in his eyes made her want to bury herself under the ground. He opened his mouth but then fell silent, his face twisting in pain.

"Ted, what's wrong?" Victoria said with alarm, seeing that something very, very bad was happening.

Ted's eyes widened and his breathing became labored. He grabbed his left arm and gasped for breath, reaching out for Victoria. He made an inaudible choking sound as he began to sink to his knees.

"Oh, God!" Victoria screamed.

Parker immediately knew what was happening and was over to Ted's side before he hit the ground. He propped him up under his arm as the school security officer on duty rushed over to help. Parker quickly fired off commands, speaking in a voice that was fatal yet calm. "Victoria, call 911, get the kids and keep them with you."

Victoria stood with panic in her eyes and fear on her face.

"Do it now," Parker ordered. He wasted no time as he and the security officer hurried Ted inside the school building.

Victoria reached for her cell and dialed 911, while concerned parents looked on, giving her words of reassurance. She glanced up and saw Alexandria peering through the car window with a wild-eyed look on her face. PJ had already undone his seatbelt and climbed out of his father's truck.

Victoria finished the call, looking from the closed door where Ted and Parker had just entered, to her daughter, who's eyes were now streaked with fear.

Ms. Snow rushed over to Victoria, "I'll watch them, she said, grabbing hold of PJ's hand as she headed toward Victoria's car to get Alexandria. "You go and see about your husband."

Victoria rushed up the steps and into the building.

Chapter 19

I Don't Know What I'll Do...

"Yes, Sweetie, your father's going to be just fine," Victoria said to Alexandria as she spoke into her Bluetooth. She was sitting in the waiting room of the Carlye Fraser Cardiac Care Unit, at Emory Crawford Long Hospital. "Remember when we were riding over to the hospital and I explained to you about how sometimes when you don't feel well, and Mommy has to take you to see Dr. Hutchins? Well, that's what we're doing with your father," she said, forcing herself to sound steady. "Those men who drove your daddy here in the ambulance were taking him to the doctor, and the doctor's going to make him feel all better."

Victoria had to pause as she choked back a tear, then suddenly, her mind went back to a moment that made her nearly loose her train of thought. She remembered the Saturday morning two months ago when Alexandria had burst into their room and pounced on their bed, excited about her pending Jack and Jill play-date and sleepover later that afternoon. Ted had pretended that her loud commotion had caused him to have a heart attack, falling back on the bed as if he was in cardiac arrest. Alexandria had put her hand on his chest, looked into his eyes with worry, and said that his heart wasn't right.

Just as her daughter's words had put a chill on her arms that morning, the same feeling ran through her now. Victoria shook her head, thinking about how strange and surreal Alexandria's premonition had been. And the fact that it happened on the same day that Parker had walked back into her life made her shiver from the eerie foreboding.

She tried not to fixate on the events of that day, forcing herself to push the troubling thoughts to another place, to be examined at another time. She knew she had to deal with what was happening in the present.

"I love you, Sweetie," she said to Alexandria. "Now be a good girl and put your Aunt Denise back on the phone,"

"How're you holding up?" Denise asked, taking the phone from Alexandria.

Victoria leaned back in the uncomfortable waiting room chair. "I can't loose him, Denise."

As soon as Victoria had rushed back into the school building she nearly lost her breath as she looked at Ted, sprawled out in front of her on the cold, linoleum tiled floor while Parker hovered above him.

Parker looked up when he saw Victoria enter, but then turned his attention back to his patient on the ground. "There's a small leather bag in the back of my truck, go get it and bring it to me quick," he instructed the security officer.

Victoria stood motionless as the man rushed by her, obeying Parker's command. A small crowd of teachers and parents looked on, standing to the side of the hallway in order to give Parker room to work. The scene looked so bizarre that Victoria could barely believe her eyes. She stared at her strong husband lying helpless as Parker knelt on his knees beside him. He slid his hand down to Ted's wrist, resting his fingers there as he looked at his watch and counted the beats per minute. He brought his hand back up to Ted's shoulder, leaning in close to him.

Ted's breath was labored. He squinted his eyes, opening and closing them tight as he tried to shift his body.

"Don't try to move," Parker told him. "You need to lay as still as possible."

In less than a minute the security officer was back, handing Parker his bag. Victoria watched motionless as Parker put his stethoscope to her husband's chest, listening with care, before pulling out a small light as he looked into Ted's eyes.

"Oh, God," Victoria finally spoke, rushing up to them. "What's wrong?"

Parker spoke in a voice so calm that if it had been any other situation Victoria would have felt at ease. "He's having a heart attack."

Victoria dropped to her knees. Her skirt twisted up her thigh as she crouched next to Ted. Despite her shaking body and frantic state of mind, she reached down and stroked Ted's shoulder with gentle, delicate care. "You're gonna be all right, Honey. Everything's gonna be fine." She turned to face Parker. "He's gonna be all right?" she said to him, asking the question.

Parker had a pressed expression on his face that she didn't like.

They both looked up when they saw the double doors open and the paramedics come through with their equipment and a gurney. "Stand aside," Parker told her, speaking as gently to her as he could.

Victoria looked on, helpless, as she watched people moving about her husband's limp looking body. The more they talked in rushed tones, the deeper her fears plunged. Parker showed the medics his hospital ID badge, and gave them Ted's stats while they started an IV drip before lifting him onto the gurney. They rushed through the door, wheeling Ted toward the ambulance waiting outside. They moved through the small crowd of concerned parents and curious children as the security officer and teachers cleared their way.

"We're taking him to Emory," Parker said, looking at Victoria. He gripped his medical bag under his arm. "Ask Ms. Snow to call Olivia, she's PJ's nanny," he told her in a hurry. He looked over and saw Alexandria and PJ standing with their teacher, looking bewildered and frightened. "You and Alexandria can follow us. We'll meet you at the hospital...I'm riding with him.'" Parker looked at Ted who was loosing consciousness, and rushed around the side of his gurney.

Victoria grabbed Parker's arm. "Don't let him die," she pleaded, too panic stricken to cry.

Parker took Victoria's hand in his. "Don't you know he's in the best hands?" He gave her a smile that he knew did little to ease her worried mind.

Back in the present, Victoria thought about the circumstances that had led her to where she now sat. She wished that she'd looked at her phone earlier instead of ignoring it. If she had, she would've seen that Parker had called and then sent her a text saying he needed to see her and that he'd wait for her at the school if he had to.

She continued her conversation with Denise, speaking in a low voice. "He's still in surgery," she sighed.

"Girlfriend, God will see you through this. Ted's gonna be just fine. You hear me?"

Victoria gave a silent nod that Denise couldn't see.

"He's in good hands," Denise said. "We both know Parker's the best. He may be an asshole, but he's a damn good surgeon."

"I'm just so scared."

"I know, but have faith. As soon as Alexandria finishes her reading assignment we're going to eat dinner, then I'll put her to bed a little later."

"I can't thank you enough."

"That's what friends are for. If you need me to come back down there, I can get Vernon to watch Alexandria after I put her to bed."

"No, that's fine. Tyler's here, I'll be okay."

"All right, but be sure to call me after Ted gets out of surgery and let me know that he's all right."

"I will."

Victoria ended the call and looked up at the large clock on the wall. It seemed as though the hands were moving slower and slower with each passing minute. Everything had happened with lightening speed before they reached the hospital, and now time was crawling like rocks through an hourglass.

"You want me to get you something to eat?" Tyler asked.

Victoria shook her head. "No thanks." She placed her elbows on her knees and rested her head in her hands. "God, let him be all right," she said aloud.

Tyler rubbed her back. "Like you told Alex, he's gonna be just fine. Ted's a strong man."

"That he is."

"And he's in there with one of the best heart surgeons around.

One of the nurses was telling me that last year Parker was ranked by the JAMA as one of the top cardio thoracic surgeons in the country. That's huge," Tyler said, patting Victoria's hand for encouragement. "He might be an asshole, but the brothah knows his shit cold."

Victoria managed a small smile. "That's what Denise just said."

"She's right. Parker's gonna make sure that Ted pulls through this."

Victoria lowered her head. "This is all my fault."

"Don't say that"

"Why not, it's true. I saw the look on Ted's face when he put two and two together and figured things out. If I hadn't been screwing around on my husband, none of this would have happened."

Tyler took her hand in his. "Listen to me. You're not the cause of this."

"Yes I am, and you know it too. Finding out that I cheated on him pushed Ted over the edge. If he doesn't make it…Tyler, I don't know what I'll do."

"He's gonna make it. And you have to pull yourself together because Ted's gonna need you to be strong for him during his recovery."

"Hmph, I'm sure he won't even want to look at my face."

"He'll be hurt and mad as hell, but that man loves you, Victoria." He looked at his friend with sincerity. "It won't be an easy road ahead, but believe me, far worse shit than this happens to couples every day. Trust me on that. Life's not wrapped up in a neat bow, and now it's time for you to dig deep and see what you're made of. You have to stand fast and fight hard for your marriage if that's what you want." Tyler paused, nodding his head. "You have to face your fears and love through the hurt and pain. Like I said, this ain't gonna be easy, but if you love him like I know you do, you'll find a way." Tyler was speaking as much to himself about his own budding relationship as he was to Victoria about her marriage.

"What would I do without you?"

"Stumble and fall worse than you already do," he joked.

Just then Tyler's cell phone rang. Victoria listened as he spoke in a slightly higher tone, letting Samantha know that he was still at the hospital. "Okay, I will. I'll see you later," Tyler said before ending the call. "That was Sam," he smiled. She got in town this morning, she told me to tell you that you and Ted are in her prayers."

"That's sweet," Victoria nodded. "This is getting serious, isn't it?" Tyler smiled again. "Could be."

Another hour went by. Victoria got up and went to the restroom. She splashed cold water on her face, wiping away dried tears from her cheeks with a hard paper towel. She stared at herself in the mirror. Her eyes were puffy, her hair was disheveled, and her lips trembled as she let out a cry. She shook her head back and forth, releasing the pain, regret, and fear that had been holding her hostage.

After she finished her cry, she splashed her face again, then raked her fingers through her hair as she tucked her stray strands into place. She reached into her handbag and pulled out her MAC compact, dabbing a small amount of cocoa-colored pressed powder over her face before tracing her lips with her plum berry lipstick. She stared at herself in the mirror, then closed her eyes, praying to God for strength and forgiveness.

Victoria returned to where she'd been sitting with Tyler, looking tired, but also much better than before she'd left.

"You all right?" Tyler asked.

"No, I'm not. But you know what?...eventually, I know I will be."

"That's what I'm talking about."

A few restless minutes later, Victoria looked up to see Parker walking toward her. She leaped out of her chair and rushed over to him.

"Is he okay?" Were her first words upon reaching him. She held her breath, studying Parker's solemn looking face.

"He came through just fine."

Victoria brought her hands to her mouth. "Praise God."

"After we went in we found a bit more damage than we initially saw on the tests we ran. He had significant blockage, but he also had a slight enlargement which isn't unusual with congenital anomalies." Victoria looked at him with a question mark over her face. "That means the enlargement was the result of a condition he's had since birth and it's now rearing its ugly head. It's not serious, but he'll need to monitor it."

Victoria nodded with new understanding. "I know that stress makes things worse, and with what happened..." She let her thoughts trail off.

Parker knew she felt guilty. "Victoria, he would've had a heart attack regardless of what happened today, and I'm surprised it didn't happen before now. He had ninety percent blockage in five arteries. That, combined with the enlargement made him a walking time bomb. The truth is, he was on borrowed time with his condition."

"Is he really gonna to be all right?"

"Yes, he's going to be fine. Other than this trauma, he's healthy and strong and I don't see any reason why he won't make a full recovery."

Victoria let out a genuine smile. "So what's the next step?"

"We'll keep him here for a few more days, then he's free to go home. I'll consult with his primary care physician and you should take him in for a visit early next week."

"Thank you, Parker."

"Didn't I tell you he was in the best hands?" Even though he didn't feel like it, he made himself smile because he needed something to hold on to.

Victoria looked at him through serious eyes. "You saved my husband's life, and I'll be forever grateful to you for that."

"I did my job." Parker didn't tell her that as he rode in the back of the ambulance, looking down at Ted, a small part of his mind had drifted to thoughts of a future that he and Victoria could share if her husband wasn't around. But just as quickly as he thought it, the fleeting moment passed. The man who he despised, whose wife he coveted, was lying before him with his life in his hands. He'd been trained by profession and groomed by nature to handle the situation in front of him. Right after they closed the ambulance doors and headed to the hospital, Ted had stared up at him, wanting to speak but unable to. Parker had seen the same desperate look that was etched in Ted's face hundreds of times on other patients. *I need to live. I can't leave my family*, was what their eyes said when their mouths couldn't.

Parker stared back as they locked eyes, like two bulls locking horns. "You'll make it," he told him.

Ted closed his eyes, letting the IV drip work its magic. Parker turned his head and looked out the back window, watching Victoria as she trailed in her car behind them with a determined look on her face. At that moment his own heart sank as the realization settled in that he'd never have her.

"You did more than your job and you know it," Victoria said.

Instead of telling her what he really wanted to say or what he thought she wanted to hear, he simply nodded. "He's in recovery. It'll be another hour before they can take him up to one of the rooms. I'll make sure that his nurse lets you know when you can go up and see him." He turned to walk away, then stopped. He leaned forward, giving Victoria a small kiss on her forehead. "Take care of yourself." And with that, he walked away.

Mistakes Have Been Made...

Three days later, Victoria sat perched by Ted's side in a large reclining chair. He'd just finished his second walk down the hallway and was a bit winded. They looked up as the nurse came in carrying a large vase of flowers and two balloons. "We're going to have to start sitting them on the floor," she joked, clearing a spot on the crowded windowsill. "You have a lot of people who care about you, Mr. Thornton. You're a very blessed man."

"Yes, I am," Ted nodded.

Victoria stared at the cards, flowers, and balloons that covered Ted's room. She concentrated on them because she couldn't bring herself to look into his eyes. She'd been by his side since he awakened from recovery and was brought to his room a few days ago. She'd smiled at him, and he'd smiled back at her. But aside from that initial tender moment, they'd kept their emotional distance, and hadn't spoken to each other outside the perfunctory matters concerning his health.

She'd been the dutiful wife and asked questions as the nurses and doctors flowed in and out of his room. She held cups of water up to his mouth when he was thirsty, and helped him in and out of bed when he needed to use the restroom. But she had yet to look at him the way she wanted to, or the way she knew that she should. A part of her was afraid of upsetting him for fear that she'd cause him a set back, and the other half of her was afraid of looking into his eyes and seeing the finality that might be resting there.

After the nurse left the room they were all alone. Victoria could feel Ted staring, boring holes through her. "Can I get you anything?"

she asked.

"I'm fine."

"Are you thirsty?"

"No."

She would have felt better if he'd cursed her out and called her a cheating whore because anything would have been better than experiencing the pain of his indifference. She braced herself, worked up her nerve, and looked into his eyes. "I'm sorry." She rose from her chair and sat next to Ted on his bed. "I kept secrets from you and I lied. I've made some terrible mistakes, and I expect to pay for them. But I love you, Ted. I love you more than you can possibly know." Victoria held her head low, waiting for him to say something.

Ted had carried on numerous, but very discreet affairs during his first marriage. He didn't believe he'd ever experience true love, then he met Victoria and his entire world changed. He still admired beautiful women when he saw them, but the thought of being with anyone other than her was like a foreign concept to him. "Why, V? I know things have been rough lately, but haven't I been a good husband to you? What did I do to drive you into another man's arms?"

Aside from when he was lying on the gurney, it was the first time that Victoria had ever seen him look and sound helpless and vulnerable. "You didn't do anything wrong. I'm the one who messed up, not you. I jeopardized our family and I'm so sorry. I was weak, and careless."

"Do you love him?"

Victoria forced herself to look into Ted's eyes again. She wanted him to know that even though it was going to be painful for her to speak it, and for him to hear it, he had to know that what she was about to tell him was the complete and honest truth. No more hidden secrets, no more lies. She nodded her head. "Yes, Ted. There's a part of me that loves him. But if I'm hearing you, you're asking me if I'm in love with him? If I want to leave you and be with him?"

"That's exactly what I'm asking."

"Then, the answer is no. I have no intention or desire to leave you, ever. Even through everything that has happened and all the bad decisions I've made, I never thought about ending our marriage," she sighed, shaking her head as if trying to pull herself from a bad dream. "Sometimes the fantasy of something is more enticing than the reality."

"This was a fling?"

"It was a colossal mistake."

They sat in silence again.

Victoria swallowed hard, asking the question that had been on her mind. "Do you want a divorce?"

There was silence. Finally, Ted spoke. "No."

"Do you think you can forgive me?"

"V….," Ted paused, bringing his hand to his head. He looked at her without responding because he didn't know what his answer was going to be. He knew if she could forgive him for what he'd done, he should forgive her too. He knew that she loved him, and despite the overwhelming hurt she'd caused him by her betrayal, he still loved her more than he could put into words.

"Ted, I know that I've hurt you, and I know it's going to take a long time for me to regain your trust. But the only way we can survive this is if you can forgive me."

"I feel like everything that we've built together over the years suddenly crumbled in just a matter of days. I lied to you and you lied to me. We both kept secrets from each other. We both betrayed each other's trust." That was his way of telling her that he didn't have clean hands either, and that they'd each made mistakes. "Betrayal is a hard thing. How do we get past this?"

"Together…that's the only way we can move forward."

"When I was lying on that stretcher, the only thing I thought about was you and Alexandria, and how I wanted to live because I didn't want to leave you." A small tear escaped the corner of his eye. He wiped his hand across his face, talking in a steady tone as another one rolled down his cheek. "I don't want to lose my family."

"You haven't lost us. I'm here where I'm supposed to be." Victoria reached for Ted's hand and held it. "I'm gonna work hard to fix this…this mess that I've made. Yes, mistakes have been made, but we can get through this. If we can forgive, we can heal."

Ted nodded.

"Do you think you can forgive me?" she asked again.

"I love you, V…but it's going to take time."

"That's all I can ask for."

Victoria slipped off her sandals and curled up in bed beside him, gently resting her head on his shoulder. Ted planted a soft kiss on her forehead as she draped one arm around him. It didn't feel like old times to either of them, and they knew that it might never feel that way again. But what they were sharing now was real, and it was pure, and it was love, and they were ready to ride it out to wherever it was going to take them.

In the story, Victoria volunteered with the Atlanta office of Dress for Success. Read here and learn more about this worthy organization!

The mission of Dress for Success is to promote the economic independence of disadvantaged women by providing professional attire, a network of support and the career development tools to help women thrive in work and in life.

Founded in New York City in 1997, Dress for Success is an international not-for-profit organization offering services designed to help its clients find jobs and remain employed. While best known for providing suits to women, it is the employment retention programs that are the cornerstone of the organization. Dress for Success recognizes that finding work is only one step in a woman's journey towards economic independence; remaining employed and building a rewarding career are essential if a woman is to become self-sufficient. The organization provides the Professional Women's Group (PWG) program, which offers ongoing support as clients successfully transition into the workforce, build thriving careers, and prosper in the workplace.

If you would like to donate to this worthy organization and/or find a Dress for Success location near you, please visit the web site at www.dressforsuccess.org.

Reading Group Discussion Guide

1. Which character in *Keeping Secrets & Telling Lies*, did you connect with the most and why?

2. This story picks up six years down the road in the lives of the main characters from *Unexpected Interruptions*. Which character's life do you think is the most changed and why?

3. Victoria and Ted had a seemingly happy marriage, yet they came to a damaging crossroad in their relationship. What factors do you think led them down the paths they each chose?

4. Think about these two quotes; "There is no big lie or small lie...a lie is a lie." "There is no big sin or small sin...a sin is a sin." Victoria and Ted both kept secrets and both told lies. Given their situations, do you think they were even in their deceit, or do you think one betrayal was worse than the other?

5. Family dynamics played a significant role in the lives of Victoria, Ted, Parker, and Tyler. How do you think their individual backgrounds and experiences affected the decisions they made?

6. Was there any part/scene in the book that took you by surprise?

7. Traditional roles are changing, and statistics have shown that infidelity among women is on the rise. What factors do you think have attributed to this increased behavior?

8. Initially, Victoria and Ted had differing views on racial identity as it related to raising their daughter. In America's changing cultural landscape, do you think individuals of bi-racial descent are still labeled as one race or the other, or do you think one's racial identity can fly at half-mast?

9. What emotion(s) did you feel once you finished reading the book?

10. Although the book ended, do you think the story is over for these characters? If not, what do you see in their futures?

If you would like the author to make an appearance at your next book club meeting, in person or by phone, please send an email to tricehickman@yahoo.com.

About the Author

Trice Hickman, is the author of Unexpected Interruptions, which was the recipient of the Southeastern Virginia Arts Association's 2008 Afr' Am Literary Award for Best New African-American Voice, and the Best Romance Novel Award at the 2008 African-American Literary Awards Show. Prior to writing, she worked in management positions for both corporate and non-profit organizations. She holds a Bachelor of Arts degree from Winston-Salem State University, and a Master of Arts degree from Wake Forest University. She currently resides in Washington, D.C.

Visit Trice at www.tricehickman.com